Books by Anthony Huso

The Last Page
Black Bottle

Black Bottle

Anthony Huso

A Tom Doherty Associates Book • New York

BLACK BOTTLE

A Tor Book
Published by Tom Doherty Associates, LLC
175 Fifth Avenue
New York, NY 10010

www.tor-forge.com

Library of Congress Cataloging-in-Publication Data

Huso, Anthony.
Black bottle / Anthony Huso.—1st ed.
p. cm.
"A Tom Doherty Associates book."
ISBN 978-0-7653-2517-4 (hardcover)
ISBN 978-1-4299-8553-6 (e-book)
I. Title.
PS3608.U82B53 2012
813'.6—dc23
2012017275

First Edition: August 2012

Printed in the United States of America

0 9 8 7 6 5 4 3 2 1

FOR

BARNO

&

JADA

ACKNOWLEDGMENTS

I WANT to thank Ricardo Bare, Alan Blomquist, Christopher Duden, Joe Houston, Marc Laidlaw, Andrea Lee, Brady Monson, and Gary (William) Webb. I also want to thank Sandy and the Öyster boys for more inspiration than I can shake sticks at.

With regards to other details such as patience, answering my questions, and generally being cool: thanks to Tobias Buckell and Alan Campbell. To my agent, Paula Guran, thank you again. To Paul Stevens in particular: I couldn't have finished this without you. And the rest of the crew at Tor, also and again: thank you for the opportunity to tell this story. To my girls, I love you.

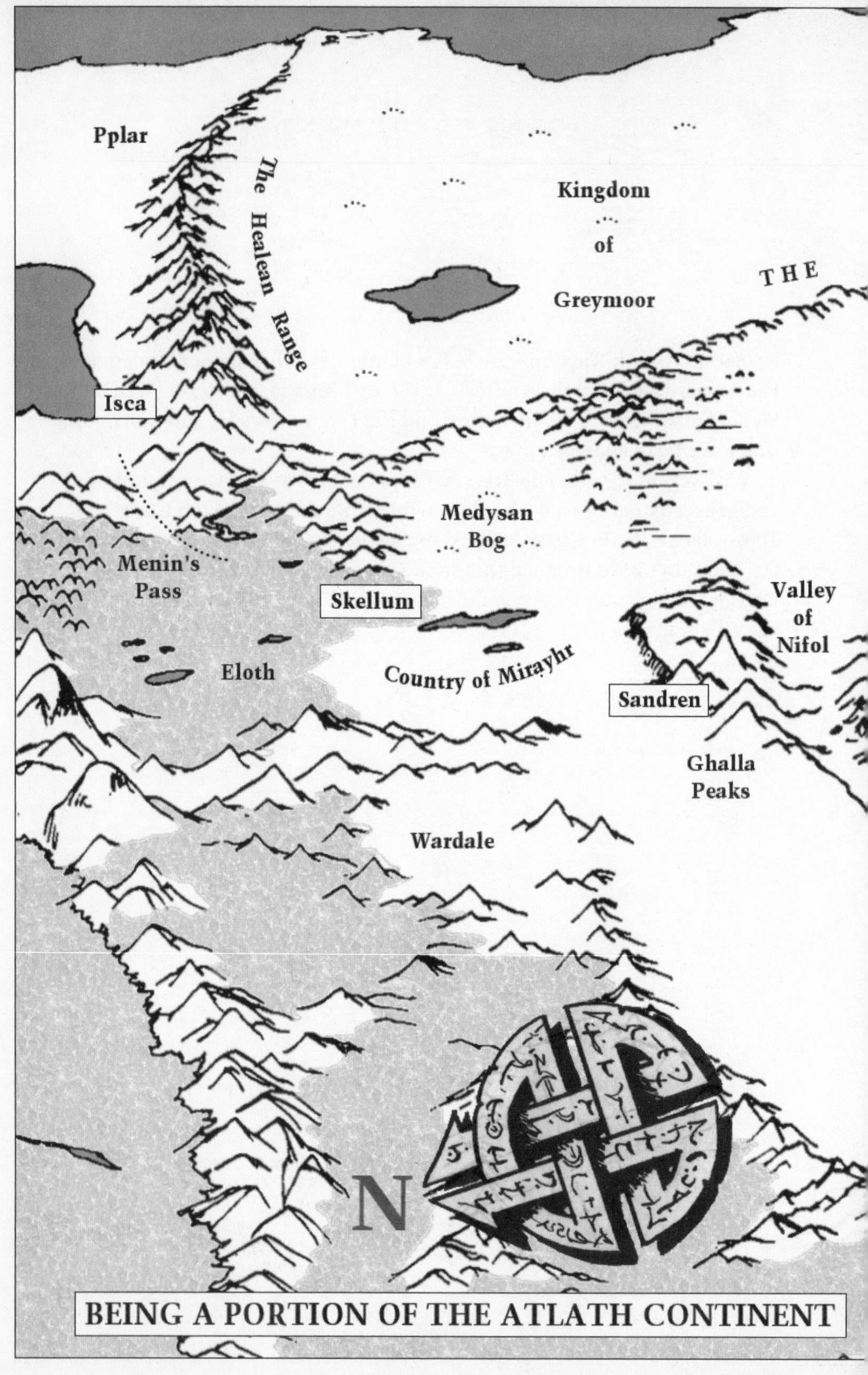
Pplar
The Healean Range
Kingdom of Greymoor
THE
Isca
Medysan Bog
Menin's Pass
Skellum
Valley of Nifol
Eloth
Country of Mirayhr
Sandren
Ghalla Peaks
Wardale
N
BEING A PORTION OF THE ATLATH CONTINENT

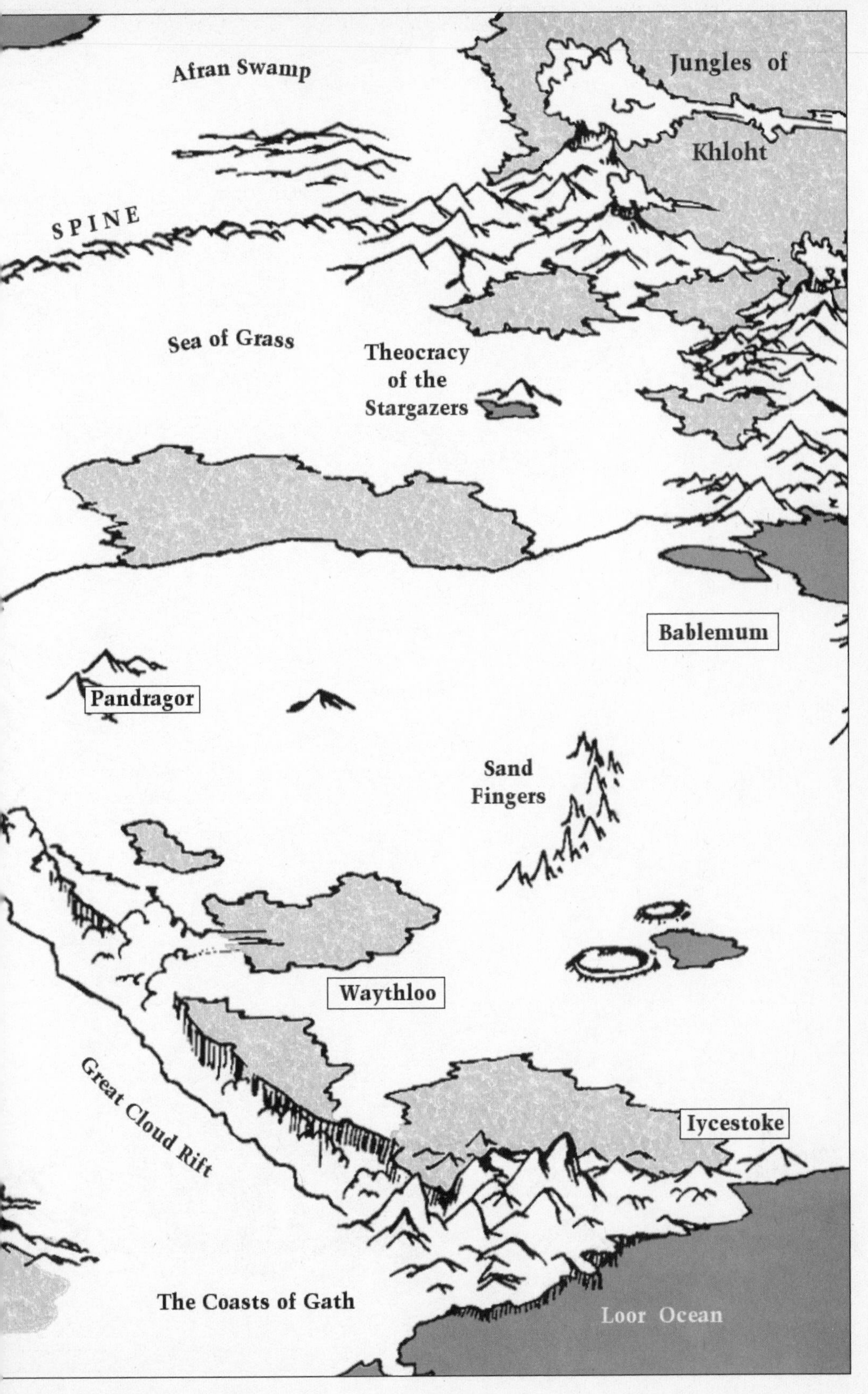
Afran Swamp
Jungles of
Khloht
SPINE
Sea of Grass
Theocracy
of the
Stargazers
Bablemum
Pandragor
Sand
Fingers
Waythloo
Great Cloud Rift
Iycestoke
The Coasts of Gath
Loor Ocean

Part One

There is an island paradise
where truth is absolute.
Once you arrive, you cease to exist.

—Yacob Skie

CHAPTER I

Love and warmth and family portraits were gone. Taelin had said good-bye to all of her friends. She walked resolutely, powered on disdain and a small cold brightness between her breasts.

Her journey stretched out behind her like a continental seam. She had *struggled* to get here, clawing out of the south, away from her father, across Eh'Muhrûk Muht[1] and up through the raw drizzle of the Country of Miraỵhr. Her most recent complication had been the bone-jarring twenty-one miles between Clefthollow and the spot where her chemiostatic car had whined to a halt in deep mud. She had left her driver two miles back with half-fare, opting to slog alone with her only suitcase through freezing rain. Now, at last, she stood within eyeshot of this dismal country's heart: the capital of the Duchy of Stonehold. Huge walls appeared from the weather, hammer and tongs, strung with vapor and steam, like pig iron pulled from its first bath.

Glaring at the towers, Taelin lifted her crimson-lensed goggles back from her eyes and let them snap into brunette shadow. *So this is the top of the world?* she thought. *This is the barbaric Naneman stronghold no one dares touch?*

Stonehold had been founded by criminals. In 700 S.K. Felldin Barâk had pardoned several thousand Naneman murderers on the condition they explore and settle the north. The ruffians' progeny had sunk deep into the mountains, turned their backs on the south and—eight hundred years ago, give or take—declared their independence. This cold, rugged land subsisted on fisheries and metholinate gas and a modest export of caviar and other luxury goods. She would have struggled to find it on a map until last year.

Now, being here, wrapped in winter, awash in the legendary ferocity of this place, a chill deeper than weather sank into Taelin. This was what she was up against.

She remembered the day, the place she had been sitting and the cool

[1] P: Great Cloud Rift.

prickle that had traveled across her forearms when she had heard that the diplomatic vessel *Baashạ One* had been shot down over the Valley of Nifol. That was the summer before last, when the world had changed and the whole south had erupted into a hive of buzzing opinions. It was the day that had brought the Duchy of Stonehold to her attention.

The short, horrible story was that the victims of the crash had been picked over by northerners. Everyone in Pandragor was appalled. Taelin had shared a national sense of disgust.

Then it had leaked that solvitriol blueprints had been in *Baashạ One*'s wreckage. Solvitriol secrets had fallen into the barbarians' hands!

The papers had kept the drama going, an entire summer of real-life cloak and dagger. Taelin had to admit that despite her fear over Stonehold's solvitriol program, the daily news had offered a kind of terrible entertainment. Shame had followed her to the newsstand every day where she indulged in Pandragonian accounts of her country's diplomats: arrested in the far north. The saga of accusations, interrogations and executions had lasted for several weeks. Everyone had assumed that Pandragor would get involved.

Her father had told her that was precisely the articles' purpose: to whip up public sentiment. Pandragor was going to throw the gauntlet down right in the middle of Stonehold's brewing civil war.

And it had almost happened.

But one day, all the propaganda, all the support drummed up by the press had fallen flat when a Pandragonian airship full of diplomats had gone down under Stonehavian guns. Not the guns of Caliph Howl, the High King that Pandragor opposed, but the guns of Saergaeth Brindlestrọm, the provincial leader Pandragor had been backing.

When the very arm that the emperor had been sponsoring stabbed him in the back, what else could Pandragor do? Emperor Jünnũ had backed down. He had said in an address that the south would "let the north sort out the north."

TAELIN looked hard at the walls of Isca City.

Despite her objectives, she had never really trained with a velvet gun or a compression sling. But not all assaults required weapons. Taelin wasn't going up against the government. She wasn't going to be a spy like her father wanted her to be. Not exactly. She was here on a mission of famicide, tearing down a reputation rather than a body.

What had driven her here, alone, was not what anyone would have guessed. Her reason for undertaking this crazy personal quest was not related to the diplomats who had died or the possibility that solvitriol weapons were being made in the north.

She didn't count herself smarter than Emperor Jünnũ but she did believe that her reasons for being here were above politics.

Weary to the bone, she stumped along, steam escaping her lips with every step.

She imagined Isca City at the center of the deepening cold, the stronghold of the ice-blue eyes that had mocked her from glossy magazines. She had never met Sena Iilool, but lithos and rumors described her well enough.

Taelin reached for the demonifuge[2] beneath her jabot. It moved between her breasts like a living thing. The heartbeat of a mouse. Its cool smoothness reassured her.

The demonifuge had not always been a necklace. Discovered in her grandfather's trunk along with a menagerie of other heirlooms, she had taken it to a jeweler to have the chain affixed. The jeweler had been nonplussed. A perfect ring formed the pendant portion. On the back side, a disc of gold turned beneath her fingers, riding a bearing-lined groove. The disc was engraved with a deep glyph:

Taelin tugged it from her cleavage. The front of it blazed with an exquisite golden mote. As she rubbed it, it moved like a stirring chrysalis, almost too bright to look at, which was curious since it produced no visible light, failing even to illuminate her fingers. No one had been able to tell her what it was. Not even her father. But that didn't matter. All that mattered was that it bore Nenuln's mark; that it was beautiful and that it calmed her.

Nenuln's sacred light could free this land; bleach the journalists' profane ink from north-south periodicals. Taelin tried to focus on this bright thought as she passed deep ditches that crepitated in the wind, stirring fitfully with the zombies of summer bog hemp.

Nenuln would keep her safe.

[2] Pandragonian charm against evil spirits.

Rain sprinkled her shoulders and cheeks. As she trudged, she thought about her aunt and uncle. Years since the last family reunion, all she knew about them was that they had little love for the Stonehavian government. Tonight they were leaving the light on for her.

Their letter had mentioned that seeking an audience tomorrow on the *Funeral of the Leaves*—a fitting holiday for such a dank, dripping land—would be her best chance at a face-to-face with Sena Iilool. Neither of them had expressed much optimism in her chances, but Taelin felt differently. Sena would not be able to ignore her. Taelin held political status in the south. Sooner or later, the government of Stonehold would have to acknowledge her.

The caramel mud of the road reared up before the vast dark walls of the city, crowned with ancient cobbles now and patched with snow and modern cement. The pooling ditches gave way to gushing culverts. Stone and metal supplanted dusk and fog-draped fields. Streetlamps buzzed. Gargoyles threatened. Dogs clucked in the shadows.

She entered the tenebrous bulk of West Gate with its acres of bricks arching overhead. Her fingers were cold. Her hands and arms throbbed from the burden of her suitcase. She smelled greasy food and heard laughter, saw that there were pubs and restaurants inside the gate. Her stomach growled but she would wait until she reached her destination. It took her only moments to secure a cabbie. The vehicle's windows glittered with purple lights amid the chaos of the gate.

She got in.

The cabbie took her into the city, along a street labeled Sedge Way into the borough of Three Cats. Even after she smeared it with her sleeve, the window fogged quickly thanks to a bulky black heater that cramped her feet. She couldn't see out. Inside the lantern-shaped cab, it was warm at least, but the leather seats were sticky and exuded a cocktail of sour odors.

Her driver remained silent.

She glanced at the address on a slip of paper.

She had told him to drop her at Heath Street.

"I'm starting a church here," she said.

For a moment, he glared over his shoulder. Then his face returned to the windshield, lit wildly by a glowing purple cat that swung from his mirror.

"If you're wondering why you go to the same job, the same bar or tavern every day. If you feel like you want to talk about . . . anything. Well, we don't have a chapel yet. But we will soon. In the meantime, you can reach me by air."

She pushed a card over his shoulder. He took it and glanced at it.

CHURCH OF NENULN
LADY TAELIN RAE

Taelin looked proudly at the small gem, affixed in the center of the card with a dollop of rubber cement.

She saw him raise his eyebrows in the rearview, probably thinking of the huge cost and risk of handing cruestones out to strangers.

"Ticky," he said. Then he tossed the card on the dashboard amid sandwich wrappers and mini Pink Nymph Whisky bottles—all of them empty.

Taelin didn't sulk. He wasn't ready for her message. That was all. After several more minutes of silence and bouncing on the ice-crusted roads, they arrived.

She handed him the fare and watched politely as he counted the coins and logged the trip on a clipboard. When he jumped out, freezing fresh air rushed into the cab. He dragged her suitcase from the trunk and set it in the snow.

Taelin climbed out into the foreign cityscape and maintained her smile until he and his bad-smelling contraption had coughed into the night. She opened her pocket watch. The skeleton gears flickered with ghostly, pastel lights.

Nearly midnight. And still a mile from her destination. But her aunt and uncle had warned against taking the cab all the way to their address. "The High King is watching us. Make sure you come on foot . . ."

There were other instructions as well. It felt vaguely criminal, but Taelin understood precautions had to be taken. This was a dispiriting town with a violent government—unlike Pandragor.

She followed the leprous masonry of Heath Street south, out of C Sacrum's foggy desertion and toward the upscale twinkle of Lampfi Hills. At the corner of Knife Street she thought she saw something gau and exaggerated standing under a streetlamp but when she looked at directly, there was nothing there. An old man perhaps. That had been h impression. Stooped and dark.

She stood for a moment with her heart pounding. She pulled her g gles down to double-check. Nothing stirred across the street. She im ined spies and worse but after half a minute, she adjusted her grip on suitcase and trudged on.

The streets of Heath and Mark met in a sullen quadrangle whe ae- lin found the beginning of a lane that ascended a hill lined with rren trees. She climbed to a point that gave her a broad view of the a and the alleys between what looked like thin brown tenements brooding beyond an empty field to the south. Across the field, small golden windows flared in some of the floors but mostly they were dark. A shout caused the air to quaver spontaneously, as if someone had dropped a street sign off a distant roof.

"Keep me and protect me," she whispered and made Nenuln's sign in the air.

Isca scintillated; some of the humidity was turning to snow. Even the slush above the sewer grates was beginning to crunch underfoot when abruptly, glowing in the icy haze, Taelin met the High King's witch in the gloom.

Sena Iilool's eyes burnt up at her from a billboard that topped a clutch of buildings below the hill. So blue. They were wicked, sultry eyes, lined with black. Golden curls splashed together with white downy fur. A Niloran cocktail. Liqueur splashing into cream. The mix cascaded over her naked shoulders. JESUEXE FURRIER! 1319 S. OCTUL BOX. The letters wavered in reflective gold.

Magazines as far south as Iycestoke and Waythloo had printed articles about this carpetbagging beauty. Her history had thickened like something delicious that periodicals then whipped with sweetened words and ambiguity into a theosophic meringue that sold faster than it could be printed. All stories shouted the same cock-and-bull fabrication: *there is a demigod in Stonehold!*

No one really believed it. But when lithos snapped by dressmakers hit the papers, black-and-whites revealed the woman was a peri: shivering demonian eyes and an ecdysiast's smile. Iycestoke the political entity, with its gruesome history of witch executions, officially snubbed her but the populace roared for more. Especially the gentlemen's periodicals. Pandragor was equally guilty. The whole of the south couldn't get enough of Sena Iilool.

Taelin had bought papers and magazines. She had heard the street preachers shouting, decrying the sins of Stonehold, indistinguishable at first from political propaganda.

They claimed that High King Caliph Howl's enemies had been crushed the end of his civil war by the most outlandish phenomenon ever re-ted, some kind of holomorphic weather system. The event had been so espread and so devastating that it had obliterated entire towns. Caliph l himself had wound up a casualty, which should have allowed Em- Jünnü and the rest of Pandragor to finally exhale.

cept for one thing.

e an evil gift to the browbeaten citizenry of the Duchy of Stonehold, a fable was slapped together that the infamous witch queen, Sena Iilool, had somehow managed to raise Caliph Howl from the dead. With fearless leader restored, rehearsed cheering had no doubt been queued. The tyrant lived on.

What had really happened, Taelin found impossible to tell. Details trickled rather than flowed from this reclusive northern country. But portraying the High King as a resurrected being and his witch as some kind of demiurge? Taelin understood this was the oldest and simplest kind of control: presentment of government as god. And that was why she was here. That was why she had come north. She remembered one magazine article in particular that had startled her into action:

> There are those who worship Miss Iilool. In fact, the temple of what some term to be a fad-religion with partisan[3] popularity has sprung up on Incense Street at the corner of . . .

Well, that had sealed it. Something had to be done to stop this kind of blasphemous lunacy: people worshiping people.

Despite the cancellation of Taelin's wedding and the very private transgression that had caused it—a mistake which still echoed painfully in her heart—her family's temple had, in the end, not taken her back. But her sins didn't make her any less of a believer, so she had formed a new church, her own church, and begun down a different road. She had focused her ire on the god-myth in Isca and tracked Sena Iilool's inexplicable ten-month circuit of the Atlath Continent through the papers. Taelin had planned her arrival in Stonehold to coincide with Sena's return.

Taelin lifted her eyes from the billboard and found her goal in the darkness, an impressive and ornate house on the edge of the hill. It stood in black counterpoint to the fog. The silhouette of the House of Mywr'Din was tall and grim, much different than styles found in Pandragor. This was her uncle's house. Taelin trudged the final thirty yards through the swirling snow, lifted the door's heavy knocker and let it fall.

It bounced loudly against the brass plate. A few moments later the mascaron swung back, a young man's face appeared in its place and bid her welcome to Isca City.

[3] Not everyone would have wanted *High King* Caliph Howl raised from the dead.

CHAPTER 2

High King Caliph Howl tapped his fingers on a sheaf of paper. It was one hundred twenty-three pages of fresh print that had nothing to do with the parlor full of cigars and music that twittered just the other side of a twelve-foot cherry wood door. The evening of entertainment was not for him. It was for Nuj Ig'nos and the other diplomats.

The papers puffed slightly at the edges every time Caliph's fingers struck them; the desk lamp imposed a sharp, ice-bright rink of light onto sentences filled with names and commerce and promises and threats. He was supposed to be thinking up enigmatic calculations that would transform the stack of Pandragonian demands into something that would serve the Duchy of Stonehold rather than undermine it. But after an hour he felt the hot itch of pressure at the back of his neck. Despite the coolness of the room, heat coursed over his shoulders, under his arms, up into his face.

He pawed at his chin. The cup of warm milk and honey on his desk—gone cold—had failed to help.

Finally, he opened a drawer and raked through staplers and gadgetry for a bottle of artificially flavored tablets. After eating two, he tossed the bottle back into the drawer and kicked it shut. The gurgling pain in his stomach subsided.

Maybe there was no way to satisfy the Pandragonian demands. Apart from turning over the throne and making Stonehold an unincorporated, organized territory of the empire, something like the tragedy that had befallen Bablemum, nothing was going to make Nuj Ig'nos happy.

You fuckers, he thought. *Out there eating Iscan caviar, drinking comets, staring at the ensemble of violinists wearing bare-backed dresses in the middle of Oak just for you! And you hand me this—koan. And you already know how it's going to end.*

A soft, persistent knocking resonated from the room's official entrance.

Caliph picked up the stack of papers, tapped its edge on the leather surface of his desk and took it across the room to the trash. The trash consisted of a black envelope. It would bear the document's name and date until it merited resurrection. Caliph sealed it and placed it in a wire basket.

He smiled wanly as the knocking persisted. Only one man knocked in such a fashion. Caliph strode from the bookshelves, over the patterned carpet and cracked the door. A volcanic glow immediately widened and burst across the threshold.

A thin figure bowed from the waist, shadow streaming into the room. Alani's head, as always, was shorn and his powder-white goatee was diplomat-perfect. Slender liver-spotted hands folded reverently across his black vest. Stuffing the vest, pleats of white silk had been stamped with an asymmetrical brooch of featureless silver.

Caliph stepped back and made a theatrical gesture with his arm. The spymaster straightened and walked in.

As the door shut, Caliph started talking. "The accord is a sham."

Alani's voice, like whisky, came with a warm ripple of corrosion. "Of course it is."

"And this conference in Sandren we're supposed to go to . . . is starting to feel like a trap," continued Caliph. He returned slowly to the cold oasis of light on his desk.

"This came for you." Alani handed him an envelope.

"You've read it?"

"Yes."

Caliph unsheathed the note and snapped it open.

" 'King Howl,' " he read aloud. " 'We feel compelled to make it abundantly clear that your speech on the fifteenth is of critical importance. Do not deviate from the clear and narrow dialogue that will lead to warm relations with the Six Kingdoms.' "

It was not signed. Caliph snarled at the page. The Pandragonians were far from subtle.

"Do you still plan to go?" asked Alani.

"Of course."

Alani reached into his vest. "Good." He drew out a pipe. "Understanding their motives, you can't fault them for being unhappy over the reunification. They'd rather you were dead . . . and all of Stonehold splintered."

"Well, I'm not dead," said Caliph. But the assertion forced him to reflect. *At least not anymore.*

It had been what? Twenty months since his failure in the skies over

Burt? He wouldn't allow himself to relive the full tragedy of the war in front of Alani, but he felt it. Enough sour, cold regret to pucker his insides.

Alani waited quietly, patiently. He had once waited for two days for a man's head to cross in front of a three-foot pane of glass. Caliph pondered this little-known fact as he watched the emotionless lines in his spymaster's face.

Finally Caliph said, "Metholinate has to be a factor." He moved around behind his desk and leaned against a windowsill that supported enormous slabs of glass.

Alani made a grunt. "They don't want gas for Iycestoke, or Pandragor . . ."

"No," said Caliph. "They have solvitriol power and bariothermic. They just want to own us outright. They'll keep our trade agreements intact but they'll be inside the government then. They'll be here, in the north. For the first time. And you know what that means?

"They'll control how we use or don't use solvitriol tech."

Alani snicked his tongue against his teeth several times. "Are you sure? Are you sure that's what this is about?"

The way Alani asked, Caliph felt as though a drop of melt water had fallen from the great casement behind him and trickled down his neck. "You think it's something different? Why?"

The spymaster had not lit his pipe. He folded his arms and relaxed against the desk. "It's a long way, reaching across the Cloud Rift, through the Healean Range, to this patch of mud and ice; especially when they have enemies grinding at them from next door. Even if we opened the floodgates on solvitriol development, we're ten years behind them. They don't need to be pushing so hard. Not now. By all accounts, as the saying goes, they have bigger fish . . ."

Caliph pulled his lip. It was true. Why *were* the Pandragonians willing to extend themselves all the way to the top of the world—to the Glacier Rise? Preventing solvitriol secrets from leaving Stonehold was in the south's interest. But could they really stop *that* with broad political maneuvers? No. Alani was right. That sort of thing fell to espionage.

Why was Pandragor pushing so hard?

Neither of them spoke.

Finally Caliph broke the silence. "Maybe the conference on the fifteenth will turn up some answers. I want you to come with me."

"I was planning on it," said Alani. "Did you really think I'd let you go alone? They're going to try and end this whole thing while you're there. And I mean end it."

The conviction in Alani's voice gave Caliph pause. "Well, that's why you're coming with. If I don't scratch out some allies while we're there, it's not going to matter. Maybe the Stargazers—"

Alani touched his beard and seemed to wince.

"What?" asked Caliph. "You don't think we can win them over?"

"It's not that. I'm sure they're the best chance we have of finding an ally south of the Rift but—"

"But what?"

"They don't have much to offer. Bablemum is a better representation of how the south feels about us, your majesty."

Caliph scowled. "Those priests in Gas End demonstrating again?"

"Yes." Alani rolled his pipe in his fingers. "They don't like Sena."

"Well, I don't like the south." Caliph felt his face flush. What right was it of theirs to have a say in who he slept with?

"Along those lines," Alani shifted gears ever so slightly, "the House of Mywr'Din has a visitor."

"From the south, I take it?" Caliph lifted his eyes from the desk lamp. He read the information in Alani's expression. "Pandragor? Are you serious?"

"Indeed. She arrived at West Gate and took a cab, which let her off early. She walked the rest of the distance to Salmalin's house via back streets."

"Reeeeally."

Alani held up a tiny black gem in his fingers. "What I don't understand is, if she's a spy, why is she handing out these . . . to strangers?"

"A cruestone?"

Alani placed it in Caliph's hand along with something small and white. "Yes, and here's her card."

"'Church of Nenuln'?" Caliph read.

Alani smiled for the first time. "She's the daughter of Pandragor's attorney general." His smile broadened. "We can use this."

After the spymaster had left, Caliph turned down the gas lamp. The resulting ineffectual ringlet of blue flame allowed moonlight to resurface the room; it rolled from the window over the desk and down the Greymoorian carpet. He noticed patterns moving across the floor and turned to discover that it had started snowing.

He flipped open the brass latches and pulled the windows in. Icy air gushed over his body. It smelled of smoke and pine: urban and rural mixing here at the edge of the city.

Sena's arrival had been delayed by weather. Her airship would dock tomorrow rather than today, a homecoming that carved his internal calendar up with anxiety.

Theirs had not been a warm intimate coupling, sharing breakfast and mutual goals on the balcony. Rather, Caliph found it discomfiting that scandal sheets like the *Varlet's Pike* had mostly gotten it right, painting their relationship as a hot and cold bodice-ripper headed for emotional destitution.

Maybe it was his fault. He wanted daily rituals with her that somehow fit his impossible schedule. That might have been feasible if she had been a bauble, content with parties and shopping and interior design.

But Sena showed up for parties only as a favor to him, seldom went shopping and left the look of Isca Castle to designers who marketed their taste as hers and thenceforth made a killing. Sena had her own schedule. And it was rigorous. When it did mesh with his, the outcome was never predictable.

After a long time Caliph closed the windows and snapped the latches. The Pandragonians had gone to bed.

He left the room, head floating down the endless cavernous hallways, past the banks of palladian glass and countless twelve-foot doors to other rooms. His tether to his exhausted body felt tenuous. His skin itched. But he knew he wasn't going to sleep.

Insomnia had vexed him ever since the wake.

In the grand scope, his life had remained unchanged by the events of Thay second, Day of Charms. He could remember the taste of the metal sticking through his chest. So strange that he could *taste* it. The fire. The crash. All slowed to the speed of a parachute seed drifting over Thilwicket Fen. That was the strange part. The part that *had* changed.

He could remember, back at college, standing on North Oast Road west of the cemetery, looking out across Thilwicket as dawn hit the trees; standing there, watching the swarm of gossamer seeds float above the fen like a million illuminated insects. For some reason he connected that moment to the moment of his death: that was the subtle way Thay second had changed him. That morning on North Oast Road was important. Had become important. And he didn't know why.

Caliph sorted through a ring of keys and tried several before finding the right one. He hadn't been to the library since Sena had locked it ten months ago and boarded the *Odalisque* for her trip.

It felt like trespassing even though she hadn't explicitly forbidden him from coming here. In fact, she had used only three words to describe her desires concerning the place where she kept all her precious notes and books: "Keep it locked."

The key scraped hollowly inside the metal aperture, a sound that traveled through Caliph's bones. He pushed the door open and paused at the threshold, looking in. It had stopped snowing and a thin, watery band of moonlight ghosted the blackness, streaming from a small upper window. It touched nothing. As if the pillars and bookcases shrouded in midnight were being given deferential treatment. As if the southern moon had decided it was better to leave this dark socket undisturbed.

Why am I here? He supposed it was prologue to her return, a way of reacquainting himself by standing in the place that very nearly defined her.

Except that it didn't feel like Sena.

His hand nearly trembled. A presence resonated from the blackness. It beat his cheeks as if the darkness itself were trying to push him back. A drapery charged with static. Galvanic waves throbbed against his skin.

He took a step into the room and stopped: the animal part of him was afraid. Had some tendril drifted? Some shroudlike form? Maybe a cloud brushing the moon?

Caliph groped for the switch like a child. His pulse fluttered, puerile and timid. While his body cooled, terror gelling around him, his face clenched defiantly. He stared hard into the darkness.

There was a snap followed by a hiss as the gas lamp bubbled to life and spread rheumy light through the chamber's wood and leather angles. His heart caught as if a cog had been spinning, out of gear. Now re-engaged, it slowed.

The room's fireplace emitted strangled sighs; breathed on a blackboard smeared with formulae. There was an empty lectern nearby. A stray draft disturbed the powder and a specter of dust spiraled off the chalk rail as Caliph, very slowly, crossed the room.

Before him, a table with mammoth legs supported a sprawl of books, maps and loose pages. The table's vast leather surface was further arrayed with colored notes stuck to manuscripts, pages, even the table itself. Gnawed pencils in the lair of an academic fiend seemed to be the only things not in meaningful locations.

Caliph circled the enormous table, looking at Sena's meticulous research. Her lanthorn hung above the middle of the sprawl, too far for him to reach, its lenses gray and dark. There was a single chair with comfortable-looking leather upholstery that Caliph tapped thoughtfully. *What is the harm,* he thought, *in seeing what she's been working on?*

Back in the house on Isca Hill, his uncle had taught him a small obscure word that required no blood. A curiosity that had earned fear-based opprobrium from several college professors. He spoke it now to ignite

Sena's lanthorn, which smoldered into absinthe-colored light, immediately soothing his tired eyes. A warm woody smell of spice and flowers flowed out from it and pushed Caliph down into the chair. The light picked words from the pages more clearly, it seemed, than direct sun.

Soon, he was following arrows in the notes, reading bracketed paragraphs, flipping to cross-references and devouring a terrifying set of journal entries that fed him ceaselessly into the brilliant ache of a morning unbacked by sleep.

CHAPTER 3

Journal Entry: C. Wind: 492, Y.o.T. Betrayal:
E—Black Moon, 24th: Arkhyn Hiel.

All my servants are dead.

I watch the nilith ooze across ubiquitous wet jungle stones and banyatha leaves. Gaudy blue and orange-speckled bodies burble across the slabs of my fallen estate, make sucking noises under Naobi's light and leạve trails like alien wine—the last traces of madness, one might think, from dreams of bygone revelry.

But there were never any parties at this house. Never any guests that surreptitiously made love in the flowering gardens or stumble-danced to the tune of the mẹlîkon.[4]

As I write in the stifling ruin of my study, I feel little remorse that my fantastic estate has fallen to the slow, quiet suffocation of the jungle and the weird mating rituals of giant slugs.

I was born in Pandragor where the skies sear your eyeballs with blue and the sands are the color of crystallized honey. I grew like the greenery in a narrow strip along the Bainmum River, but did not stay there long. My people, the Despche, have a saying: *a standing man withers like a tree on the dunes.*

I moved with the sand, blowing south and east off the Tebesh Plateau. Beyond the Sea of Grass and the Theocracy of the Stargazers, I went south between the Great Desert Rauch and the Afran Swamp. I have been to the north but most of my life was taken by the jungle.

Five years ago I turned from exploration and treasure hunting in order to carry something special out of the rain forest. Its aperture was small. We had built a forge around it and ringed it with numbers.

I was meant to deliver it to the priests in Iycestoke, but decided not to. I knew what I had.

Tonight is the anniversary of the night in 487 when my indignation for the priests finally boiled over and I achieved my smallest

[4] O.S.: A stringed instrument with a woodwind built into the neck. It is held vertically in front of the body and played by blowing and plucking at the same time.

nevertheless most notorious crime. I butchered the conclave. They were more *and* less than human. I piled them on the altar. Their arms drooled a final offering. After that I fled, bringing half my servants and much of my wealth with me. The journey south took several months but the Iycestokian constables took longer—too much longer—to solve my crime.

It was after nightfall on the twentieth when I crested the final hill. In the volcanic glow of K'rgas and Jag'Nạrod I beheld again as I had so many times before, crawling like a cheerless riot of kudzu, the endless expanse of the Ķhloht Jungles.

Behind me was the roar of the twin mountains; ahead of me the roar of insects and inside of me the roar of insoluble guilt, not for what I had done, but for what I was about to do.

Hidden from city detectives by artifices stolen from the Cabal and supported by a host of machetes that flickered in unison from the grips of my pale servants, I cut our path into the ruffling black rib cage of a fungal-smelling shadow of a land, never to return to the sprawling urban sweep that had been my occasional home.

Ķhloht is a Veyden word and the Veydens are a tall, olive-skinned, rusty-haired, heavily tattooed people that live in the fringes and murmur fearsome myths about the depths of a homeland they have never fully explored. I speak Veyden well enough to be confused by their legends and poorly enough to be incapable of adequately translating *ķloht* into Southern Trade. The closest synonym I can offer is *complacent*. The Complacent Jungles. Although lurking, listless and indifferent might be equally correct. Apparently there is a Veyden saying that when the end of the world comes, the jungle will not care.

We carved our way south, all the way through Ķhloht and out the other side. Near the great necropolis of Ooil-Üauth, on the luminous shores of a pink ocean below the equator, my servants built a palace of stone to withstand the decay of the climate and I began my long wait for the end of the world.

Caliph noticed movement in the room. It disturbed him. A page drifting from a shelf had settled against the floor. He looked toward it with uneasy curiosity, trying to gauge the limited strength of the fireplace draft. Eventually he turned his attention back to the journal. The handwriting of Arkhyn Hiel was vaguely familiar and he followed one of Sena's notes to another entry in a separate volume.

Journal Entry: C. Tides: 557, Y.o.T. Meeting:
Li—White Moon, 3rd: A.H.

In the far north, near the Glacier Rise, the red-bearded Nanemen have many myths, more perhaps even than the Veydens. In Naneman mythology they speak of the Hjolk-trull, the *Ones Before.* But even the Hjolk-trull had ancestors, those called Gringlings: *the Writers and Eaters of Time.*

The archives at Shærzac University, which will survive the Civil War of '61 . . .

"Will survive?" Caliph whispered. He glanced up at the dates. One of them had to be wrong. He felt something cool drag across his neck and slapped at it. More drafts? His stomach turned cold and rolled up on itself as if fists had clenched the ropy mass of his entrails. He looked at the date of the journal entry, a full four years before the Civil War of '61, and tried to find some reasonable explanation. The second five could be a six, he decided. And maybe the seven was actually a two with an overly short base stroke. Five sixty-two. That would make sense. Except for the inexplicable future tense associated with the war. Nevermind. The whole thing was handwritten, unedited and therefore certainly full of mistakes. He was too tired to care.

. . . which will survive the Civil War of '61 house texts that describe the Gringlings in the words of scriveners from the previous century. *Besom's Dictionary of Unusual Legend* defines the Gringlings with a single sentence that sounds suspiciously like plagiarized fable:

> A mythological radiant people endowed with the gift of prophecy who authored legendary books until the Rain of Fire.

This is, by my own account, an accurate description.

But at the High College of Desdae there are private collections. There are deeper myths crawling out of White Tongue, Mạllic and Old Rîlk. Many of the pages have been translated. Many more have not.

I was there . . . or will be there. I went through the entire library and afterward compiled the Sọthic Myth: *The Fallen Sheleph of Jôrgill Deep,* by Arkhyn Hiel. It was a task for which I . . . would be . . . commissioned by the Cabal whose *fingerlings* I later killed.

Writers and Eaters of Time. I am a Gringling, you see. Not in flesh but in spirit. I once tapped a holomorphic hybrid of floro-dririmancy to check the heartbeat of the north: the color of the petals, the way the blood dripped from the zebrian orchid's ovaries and anthers. I knew soon. Soon—soon the Sslîạ[5] would open the book.

Caliph scowled. He had little patience for this sort of drivel and had to force himself to keep going. Sena's notes now pointed him toward a different stack of papers. He rummaged and found the reference.

Excerpt: pages 23–27
The Fallen Sheleph of Jôrgill Deep
Precipice Books © 1546 S.K. by Arkhyn Hiel

Caliph stared at the colophon for a moment: an engraving that depicted a man falling from a cliff into an abyss. He had never seen it before and it must have come from some small press, perhaps even privately owned. The perspective was from overhead, looking down at the back of his wind-whipped hair, his spread fingers. It seemed a bizarre thing to transfer into an excerpt. As Caliph stared at it, he thought about his uncle and the way he had died, leaping from the cliffs at the north end of the city. As he sank deeper into the chair, a morbid chill crawled on to his chest and squatted there.

Arrian must have looked like one of those leaning sensual forms carved along the Coasts of Gath: a white statue of a woman cradling an urn beneath empty eyes, lovely limbs tangled in the vines. Her chin would have been proud, her lips thin. She would have had hair the inhuman fluid color of pearl and eyes like tiny plaques of jade.

And, in fact, all of this is true.

Few people would believe I saw her again . . . from the inside. But in the Ķhloht Jungle there are secrets carved in stone. Memories, you could call them. At Ooil-Üauth, bizarre mathematics have been graven into oblate rhombohedrons. They are alien things, cracked and decayed long before they were reused and fashioned into canted bee-

[5] A possible transliteration of Jingsade (or Gringling script) into Mḁllic (or the language of the Lua'grọc) and a word whose meaning is generally described in Trade as "deliverer/rescuer" but contextually *often carries* the connotation of "forerunner."

hive tombs. These are the buildings in a vast necropolis with no way out, whose inscriptions provided the recipe for poisonous shuwt tinctures that the Veydens now use to suspend the shadow of their body in the solvent of another's soul. They are Gringling secrets. And I should know. From these conical ziggurats, the Veydens condensed that time travel was impossible. But that fact is wholly unrelated to accessing events. To inhabiting non-time.

This has ever been the secret of the Gringlings, whose knowledge the Veydens first discovered. We were the builders of the Staircase to Infinity, which bore our memories but did not survive the century of terror that the Ublisi unleashed—when the Yịllo'tharnah scoured the world.

Our Staircase was sundered, refashioned into the necropolis at Ooil-Üauth. But our memories and our recipes remained.

These are the carvings that the Veydens found. Through judicious use of shuwt tinctures and other holomorphic secrets that I relearned from the jungle, I compiled the Sọthic Myth, a piece of work that I have no doubt will be ridiculed as pure fabrication by any scholar of "serious disposition." The toxins have caused intracranial bleeding, and I myself can see the way my meninges have seared to the inside of my skull: a feat that only detracts from my credibility, no doubt.

But I did not compile the myth for scholars. This is my own press, purchased with my own funds, for my own reasons: to remember my daughter.

And I will gladly burn the feckless cells of this pathetic mind with potion after potion of shuwt tinctures in my quest to see her again.

For the inexperienced, shuwt tinctures provide a mishmash of hallucination and truth—the first several journeys take the drinker into the youth of self rather than into the minds of others—Veyden spirit guides are able to enter the vision and teach the user how to focus the lens. But I am no novice. I am a Gringling, despite the flesh I have lost. My mind is quite intact.

I will begin by saying that Arrian was a sheleph.[6] Her power was supposed to one day match her beauty when she inherited all her father's holdings.

I am, of course, her father.

But at fifteen, her only love is sitting in the fortress walls, watching clouds blow in above the ocean. All day, she sits and watches and

[6] O.S.: A Gringling princess.

sketches with colored sticks of pigment, blending with her fingers, greasy pastel hues into sheets of parchment that are made in Lewyl and shipped to Sọth specifically for her.

When she tires of sketching, she lays the sheet aside and listens to wind come between the paper and the stone. Finally, the drawing is pulled off the wall and carried out over the surf that foams three hundred feet below. She watches the colors in the sky change from morning yellow to midday blue to evening indigo. She watches all day, nearly every day, soaking her jade eyes in the colors, infusing her brain like a sponge.

"Cor, come here," Arrian calls.

Corwin looks up from where he is teasing a centipede with a stick. He has it cornered in a shady damp niche of the parapet. The centipedes on Sọth are nearly a foot long and offer plenty of fight. The iridescent black-blue and yellow striped body coils around Corwin's stick and stings the dead wood repeatedly.

"I'm rather busy," he says. He has thin blond hair which blows straight back in the wind but his eyes betray a weakness of the heart that causes him to look at all girls with a form of awe. He flips the centipede across the battlement with his stick. I can tell he ponders crushing it for an instant.

"Cor?"

"I'm coming."

"Fetch me my colors," Arrian says when he is close enough that she does not have to yell.

Corwin sighs. "Can't we do something else?"

She pulls a strand of pale hair down in front of her eyes. "I want to draw, Cor." She knows he will succumb but she does not know why. Even at fifteen, love is a far-off thing; her mind is green and innocent from her isolation on the island. That is my doing. I know that her Gringling bones will carry her out of childhood soon enough, into an eternity of adulthood.

"I spend all my time with you and you'd rather draw," Corwin complains.

"Rather? Rather than what? As I recall, you were off playing with bugs."

Corwin raises his eyebrows.

Arrian makes a pained face. "Cor—!"

"I'll get them," he grumps. It is a long way to her room on the other side of the stronghold, a good ten minute walk in both directions.

Sometimes he walks it five times a day and only now, toward the end of summer, has he started to complain.

Arrian watches the ships come and go bearing her father's loyal emissaries. They have empty hands but carry rumors on their lips. They speak of frightening creatures in the south, hated races: Groull and Yịlthid. It is a strange time, I tell her, though she does not understand what makes it so any more than she understands the way Corwin looks at her.

She watches the ships come and go as she watches Corwin come and go, with colors and paper and pitchers of icy things to drink. It does not occur to her that Corwin is her only friend.

While she waits for him, Arrian sees a strange ship move into the harbor. It has turquoise sails and rigging like gold thread and from the main mast blows a pennant with a symbol of both moons intersecting. By the time Corwin returns, it has docked and she points it out to him. "I'm going to draw that ship."

"I can't even see it from here," says Corwin. "Just a speck of color."

"I can see it very well," Arrian replies, picking up one of the blue-green sticks he has brought. "Even if I never saw it again I should remember it always. Have you ever seen a boat so lovely?"

Corwin looks over his shoulder for the centipede but it has slithered off. "No. Maybe we could go down and see it better."

"Father doesn't like me near the docks." Arrian's voice is like a fife.

"I don't think he'd like you dangling your feet this high above the surf either but he doesn't seem to notice that. Why would he notice the other?"

"If we go down you'll have brought my colors for no reason."

Corwin shrugs. He knows indifference is the only way to coax her.

Arrian gathers up her pigments and lays them in the little wooden case. Corwin offers to carry it out of habit. He picks up the parchment and follows one step behind.

Jôrgill Deep gets its name from the cleft between the mountain and the sea cliffs where it rests. The fortress itself is the only spot of civilization on an island whose ancient name comes from the mountain: Sọth. Sọth is a great hooked horn of blackened rock that casts a nearly eternal shadow over Jôrgill Deep. The stone here is mostly volcanic and the fortress was hewn of basalt by Gringlings and beings that the Gringlings once called Limuịn: the *Infinite Ones.*

Some Limuịn remained behind after the Banishing. They renounced Limuịn prophecy and surrendered their titles. *Limuịn* became an offensive slur synonymous with elitist and disparager. *Infinite Ones* was replaced with *Ublisi*, a title that means *Smooth Thinker.* The Ublisi now use their intellect to expand and secure the Gringling Empire against the expansionism of the southern Yịlthid and their Groull slaves.

The vast prismatic panes of Jôrgill Deep now reflect the sunlight in proud white-gleaming sheets, glaring out from the nullifidian bulk and heavy tracery of the walls. Arrian feels coddled behind them, safe inside a structure that has scoffed for millennia at every kind of storm. She gazes at the splendid ship in the harbor and walks gracefully out through black arcades atop the battlements. Flowering vines grow here and frame the sky with perfumed boughs drooping with white petals.

"What if it's an Ublisi come to visit your father?" Corwin says quietly. "Would you be frightened?"

Arrian is surprised that his thoughts have been identical to hers. She is peering curiously toward the harbor. "I don't know," she says slowly. "I've never seen one before."

"I hear they have no blood. That's queer to think of. They can't die. Ever."

"Oh, Cor! It's probably just an ally. A household from the south. They say southern ships are grand to look at."

"I want to get off this island!" Corwin suddenly spouts. "I want to see the mainland. Go places. Do something important."

"Father says it's safer here on the isles."

"Your father doesn't know everything!"

Arrian stops and turns with a look of shock on her small dark lips. It has never occurred to her that anyone might have ideas that oppose those of her father and the sudden realization forces her to stop completely in order to digest. "By the Eyes, Corwin, why are you so upset?"

Corwin looks down at the box of colors in his hands. The sunlight on the wood shines gold and turns his fingers copper. He bites his lip while color flushes his ears and cheeks. Only when Arrian begins walking again does he venture to respond. "I'm just tired of being here and never seeing the world."

"What does that have to do with my father?"

"Nothing."

He wants to say that he is upset with himself. I know he is angry for not having been braver, brasher. He should have killed the centipede. He should not have gotten her colors. He should have kissed her, brushed his hand across her waist and then . . .

There are noises coming from the harbor, excited shouts and the roll of drums. Corwin and Arrian take a tertiary staircase down to a small balcony the guards seldom use. It looks out from a tiny room that punches clean through the fortress wall and grants a good view of both the docks outside and the courtyard within. From here, they can see Arrian's father standing with a body of men in robes, personal advisors who whisper in each other's ears. It is strange that I know what they are whispering. The drums are also those of her father's men: sea turtle skin stretched over hoops beaten with soft leather mallets.

But Arrian is staring at the ship. The prow, covered with beaten copper and silver studs, seems to burn its reflection into the dock waters. At the center of one of the sail's moons, a silver eye is painted. Arrian can see a dark-skinned woman in white silk stepping gracefully near the landing while bare-chested albinos flex their muscles to get the moorings tight. Their shoulders are red from the sun.

It is a delicious scene.

The woman wears a copper carcanet with red jewels, anklets and bracelets that explode in the sunlight. Part of her face is lined with a curious black design—even darker than her skin—which seems to hold her eye like a diamond in a claw.

The drums fade and Cendrion harps fill the air with soft music. Arrian notices green and blue veils hanging in the gate. They bloom fatly in the wind while the woman and her servants seem to float toward her father.

Caliph checked the time with bleary eyes. The soothing aroma pouring from the lanthorn was a natural stimulant but he closed the book across his stomach. His head ached. He didn't understand why Sena must have been reading this particular account, for long hours, locked away in this freezing chamber just before she left.

He turned his thoughts toward her return. The possibility of sex and quiet conversation made him long for her. Fire and wine would warm the moment of her arrival. He had already informed the staff of their duties, he had orchestrated everything.

She would tell him all about her trip, what she had done, where she had been. He in turn would tell her about the problem with the Pandragonians. They would sit close together, feet touching.

As the High King, he was forced to keep certain secrets. Maybe that was why he didn't begrudge her a handful of locked doors; or judge her based on the books she read. In fact, her secrets were part of the allure, part of her intractable luster. The unfathomable still looked out at him from behind her mirror-like eyes.

Caliph felt his lids droop despite the lanthorn's light. He turned into the bow of the chair and barely heard the journal clatter to the floor.

CHAPTER 4

In Octul Box, the infamous witch's skin up-welled with a fantasy of jewels that beaded from her very pores. Dark and dazzling, both the expression on her face and the diamonds, like droplets of night sweat, seemed products of wild ecstasy. Taelin could see flexuous clones of precise lamplight in each gem, positioned by the jewelers who had engrailed her body, snapped lithos and presumably left her with the treasures.

The posters were everywhere: INDULGE YOURSELF. GET TICKY!

She passed Jesuexe Furrier where Sena's pavonine eyes stared back at her.

Taelin shivered.

A letter had come from her father by bird that asked her to do things she didn't want to do—that she had no intention of doing. She wandered the streets to clear her head.

The morning had remained dismal. Clouds grazed single-story structures, astonishingly low.

While she browsed the upscale streets where ice had been salted away, people passed her with ostentatiously manicured creatures on glittering leashes. In shape, the small faceless monsters resembled furred maggots with bizarre haircuts. Stubby legs propelled them around while drool flowed from gaping holes at the front of their bodies.

Taelin sat down under one of the smooth patinated bronze dragons whose sinuous body made a shape like lightning over Octul Box's fountained mall. Lily white spatters had put the sculpture in a sour mood. Its eyes indicated it wanted to tear something apart. Taelin could relate.

She had tried to console herself with a bottle of Pandragonian perfume. Sena's return had been delayed by weather and no new audiences were being granted. Nevertheless, Taelin put her name down for an appointment at the earliest convenience and left a cruestone.

She glanced toward Isca Castle. Even from Octul Box, the blue-black carrion birds played an evil game: leading her gaze repetitiously toward cages made hazy by two hundred yards of intervening mist.

Assuming the Iscan staff (or Sena) granted her an audience she couldn't help morbidly envisioning herself suspended there, left to rot, while the castle's mythic spindles marked her grave. Would even her father be able to save her if she wound up on the witch's bad side?

Pandragor had not executed anyone in over two hundred years. Not that Pandragor was perfect, Taelin mused, but if some of its values rubbed off on these northern backwater rogue nations of the world . . . well, maybe things would improve. It was simplistic and imperialist and she knew it. But Pandragor was the freest country north or south of the Tebesh Plateau. She believed in it. She trusted it.

She opened her box and took out the pearlescent bottle, fingering the snowy braided cord and ball: its every detail spoke to her of home. It was indulgent but she couldn't help herself. She pumped the atomizer once and the crisp spices of the desert infused Isca's icy air, transporting her over eight hundred miles to the south. She lifted her wrist, closed her eyes and inhaled.

Her choices for the rest of the day remained open to possibility. Her list of "to-dos" included finding an architect (at the top) and applying for a permit that would allow her to stand on street corners and talk about religion (at the bottom). She quickly settled on an item in the middle that had been chewing on her thoughts, bothering her irrepressible curiosity.

Having made up her mind, Taelin repacked her perfume and stood up to hunt Isca for *the abomination*.

She had heard it was monumental, gluttonous and shocking; fed regularly by the city's eccentric types.

According to her map, purchased earlier at a tobacco shop, the path to its lair was a straight line, by streetcar.

Taelin walked to the nearest stop and waited with a small crowd. A thin Naneman in pinstripes scratched his tatty beard. He stabilized a unicycle in the other hand and stood patiently, trying to ignore a pair of strawberry tufted twins that brawled around his ankles. Taelin smiled and gave him one of her cards.

When the streetcar arrived she boarded and found a seat behind one of the oval windows. With a lurch and a flatus of ozone-smelling gas, the car pulled away and soon ducked through a mildew-cankered tunnel where light dwindled under the Hold. They emerged again into sunlight and soon Taelin realized it was time for her to get off. She climbed out onto the tomb-shaded slope of Barrow Hill's east side, well within view of the startling Avenue of Charms. Startling because of the view.

From the station, framed by decorative wrought iron, Taelin gazed through Temple Hill's blackened fingers. They groped out of theophanic fog banks, glittering through amethystine piles of smoke. The temples' myriad spires looked arthritic and lost, floating free of their foundations.

Incense Street broke east from the avenue and snarled with awesome statues and strangely dressed people. Taelin marched down into the morass where vendors sold aspersories and vials of chrism.

Choking-sweet clouds that gushed from thuribles stung her eyes. She pulled her goggles down as she passed a chiseled font depicting a bearded ancient whose mouth let flow a never-ending vomit of cinnabar-colored water. She couldn't help a second look. His tongue blistered and flagellated with unbelievable growths of rust-colored algae, consuming his lips it seemed with unbridled disease.

People shoved past as she stared.

A pair of giant idols offered her a route between their legs and she took it, raising her palm to a hawker who thrust something like a chicken bone into her face.

She darted out from under the idols, down three marble steps and entered a thicket of black feretories overspread with white latticework. There, between a massive copper cage shaped like a teakettle and an engraver displaying sarcophagi, she found *the abomination*: Sena's temple.

It welcomed her with blood and screams.

From the tumult of the street, a shriek of pain squealed up into the sky like a firework. A circle opened in the crowd and Taelin found herself on the edge of the ring, watching in horror as four white-robed suffragans from the Church of Kosti Vinish wrestled a group of Nanemen sentries. The southern priests were Ilek, certainly out of Bablemum judging by their purfled hems and shorn heads. The giant red-haired Nanemen opposing them clearly subscribed to Sena's church.

Taelin flinched as one huge northerner hurled his assailant into a brick wall behind the engraver. The Ilek man's head gashed open and he fell, bleeding into the gutter. Enraged, the other suffragans drew knives.

But now the city was moving in.

Men in tall rubber boots with dark suits and chrome-blue goggles emerged from the chaos. The cobbles of the ancient street crackled under their feet as chemiostatic swords ripped out into the air and lanced the stones with bolts of lightning. The crowd fell back, instantly cowed. Two of the police drew batons and beat the southerners to the ground.

Taelin covered her mouth and recoiled as the Nanemen sentries stepped back, allowing the Iscan police to twist the unconscious southerners' arms behind their backs, cuff them and drag them away. One of the suffragans' heads hung so low his face bounced along the uneven street, slack-jaw snagging momentarily on a brick. Taelin quailed at the sound of snapping teeth.

The Nanemen sentries were not questioned. The police simply disappeared. Taelin wanted to scream. She wanted justice. But already the scene was being effaced by thronging people and she knew she risked everything if she made another scene. Taelin stood with her fingernails gouging her palms.

She was only a few feet away from where the Nanemen had repositioned themselves on either side of the temple's entrance. Snowflakes dissolved into fuming columns of steam that poured out of grilles flanking the way in. She half-expected the guards to accost her as she took a tentative step forward.

They did not.

There was no edifice in sight. Rather, a disc embedded in the first of a broad slope of steps decreed in several tongues that this was: *the Fane of Sienæ Iilool: Omnispecer.*

Omnispecer?

The iron-trimmed disc bore a stunning alabaster relief of Sena at its center, eyes poured from pure blue glass.

Bemused, Taelin ascended the white steps, slowly at first, still cautious of the guards. The steps abutted a massive wall of troglodytic clinker brick, encrusted with city soot and birdlime, far older than the smooth cream of treads below her feet. After several yards she had risen above the feretories and could gaze down into the befuddled warren of Incense Street. With no opposition from the Nanemen, she traveled another hundred steps, which put her around a corner. The ramp now climbed east, still hugging the mountain of ancient brick. *Where can this be going?*

Ahead she could see the staircase end against a blazing sheet of clouds. To the left: open sky and the tumble of rooftops that spilled down into Ironside. To the right: the vast pile of masonry ascended. The climb burned into her thighs. She stopped to rest and walked over to the safety chain that served as a railing. Four- and five-story buildings piled up over fifty feet below.

The trauma of seeing the clash in the street still lingered. She felt light-headed. Queasy. But mostly she felt alone. She missed the blue-gold streets of polished marnite, the tittering sands and whispering tea trees. She missed figs and honey cakes and the vast bulrushes beneath Pandragor's palatial quartz terraces where the Bainmum spread out into the White Marshes and fed the irrigation lines.

She missed warmth.

Inhaling the thick smoke-filled cold of the city and fighting off vertigo as zeppelins wheeled overhead, Taelin started climbing again. By the next corner she had doubled her height above the street. From her new perspective she could see that she stood on one of the edges of an enormous pyramid of brick whose slopes continued to rise above her. The steps led on, traveling south, but she could not yet see the peak. Or could she? She pushed herself up the broad treads toward the next corner.

Reaching it, she found herself on a dizzying precipice with a historical marker that told her she stood two hundred sixty feet above the city. The marker formed the southeast corner of a vast plaza that topped the immense frustum of brick.

From the top of the stairs she overlooked the entire city with the exception of the Hold: Isca Castle reared triumphantly to the north. Everything else spilled away into brown-black spindles of shingle and stone.

From the enormity of the sky, Taelin turned her attention inward, to the objects at the center of the square. A dais of some buttery white mineral seemed to levitate just above the acre-wide surface. It consisted of three layers, or steps, topped with a hypaethral grove of black columns. Although the exact arrangement spread too broadly for her to be certain, she got the impression that the dais formed a huge disc and that the columns spiraled into its center.

Her skin prickled. Tapestries of red silk undulated, effecting a kind of sanctum that seemed to float, cordoned from but flirting with the sky. It felt like the ground was tipping beneath her feet as she caught provocative, dizzying glimpses of people bending amid the black pillars, cradling silver vessels, glancing in her direction before vanishing again into the billowing scarlet canopies.

Everything was in motion. The clouds, the distant zeppelins, the sails of cloth and the people behind them. Even the vast milky dais that supported the columns seemed to bob slightly . . .

Taelin felt her stomach pitch. She closed her eyes but her balance was off. She had to kneel down. She felt grains of stone roll under her fingers.

Her esophagus clamped down on an airy pressure that climbed up the back of her throat. She got control of it. After a few moments the feeling subsided and her head cleared enough that she risked opening her eyes.

At the edge of the dais stood a man, exceptionally tall and pale, wrapped in a single luxurious heap of long dark fur. His feet were similarly booted to the knee. He was talking with a journalist who had just ended the conversation by saying something she couldn't parse in a loud, cheerful voice. Then the journalist and his shoulder bag turned in her direction. He smiled at her, raised his bulky camera and snapped a litho.

Fantastic.

Caught for all time: kneeling at the temple of Sena Iilool.

She struggled to her feet and rested a moment. The man in the fur wrap came over. He smelled of overly sweet perfume and his smile was too symmetrical, like something coming out from behind a mirror.

"May I help you?"

Taelin pushed her goggles back into her hair. "Yes, I'm wondering if you . . . if your congregation . . . if your *religion* really believes that Sena Iilool is a god?"

"You smell like apples." He looked down at her with lavender eyes, deep-set under yellow brows.

Taelin scowled. She wanted to tell him that he smelled rather cloying himself but she wasn't interested in a pissing contest. "Is that right? You people believe she's a god? Goddess? Whatever?"

The man said, "Belief is not required."

"This is a temple, isn't it?" said Taelin.

The man's smile diminished but his eyes almost incandesced in the sunlight. "We do not answer questions here." His head was shaved but a nap of blond velvet covered his pure white skull.

"You're not interested in converting anyone?"

"No."

"Can I look around?"

"Yes. But please, do not disturb the colligation."

"What's a colligation?" Her father being a lawyer, she understood a colligation of facts used to support an argument but . . .

"We do not answer questions here."

"Oookay. I'll just look around then." She gave him a smile that he did not return.

The dais hovered twenty feet behind him. She wanted to crouch down and look under the bottom step, discover if the whole massive thing were really floating, but to do so felt childish.

Instead she walked toward it, set one foot on the impossibly smooth monument and stepped up. As she did, she felt her nausea return momentarily. Just a flicker at the bottom of her stomach.

She paused, then climbed the other two steps and passed one of the red veils.

The scene that greeted her sent her vision rolling. Among the snapping silks knelt a stunning host, mostly pale Pplarians. They faced north, knees on cushions of scarlet embroidered with black. In front of each worshiper stood a two-foot amphora of dark glass. The mouths of the amphorae were wider than their bellies, spun into broad funnels by whatever glassblower supplied them.

To the right of each worshiper knelt a man or woman in red silk who assisted them through the act of oblation: inserting the needle, depositing the other end of the vacuum tube into the mouth of the amphora. Taelin watched in horror as row after row of phlebotomists methodically went through the venepuncture, then bandaged up their patients and helped them lie down, heads on the pillows that had previously cushioned their knees.

Once their patients were comfortable, the phlebotomists raised smaller silver amphorae, spilling liquid from these sparingly into the larger vessels before capping the tall black amphorae with ornate lids.

Young vergers with silver trays of fruit, drinks and biscuits glided the spiral aisles.

Eventually the devoted were led out along the spiral and a new worshiper was guided in to take their place. The turnaround was slow; people trickled in and out. They seemed to both come from and disappear toward the region farthest from where Taelin stood.

Taelin watched as a phlebotomist lifted one of the black amphorae. She clutched it close to her body with both arms, and hauled it north to yet another dais where she ascended three more steps and entrusted her burden to a muscular Pplarian. He in turn labeled and hung it at a forty-five-degree angle from a magnificent silver scaffold. It swung gently with others that had been filled and made Taelin's stomach hurt.

None of the worshipers spoke, but Taelin could hear even above the snapping silks, the dribbling echoes of the hollow amphorae, the colligation, the vast sound of blood collecting drop by drop, which she now realized had to be linked somehow, impossibly, to Sena's use of holomorphy.

It was not so cold here. Whatever the custard-colored dais was made of, Taelin could feel a mild warmth coming off it. The whole thing repulsed her. She backed out of the temple, down the steps and nearly into the towering Pplarian who had snuck up behind her.

Her fear, both at the Pplarian's sudden proximity and the memory of what she had just seen, boiled out as anger. "How . . . what are you doing here?"

The man's face twisted like white plastic at the edge of a fire. Taelin backpedaled, nearly falling in her effort to widen the distance between them. His words barely reached through her shock and horror. "The Omnispecer is not like you," he said. "Axioms do not require belief."

Taelin gaped. One of his lavender eyes glared at her, bulging and cycloid while the other seemed to have been sucked back into his head, partly hidden by a wrinkled sphincter of bleached flesh.

His grin returned, broad and venomous.

"We do not answer questions here," he called out to her as she turned, still stumbling, dashing for the stairs.

CHAPTER 5

Caliph woke with a silverfish on his face. How it had survived the cold, he didn't know. Nor did he know what time it was. He was wrapped in a blanket (another mystery) with the leather desk chair reclined beneath him like a sling. The muscles in his neck had stiffened. He rolled forward, chair tipping upright, and noticed a fire burning on the hearth.

Clearly, his staff had found him.

He picked up the book that had fallen to the floor. Curiosity about the characters in the journal drove him to find the next entry.

Journal Entry: C. Tides: 543, Y.o.T. Crow: Mas—Harvest, 15th: N.H.

Arrian Glimendũlạ lived roughly twenty thousand years ago. Scholars place her at nineteen thousand, nine hundred fifty years old, give or take a year or two. My ruined estate in Ķhloht, overgrown with seventy years of jungle is still new by comparison. My poisoned servants are fresh gossip, sweet golden dates rotting in the sun. In the company of such a beast of legend, I am nothing. In this, I take comfort . . . despite the fact that it is a lie.

With sweet shuwt tinctures I was there, inside of her as I have been inside of others. My sense of self is muddy. As is my sense of time. I look out through Arrian's eyes, see and sense Corwin's adolescent frustrations. When Arrian met the woman on the ship Corwin stayed in the shadows, watching. After a while, he turned and marched up the coast, skipping stones into the Loor. The woman was Ublisi. She had come to Sọth carrying the Red Book.

By then, the *Cịsrym Tạ* was already nearly three thousand years old (H.X.) yet it glistened like the day the Ublisi had bound it. The Ublisi stayed at Sọth for three years; then, on Arrian's eighteenth birthday, I returned through a poisoned stupor, escaping the jungle's sultry spell on what fools might call *bent time.*

Cịsrym Tạ! This was the name that Sena had always used for Caliph's uncle's book—the book that she had discovered and brought into the north—the book she had studied day and night and rarely let out of her sight.

If these accounts revolved around the *Cịsrym Tạ,* Caliph had a much better understanding of why Sena would be reading them. He turned the page and was once again confronted by the colophon of the falling man.

Excerpt: pages 49–51
The Fallen Sheleph of Jôrgill Deep
Precipice Books © 1546 S.K. by Arkhyn Hiel

The upper arcades of Jôrgill Deep are cleared. The floors are swept in both directions, inviting a menagerie of guests to dance atop the battlements. As the music begins, Arrian watches Corwin flirt ridiculously. He has become a sailor this last year, grown tan and arrogant. He no longer carries her colors.

Tonight, he looks fine, still damp from ocean spray and graceful from ever balancing on ship decks. Arrian banishes the annoying thought and goes to the high table where sweet-fig pies have been laid before the merrymakers. She samples the desserts and licks her fingers when she hears him stop directly behind her.

His voice and the clean smell of the ocean carry over her shoulder.

Arrian turns and smiles. "I thought you came to see *her* instead of me." She gestures with her eyes across the battlement.

Corwin laughs a half-embarrassed laugh. He is only seventeen. "I doubt you know how to be jealous."

Arrian's eyes flicker. "You don't know me well anymore."

"Maybe not. But I sense your influence at this party. You've had the decorations hung exactly to your taste, probably fretting over them until early this morning."

She nudges him with her elbow, enjoying his nearness. Wreaths holding candles bear indigo ribbons and the flames illuminate white flowers overhead. The pergola above the arcade is burgeoning with blooms. "I brought you a gift from the mainland," Corwin says. "Since you've never been away from Sọth, I thought a little something foreign might be good."

"I love it here," Arrian says defensively. "We have perfect seasons all year round."

Corwin replies with slow enticing words. "On the mainland they have snow."

"Snow?"

Corwin grins. He reaches up and shakes the pergola, generating a storm of petals. "It's white and cold and flutters from the sky—like rain but more slowly." Arrian watches his lips move.

"I belong here, Cor. You're the traveler, not me. Besides, father says I should marry."

Corwin laughs. "You!—who've never had a suitor or anyone you loved, what would you do with marriage?"

Arrian bites her lip softly. Her father is calling her from behind the high table. "I'll be right back."

Corwin watches her go. The ghost of an old ache passes ever so faintly through his face.

The party is for celebrating both Arrian's birth and the anniversary of Jôrgill Deep's desecration. All the guests know that Arrian's father has something special planned and servants are beginning to usher the party downstairs toward the courtyard.

In a chamber off the arcade where the music is only a murmur, Arrian meets her father. It is strange to gaze on what is no longer me. As usual, the Ublisi stands at his side. Maelstroms of stars turn in each of her unsettling eyes. Arrian has never seen her eat or sleep. She has heard that Ublisi have no need of mundane necessities.

Her father has told Arrian that tonight will be the culmination of higher things. Deeper studies. The Ublisi has worked out some holomorphic secret of unlocking, which will redeem Sọth, an equation that will bring back the radiance of Ahvêllẹ.

At Jôrgill Deep, there is a knot of stone, a weird whorl of minerals: cream-colored, spiraled into blackish and brownish granite—all of which swirl up into something like a protruding navel on the ground. It is the remnant of where one of the chambers[7] first landed. A backward crater that defies standard physics. It is graven with glyphs not even the Ublisi remembers how to read and it rests in an unused alcove in an overgrown section of the courtyards of Jôrgill Deep.

"Arrian," her father says. "We will be going down to the courtyard. My gift to you tonight," his voice—my voice—softens, "will lift us to a better place." He has green irises that I remember from the mirror, blunted with age, and he rests his hand gently on his daughter's shoulder. She is the only creature that he still dares to love.

The Ublisi says nothing but, with her cosmic white eyes, stares all the way through Arrian's face.

[7] Ambiguous capitalization. Does he know what these are?—Sena.

A chill goes through the birthday celebrant as the Ublisi turns slowly.

"Come." Arrian's father puts her hand on his arm and leads her to the courtyard where the guests have already gathered under a pavilion of midsummer blooms. Glasta[8] flutter through the garden and fan the smell of nectar.

The Ublisi's tall form seems to float across the lawn to where the stone knot has been extricated from an overgrowth of black pimplota. The Ublisi holds the bright red book in her hands. Its corners are shod in sparkling metal where proud Neķrytian serpents tense in intricate designs.

Arrian knows about this book. It is occasionally still called the *Gymrę Tą,* the Banishing Book: because of its role in locking D'lọig in a prison in the stars. Its creation supposedly took a thousand years. But these days, it is simply called the *Cịsrym Tą,* the Red Book—not only for the color of its cover, but for its fearsome results in the ongoing Yịlthid War.

The Ublisi stretches her arms beneath the moons and all the guests grow quiet.

Only the glasta still flutter.

Arrian stands near her father, his large hand clasped over hers. She can feel his anxiety. He has helped with the study and the preparation for this night, being a great mathematician. He waits now, breathing hard, for the golden lights that will soon fill the courtyard.

The Ublisi begins to speak in the Unknown Tongue. Her numbers fill the air, bloodless and clean. Her voice sounds like a chyrming creature far away on the mountain of Sọth. For an instant, molten glassy shapes distort the courtyard air. A sudden plunge in temperature reveals every exhalation. Inaudible frosty notes pluck a staccato stillness in the yard.

The formula does not last long, but the moment of silence that follows feels eternal. One guest looks to the next, anxiety smoking between their lips. Arrian's eyes meet Corwin's and she sees a ghost of apprehension, a sailor's instinct, perhaps. His body shifts in that infinite moment of doubt as he begins his first step toward her.

The old obsidian-crusted mountain seems to shiver with the sudden chill. Then the world shakes itself like a wet dog. Stars become slits of light that streak two directions at once. The great horned mountain of Sọth cracks open like a jungle flame. Rocks three times

[8] A species of luminous moth extinct c. 11062 (O.T.R.).

the size of Jôrgill Deep tumble down into the fissure where the fortress stands.

Arrian's eyes sweep the yard in desperation. Amid the roar, she sees her father unscrew a metal capsule. He tips it into his mouth.

Then the clouds of ash sweep in. The Ublisi stands in a halo of soot and rose-colored fire. Shards of granite and molten flowers of glowing rock rain down in every direction. The heavy hail stones the guests to death then prudently piles them under rocky graves.

Arrian is knocked into an alcove where great falling boulders have already formed a cave of sorts. Someone has pushed her. She turns to see Corwin's eyes. They are large and wet and desperate to help. A great jagged stone comes down. He disappears into ashy blackness. All of them are crushed like sweet-figs in a pie, buried in the courtyard in a great round of clay.

Arrian's eyes soak up the blood and broken bones, the fallen rock and glowing embers. Beyond the horror of their death, she sees the most terrifying thing of all. The Ublisi formula is still unwinding. The knot of stone has come undone, the whorl of colored rock, where one of the chambers left its mark, has opened, stretched itself into a hideous hole, as if the world is giving birth. Then, in grotesqueness too ripe to describe, abortive things haul themselves out. Great, translucent, protean limbs, eely monstrosities wrangle from the void and ooze and lurch and burble. The sweet stink of their decay fills the air. The gardens and the glowing moths wilt beneath rocks and huge putrid carcasses that cannot walk, but hump and slither across the liquefied land.

My daughter must have used up every lamp and candle. And when the final wick burnt low, she must have screamed and clenched her teeth as she entered a darkness that would last twenty thousand years.

She is a Gringling. An Eater of Time. Her blessing and her curse: to outlast the darkness.

All of us were burnt and crushed but her—minor inconveniences you might say. What killed us was despair. We despaired in the face of those Abominations and gave up our immortality willingly on that hideous fiery night. We had no means of escape and did not wish to suffer the endless blackness of a living tomb. But she, my daughter, in that miraculous niche of canted stone, she alone refused to go. She held onto her Gringling skin and in so doing condemned herself to the bottom of the Loor as Sọth sank beneath the waves.

She went mad, of course, cursed with immortality that the rest of us had cast off, while she waited in the dark.

On the night it rained fire, I did not expect her to stay; so I left on the sweet toxins of a final draft of shuwt tincture and found my way permanently into another form—one lacking the perfection of my Gringling corpse. But one day I will go back. I will find my little girl. I will pull her from the darkness and return to the shining lands of Ahvêllẹ.

For all its wild fantasy, Caliph found the account compelling. He blinked and rubbed crust from his eyes. Light was coming through the room's single window and his duties as ruler of the duchy swung back on him like a punching bag.

Nuj Ig'nos and the other diplomats were scheduled to leave today. Sena would be returning—late. And he had a ceremony to attend in conjunction with the holiday.

What time is it? He checked. *That can't be right.*

He pushed himself out of the chair and walked briskly to the door. Sorting through his disheveled hair, he poked his head into the hall and asked the sentry stationed in the corridor for the time.

"A quarter of seven, your majesty." Already nearly noon!

CHAPTER 6

Caliph massaged his fingertips deep into his brow and grunted.

"Should I tell the seneschal you're awake?" asked the man.

"No," said Caliph. "No, no." He struck out down the hall, headed for his bedroom.

The day swelled around him, burgeoning with details and unexpected events. It was bathe, dress, lunch, bid his so-called guests good-bye and burn wooden masks in a leafy bonfire by half past ten. After that, the Blue General briefed him before he took loring tea with the burgomasters at twelve. Twenty minutes later he met the papers and answered questions regarding diplomacy with the south. He left out the parts about Pandragor wanting immediate unconditional access to twenty different sites and mostly stuck to his lines, "We've both agreed to more talks and I think Ambassador Ig'nos shares my optimism . . . we're looking forward to a positive dialogue in Sandren."

By fourteen o'clock, just before dinner, Caliph had managed to clear his schedule and wriggle out of obligations at a maskless party in upper Murkbell where two-hundred well-heeled guests planned to close out the Funereal of the Leaves in style.

For Caliph, the cycle of days being High King, month-in month-out, resonated as a kind of unrelenting frequency. An insufferable pattern of noise and sound that he felt abrading him, disintegrating him slowly, both physically and mentally. To rule a country, he had established that you needed one thing more than any other: *to want it.*

But what Caliph wanted was tranquility. He wanted to polish his own shoes, get black marks on his fingers. He wanted Sena to come home, stop her endless research and take breakfast with him as the sun rose out of the west. He wanted time—with her. He wanted a family, fruit trees and idle chatter around the kitchen table.

Sena had offered that once. Did she still want it? A year ago they had been so close. Right after the war had ended, their goals had been braided into one line, reeling them forward.

But that had changed. She had stopped leaving the library. At one point the servants claimed that she had remained on her stool for an entire week while Caliph had been away handling affairs in Mortũrm. One hundred eighty hours in an ice-cold room without food or water, perched on a stool without a back? Was it even possible? The servants said they often found her in the dark with the lamps gone out. They said she didn't move, but stared at the books, as if she was reading them.

Caliph's thoughts lifted as a message arrived that Sena's airship was coming in from the west, over Octul Box. He strode quickly through the statued opulence of a hallway overlooking the east courtyard, toward the castle's zeppelin deck.

When he arrived, the evening was gray and dripping, not quite cold enough to sting. Caliph's stomach felt loose, like it was lying on the blocks beneath him. He insisted on standing alone. The small army of servants in charge of the arrival had organized themselves half a dozen yards away.

Caliph kept waiting and watching . . . and waiting as the clouds churned.

Finally, the *Odalisque* materialized like something conjured out of magic smoke. It slid into position above the zeppelin deck and immediately, a terrifying chill coursed through him.

Sena had been gone nearly a year. It had been months since he had heard from her and, for him, the hiatus had metastasized into irrational unfamiliarity. He couldn't wait to put his arms around her. Feel her. Smell her. Hear her voice.

The craft's wicked mulberry skin might have shown traces of purple under direct sunlight but currently it looked black, dangling from a claw of cloud. The *Odalisque*'s silver filigreed fins and spines marked her as an exclusive pleasure ship and though they tantalized the air with their femininity, they were also vaguely threatening.

Caliph shifted from one foot to the other. He watched the lights flash, signaling that the ship had successfully docked. People began to move.

The airship's cargo doors opened and casket-shaped boxes began sliding out, pulled by rope handles, maneuvered by giant men. A small, fierce woman, clearly in charge, barked at the unloaders. The men adjusted their grips, used tarps to shield the containers from the rain and lugged the heavy loads toward the castle without complaint.

Caliph took a flight of cement steps up to the parapet that would conduct Sena from the *Odalisque* to the castle's warm interior. There were already servants moving back and forth along the narrow pathway hedged with crenels. He made his way toward the airship and spotted the captain. A big man with blond thickets on his forearms stepped out and addressed him with a quizzical smile. "Your majesty? Did she forget something?"

"What?"

The captain kept grinning. "Did she leave something behind? I'll help you look." He turned toward the ship.

Caliph stopped him. "She's already left? She's already gone inside?"

The captain turned back around, lips puckered, eyes wide. "Well . . . yes."

"And she came this way?" Caliph hooked a thumb toward the narrow parapet.

Now the captain showed traces of concern. "Yes, she did. Is something wrong?"

Caliph looked back through the rain in the direction he had come, feeling dizzy. It was impossible. He couldn't have missed her. He didn't know whether to board the *Odalisque* and search for her or return to the castle. Finally he forced a grin and waved his hand dismissively. "No. Nothing's wrong. I must have gotten here late."

The captain saluted as Caliph turned and ducked back over the busy walkway, rain pounding him. By the time he entered the castle, he was soaking.

A short, thick maid with breasts like gun stones nearly walked into him before declaring that he was drenched. She insisted on getting a towel.

"Where is Sena?" Caliph followed her to a nearby linen closet.

The woman didn't know. People milled near the doors; some glanced at him curiously.

"Did you see her come in?"

"Yes, I did. But I don't know where's she's gone. Let's get you dried off."

Caliph took the towel but left her immediately. He headed for the library, reached it in under a minute and found it locked. He grabbled through his keys, dropped them twice. When he finally unlocked the door, the space beyond was dark and empty.

He headed for the kitchen, feeling strangely panicked. Sena wasn't there. By the time he reached his bedroom—their bedroom—he was huffing. Two servants looked up at him, eyes turned saucer. They were folding down the sheets.

"Have you seen Sena?"

They shook their heads. *Am I going crazy?* He checked his choler. Was she doing this intentionally? Just then, a young butler Caliph knew appeared at the bedroom door and spoke with an irritatingly cheerful tone. "Pardon me, your majesty. The door was open. I hope . . ."

Caliph's frustration slipped out. "It's fine, Gilver. What is it?"

The butler continued smiling. "Her ladyship would like to meet you in the east parlor in half an hour. Can I tell her yes?"

Caliph felt stunned. What could be more important than seeing him after so many months? Where was she? What was she doing?

"No. Tell her I'll meet her *now.*"

Gilver's smile vanished and his cheeks went pink as if Caliph's displeasure had seared him. The butler turned, trying to maintain decorum. He gave up. His stride broke into a stiff-legged run.

SENA disregarded the summons, which put Caliph at the table for forty minutes working his way through spinach leaves and creepberries and almond-crusted tenderloin—alone. When he was done, he stalked back to the great east parlor where a salver of ice cream and wine waited.

Sena liked ice cream regardless of the season.

He wound the thermal crank and flicked the lid on his chemiostatic watch. He was fuming. He plunked down and dished himself some dessert. She was uncontrollable. Unreliable. Unfathomable. And what was he going to do about it? Evict her?

After nearly two years on the throne, he had a grip on most aspects of his domain. He knew how to handle the burgomasters. Multinational relations were a work in progress. But Sena?

There was a steaming cup of milk and honey on the table, recently placed by one of the servants. He pushed it aside and opened the wine.

Partly because he didn't want to think about her and partly because he couldn't help it, he tried instead to focus on his country's politics. He could already hear the journalists.

Have the Pandragonians given us any ultimatums, your majesty?

Is solvitriol research still going on at Glôssok?

No and no.

But the problem of the solvitriol accord dragged him down onto the nearby chaise. He grabbed a pillow and lay back, staring up at the ceiling. *No ultimatums yet,* he would lie.

What would Nuj Ig'nos report once he arrived in Pandragor? Caliph had seen machinations like this before: the charade of diplomacy laying the groundwork for a bloody inevitability. He sat up and poured himself another glass of wine.

He had tried to assure the visiting diplomats that Stonehold's solvitriol research had been abandoned; that the facility at Glôssok had been shut down. But tours hadn't satisfied his critics. Now they were demanding access to Stonehavian factories, warehouses, even the cellars of Isca Castle.

"I can't do it," he said aloud. "Letting them in is a no-win. We'll wind up like an old circus beast, limping through hoops, extending our paw every time some ticket-holding monarch wants proof we've been declawed." The second glass . . . or was it the third? . . . went down like the first (or the second). Too fast. It puckered his mouth.

No proof you give will be enough.

Caliph frowned. "No. It won't." He almost looked around for the speaker.

Solvitriol's just a pretense. It was a breathy scratch inside his head more than a voice. Caliph looked at the bottle of wine and noticed it was over half gone. "Yore absolutely right. Alani and eye whir thinking the same thing. Why wood they come awl the whey up hear win they've got wore on they're hands rite next door?"

The voice in his head was asexual and monotone. It reminded him, for blurry reasons, of his childhood. Its answer felt miraculous.

Caliph scowled."What dew yew mean, 'the whiches told the south'?" he asked the invisible speaker.

He pictured his uncle's book, the *Cịsrym Tạ.* For no reason that he could think of, its faded red and filthy hide rose up in his mind. The room had grown distant, it reached him only through a filter of gauzy impressions, one of which was that the presence he was talking with smiled like a sarchal hound.

My uncle's book . . .

In his head, he heard the words: *It's mine!*

Caliph didn't find it strange. He almost laughed as he took another drink. It tasted like brine.

Caliph pawed his face with clumsy fists. "Why everyone care about an errant text ewe bot in Sandren four five scythes?"

You mean arrant?

Caliph laughed. A moment of clarity seized him. "Ewe told me its pages were pounced from stillborns! That's fucking errant!"

He spoke as though the voice in his head belonged to Sena, though he knew with vague growing terror it did not.

"Why the Pandragor want that book?"

Iycestoke wants it too.

Caliph felt the words sink through the wine in his stomach and settle at the bottom. "Do they? Then why dun the Three Kings jush bye it? Ice-stoke can by anything. Ann if we're don't selling, they can shend there thieves two steel it . . . bam!" He clapped his hands.

He looked toward the voice but saw only his empty hand. He heard a padded thud. The glass was empty too, rolling on the rug.

Caliph eased back into the chaise, watching his hand flicker as twilight wobbled through the wet windows across from him.

He could feel the wine smoldering in his cheeks. The chaise was rotating on a slow teetering axis.

If I can just survive this year, he thought, don't get assassinated at the conference on the fifteenth. Just make it through the year. He closed his eyes. The voice was gone. He heard the wind pick up and the rain turn flaky and cold. *Make it through the year and I'll walk away from all of this . . .*

He envisioned snow creeping down into the courtyard where black trees stretched spidery vaults over a late milk-and-sugar sky. The door opened and the scent of southern perfume slunk over him while the world sank into huckleberry night.

"Caliph?" This time it was real. It was not the hissing in his head. This time it was Sena's voice. He struggled against the darkness to find her. He had missed that voice. So much. "Caliph?"

But he was feeling warm and silly, head curled around the wine. He muttered something to the darkness as her cool fingers touched his burning cheek.

"PEW . . . smells like *boy.*"

Sena drew back from Caliph's flushed skin.

But the stuffiness was different from the numbers and the presence that had been here. She stared through the wall at a residue of integers—which was something she could do.

This was her new life, her new eyes, just one year old, encapsulated, isolated and different from everyone else. This life beyond life had stranded her on an island that was both unapproachable and incomprehensible to the people that moved around it. People shrunk away from her. People feared her.

It was not so different from being insane. Indeed, she still wondered if that wasn't a more elegant solution. It was impossible to relate to anyone anymore. In the sunlight that slipped around her season-to-season, melting away her days, the busy milling throngs had become high-speed patterns. People were predictable static. Background noise. Faint chemical-electrical residues in air. She had little patience for them: self-absorbed and oblivious under the racing cycles of the sky.

Only the Pplarians understood.

In her hand she held a crumpled letter from Yũl, her "humble servant." It contained numbers important only to her. A key to the chambers. Chambers inside of chambers. The numbers were soaked in blood.

She had read the letter without looking at it. She would always be reading it.

Yũl was Pplarian. He did not worship her. But like the rest of the Pplarian nation, he understood the gravity of her situation. Once, the Pplarians had come here, out of the dripping blackness. They had distilled on the mountains, seventeen thousand years ago. Because of their origins, they recognized the markings on her skin, and took pity on her. They had seen this before.

Sena scooped herself a cup of melting ice cream and looked around the room.

The presence that had been here with Caliph had burnt numerical anomalies into the air, like the trace of cigarettes hours after the smoker had left. It troubled her.

She watched over Caliph's sleep with involuntary math, hexing and double-hexing the doors and windows to the parlor without blood, making sure they were secure at the same time she concentrated on finding the intruder. Her brain no longer focused on only one thing at a time. She stepped across the hall, into the ballroom. Her eyes, cut with tiny sigils, sorted through the glitter of New Market beyond a terrace of three walls.

Out in the darkness, she discerned people talking, journalists finishing up articles for tomorrow's editions, digging through her affairs with spade-like tongues. She collected all kinds of information, most of which she already knew.

As she searched for the specter she exhaled softly on the windowpane and drew a flower-like shape in the glass, something habitual and only tangentially related to her current concerns. She looked through the shape. Out amid the pale sizzle of Isca's blackened streets she found it.

It had departed from the parlor in haste, low and ebeneous. He—*it*—knew she was furious that it had dared to speak to Caliph. Now it thought to hide, hanging away, between the upright fingers of buildings, levisomnous and horrid.

Why was it here, bothering Caliph? A charade of affection? Trying to fool her into believing that it could care for anything outside itself? Or did it know?

She whispered to it—the thing—miles away, warning it not to come again. She threatened it softly, carefully, telling it that she could change her mind. She reminded it that she was not obligated to do its bidding.

The thing dislodged itself from the district of Maruchine. Unafraid, it sneered and exited the city, billowing out through West Gate. It skirred beneath winter trees that clutched over Howl Lane. In an instant it had vanished, not into, but *through* the house on Isca Hill.

"Soon," Sena whispered. The word fogged her drawing. "Soon—soon." Then she left the ballroom and wandered through the hallways until dawn.

CHAPTER 7

In less than a week, Taelin resigned herself to the fact that snow and ice made new construction an absurd proposition. Men in the business simply laughed at her when she suggested breaking ground in Phisku—or the month of Tes as they called it in the north. Laying foundations was simply not plausible in the Duchy of Stonehold at this time of year. Taelin fretted a whole day before making up her mind. On Day of Whispers she packed it in and bought St. Remora instead.

What she got in place of a church built to her specifications was a dark ruined hulk in Lampfire Hills and a hundred thousand beks in savings.

As part of the break with her father, she had transferred her entire portion of the family's wealth to Isca's Crullington Bank. She knew many people would see it as a half-witted purchase: Saint Remora's time-blackened façade of leaping creatures had melted from centuries of sour rain. It had been boarded up where Knife Street met Mark and squatters and worm gangs had taken up residence in it despite legends that pervaded the area.

Taelin discovered most of the bad history after she had signed the title, never hearing from the bank about the murders or the whore's guild that had installed the crimson glass. Prostitution candles still littered the building. Taelin didn't even know what they were until one of the squatters explained *fast burners.*

There had been drugs and violence and profiteering here, not to mention the questionable myth of the bortghast. Some urban specter the homeless siffilated about.

To the positive, St. Remora lay only ten minutes' walk from her aunt and uncle's house. And she had successfully filed for the city to patch the building's circulatory system on the basis that the church qualified as an historical landmark. Happy to trade the ancient foreclosure for a public record with his name stamped on the building's promising new future, Mayor Kneads quickly capitulated, pulling down the last board and handing her the key (a moment captured by litho which subsequently made front page). Only when they flipped the power back on did she notice that the cathedral's façade had not flared with oily orange and brown-green light.

Rather it had glowed dimly all along.

"Yeah," the man from the city had said with something between boredom and condescension. "We don't really know where those draw juice from. There's a file on 'em down at public. You can check it out for yourself if you want."

The story behind the garish colors was that two decades ago, some eccentric investor had installed the dials asymmetrically across the building's front before letting the loan lapse. He had replaced the rose window with a cluster of glowing clocks that didn't seem to have much to do with telling time. The metholinate boilers in the basement did siphon some of their power into turbines that charged chemiostatic anomalies at the front of the building. Every time the boiler fired, the eleven large hermetic dials flickered with a slight surge of luminosity. But boilers or not . . . the dials never dimmed completely.

Taelin hated them. Come spring, if she could spare the money, she would have them torn out.

On the second of Tes, she bought detergent and wire brushes and put the squatters to work. Those who wanted could stay, with the provision that they earned their keep and followed her rules. Grinning dutifully, several bedraggled souls helped her scrape candle wax from the floor and scrub where campfires had blackened the frescoed ceiling.

In the afternoon, Taelin caught Palmer smoking beggary seeds on the postern steps.

When she scolded him, he handed them over with nothing more than a tilt of the head and a shrug of the shoulders. She was surprised by his acquiescence but pleased as she slipped them into her pocket and guided him back inside.

The two of them spent the next couple days bringing some of the original polish back to the front doors. None of the imagery related to Nenuln, but Taelin didn't care. The carvings and paint offered bright alternatives to worm gang graffiti and soot. All she needed was a warm, relatively clean place to shelter her flock.

The flock consisted of nine people, three of which had been squatters. Taelin fed them twice a day so that, with the boilers restored and the windows replaced, the comfort of their former haunt far surpassed what it had previously been.

On the sixth, Taelin woke up to the smell of Palmer's body, right next to hers. He smelled of beggary smoke and was difficult to rouse. Her room didn't have a lock, a detail she knew she would have to remedy later that day.

When she finally got Palmer awake, he smiled sheepishly. She frowned and told him kindly but clearly that this was her space and that he couldn't just plop down and sleep wherever he wanted. He looked confused with the sunlight blasting his bright blue eyes, pale skin and orange hair in a mad snarl on top of his head. A scrawny Naneman, wasted by the streets, but with a decentness and a sincerity still present in his eyes. He didn't argue, just nodded quietly and gathered up his clothes.

She made him breakfast. Tebeshian coffee for herself.

After that she put him to work caulking cracks in the basement and set herself at a small table to formulate her budget and forecast expenses. The savings made by buying instead of building had stacked up in the church's larder: great sacks of wheat and shelves of canned goods. The northern brands offered no reassurance, all of them strange. Without a sense of quality, she chose the canisters of powdered milk that seemed the most welcoming: cartoon faces of bovine happiness shining in purple ink.

By the end of the day, she judged her stores sufficient to maintain the shelter for several months. She could begin pulling some of the burden off Cripple Gate, planning to feed one hundred twenty meals a day. The larger soup kitchen, two miles to the west, served nearly five hundred. But Cripple Gate was supported by Hullmallow Cathedral and the Church of the Mourning Beggar. They had more resources—a fact that didn't keep them from noticing her efforts.

Taelin read the paper on the morning of the seventh and smiled. She was making an impact. People knew who her father was. The government couldn't ignore her for long. And it didn't. Mail arrived shortly after the paper indicating she would have her audience with Sena Iilool.

Taelin tried to contain her joy—and her anxiety. *Don't be rash. Be persuasive.* This was her chance. The one she had been waiting for. Everything else she had tried in her life had ended in disaster. But this was going to be different. Deep inside, Taelin knew she was still young and inexperienced, perhaps even a bit naive. But she also knew that she was special because, unlike so many other people, she had the desire to do great big fabulous things and that was what she hoped to accomplish here in Isca.

She wanted to unleash something that would change the world, something they would remember her for. Forever.

But before attempting to bring public censure down on Sena Iilool,

Taelin wanted to meet the woman face-to-face. After all, none of the papers or magazines Taelin had read indicated that Sena's church had been established *by* her. Rather, the phenomenon had come out of the Pplar. Whenever a journalist had put forth the question about people worshiping her, Sena had always politely declined to comment. It gave Taelin hope that eventually the blasphemy would end.

Taelin spent the rest of the morning rehearsing what she would say. She left the midday meal service in Palmer's hands, caught a streetcar at five before the hour and arrived on time, eighty minutes later.

The gates of Isca Castle were free of snow and a traditional Stonehavian carriage shuttled her from the gatehouse, through the south bailey and up to the castle doors. It was a cold ride.

A butler with the name GILVER pinned on his lapel signed her in.

After a brisk walk they arrived in a distant wing of the castle. Gilver stopped outside a set of oaken doors, knocked lightly twice then turned the polished porcelain handles and stepped partway in. His body expertly fenced Taelin off in an unobtrusive way. "My lady, the missionary Taelin Rae to see you from the new—"

"Reestablished," corrected Taelin.

Gilver gave her a tight smile then continued. "Reestablished Church of Nenuln." His voice echoed as if he were talking into a metal drum.

Though Taelin heard no response, Gilver stepped aside, granting her access to the chamber. This single gesture, and the demeanor with which he performed it, seemed to elevate her from stranger to guest.

Taelin walked into the stark room.

A sheet-draped piece of furniture despaired in the southwest corner. Aside from that and a ticking thermal crank the space was empty.

A woman in tight black riding pants straddled a wooden stool. Blond as a candle flame, she perched proud, silent and eerie.

Maybe it was her irrational sense that this was an ambush that caused Taelin to look up at the frescoed ceiling. Against the gray plaster, resplendent egg temperas of creepberries and vines had darkened with the centuries.

The ticking of the thermal crank was deafening.

Is she going to welcome me?

Despite the chill, the High King's witch wore a white summer blouse. Ruffled off the shoulder. It revealed too much of her in equal directions, up and down. Taelin found herself staring at the woman's bare trunk and the gem, like a lustrous black currant, that occupied her bellybutton. A heady mix of sensual physicality and dream-like etherealness volatilized the air. A fever-dream.

Gods! Those eyes! Empty and glyptic—litmus blue—so different from the billboards and yet—

Gilver shut the door. The sound tipped Taelin back on her heels. Stiffly, she looked over her shoulder but the butler was gone. When she turned, Sena's eyes pierced her.

The High King's witch held an ancient red book with one hand, vertically, like a ledger pressed into her thigh. The faded black sigil decorating its cover delivered a jolt to the center of Taelin's head.

Taelin looked away.

In the other hand, Sena twirled a fountain pen languorously across her thumb. She was radiant, powerful and relaxed. Taelin began to understand by increments that this was not likely the place or manner in which Sena took most of her appointments. This had been blocked out, carefully. There were no curios. No distractions. Even the anemic lemonchrome glow of a tiny window, which must have been unique to this quarter hour, kindled a halo around the witch's head and enflamed the highlights presumably burnt there by the sun. Taelin got the feeling that everything had been perfectly timed and staged.

Finally Sena stopped spinning her pen. "Lady Rae, would you care to sit down?"

Taelin managed to keep from curling her lip. "No . . . your majesty. I wouldn't dream of taking your stool."

Sena smirked, showing spare amusement. "You don't have to call me that."

"What would you like to be called?"

"Sena."

Taelin watched the woman tousle her curls. *Pure swagger.*

Then Sena's neck extended slightly in Taelin's direction. A feral cat catching the wind. "You smell like apples."

Taelin laced her fingers. "Strange. Your priest said the same thing."

"My priest?"

"I assume he was a priest. I visited your temple, what? Over a week ago now, I think."

"Really?" Sunlight basted Sena's naked waist as she leaned back on one arm. "What did you think of that?"

"It didn't make me feel like I think a temple ought to make you feel. Let's put it that way."

"Haugh." Sena pushed her tongue into her upper molars as she made the pensive sound. "Well it isn't exactly a temple."

Taelin sneered. "Then what is it?"

"It's a colligation."

"My father is an attorney. I—"

"I know who your father is. He used to come to Sandren."

Taelin laughed. "No offense, Miss Iilool, but I doubt you and he were in the same circles back then."

"Well, it was only a few years ago. Summer of '59? Bishop Wilhelm introduced us. I had dinner with your father one night at the Black Couch." She smiled thinly.

Taelin's face turned hot as a lightbulb. "What are you suggesting?"

"I'm not suggesting anything. I'm just telling you that I know your father."

"I doubt it. My father is a good man."

"Is he? I'm glad to hear it. You asked about the colligation?"

"No, I don't think I did."

Sena smiled.

"I've come to build a mission in your city . . . and to speak with you . . . candidly." Taelin took a breath, ready to begin her rehearsed admonition.

"It's all right," said Sena. "You're not the first impassioned clergy that's wanted me to publicly disavow all this"—she stirred the air with her finger—"*blasphemy.*"

Taelin's mouth twitched. The witch was hard to read.

Sena grinned, not maliciously. "You are, however, the first I've granted an audience."

"Thank you," stammered Taelin. "Thank you. I . . . which I, appreciate . . . of course." She wrung her hands behind her back. "Why did you grant one to me?"

"Someone from the south put in a good word for you. And besides, you were called here by Nenuln, weren't you?"

"What? Yes." Taelin had just noticed the faint glimmers that decorated Sena's waist, tracing the muscular hollows as if a spider had crawled crazy over her skin. She was so distracted by the designs that the question hit her broadside. "Have you? I mean . . . who is it that you know? From the south?"

Sena's eyes moved from where they had been boring holes in one of the room's featureless walls and centered on Taelin's face. "Can I ask you something?"

"Of course."

"Does your goddess love me?"

Taelin fumbled mentally. Finally she said, "Yes. I mean . . ."

"Does she love me as much as you loved Aviv . . . or your son?"

Taelin's blush returned. *Unfair!*

But before she could respond, Sena's cool, gravelly voice scraped over her. "Let me tell you what you were sent here to learn."

"I wasn't sent here to lear—"

"You were sent to learn that I am, in fact, going south. I'll be passing over Mirạyhr, over Skellum, near midnight on the twelfth of Tes. You will be unable to stop me there and I will proceed to Sandren. Send whomever you want. The Stairs will kill them."

Taelin felt Sena's words dissolve reality; the logic of the moment was crumbling into chunks. *What's going on? What is she talking about?*

"From the Stairs, I descend toward Bablemum. If you're still following me after that, I'm afraid I'll have to drag you through the jungle."

She's insane. Of course . . . Taelin felt the Duchy of Stonehold as a political entity wrap itself around her, more sinister and entangling than before. This wasn't about bringing some power-hungry shakedown artist to repentance. That clearly wasn't who Sena Iilool was. No. Sena Iilool was crazy. Maybe the king too, if all of this was true. *Or maybe . . . what if? Maybe this was all an act.*

Taelin fixed Sena with a dubious scowl. "I'm sorry . . . I don't . . ."

"Shh." Sena put her finger to her lips. "They'll hear you."

"Who will hear me?"

Sena unleashed the perfect white smile from her billboards. "It belongs to you now. Don't let them take it."

Enough nonsense! "Nenuln sent me here to—"

"Nenuln sent you here as part of an agreement."

Taelin gave up. "I think I should leave."

"Only because you're frightened and you don't know what to say."

"Yes. Exactly."

"I'll keep you safe, Lady Rae. Don't worry."

"Stop it. Stop it!"

"Better than your grandfather's amulet . . ." Sena held out her hand, sideways, fingers extended ambiguously. Whether she was pointing toward it or asking for it, Taelin couldn't tell. Her hand shot up to protect the demonifuge. "No! You can't know that. It's impossible that you know about that!"

"Impossible? What about the scroll from the Valley of Dust that you translated so painstakingly out of Veyden: Gnôr-ak Gnâk Zith'yn Ǻuth-ịch Aubelle Aubiel Gnâk Næn'Ṹln Thũ-ru Ryth-ịch El? And what it means to you is: 'In the darkness there are many lights; Nenuln is One that will end an Age of Sadness.' "

"Stop it. Stop it!" said Taelin. "You can't know that. It's impossible! Your holomorphy . . ."

"Shh—" Sena hushed her again, gently, as if tending an infant. "We aren't enemies." Then she spoke in the Unknown Tongue, which Taelin recognized mostly from those short examples of blasphemy handed out by priests at the church her parents attended, two or three phrases uttered as warnings, as examples of what to fear. The dark glottal sounds popped from Sena's throat with the sound of volcanic glass cracking.

Taelin clenched her grandfather's demonifuge as the panicked sunlight withdrew from the window. A thickening cocoon of shadow concresced over Sena's body.

Darker. Sena became a spectral pit of blackness straddling the stool. Instead of sunlight, a halo of dust or smoke obscured the shape that might or might not have been what Taelin was looking at. Taelin felt her eyes being pulled out of her head into the relentless gravity of the thing. Thin platinum lines, like starry charts, fluoresced within the blackness and a pair of burning eyes opened: white and blue.

Taelin's heart pounded in her skull. She closed her eyes and began to pray. "Sweet Mother of Light, I have been deceived. Your warmth and glory come around me. Protect me and—"

Taelin felt her thoughts lose traction. Her fist was numb from clenching her necklace.

Sena's cool husky voice penetrated the sanctum of her prayer. "You told me your goddess loved me."

Taelin did not dare open her eyes. "Y-yes"—she bit her lip—"she loves you—"

"Of course she does." Sena's voice was right next to her temple, bouncing off her blood vessels. "All the gods love me. You saw their love poems—written on my skin."

Taelin opened her eyes. The doors were still shut but the room was empty. The thermal crank had stopped ticking.

Taelin sank down on her knees and cried.

CHAPTER 8

"If I's there, I'd a smacked her," said Palmer. "She got no business treatin' people like that."

"No, you wouldn't," said Taelin.

"Yes, I woulda and you couldn't a stopped me. She's nothin, she's less than nothin. Got her face all over town like it's somethin special—but it ain't. What you do is special, Lady Rae. What you done is special. Helpin us."

Taelin smiled but the horror of her visit still haunted her. When that awful tangible darkness had surrounded Sena, Taelin had *felt* it. More than a change in light. It had been a power, a sign, a bellwether. The experience still tingled in her pores.

For the next few days, Taelin shook off her fear by serving meals and handing out blankets; delivering evening services and passing around flyers. Every day, without fail, she got the questions.

"You from Pandragor?"

"Why you come up here?"

"Must be crazy. Trade that warm sand for snow!"

She took pride in being from the south and enjoyed the attention. But her escape was short-lived. On the eleventh, a stooped, vile-looking bird planed in through the dreamhole in St. Remora's steeple where Palmer had been stationed to operate the volucroria. When Palmer rang the bell Taelin darted upstairs, giddy at hearing the signal that meant correspondence had arrived and that Palmer had determined it was important.

Perhaps it was from the mayor. Or maybe Travis Whittle had decided to support her with a grant.

She entered the volucroria and boggled at the three pigeons she had purchased from a local duffer. They churned through a series of conniptions inside their cage. The fits looked and sounded more like feathery explosions than anything real birds could accomplish. Taelin marched across the room and wrenched a heavy quilt over the volery.

"Palmer! You have to cover them when they do that."

"Yes, ma'am." Palmer was looking quietly at the sinister bird. Taelin saw it now that the commotion had ended and it gave her pause. The four-foot creature stood on a wooden perch near the dreamhole, shaking out a black ruff with tiny irisated markings. It glared at her. Eyes, dark as blood; the curve of its long ibis-like beak, white—softening into blue near the skull. The creature seemed to know to stand quietly so that she could use an extractor to pull the cruestone from its skull.

Taelin swallowed and picked up the tool. She approached slowly, wary of the sharp beak that resembled one half of a pair of ice tongs. The thing shrieked at her, revealing the pale pink interior of its mouth, urging her to hurry.

Taelin steeled herself and untied the bundle from its leg: a message and a hood. She secured the hood first. An eyelet at the top of the skull allowed her to pluck the cruestone out. Freed from the fire, the creature shook its head again.

Taelin's heart was pounding, not from the ferocity of the messenger but from the seal on the golden tube.

Palmer's voice trembled. "Is that . . . is it uh . . . ?" He was pointing toward the seal.

"Yes." She felt breathless.

It was the seal of the High King.

"Fuckin' ticky," Palmer mewled.

She opened the golden tube and pulled out a single sheet of paper. Affixed to the bottom was a gem that would undoubtedly send the bird back whence it had come. Taelin read the few words on the page and felt her entire body flush with a mixture of pride . . . and fear.

Madam,

His Majesty, High King Caliph Howl, welcomes you to the Duchy of Stonehold. It would please the crown to acknowledge your recent charitable efforts here in Isca City with a token of his gratitude this evening at St. Remora at thirteen o'clock.

Please feel free to use the enclosed cruestone in order to confirm or decline at your earliest convenience.

Drown Vicunt,
High Seneschal, Isca Castle

Taelin's knees, despite the reason for her coming to Stonehold, promptly gave out. She sat down in a wooden chair, clenching the note as if it had been delivered by Nenuln herself.

She worried that Sena was behind this but Palmer interrupted her thoughts.

"Lady Rae?" he whispered. "Lady Rae? Is they shuttin us down? Is that what it says?"

Taelin made the hand sign for no.

"He's coming," she said, looking at Palmer's pale, wasted face, which hung in astonished folds like a wet sock back in the shadows of the volucroria. "He's coming here. Tonight."

"YOU'LL want an engineer," said Alani.

"Sig."

"Sigmund Dulgensen?" Alani clarified.

"There's only one Sig. He'll come. He owes me. He owes me for the rest of his natural life."

Alani wrote the name on his ledger. "Anyone else?"

Caliph tugged his lower lip. "I don't think so."

"I suggest we bring Lady Rae," said Alani, "from the Church of Nenuln." Dappled, snowy light danced through the office windows and played across the spymaster's unsmiling features.

Caliph chuckled. "Why? And why would she agree to come with us?"

"Because I have it on good authority that her reason for being in Stonehold isn't to assist the poor."

"She's a spy then?"

"Worse. An idealist."

"I'm an idealist."

"Hardly." Alani's scoff was brusque. His sharp features peered against the light, out into the city. "Lady Rae isn't fond of Sena or the fact that there's a temple in her name."

Caliph steered his thoughts away from Sena. "So this Lady Rae is here because she's upset over some crazies worshiping my—?" He wondered why the daughter of an attorney general had nothing better to do with her life.

"Precisely," Alani cut in. "Did you know she had an audience with Sena last Day of Charms?"

"Sena does a lot I don't know about."

"The priestess left the castle looking flushed. What intrigues me is why Sena granted her the appointment."

"I don't know," said Caliph. "But if she's here because she hates Sena, why would we want to invite her—"

"We don't care about her on that level," said Alani. "We care about how we appear to the south and what they print. I'm sure if you make a donation to her church tonight . . . she'll see you in person of course in the best possible light . . . and then I'll invite her to accompany us tomorrow. Not only will she feel obligated, but I'm sure she'll also view it as an opportunity to go another round with Sena and perhaps this time get the upper hand."

"Not very subtle."

"Subtle enough. Did you know she spent time in a mental ward?"

Caliph raised his eyebrows. "How do you know she's free for a visit tonight?"

"I've already made arrangements."

Caliph grunted. "You know I don't like it when you—"

"Yes. I know." Alani's lips formed an immaterial pout.

Caliph couldn't help smiling. Just slightly. "I'll trust you on this. Whatever edge you can get us with the Pandragonians, I'll happily take."

Alani inclined his head slightly, tucked his ledger under one arm and quietly left the room.

WORD of Taelin's efforts with the poor had fueled a hot controversy. After all, St. Remora was in Lampfire Hills. This wasn't Maruchine, or Thief Town. Outside of the little cavities of decay along Knife Street and Seething Lane, Lampfire Hills was an upscale borough. Critics were already blaming her for luring unsavory elements out of Winter Fen's slums and into the proper neighborhoods of Heath Street. Others decided it had become chic for the upper crust to stroll down and serve food at the shelter.

That the High King was willing to publicly recognize and support her efforts clearly meant that he wasn't worried about criticism. Even the squatters took pride in scrubbing the church anew, with the understanding that the supreme leader of the duchy would be arriving today: to see them.

Taelin expected them to utter slurs but, to her surprise, not one of them did. In fact, she began to understand that they did not blame the crown for their lives. Rather they blamed themselves and, in Palmer's case at least, thought of it as a personal choice.

Early in the afternoon, Taelin reread the message.

She still didn't trust it. This was not Pandragor and Sena Iilool was certainly not her friend. She sorted through her larder for ideas, pulled out a can of freeze-dried berries and sighed. *He won't eat. But I have to put out a spread . . . something for his bodyguards at least.* She guessed there would be journalists and ambrotypists and city watchmen by the dozen.

Slightly after noon she began to notice that the whole of Knife Street between Mark and Heath was barricaded off.

His motivation must be purely political.

She couldn't imagine Caliph Howl taking a sincere interest in Nenuln's church. Not that it mattered. She wasn't going to take his money, even if he offered any. *What would a "token of his gratitude" consist of, anyway?* She tried not to think about it. Besides, she could afford her current expenses better than she could afford to be financially obligated to the entity she had come here to depose.

Tonight was going to be *her* stage with litho-slides and editorials; her chance to politely decline his assistance and tell the press what Nenuln's church was really about.

By half past twelve, winter hurled night at the city and the sunset transformed icicles on St. Remora's eaves into jewels. This far north, the planet's angle around the sun produced sunsets that lasted for hours.

Shortly, a knight in chemiostatic armor pounded on the front doors just as Taelin was opening them to check the approach. When they swung into the vestibule, the narthex seemed to lose one of its walls, staring vastly down on Mark Street.

The knight greeted her with a brusque smile and stepped out of the cold strawberry evening, armor glowing from little emerald panes of holomorphic glass. Once she had invited him in, a detachment of men poured into the church, inspecting rooms and establishing a perimeter with gate-crashing efficiency. It took less than five minutes. Taelin could see men holding flash handles. Bulbs popped in the murky street where gas lamps dwindled toward Knife. Then, Taelin heard the jingle of bells. A dark shape slipped off Mark, up St. Remora's private causeway and came to a stop on the terrace.

Against the sky's pennants of ripped pink and winter turquoise, Taelin saw a man dressed in black step from a sleigh heaped with luxuriant fur. He wore a gold clasp at his throat and looked directly at her.

I am an emissary of Nenuln! She chastised herself as the High King's hand floated up to help Sena.

Twined in white fur, immaculate as the snow-draped roofs, the High King's witch drew her hood back while Caliph Howl waited for her. In the twilight, Sena's short gold curls tossed fitfully in the wind, eyes searching momentarily, wary of the subjacent streets.

Her gaze found Taelin as the eleven lenses on St. Remora's façade dumped muddy orange light over her face. An eternal instant passed between them. Then the High King caught Sena's hand and pulled her like a kite through air.

* * *

TAELIN imagined decadent sweets imported from Yorba, silk sheets as rich as cocoa butter. She imagined gorgeous, wrought-iron lanterns throwing candlelight across a lavish palace bedroom dripping beneath the moons. Under creamy light, the High King and his witch were moving together. Perfect bodies. Serpentine rhythms. Indulgent. Erotic. Pernicious to the soul. Sena's lips pulled earnestly, her perfect teeth bit tenderly, siphoning the High King, drop by sparkling drop into an ewer full of souls . . .

"YES. Come in." Taelin inhaled sharply.

The narthex was freezing. The knight helped her close the door. A crowd of people with official clearance milled as another flashbulb branded its ugly ghost onto her retinae.

"Thank you. Nothing for me," the High King was saying. His smile was cordial. The smells of mocha and warm, iced pastries (filled with rehydrated berries) had already fogged the air.

Taelin watched Sena's delicate fingers pluck snowflakes from her hair. "I'll have loring tea," said Sena.

More flashbulbs and conversational laughter. Taelin watched the press fawn over the High King's witch while Sena reciprocated.

"Lady Rae," a man in business attire leaned into her ear, "we're going to do the donation over here." His hands, one behind her back and one gesturing in the direction he meant for her to go, never actually touched her.

More flashbulbs. Taelin was getting a headache. She smiled and blinked and followed the man's directions.

Caliph Howl stood near a table with a coffer on it, smiling exactly as all politicians smiled. His hands were folded in front of him until the man guided her into position. Then a spot right next to the High King opened up and Caliph put his arm around her.

That was precisely the moment that a huge amorphous shadow burst out of the chancel into the hall and caused Taelin to cry out. No one else seemed to notice the shape. They looked at her instead.

Taelin looked from the undulating apparition toward Sena.

Forked, interwoven shadows fluttered over the witch's cheeks. Her stare seemed to gouge Taelin's body, excavating flesh and bone and soul like an occult steam shovel. *What's happening? Why did I come here? Why am I in Stonehold? This is . . . anserine.*

TIME seems to change. Chemiostatic mechanisms in the church's walls are groaning. Everyone is talking. Sipping cups and smiling while the

High King reveals a coffer. Litho-slides of the moment are flashed by journalists in the wings.

Glowing dials are spinning. The air is warped. Taelin can see a mansion on a hill . . . its windows swell with red skies. Sena's mouth is full of whispers. Her curls are blowing. Her sapphirine eyes drool perfect rivulets: chokecherry red. Taelin hears the great black shadow that has slid out of the chancel shriek like gulls above the sea. Its shape is enormous and impossible to describe. Taelin feels herself stumble and fall. Then a woman's beautiful lips—perhaps Sena's—are pressed against hers, kissing her deeply. She feels the probing of an eager tongue.

Taelin opens her mouth to scream but something heavy dislodges from the back of her throat. It bubbles out of her mouth like semi-molten beef fat . . . with the exception that it ululates and squeals.

"There she is."

A smiling face hovers over her. Not Sena's.

"We lost you there for a minute. Let's move her to that cot." She can feel strong hands lift and position her on the uncomfortable canvas. She lets the nightmare go, gladly trading it for reality—even though it doesn't feel real yet. Things are only marginally better.

Caliph is leaning over her with eyes the color of wet snakeskin. He is looking at her pupils. She can tell he is attempting a prognosis. But his anxiety over her is the anxiety of a stranger for another stranger.

For a moment she lets herself look into his eyes.

What's happening? She feels frantic and confused.

From behind the High King, she hears someone break the silence with a joke. "It's okay folks . . . she's just never seen that much money before." A chorus of good-natured laughter.

But a flashbulb pops and Caliph's irritation shows. "Please! No more lithos!" Caliph's voice is smooth but forceful. She sees a knight grab the offender and move him instantly toward the door.

A woman in a red trench has appeared.

"I don't know what I'm looking for," says Caliph. "Is she all right?"

It is the physician's turn to look at Taelin's eyes. She makes Taelin squeeze her fingers. Her face is kind but not as kind as Caliph Howl's. "I think she'll be just fine," the doctor says.

Taelin sits up and summons a smile for the crowd. "I'm sorry." Dazed amity leaks out of fractures in the resolve she has put on specifically for the event. "I don't usually faint." There are more jokes . . . this time about the High King's good looks.

Taelin sees the chapel as though its gravity has shifted and the witch is at its core. The huge shadow has disappeared. Sena is looking at her with a curious smirk. Not cruel. Rather ingratiating . . . as though she has done Taelin a favor.

Taelin scowls and stands up. She remembers she is being scrutinized. She smiles again and touches her forehead where there is a faint scar.

The physician produces a glass syringe.

"Oh Gods, no. No. I'm fine." She holds her hands up and maintains the artificial grin despite the fact that the room is spinning. "I'm so sorry. I haven't eaten much today." She sits down again, this time in a padded chair that has been scrambled from a nearby room.

Caliph pats her gently on the back and puts a glass of water into her hand. "We don't have to do this tonight," he whispers. His voice is only for her. Too kind. She suspects him of ulterior motives but smothers her skepticism with graciousness she coughs up for the press.

"No, really. I'll be all right." She stands up. Everybody claps.

She can see the Iscan trade bar in the coffer. Gold. Its value must be extraordinary. She doesn't know what to say. She says thank you. She lets the High King's aides move her into position by the table. They shine lights on the two of them. The ambrotypist begins with a litho for the papers and then takes two images on treated plates of glass.

She doesn't want this. She works her demonifuge nervously between her fingers. She remembers that it is too much money. She must stop this. She must decline. She must turn this event to its one true purpose and the only reason she agreed to the High King's donation in the first place: so that she could refuse it in front of the press, then tell all the journalists what she intends to do . . . how Nenuln will change the north forever. But it is too late. Is it too late?

The litho-slides have already been taken. If she declines now, they will print the slide of her accepting and then write that she changed her mind. She will look foolish and capricious. If she accepts, her entire goal will be compromised. But it is too late. She has been thinking while the flashbulbs pop and the journalists scribble. She has been smiling and nodding while her eyes circuited the room.

The ceremony has been abridged for her sake. The High King is already leaving. Taelin sees Sena standing by one of the crimson window panes. Wait! Weren't all the panes replaced? *The witch breathes on the window and then draws something on the frost-covered glass. The knight has reopened the front doors and the air is freezing. Sena gives Taelin a private smile and floats out into the snow.*

CHAPTER 9

Royal Charity Backs Pandragonian Religion
by Willis Bothshine, Journalist

In a move some have called political desperatism, High King Caliph Howl gifted three hundred forty thousand beks to the reformed Church of Nenuln in the form of a solid gold trade bar. The king's public donation took place at thirteen o'clock on Tes eleventh, Day of Whispers. The gift was accepted by Lady Taelin Rae, currently the church's only acting clergy, before royal knights escorted it to Crullington Bank for deposit . . .

Taelin's eyes skipped down, passing over details of her arrival and purchase of St. Remora.

But according to Dr. Yewl, professor of Stonehavian Politics, "Even if the [High] King's donation doesn't ease the tension between [Pandragor and Stonehold], it's a smart thing for him to do, locally. He should do more of it. Shelters bring order [instead of] rogue panhandling to pay off squat lords. We need more infrastructure for rebuilding [people's] lives."

Before it came to its smug conclusion, the article turned out another line or two about the High King's failure to build relationships with the south.

Taelin set it aside with a feeling of despair. Papers were for entertainment, skepticism and veiled malice, not messages of hope.

What had happened? But she knew. Last night she had had a dream. A beautiful white figure had appeared to her, standing in St. Remora. Haloed in gold, and orbited by fantastic lights, the being had told her, in a pure high language, about the blackness that had come crashing through her chancel.

So much like a train . . .

All darkness and smoke and dials spinning. Like a locomotive bursting into a station.

It was the witch's train.

And Sena had her bags packed. She had used Stonehold up. She was done here, on the edge of escaping . . . far away.

The language was so simple, so beautiful and perfect, that Taelin hoped Nenuln would never stop talking.

Don't let her get away, Taelin.

But I don't understand the other things I saw. There was a man's body, I—

You saw the future, Taelin. It is a gift.

TAELIN touched the demonifuge against her chest. So it was meant to be. She was meant to accept the High King's money. She was meant to meet Caliph Howl.

Yet her dream had given her no clue *how* to chase Sena down. Taelin didn't know any holomorphy. She had never been good at math. *Nenuln will provide a way.*

She set her cup of coffee down and got up to shovel snow.

As she approached the front doors, she stopped.

A single pane of red glass confronted her. How had she missed it? Its ill-fitting edges leaked cold air. Taelin looked at it closely. There was a finger-drawing melted into the ice, flower-like.

She wiped her hand across the mark. Strangely, she couldn't make it go away.

She rubbed harder, scrubbing with her sleeve. She began to panic. Why wouldn't the ice melt?

"Lady Rae? Is something wrong?"

Taelin whirled. "I thought I told you to have all the panes replaced!"

A former squatter named Vera, nearly Taelin's age—whose youth had been rasped off against sidewalks and back alleys—put a worn, ruddy hand emphatically against her concave chest. "I did."

"Then what do you call that?" shouted Taelin, thrusting her finger at the glass.

Vera shook her head, utterly confused.

Vera liked to remind everyone that she had been a landlord and had once taken good care of her properties. Taelin now doubted that was true and regretted having given charge of the church's restoration over to her.

"I want that red glass changed out," said Taelin. "Today!" Then she hefted her shovel and opened the door, squinting against the sudden brightness of the snow.

There had been no knock which was why, when she stepped out onto the powder-laden step, the man standing there startled her.

Thankfully, he gave no indication that he had heard her yelling. He wore a long black coat of felted wool that fell to his ankles and his smooth head, dappled like an eggshell, framed a warm face that smiled through a soft white beard.

"Good morning," he said brightly. "My name is Alani."

Vera poked her head out, interrupting. "Pardon me, Lady Rae." Vera's tone didn't indicate that she wanted to be pardoned. "But there ain't no fucking red glass to change out!" Then she disappeared and slammed the door, leaving Taelin outside.

"THOUGHT she was exotic, did you?" Sena smirked. "It's all right. I'm not jealous."

"Why are we talking about this?" asked Caliph. His neck was hot from the conversation.

"Oh, be serious. That priestess costume she wears? That's just for show—"

"Just for show?" Caliph started laughing. "Well she's a damn good fake then. She bought that horrible ruin with her own money."

"Not her money."

"Whatever. It's her money now. Daddy's name isn't on the account at Crullington. Maybe I just handed a trade bar to a theologaster but—"

Sena's smirk faded away. "Maybe you did."

"Maybe I did. It doesn't matter. It's political."

The night of her arrival had blown over. His desperate search, the way she had avoided him: the argument had already come and gone. Another stone tipping the pan toward something he didn't want to think about.

The thermal crank's fan had kicked in. He sat across from her in the east parlor watching the hot breeze tug her oiled ringlets. When she leaned forward in the chair, legs braced in an elegant *K*, shoulder extending so that her fingers could deposit an unfinished cup on the coffee table, Caliph coughed.

An angelus bell sounding from Temple Hill cleared his thoughts, reminding him of the time. "You're sure you want to come with?"

"I'm all packed." Sena looked up from her position, stretched between cup and chair. The filigree in her skin went chromium with the dawn. Caliph remembered phrases: *crystallized guanine in the dermis.* She had once called the markings her *iridocyte idiom.* Words he had been forced to look up.

"Caliph?"

"Sorry. I'm . . . tired." He stood up and stretched. "You're absolutely sure you want to come?"

"You already asked that."

He rubbed his temples. "I know. It's just that this trip might not be perfectly *safe.* This speech I have to give . . ."

"Important one. I know."

"You could say that."

"There's a lot riding on this trip, Caliph." The way she said it made it sound more like a warning than an acknowledgment.

"All right. But we have to leave by twelve."

"My ships are ready."

"Ships?"

She sat back. "I'm taking the *Odalisque* and the *Iatromisia.*"

"I see. So we're taking three . . . three airships," he spread his pinkie, ring and middle finger like an array of weapons, "when we only need one? Why do we . . . I mean, why do *you* want to do that?"

She stood up, walked over to him and draped her hands around his head. Despite a cup of loring tea, the scent of her breath remained almost perfectly neutral. "Caliph, you're bringing the Pandragonian priestess. I haven't asked you why."

It felt like she had punched him. "How did you know that?"

She breathed—which he knew was a presentment—and closed her eyes. When her lids slid shut she looked almost exactly as he remembered her from college. But when her lashes unzipped, like black vinyl, they revealing glistening alien pools.

"Trust me," she said.

But he couldn't.

"You know I brought you something," she said. "But you were so upset the other night, I didn't give it to you."

"Oh? Was it a birthday present?"

She nodded and her fingers produced a wooden carving that resembled his collection of tiny figurines in the high tower's display case—except that this one's workmanship was not as elegant. It was a man with a young girl on his shoulders.

"Thank you." It was nice of her to remember his fondness for those wooden figurines but she apparently lacked understanding. He was not a collector. The set in the high tower was not an array of pieces purchased from upscale shops. He kept them because of the person who . . .

Caliph's heart skipped. He turned the thing over and saw the familiar words carved into the piece's base.

"For Caliph." The same that marked each of his other figurines.

He felt elation and confusion at the same time as he pictured how Cameron's hands must have aged, how whittling a hunk of wood must have grown more difficult with the years—

"You saw him? You went to Nifol?" Caliph interrupted his own thoughts.

Sena nodded.

The dream man had left Stonehold just before the war, heading for the warm south. But this carving pulled him back across the miles. Caliph stroked the wood lovingly with his thumb. Upon closer inspection, the carving seemed to be of Caliph himself. He noticed how Cameron's knife had picked out the smile of the girl on his shoulders with particular care.

Sena had told him nothing about her trip. Ten months of mystery. The casket-shaped boxes unloaded from the *Odalisque* had carried books. They were stacked three deep, creating blockages in all the hallways adjacent to the library.

Well, now he knew one more thing.

Seneschal Vicunt knocked on the parlor door. Caliph recognized the two-stroke tap, light-handed and expressly unobtrusive. He slipped the wooden carving into the pocket of his long coat. Sena withdrew her arms from around his neck and walked slowly back to the glass coffee table where she retrieved her cup.

"Pardon me," said the seneschal as Caliph opened the door. "There's a diplomatic package here, addressed to the lady of the castle. It's from the Grand Arbiter that's been holding rallies in Gas End."

Caliph glanced over his shoulder to where Sena stood, blowing across her cup, watching him.

"It's a bit heavy." Vicunt's voice communicated strain.

Caliph opened the door and directed him to bring it in.

The seneschal placed it on one end of the coffee table. It was a square wooden box, roughly two feet on a side and eight inches deep. The label bore the diplomatic seal and was clearly addressed to Sena.

A strange aroma surrounded it. It smelled of ointments and spice.

Caliph lifted a butter knife and offered it to Sena, gesturing for her to break the seal.

She sipped her tea and did not respond.

"You're not going to open it?"

"No. Take it out and bury it."

"Bury it?" Caliph smiled quizzically. "What's in it?"

"Nothing good," she said.

Caliph brandished the knife at the seal but Sena only shrugged. A pavid chill crawled across his back. It was addressed to her. He had no right to open it.

"You know what's in it?"

"Take it out and put it in the ground," she said again. "The Church of Kosti Vinish feels threatened by me. If you open it, it'll be public knowledge . . . and it will derail our reason for going to the conference."

Caliph hesitated, still holding the knife. He could not fathom what the box might contain that would prevent him from going to the conference. He looked at Sena's unreadable blue eyes, hovering an inch above her cup. Finally he put the knife down. "Drown?"

"Yes, your majesty?"

"No one opens it. Take it out to the bogs. Make sure it's never found."

Drown bit his lip nervously. He approached the box with brand-new, highly-visible dread, picked it up in both arms and hauled it from the room.

"See," she said after he had left. Caliph scowled at her. "You *do* trust me . . ."

CHAPTER 10

Suspicion nagged Taelin. Her invitation to accompany the High King's entourage bore the stink of contrivance. Especially since the high-profile conference in Sandren was going to be the first real forum between the Tebesh Plateau and what was collectively known as the Hinterlands in over eighty years. Her father had instilled in her an awareness for what he called *the wire-pullers*: people who maneuvered other people in order to protect themselves from legal or political harm. Her presence on such a trip, amid the High King's staff, would certainly classify.

On the other hand, Taelin had come north with a keen understanding of her social status. Her whole goal in transforming St. Remora into a mission home was to gain the attention of the crown.

In light of how her journey had unfolded thus far, it was only natural that the crown would seize the opportunity to pose her next to itself. And that was precisely where she wanted to be. Only from such a position of privilege would she have access to Sena Iilool, to the possibility of persuading her to denounce the groups that had elevated her to the status of a goddess, or in the case that Sena was insane . . .

Taelin had not actually planned for such a contingency.

Nevertheless, she equivocated only a few moments over Alani's invitation. Though she initially had no one to entrust her shelter to, speaking with clergy from Hullmallow had quickly produced a solution. She dropped the keys to St. Remora off with Hazel Nantallium on her way to the Hold. The trip to Sandren would only be three days. She packed light.

THE three airships were leaving Isca late, under snowfall, far past noon. They had waited for her.

The *Bulotecus*, the *Odalisque* and the *Iatromisia* were all relatively small. Taelin surrendered her flight bag to one of the handlers. He knocked a finger against his brow and smiled at her while chiding playfully that the daylight would leave without her if she didn't hurry. Taelin boarded the *Bulotecus*, which was the High King's vessel—though he was not on board.

She had overheard from men on the platform that he would be on the *Odalisque* with Sena.

Taelin glanced around the swank quarters, impressed with the décor. As the airship uprooted itself from the castle, she found a bar and poured herself a sherry, which she finished before leaving the glowing cabins for the observation deck. Her boots gripped the textured steel and her lungs filled with cold air. She reached for the icy railing to steady herself and gazed down.

Gray towers, drifting with snow, fanned below her: a rolling parallax that accentuated the third dimension and made her stomach pitch. The sky, identical to tarnished silver, burped uneven flurries. The flakes swirled past her, vanishing into the fissures of Isca's gaslit abyss.

Taelin slid her crimson goggles down over her eyes, enjoying their power, then hugged herself and shivered from the beauty of the moment. As the craft ascended, the buildings became phantoms, the streetlamps: dreamlike phosphors. She felt the wind increase as the engines' hum modulated toward crescendo. Then, all at once, Isca City disappeared, and the void swallowed Taelin whole, churning like a ghastly white stomach.

"Hi!"

Taelin spun around. The voice was high and bright as someone banging a toy cymbal. "I'm Specks."

A thin boy, pale as the snow, dark brown hair windswept to the side of his face, hovered spare inches above the *Bulotecus*'s deck. His legs hung useless as crumpled straws. "Do you like snow?" he asked.

"I'm from the south. I've never seen snow before. But yes, I like it. You're floating—"

"Yeah," he said, face beaming. "It's ticky!"

"How old are you?"

"Seven." He was small for seven. His thin right arm was shod in a heavy leather bracer that pulled that side of his body down, forcing an uneven slope to the hang of his shoulders. The bracer ticked and Taelin noticed a drop of blood under Specks' feet.

"Oh, gods . . . you're bleeding."

"Yeah. It's okay. I'm a holomorph." He seemed proud to say so. "That's what the doctors say." His left hand held a small cup of something warm and steamy, which he lifted to his mouth and drank.

Taelin crouched down in front of him. "Can I look at that?" she asked, gesturing to the bracer.

"Sure." He extended his arm with visible strain.

The bracer was made of thick chrome-tanned leather. Adjustable straps with copper buckles ensured that it remained cinched tightly to his arm. There was a compact engine stitched into the thing, also made of copper and steel, barely larger than a pocket watch. It gave off the whispery sounds of fine clockwork. A tiny chemiostatic cell powered it and outlined, in green, a spigot that jutted from the side of his wrist.

From the spigot, a drop of blood beaded and fell.

The purpose of the contraption was mysterious at first until Taelin listened carefully to the ticking. Like tapping codes for the blind, the little engine pinged out a stream of numbers, over and over, ringing off the duralumin railings of the zeppelin deck. The sound was subtle, thought Taelin. She supposed you could get used to it.

At the end of the long series of precise pings and ticks, which Taelin now guessed was a complex but automated equation, the valve on Specks' arm snicked open, then shut again, and another drop fell.

"You *are* a holomorph, aren't you?" she whispered, genuinely amazed. "This thing keeps you floating?"

"Yes, ma'am. My dad says my legs are in this arm."

"What are you doing here?"

"My dad works for the king and we don't have a mom so I comed with."

"I see. What does your dad do?"

Specks showed teeth, a sly smile that he seemed to have been saving up. "He's the captain of this ship."

"And I see you're quite proud of him."

"Yes, ma'am."

Taelin looked around but they were alone, plowing through the snow in the empty clouds over Stonehold. "Who looks after you while your dad is flying?"

Specks' eyes got wide and serious. He nodded his head up and down as he spoke. "I know the rules. I stay safe. I don't need no babysitter."

Taelin felt a smile creeping into her face but she didn't want to belittle him. She brushed a whip of dark hair from his cheek and said, "No. Of course you don't. But who's this?"

A plush toy peeked from a backpack over the top of Specks' shoulder. It was dark brown and ferocious with black plastic eyes and felt teeth and Taelin shook it gently by the ear.

"That's Rot. He's a sarchal hound. He'll bite your hand off if you're mean to me. But not really. And not you anyway. Cuz you're not mean."

"He's all the protection you need then."

"Yep." Specks pointed at the bright glitter of Taelin's necklace, which was eye-level as she stooped in front of him. "What's that thing?"

"That's what protects *me*," said Taelin.

"It looks like a light," said Specks. "But . . ." He had noticed how strange it was.

"It's a special necklace that my grandfather found."

"Ticky," said Specks. "Do you want to come see the other animals what my dad gave me for my birthday?"

Taelin smiled and took his hand as another drop of his blood hit the metal decking and turned to ice.

STOIC but afraid of what his speech to the assembly might mean for the future of the Duchy, Caliph scowled at himself in the stateroom's beveled mirror. Dim hooded lamps to either side barely exuded a woody-orange luminescence.

Behind him, Sena knelt on the bed, outlined by a vast circular window. Her arms moved gently around her head as if she was putting something on. "We could waste some time," she said.

Her words affected him instantly, like a spell.

Up until this moment he had been looking past her, to where the night sky boiled and the *Odalisque*'s six water-cooled engines lit the ship's chrome undercarriage like wet actinolite. Caliph's skin grew clammy as he listened to the extension shafts spin, powering them toward Menin's Pass. He tried not to think about last year's war or the cold spar sliding under his heart.

Startling him, diverting his fear, Sena's voice hit the back of his neck. She was right behind him. "Don't be afraid," she said.

He felt her arms encircle him, which was more than a little unnerving. So he turned from the mirror and choked up a laugh. "Afraid? Why would I be afraid? Everything's going to be fine."

Her finger tapped him on the chin. "No, it's not." His skin crawled.

"I don't want you to be afraid of me, Caliph." It started to sink in that her words were too precise, too perfectly tuned to his thoughts. Caliph let go of her as if she had become a block of ice.

"What are you doing?"

"Caliph." Her voice was careful. "Remember that night we slept downstairs? You went to the icebox, so thirsty . . . looking for a carton of milk."

Caliph took a step back.

"It was dark," she said. "You were tired. You wound up with the wrong container and when you lifted it to your mouth, the taste of citrus was so appalling that you dropped it on the floor.

"The juice hadn't gone bad. It was your expectation that soured it."

Caliph did remember that night. And she was right. The nectar—flown from Sandrenese vineyards—might as well have been vinegar.

The memory was stunningly relevant to what he felt right now. It was as if her words had flipped a switch inside his head.

She was not like him, despite her appearance. The perfection he saw in her—that everyone saw in her—had instilled in him the expectation that who she was, on the inside, should—

Her words both interrupted and finished his thought, completing it more succinctly than he could have done himself.

"The paragon of humanity is as alien as anything you can dream," she whispered.

"You're inside my head."

"I'm not going to hurt you."

Caliph imagined a heady fume coiling off her skin in the darkness. The platinum lines glittered as she turned slightly. The sound of Caliph's own breathing deafened him.

What if she was right?

What if she represented something closer to apotheosis than he wanted to admit? He was afraid to touch her. There were numbers in her. Ratios. The cunning spirals of her ears. The distance from eyes to chin. The precise width of her lips was overly perfect.

"What happened to you?" he said. "What made you like this?"

He hadn't meant it as a cruel assessment but in response, the black cutout of her head turned down into the fan of her fingers. The uncanny seduction broke off. For a moment he thought she was only thinking. Then her shoulders convulsed.

He couldn't understand what had caused this. He reached out. The instant his hand touched her, the sound came out, wretched and plaintive. All his internalized fears and postulations shed away. He was left with the sound of her hushed blubbering, the humming of the airship and her strange patchy-warmth shuddering against his chest.

"I'm sorry. I didn't mean—"

"It's not your fault," she hissed. "It's not your fault."

Feeling brutish, Caliph reached back into their past for anything that might shore up their embrace. "Hey." He tugged her chin with his finger. "You and I belong to the stars, remember?"

She laughed brokenly at that and said, "You don't know what that means. You've never known what that means." For a long time after, she was quiet.

Caliph held her. He looked over her shoulder, through the eight-foot circular window, to where the ship's starboard lights flashed and burned. Slowly, his anxiety began building again.

Other ships signaled back. They were organizing for the single file journey through the Greencaps. The *Odalisque* revved her engines, preparing to accelerate to lead position.

Caliph felt his skeleton shiver uncontrollably, as if connected to the zeppelin. The vibration centered around his heart with a curious tingle. Just as he was contemplating the strangeness of this, he felt Sena's fingertips unbutton him, slide inside and crisscross over his chest.

She pulled herself closer, soft and warm, except for those thin glittering lines of coldness. Her aberrations became toothsome. She smelled of hypnosis, of deep narcotic sweetness, sugary mint and water-flowers. Her body crept off the floor, one leg at a time, and wrapped itself around him. She was kissing his lips. Caliph could no longer see. He felt his back bump against one of the stateroom's paneled walls.

Sena's hands pushed them off and pivoted them like one creature toward the bar.

He leaned her back amid the imported liquors. She smiled crookedly, tears gone—drunk up by his shirt. Sena reached behind her head for a bottle of hard black rum. The stopper popped into her palm and she tipped it, glugging softly over the front of her body, like a dark cascade over pale stone. It pooled in her navel and wet the jewel there.

Caliph remembered a similar night in the geometry classroom, before he had stolen the clurichaun, her back pressed against the top of Professor Garavaso's desk.

"Is that where you want to go?" she whispered as if reading his mind. "Where do you want to go?"

Where do you want to go?

Caliph felt a tremor of fear but he closed his eyes and let himself slip into the device that made everything simpler, where Sena's movement could be described with angular velocity. He felt the compression. Riding the infinite plane of her back. The foundation for the catapult. Waiting for the throw. And her—waiting for the zoetrope's spinning.

ZEPPELIN light flickers on the delicate windowpanes while Sena's lips make obscene requests. Her bodice has turned into a black belt trimmed with tiny scarlet feathers—wet with rum.

Caliph has been wanting this for days. Desperate as a junkie for a hit. Unwilling to admit it even to himself.

She is dark and strange like a crow on its back. It is different than anything he has had with her before. Though he wouldn't have believed it possible, it is stronger than the night after the argument. She is cool and powerful beneath him, like a machine, like water rolling. Her coaxing is primal. He loses himself completely, not for an instant, but for several minutes . . . or more. His ability to gauge time has left him.

All he hears is her scream like a creature announcing its territory. He feels his soul slip forward, pulled partly through his skin, drawn by the inexorable singularity of something he cannot name. A deep gravity inside of her. He is leaving his body. Nearly breaking against her. He is nearly dying.

Caliph steps back from the beautiful sprawl. Dizzy, glazed. But she cannot dehorn him.

He is staring into her face. Staring at a blue sun. All that matters is his unity with the attractor inside her. He wants to dash himself against her and be utterly destroyed.

CHAPTER
II

Since early spring, three Pandragonian bureaucrats have disappeared. One leaves a sprinkle of brown flecks, dried blood like half a dozen exterminated chinches on otherwise immaculate designer sheets. The second leaves a richly upholstered bariothermic car whispering at the side of the road. The third leaves nothing at all.

The Sisterhood uses Miriam to orchestrate these minatory escalations of Shrạdnæ diplomacy not because she is Pandragonian and therefore moves unnoticed through the south, but because the Eighth House trusts her completely.

With the last bureaucrat's disappearance, summer fades and the entire coven turns restless.

Miriam returns from Pandragor on furlough and is admitted to the Sixth House. Bored, she takes a part-time post overseeing Parliament's "nursery." She wonders what is happening to the Sisterhood.

In the nursery, *she overhears girls in the Second House speaking furtively after lights-out about Sienæ Iilool and the Wịllin Droul*[9]*: the Lua'grọc . . . the terrifying Cabal of Wights. In Parliament's vast east wing, they drape themselves over iron bed frames and thin mattresses. It is hot but the windows are open. Some sit cross-legged on the floor, letting the final sweet pantings of summer lap over them. Their white gowns ripple over willowy limbs and small breasts. They speak in Withil, practicing the cant so that if they are caught they can say they have been studying.*

Miriam does not bother them. She stands in the shadows and listens to the mythopoeic fertility of fourteen-year-old mouths.

"She used to be one of us."

"Really? Stupid."

"I wonder if she's stronger than the Eighth House."

[9] Wịllin Droul is a cant term used only by the Shrạdnæ Sisterhood for the Cabal of Wights. The Cabal of Wights is a legendary underworld organization consisting of human, partly-human and purportedly *nonhuman* operatives whose goals are a matter of conjecture.

"No one's stronger than the Eighth House."

"She was stronger than Megan."

"Shh. What if someone hears?"

"Without the book, she's nothing. That's what Haidee says."

"I hate Haidee."

"Haidee's going to be Coven Mother, idiot."

"I still hate her."

"Why haven't they already picked someone? To replace Megan?"

"They should pick me!"

Mocking laughter from all of them.

"No. Me!"

"Shut up. It's not funny anymore."

"Maybe Giganalee's lost her mind . . . she's soooo old."

"I'm telling."

"You do and I'll kill you."

"Bitch!"

"Eat me."

"Maybe I will."

More laughter.

"I bet they haven't picked someone because they're scared. What if Sena just kills whoever they pick? Just like Megan?"

"They should pick you, then."

"Shut up!"

"Maybe they're waiting to get her book."

"They're all afraid of her. I bet she's stronger than Giganalee."

"No one's stronger than Giganalee."

"I bet she is."

Miriam retreats from the childish, circular talk. Over the course of several weeks she answers the Eighth House's pointless questions and fills the old woman's hookah for her with herbal fruits. Maybe the ancient woman really is losing her mind. Maybe she's just high. To Miriam, the Sisterhood feels different. She senses a change in the organization, a lack of businesslike ambition that it used to have when Megan was still alive. Instead of feeling awed and inspired, she feels ambivalent, despondent and unsure. Since Megan's funeral, the Sisterhood has felt headless.

Unofficial "representatives" from Pandragor claim the transumption hex was a failure. They say it did not dislodge Caliph Howl from the throne as promised and that they are not obligated to adhere to the bargain. They will not attempt to get the Sisterhood's book.

In retaliation, the Sixth House in particular has tried to send a message, but the Pandragonians are not afraid. They say that if any more of their bureaucrats turn up missing, Skellum (and Parliament) will be razed.

Not that Pandragor, as a government, would ever admit to dealing with witches or that those dealings had gone sideways, but Miriam knows Emperor Jünnũ is quite capable of concocting other reasons for war.

There are rumors that Pandragor has taken an interest in the Cịsrym Tạ. *The emperor may be trying to secure it for himself.*

She wonders again what has happened to the Sisterhood. Bullied by governments, murdered by the Wịllin Droul, terrified of a girl with a legendary book.

Perhaps all of it really is linked to the Cịsrym Tạ.

The Eighth House babbles incessantly about it. Every day, Giganalee mutters paranoid expletives. She is convinced that Sena Iilool has opened the book.

Miriam recalls the Sisterhood's last encounter with Sena, on a weedy road in Stonehold, surrounded by singing insects and fabricated shadows. It is a chilling encounter that Miriam remembers clearly. She alone had been privy to it.

But there have been no Shrạdnæ operatives in Stonehold since then. Over a year now. Not even half-sisters. And even if there were, Sena has cut her eyes. She would recognize a Shrạdnæ spy.

The coven needs a window into Stonehold.

Miriam spends her time thinking and waiting for opportunities.

And then it happens. Late in the year, disillusioned with her family's faith, the daughter of Avidan Mwyr comes sailing out of the south: heading for Stonehold. Her pedigree dictates that she will have access to Isca Castle.

Taelin Rae is worth using a puslet.

On the tenth of Oak, the clergywoman arrives in Newlym and disembarks for a bit of shopping at the town's rustic stores. Miriam is there with a qloin[10] *and an iatromathematique to perform the procedure.*

That night, while Taelin sleeps, Shrạdnæ witches descend on her stateroom. A thick silence settles over the deck, the halls and mooring lines.

The window to Taelin's chamber dehisces without sound. Miriam is one of the black figures that billow in. They encircle Taelin's bed and drape her in inky cloth. The witches slit their palms and whisper in the Unknown Tongue. Taelin does not wake.

[10] A hit squad of three Shrạdnæ Sisters, consisting of one cephal'matris and two ancillas.

In the south, machines are made of flesh. The Sisterhood has collected specimens and recipes. Their iatromathematique is capable of this.

Miriam opens up the jar.

The smell of apples pervades the room.

From the nutrient-rich solution the iatromathematique draws out a slick fat blob. It is ugly and nuanced as a rotting wall and does not struggle in the forceps. Rugose folds of gelatin ripple through the puslet's slippery white-blue mass. But there are other colors: obscure and myriad. Sometimes burgundy, sometimes gray and dun.

It fits in the iatromathematique's palm, a tablespoon of horrible pudding. She lets it slip from her fingertips to pool over Taelin's sleeping eye.

Taelin convulses. Her eyes open wide. But the witch is already inside it, moving its soulless flesh.

She lurches the blob without bone or muscle, a pure rearrangement of fluid and cells; then forces it to burrow gob-like into Taelin's face.

The iatromathematique is from the Fifth House. And this is not a true qloin. But Miriam knows she is skilled. She helps support the woman's weight while she is gone, guiding her new body over slippery conchae, up into the sinus, toward the ethmoid. From there, the puslet travels deep, insinuating itself through the sphenoid, up beneath Taelin's brain.

The witch positions herself carefully. The puslet's lab-grown neurons vulture up against Taelin's meninges but her memories will not be stolen. They will be duplicated. The puslet is a useful tumor and its connections begin instantly to siphon off copies of Taelin's dreams.

The iatromathematique withdraws, coming back to herself. The senseless yet ever-sensing puslet stays behind, less reactive than plant-life, gathering memory, doing only what its cells have been designed to do.

Miriam snaps her wrist and pulls the drapery away. For Taelin, the puslet, her night at Newlym: all become paramnesias.

It is almost exactly a month later when Taelin Rae gets her audience with Sena Iilool.

Miriam listens to a symphysis in one of Parliament's inner sanctums. The symphysis' hideous amorphous bones have not been osteotomically extracted from any "thing." They fit together in grotesque irregular ways: malleus, incus, hooded by a yellow tissue-thin shroud of membrane. The collective formation looks like a shattered mollusk, part chitinous ruin, part sun-stiffened mantle: a creature broken open by sea birds perhaps and left to bake in the sun.

The entire grotesquery quivers in the dim light, bones vibrating, membrane singing like scraped catgut. The symphysis speaks.

Or rather, it seems to speak, as its vibrations resonate with Miriam's eardrum, conveying from across the miles the second-old memories recorded in the puslet's spongiose cells.

Miriam eavesdrops on Taelin's audience with Sena.

She is shocked when Sena mentions the smell of apples and then, to Taelin's great confusion, lays out the itinerary for her trip:

". . . Passing over Miṛayhr, over Skellum, near midnight on the twelfth of Tes. You will be unable to stop me there and I will proceed to Sandren. Send whomever you want. The Stairs will kill them."

Sena's voice echoes in the ears of all the sisters in the sanctum. Their puslet has not gone unnoticed. She is speaking through Taelin, directly to the coven. And she is mocking them.

Miriam is afraid.

She is still afraid on the twelfth, when the three zeppelins pass directly over Parliament, headed for the south. She kneels on the roof, looking up, waiting for Giganalee to give the sign.

What is about to happen has not happened in many years. But Miriam tries not to think about it. She has given herself over to the power of the Eighth House.

Her eyes watch the old crone intently, fearing the signal.

You can cast what you can cut.

This rule is the origin of hemofurtum, of spell-slaves and the legends of vast colligations harvested at Twyrloch by Aglogoth[11]*, countersunk three thousand years into the past. Attempts to exceed the power bottled in a human body.*

But Miriam's mind has wandered. Giganalee is raising her arms now.

Pulse thrumming, Miriam draws her kyru. She sets the crescent-shaped blade against her throat. It requires both hands, one in front, one in back: reaching around behind her head. Already she has cut herself—unintentionally—on the blade's fabulous edge.

Giganalee's arms fall.

It is time. Miriam almost waits to see if the others are brave enough to follow through before embarking on this plunge into madness. Instead, she pulls the blade's handle through a complete three-hundred-sixty-degree orbit, slicing through the skin. As blood rolls down her back and chest and shoulders, Miriam speaks in the Unknown Tongue.

She feels her stomach loosen.

[11] The Shokyule witch queen, born 11,984 O.T.R., vanished 12,874 O.T.R.

* * *

Each qloin contained a cephal'matris and two ancillas. Sena saw them, some of them newly cursed. The kneeling bodies slumped over, one at a time, arms limp, kyrus clattering from senseless fingers. They did not fall instantly. Some even seemed to levitate for a moment, knees coming off the roof. The only parts of them that scraped against the slate were the toes of their boots. Torsos lifted as the guts in their midsections slid up and bottlenecked; jammed in their throats. Not until the heads finally pulled loose did the knees drop and the decapitated, disemboweled carcasses land like sandbags before rolling to the side.

The Eighth House released the flock of heads from the roof of Parliament like a flight of black balloons into the stinging sky. Space stared down, a mapach with a thousand eyes. There was no wind to speak of. Three times three—a knot of qloins—nine witches pulled free from Parliament's roof: and flew.

Sena watched them come, dragging kidneys, stomachs, lungs and yards of intestine below them: slick and tangled. Strange dark jellyfish. Luminaries bled from livers and arteries, leaving trails in the blue-black sky: organs twinkling like fireflies.

The witches' eyes glittered with carvings. Their heaving lungs steamed in the icy air.

This was not minor. This was not a halfhearted attempt. A knot of qloins ascended and Sena felt the hairs on her arms bristle with a facsimile of fear.

"Caliph," she whispered. "It's time to wake up."

Faint operatic sounds trailed through Taelin's dreams, pessimal and loathsome. Dream-paint limned a soprano warbling through the upper reaches of terror while the repeated plunge of a knife deflated the sound; the residue was a ragged rhythm of gooey whispers, soft and sick-making.

Heavy boots grumbled in the hall beyond her door. Finally, a guttural yelp propelled her up, through her incubus, and into a forward lurch, eyes wide, hands clenched in her sheets. Her ears were ringing. Had there been another sound? Some kind of thud? She stared at her lap in the dark, listened acutely. Through near-total silence she heard ticking.

Where am I?

But the smell of wood polish and the faint vibration of the propellers reminded her. Her sheets were dewy.

She swung her legs over the side of the berth and dialed down the thermal crank. The ticking slowed. She reached for her bra, dangling on the back of a chair, pulled it off and wrapped it around her waist.

Something interrupted the moonlight pouring through her room's only porthole.

Frightened, she poised mid-fasten. The back of her throat felt tacky and dry. She wanted a glass of water but pulled up her holster, thumbed its straps over her shoulders and sidled toward the window instead. An infinite indigo and silver-specked canopy sloshed around the moons.

The soprano offered up another disquieting gurgle: crossing boundaries from the province of sleep. It was faint, high-pitched and filtered through the hum of the airship. *Could it be night birds?*

Taelin buttoned up her blouse and tucked her thick cotton pants into her boots before unlocking her door and stepping into the rich paneled hallway, which felt abnormally cold.

She passed a gaslight flickering in a henna sconce. Its red light quavered down the hall and landed on the body of a man. His shoulder and head propped open the door at the end of the passageway that led to one of the fore observation decks. A harsh, freezing wind whined in.

For a moment Taelin stood staring at the slumped figure. A large shadow from the sconce moved horribly over his back like a feeding specter. She recognized it as an illusion conjured by the drafty hallway, but the flapping darkness made the body doubly terrifying. Taelin took a step back then, berating herself, scooted forward and crouched down to see if she could rouse him. He wasn't breathing.

With some difficulty, she rolled him onto his back. No visible injuries. She screamed for help then pumped his chest with her palms. The wind took the door and folded it back on its hinges. A blast of icy air tore through the hall. The light went out. For a second, she heard the gas continue to hiss, then the safety valve squeaked and Taelin was alone with the wind.

The man's body seemed to be cooling.

She tried to pull him away from the door, gripping his ankles. He was two hundred pounds of nothing she could move. She screamed again for help.

"Lady Rae?"

Taelin turned around at the voice, instantly relieved. "Mother of Mizraim, thank gods—" But her vision was adjusting to the dark. When she saw the speaker, when she saw the nightmare form that filled the hallway, she lurched sideways over the man, eyes ringent. Her feet kicked at the floor. Taelin gagged and shrieked and pushed herself through the doorway, out onto the deck. Air currents poured over her as the ship barreled south.

She scrambled to her feet.

From the blackness inside the door frame, the man's arm still extended across the threshold, gray and motionless. And above it, a woman's voice curdled, vowels strange and lilting: "Ooo fundou hiroo. Shioo osou hirioo!" The firefly twinkle of tiny lights oozed through the doorway.

Taelin tried to block out the memory of the floating head, the octopus-jumble of sickly shapes beneath it: tendrils, lumpy masses and the filaments of veins, but she could not shake it.

She turned to run and pulled up short, horrified by another body. This one lay on her side like a sleeper in a heavy leather jacket. The wind stirred her hair. Lying beside the woman was a velvet gun.

Taelin scooped it up and ran.

The weapon was heavy but it was also soft and silky, like the belly of a cat. It undulated in her grasp. She nearly dropped it, but moved her hands back from the living part to the wooden stock. It made a bubbling mucous sound.

Taelin mounted a metal staircase that corkscrewed up from the deck and onto the roof of the cabins. She nuddled into the cramped cable-strung space that ran beneath the gasbags. Tools, boxes and weights were piled on the flat roof, instigating stumbles.

She could smell the chemicals from the aft batteries and see the ebbing green patterns that bled from slender glass windows on the housings. The emerald radiance together with the gold-orange sidelights that studded the zeppelin's port skin, bloomed intermittently through the jungle of cables, creating shapes and shadows that forced Taelin to aim the gun in a host of directions.

"Hiroo."

Taelin screamed. She couldn't help it. The terror that the voice provoked was intractable. Her finger brushed the trigger as she spun on the sound—so near! The gun's deep wine-colored nap swelled like a ten-pound catfish at the trigger's insistence, ballooning for possible ejaculation. Its fur dwindled near the front where fleshy red-purple antennae drooped and curled below half a dozen perfect black pearl-shaped eyes.

Something floated in the shadows cast by the zeppelin's starboard battery. It drooled a slow cascade of twinkling motes.

Taelin, still screaming, fired.

Thick jets of milk-colored slime squirted from the gun's oral tubes. Impossible amounts. The viscous lines struck cables and walls then sagged like ropes gone slack from the front of the weapon.

The bizarre, daedal shape of the gut-encumbered head floated out into moonlight; the expression on its face grim.

Out of the sky, Taelin discerned other shapes: floating, flying, moving fast. She didn't know how many. All that mattered was escape.

The dark jungle of cables proved impossible to navigate. A pink-gold solvitriol cell burned beneath the weapon's cherry-wood stock. It powered tiny sprockets and implants that controlled the lab-grown life form's neural system. Taelin used it as a dim torch to check her footing.

She skittered forward to the edge of the roof, deliberated then turned and fired again.

Two more gouts of white ooze exploded into the darkness. One coil hit the monstrosity and pulled it down. It glided awkwardly to rest on the deck, convulsing in the sticky mess.

Taelin pulled the trigger one more time but the weapon only burped, coughing up thin lines like an infant vomiting milk. Airborne shadows loomed over her like the heads of tropical trees.

Taelin tossed the gun down and jumped.

Not well-planned. What if the airship's trajectory and speed . . .

The deck came up. The rail seemed to spin below her but she landed on the deck. White-hot pain exploded inside her knee. The gun had left her hands. It rested nearly where she had found it, next to its previous owner. She saw the oral parts bite into the woman's shoulder, slicing through meat and bone, pulling out great plugs of flesh. Its metabolism was legendary. It spewed out a digestive sauce and lapped up the nutrients. The gun was reloading.

Taelin started to crawl toward it when the airship pitched. Her knee throbbed with agonizing fire. Unable to brace herself, she felt her body slide. She scrabbled at the floor but there was nothing to grasp. Frantically she searched for a handhold and saw the gun and the dead woman roll to port, slip through the railing and tumble into the dark.

The head that had been stuck in the gun's filaments was also gone.

Taelin plastered herself to the deck, clothing snagging against textured metal, but it wasn't enough. She felt herself go.

The rough cleat-like surface of the deck scraped her face and palms. She cast her hands wildly for a shining metal bar and seized it. A railing newel. Her feet flew out into space. Her hips went with them. But her torso, her arms, were folded tightly around the post.

"Please, please, please . . ." she prayed to Nenuln. Her knee was on fire, sapping her strength. Between her breasts, her grandfather's golden artifact was slippery with sweat.

"Taelin."

Taelin opened her eyes. She hadn't even realized she had clenched them against the horror. The entire airship seemed to be listing, she dangled off the edge of the deck. Three of the gruesome faces floated around her in the cold.

As she screamed she sensed one of the faces, so close she could smell its breath. It was a beautiful face despite the cable grease that marred one cheek. Wild blond hair blew in profusion around scintillating eyes. Its stomach dragged over the deck as its mouth jerked closer.

During her scream, Taelin felt the face's lips close over her mouth. She tried to spit, bite, thrash her head but her body had gone numb. She couldn't move. Vaguely, she felt the girl's tongue inside her mouth.

She heard dark glottal words gurgling from the other faces, then her sinuses loosened painfully and she smelled apples.

A great blob of mucus sealed off her breathing. She nearly choked. The beautiful girl's tongue was there, stifling her. As the mass slid down the back of her throat she gagged. The lump rose into her mouth and the girl's tongue slurped it out.

Taelin's whole body relaxed. Her arms slipped. The fatty glob was gone, the horrible kiss had ended and Taelin realized that she was falling.

Caliph looked up at the other two airships from his position on the *Odalisque*'s port deck, mystified why Sena had woken him. His body felt empty, as though she had beaten him with a club. The original orgasm, persisted even now, sending aftershocks up through his flesh, making his thoughts roll. It was an alien, unnatural sensation. The entire surface of his skin tingled.

"It's there." She pointed. Despite the pain, it was all he could do to concentrate on the end of her finger.

All he could see were what appeared to be black spiderwebs dragging from the other crafts' bellies. The *Bulotecus*'s and the *Iatromisia*'s starboard lights sparkled half a mile out.

Caliph turned up the collar on his thick coat. His fingers already ached. Sena stood beside him in a cropped jacket, apparently unaffected by the wind.

Across the sky, Caliph watched the dark threads materialize as if spat into existence by unseen arachnids. He couldn't find their exact points of origin. They simply faded away.

Some of the threads bit and anchored into the airships' undersides, others arced then fell in graceful useless hoops toward the pitchy smear below.

"What *are* they?" said Caliph.

"Holomorphic anchors," said Sena. "They're trying to slow the ships down."

"Anchored to what?"

"Air."

Alani and Sigmund were both on the *Iatromisia.* Caliph wondered what was happening. Then, "Mother of Mizraim!" Caliph gasped and pointed.

The *Bulotecus,* without signaling, had begun to turn away from the other ships.

"They've stuck her," said Sena.

"Lady Rae's on that ship!" Caliph could see the web of black threads trailing behind, converging toward an obscure origin. "The captain'll have to kill the engines or he'll rip her apart."

Caliph wanted to ask why this was happening, who "they" were and a host of other questions but a horn sounded across the sky. An alarm from the *Bulotecus.* He left Sena at the railing and bolted for the bridge, running to inform the captain.

Matters, however, seemed to be already in hand and Caliph felt the deck tilt as the rudders cranked. They were turning east.

Other men had begun to hustle around the deck. Orders were shouted. Weapons were dispensed from lockers. Caliph didn't have to direct them. He went back to his stateroom and rummaged in the closet. Servants had packed his bags. There. He found it behind the second duffle, his chemiostatic sword.

He strapped it on and marched back out to the deck.

But now the *Odalisque* was slowing. *Some hesitation in the chain of command?* Caliph could already guess that an argument had erupted on the bridge. One side would be arguing to help the other ships. The other side would be demanding an immediate retreat: concerned only with ferrying the High King to safety. *I'm a liability,* he thought. "Mother of Mizraim . . ."

He took off down the deck.

"Your majesty—"

Caliph ran by. He skipped steps and burst from the landing into the tiny bridge. The captain was an implausibly thin man with features at once gentle and fierce. He looked at Caliph as he entered the room. The copilot seemed to be struggling with the ship's controls.

"Why are we slowing down?" shouted Caliph. "We have to reach the *Bulotecus*!"

The captain, determined but powerless, turned back to his controls. His voice was thin. "I don't know."

Caliph's gut sank. He whirled, exited the bridge and leapt back down the stairs, but it was too late. Even as he envisioned the holomorphic threads of darkness entangling the *Odalisque* from below, the attack had already begun.

Something appalling floated up over the starboard side. It was black against the deck lights, bobbing and strange. Caliph could not decipher its shape. He heard his men scream.

Caliph gripped the pommel of his sword and began unscrewing the safety ring that guarded the chemiostatic switch. A moment later the surrounding metal registered with him: stairs, deck, railings. He didn't know how a beryllium steered bolt would behave under such conditions. Thinking better, he left the sword uncharged, retightened the ring and drew it from its scabbard.

But now the deck was quiet. There were shouts, possibly from starboard or aft. He couldn't tell. Three bodies littered a blazing white circle flung from overhead magnesium lamps.

Caliph felt terrorized by the impossible alacrity of their deaths.

He looked aft into the murk beyond the cone of light. Where was Sena? How could three men die in an instant without a sound?

Maybe they weren't dead. He scanned for the floating shape and approached the bodies half-stooped, as if an additional six inches of clearance might offer some protection. The air, the wind, the sounds of the ship had become places of hiding, places that could disgorge improbable death.

Caliph glanced up repeatedly as he checked his men, willfully paranoid of sudden attack. After three hurried inspections he found no wounds and no pulses.

He listened.

The aft observation deck hung fifty feet behind the fore decks, sequestered from the rest of the ship. It projected behind the chemical cells: eight hundred square feet of elegance jutting into space. It was from this rear deck that Caliph thought he heard voices above the chug of the propellers.

He opened the deck's aft door and slipped down the hallway, past his stateroom, past the parlors and out onto the duralumin rear patio that basked in the glow of the batteries.

Sena stood, cropped red jacket snapping in the wind, holding the book he loathed in one of her hands. She faced the back of the ship.

A body lay like a hump of laundry just a few feet in front of her and to her right four men clutched their weapons, symbols of paralysis. What was wrong with them? They represented his elite staff of bodyguards. They should be moving. Fighting. Doing something—

Caliph could see past their pale faces to where, floating in green effulgence, three ghastly impossibilities threatened. Their exposed lungs swelled, withered and swelled again; their hearts twitched rhythmically.

Caliph could not think. A deep, canonical terror gripped him. One of the heads spoke in a cooing language. He imagined that Sena answered.

All he knew for certain was that her red jacket was snapping. He watched it, felt it crack with petulant regularity. Snap! Snap! A red, protective chant. Its texture, brightness and continual sound cordoned him from the shadowy things floating not quite twenty feet away. On this side of Sena, there were glowing lamps, a doorway and the pounding of his heart. But beyond Sena's snapping coat, on the other side of her confident stance, there was madness.

Caliph realized he was kneeling on the deck, looking at his sword, which had fallen from his fingers. How had he dropped it? When he looked up, he could barely see his men, standing exactly as they had been before.

Caliph stared at Sena's flapping jacket. He willed himself to reach for his weapon. *Do something!* An internal scream.

He tried to speak, to say Sena's name, but couldn't.

She didn't move. He wondered if something was wrong with her in the exact way he might have wondered whether the concrete wall separating him from an inferno was sustaining damage. She was his shelter.

Mizraim, Emolus, Fuck! He tried again to grab his weapon, to get up and power past Sena.

No.

He was still kneeling on the cold metal behind her. He could not move.

Her jacket flapped again and then the sound of something heavy clanged on the metal floor, unbelievably loud, bouncing once before the dark mass of flickering entrails.

He adjusted his focus enough to look, but found he couldn't move his head. Sena's jacket was a red blur while the deck resolved into clear patterns of grating. He could see the book she had tossed down in front of them. Was she giving it to them? Some kind of morbid joke bubbled up in his mind; that the heads had no hands nearly made him giggle. And he was giggling, deep inside his chest, nowhere near the surface. It felt like a worm struggling just under his heart, threshing violently. It was the only part of his body that he could feel anymore. Everything else had turned to stone and fear.

He heard Sena's voice, husky and commanding. "Tekioo otou," she said.

It had to be a ploy. Sena would never part with that book. Never.

One of the heads jerked, a tethered balloon plucked by the breeze. Its organs flopped against the rough deck. Caliph saw blood ooze over metal. Then the dark, obscured face was whispering, crooning, speaking in the Unknown Tongue.

And the book began to float.

CHAPTER 12

Taelin cartwheeled. Flopped. Rolling buttes spun by, rotten-apple black. The wind cut her ears. An endless procession of razors. She was on her back now, arms and legs flapping, staring up into the wet flood of stars, waiting for impact.

Through the crush of one-hundred-twenty-mile-an-hour winds, a soprano whisper returned. This, rather than her fall, gave Taelin strength to scream again.

"Taelin—"

The singsong voice threatened her. She heard other voices encircling her descent. "Taelin!"

"Lady Rae."

She felt hands on her body, restraining her.

"Get off! Get off!" She was screaming. The air at her back pushed up hard. Too hard. Like a foam mattress. Like a hospital cot. She lurched forward, covered in sweat, into the bright light, the red shapes of physicians bending over her.

"I'm not falling!" She screamed and laughed.

She felt a deep twinge in the meat of her shoulder.

"Three units of amylobar."

Such a clinical voice. Taelin laughed again, right before impact.

SENA dismissed the assigned servants. She brought cream and a bowl of sugar. She brought rolls and biscuits from the kitchen. In an unusual display of domesticity, she brought blankets and pillows and coffee into the room that Caliph had chosen as his command center.

He didn't sleep. It was after midnight. Once they had cleared the airspace over Skellum, personnel were ferried between the ships. Alani came aboard.

It was after midnight on the thirteenth of Tes and for the next several hours Caliph deliberated whether to turn back, cancel his talk at the conference and return with all three ships to Isca.

Alani's quiet voice modified and calmed the tension in the air. Plans for retaliation against the government of Miraÿhr, where the Witchocracy held sway, were quickly scuttled. The attack had been a secret. Caliph decided, and Alani agreed, that for the time being they would keep it that way. The last thing Stonehold needed was to appear weak or friendless to Pandragor.

The heads had left with the book. The skies were empty and quiet again. Six people had died. Night slipped away and light spilled with a suddenness through the portholes, into the airship's makeshift conference room. It gave luster to the discarded cuff links, the clutter of cups and the several pairs of cast-aside shoes. With the dawn, Caliph decided to go ahead with the conference.

He would not turn back. He would not be distracted from his mission in Sandren. After his talk, after he hammered out his problems with the Pandragonians, he would he deal with the Witchocracy.

"We have a floating hospital and one patient," said Caliph.

"At least she survived," said Sena.

Caliph tapped his lip. "That would've been a diplomatic shit-storm. I think bringing her with was a bad idea."

"She'll recover."

Caliph chuckled through his nose but did not smile. "She seems to have some medical know-how. Put the doctors in a snarl by telling them their diagnosis was wrong." He looked up at her. "You think it's the right choice? To go through with the conference?"

"Yes."

"I can't believe my physicians are doing the work of morticians—on day one no less."

Sena struggled with guilt. "How are you feeling?" she asked.

"Oh, I'm fine."

"It's not your fault, you know?"

Caliph looked at her quizzically but she could read his embarrassment over the night before.

"When a qloin gives itself to the Eighth House, it ceases to be three sisters. They become fingers on her hand."

"What are you talking about?" Caliph's eyes went to Alani who made a motion for coffee before slipping out of the room. The spymaster thought, like many did, that Sena was crazy.

She pressed on. "The Eighth House is the reason none of your bodyguards could move."

"I should have—"

Caliph started to blame himself but Sena snipped it off. "No." She looked out through one of the oval windows. "You were under the power of the Eighth House."

But privately she shouldered a sense of guilt. She hated to see him like this, a whisker-stippled shadow. And yet she had felt so piercingly lonely—all summer long—that she had done it anyway. She had been lonely and he had been full of anxiety over the flight. She had convinced herself that she could take away his fears.

Caliph looked at her with eyes bruised by lack of sleep. Under his clothing she saw the delicate skin fronting his hips, contused through his own struggle for unity, turned black and green. There were great dark suction marks on his chest: proof that the numbers were, quite literally, stacked against him.

He had been waylaid by math.

The proportions and ratios had piggybacked on light, entered through his eyes and been assigned a requisite level of awe. A greater than average chemical storm had swelled inside him. Her numbers were a spiral, a vortex. But they were not helping him.

Her ratios exceeded his capability to compartmentalize and, like the power of the Eighth House, it was unfair.

"Why didn't the witches just kill me?" His voice sounded confused, dejected; it turned her stomach. She answered with a measure of asperity. "The Sisterhood doesn't care about you anymore. They have the book."

This worked and he hardened to her. "Then I don't understand why you gave it to them. If it's so important—"

"It is so important. Which is why I gave it to them. They'll keep it safe, Caliph. In the meantime, I have errands in Sandren. Don't worry. The Sisterhood can't use it. Even if they open it . . . it's too late."

"Too late for what?"

She hung on his question. "To save the world," she said.

This sent a hairline crack through the invisible wall between them. She watched it creep slowly, as Caliph puzzled over her words. Soon it would turn elaborate and ugly. Sena left the room and went to stand outside in the sunlight. Caliph followed her as though leashed.

She inhaled, let the cold air fill her, but did not feel cleansed. At her feet, sunlight scoured the metal, working to efface the terrible associations from the night before.

"What do you mean?" Caliph asked. "That it's too late to save the world? You mean the Shrạdnæ Sisterhood is trying to save the world? From what?"

Sena had turned her head to watch his mouth move as he asked this inevitable question. He wore a crooked premonition, gathered at one side of his face as if he sensed what was coming.

"From me," she said. These two words tapped the wedge into place.

"I don't get it." But he *did* get it. She knew, in his guts, how the rimy dark angle of her words, worked shardlike between his ribs. He chuckled, trying to make light of it. Trying to transform the absurdity into a joke. "I thought the Sisterhood was always the, you know . . ." he popped his lips and twirled his finger, "the enemy."

"They are," she said softly.

"I don't really understand what you're saying, then." He tried to smile. Failed. "Are you sure you're okay?"

Sena turned away from the sun, away from him. She saw herself through Caliph's eyes, wanting to feel what he felt. He saw her irises flickering with tiny arcs as she turned. He saw her walk resolutely away, through the doorway, leaving him on the deck to believe finally and unequivocally that she had lost her mind.

And that was better. The fissure at least, between the two of them, would give Caliph some dignity, some space and time to claw his way back.

For several minutes, Caliph stood mystified. But then the deck boy arrived. Caliph preferred the *Bulotecus* to the *Odalisque.* On the *Bulotecus,* Specks would have handed him the message, floating and smiling.

The boy on the *Odalisque* said nothing as he gave Caliph the note.

Caliph took it and pulled it open. As he read, Sena's delusions of grandeur melted into the background.

What it said, even in the shadow of last night's attack, put a disquieting spin on Sena's insistence that the *Iatromisia* be included in this ill-fated flight.

The city-state of Sandren had seen countries rise and fall. Its rich unattainable eye had long gazed over the Atlath Continent with a kind of supreme multifaceted neutrality. The city-state's wealth was enormous. It had never been looted. It was, as it had always been, aloof to armies marching under and around it. Only one fool had ever attempted a siege.

Caliph tugged his lip, bewildered to read that during the last thirty-six hours, coinciding with a stay of warm sloppy weather, Sandren's citizens lay dying.

Details were sparse. Some kind of sickness. Rumors chased their own tails.

As Caliph's three airships neared the great jag of the Ghalla Peaks, he could see other zeppelins clustering.

A flock of balloons drifted together, enormous gasbags bearing crests and colors, each one from a different nation. The airships' ponderous bodies were lanced and strafed by light; despite this, they looked small and powerless against the mountain's cool gray backdrop.

Birds enmeshed the conflux in helices that twisted slow as summer gnats. Some of them carried messages between the ships. Information was spreading.

Caliph called for field glasses. He felt them arrive in his hand and looked southwest at the congregating vessels. There were craft from Waythloo's Iron Throne, Wardale, even the Society of the Jaw. He made out one bizarre ship from the Theocracy of the Stargazers; another, pale as a cave beetle, from the Pplar. Fane, Dadelon, Iycestoke, Bablemum, Greymoor and Yorba. They were all here. A circus of colors. A sky full of political clout.

Behind the harlequin minnow-shaped bodies, where the sun could not yet reach, Caliph made out the black arms of Sandren's famous teagle system. Great brackets of metal lunged from vertical clefts in the rock. Small only in perspective, the brackets trailed down the mountain's sheer face, ending amid a smoky cluster of buildings that broke out into the sun and glinted like overturned trash.

Far above the conflux of zeppelins, the brackets led up, carrying their threads of cable toward the hidden city-state of Sandren.

If the Sandrenese were sick, Caliph was eager to hear the details, eager to see how he could help.

Some of the heavier airships had already docked at a great platform suspended halfway up the mountain: a half disk of grilled metal supported by cables and struts. The elevators could be summoned to this platform and the airships were moderately protected from the buffeting, generally east-blowing winds.

Not all craft could make the thirteen-thousand-foot ascent to the city.

Caliph handed his field glasses off and sent a message to the captain, requesting that he motor them in.

Not forty minutes later, another bird arrived with a message from the south. This one was an invitation.

Caliph was being called to Bablemum's great flagship. There, Grand Arbiter Nawg'gnoh Pag would host the pre-conference party in the evening. It would be a way to gather and make sense of the crisis, what had happened to the Sandrenese, and how best to help.

Having had no sleep, Caliph finally gave in. He slept for several hours, woke, grabbed a sandwich from the kitchen and met with Alani in private.

"This could be it," said the spymaster. "We need to be careful tonight."

"They're not going to kill me on their own ship," said Caliph.

Alani coughed into his fist. "It's Bablemum's ship."

"Pandragor controls Bablemum. Wouldn't that be a little too obvious—"

"You're right that they won't likely make an attempt until after you give your speech," said Alani. "Nevertheless—"

"I'm not afraid of them."

"You should be."

"Nevertheless what?" asked Caliph.

"Nevertheless, we're going to put a watchdog on you tonight."

"This is crazy. We're going to be late."

"No we're not." Alani snapped his fingers at one of his men. "Bring us a dog."

"Yes, sir."

Caliph was still talking. "I hate watchdogs."

"I know." Alani sounded genuinely apologetic. "But it's the best way."

Caliph frowned. His stomach hurt.

"You look nervous now," said Alani. "That's good."

"Isn't it *your* job to be nervous?"

"Trust me. I'm doing my job."

"Well if you're nervous, then I shouldn't be. It's my job to go to this thing and keep Stonehold's head from dragging in the—"

"That will be your job later, when you deliver your speech," said Alani. "But not tonight." He raised his index finger. "Tonight your only job is to stay alive. And with a little prudent fear, that job will be made considerably easier."

Caliph growled and adjusted the button cover at the middle of his throat. He pointed to it fiercely with double fingers. "Is it fine?"

"You look perfect."

Alani's man came back from belowdecks, leading a tubby dog on short legs.

"I really don't want to do this," said Caliph.

"It's my call," said Alani. He knelt down and took the dog by the collar. It whimpered, sensing that something was not right.

One of Alani's men produced a muzzle. It was a heavy latticed thing, woven into a basket of pale boiled leather, riveted together at all intersections. Caliph found it bulky and terrible to look at; it allowed the dog to open and close its beak but obscured its small blue eyes almost entirely. The dog gurgled and clucked, then shrieked once as the spike at the back of the muzzle pierced its chubby neck.

"They're going to think it strange? Sena not coming?" Caliph asked, trying not to think about the animal.

"Hardly. I think Bablemumish derision for her is an open book. We don't want to enflame an already precarious situation."

Alani adjusted a gauge wired to a chemiostatic battery that now hung under the dog's throat. This was cutting edge, government-issue holomorphy, produced by entrepreneurs in Isca City at top-secret facilities. Caliph had to accept some blame in its creation despite the fact that the product was vastly different than the original specifications.

"You're right," Caliph said. "Let's get this over with. I want to be back on the *Odalisque* by midnight."

"So do I."

Alani flipped a toggle switch on the collar portion of the muzzle. It began whispering. This was a hideous version of the thing worn by the captain's crippled son, only the equation it repeated, ever so slowly, was of a much different bent.

The numbers in the static-filled hiss produced a ward. This ward would cover the High King, all night long. The outcome, different from the company's original proposal, was that the animal would die in the process.

Each dog offered a one-night watch.

It was an inefficient device, a prototype really. But the contract had included a tricky clause. Caliph had already decided not to renew. He might even fight it in court once they returned from Sandren. In the meantime, with the knowledge of how he was viewed by the south, for the sake of Stonehold's future, he allowed Alani to set the collar.

Alani snapped a leash to the device just as their ride flew in.

A small capsule with one pilot, a glowing orange gasbag and an array of directional fans swept over the deck. The pilot got them boarded, dog included, just as the sun slipped into a violet bruise behind the mountain.

The capsule lifted off, making Caliph's stomach pitch. It ferried them through the chilly evening toward Bablemum's great *Quadrivium*.

They arrived at thirteen o' five, stepping out onto the airship's impressive brass-like deck. The sound of music and the smells of indulgence seemed highly inappropriate considering the circumstances.

Perhaps it's cultural, Caliph thought. *Perhaps there's too much of Stonehold in me. Too much of the grim Naneman.* He tried not to pass judgment as a pair of men in ecru flight suits with copper goggles and velvet guns greeted him on the platform.

Their boots and pants were smudged with grease indicating they might have done actual work during the day. One of them stroked his gun as if he were holding a pet, letting the fur trail between his fingers.

"King Howl." The two men escorted Caliph toward the light. Alani followed three steps behind, leading the watchdog. They were guided through an open doorway, into a double-decker lounge with crisp clean lines and crisp clean women. Singular scarlet lilies with black freckles emerged from slender vases like fireworks and a metholinate fireplace bubbled on a hearth that made no attempt to simulate anything organic.

The space was lit with cool white light gushing from various fixtures. A mood, neither too dim nor too bright, sprang from the crystalline radiance of the bar. The furnishings seemed to be brass. Caliph doubted this considering the weight such objects would add to an airship.

"Here they come," whispered Alani. The spymaster ignored the looks of disgust associated with the blood-dripping dog.

Caliph plucked a stemmed drink from a tray. While an ominous group of men closed in, he took a sip and eyed them.

There was a harpist playing near the bar and a naked woman lay on her back not far away, painstakingly detailed in brightly colored paint. She lay perfectly still, each of her nipples covered with a bright red lily and another pinched between her legs. She was a small-breasted creature, which helped with her duty as a buffet table: her abdomen and chest were laden with leaves that had been piled with artful, bite-sized slices of raw fish: pink and white and red.

"Your majesty," said one of the looming men.

Caliph gave them his best smile.

"High King Howl!" chimed another.

Some of them extended hands. Some did not. It was not southern custom to shake. Caliph shook the hands offered and introduced Alani.

"By the Eyes . . . what is that thing?" One of the men was looking at the dog.

Alani made a brief explanation, which Caliph still found embarrassing. It might be cutting edge in Stonehold, but he doubted the south had need of such crude mechanisms. While Alani explained, Caliph noticed how old his spymaster looked: more like a doddering relative than an elite bodyguard. It was hard not to feel ashamed in these surroundings.

One of the men laughed. "A watchdog? King Howl doesn't trust us."

Caliph kept his chin up. "Alani might be overly protective, but he takes good care of me."

"Yes. You're famous," said the man. "Or I should say *in*famous. You're *the* Alani from Ironwall, aren't you? We tried to sign you on in Pandragor." The man was laughing but his eyes were shrewd.

"I'm not from Ironwall," said Alani. "And I don't believe we've done introductions yet."

"So we haven't, so we haven't."

Several names passed revealing the men to be mostly lesser officials.

"Would you like some fish, King Howl?"

The men turned to the living buffet table and took their time, lecherously filling their small plates. As they did, Alani leaned forward and whispered in Caliph's ear. "There's the grand arbiter."

Caliph looked up and spied a man on the second floor who leaned heavily on an art deco railing. The man was robed in white fur—trimmed with black. He had yellowish flabby-looking skin and deep-set eyes. His jowls swayed as he spoke somberly with the man next to him.

Caliph looked down, re-engaging with the men around him. "So. Do we know what's happened to Sandren?"

"We do not," said a thin overly tan gentleman with white hair who had suddenly appeared. He had a ragged mouth that looked like a badly healed knife wound.

"It's excellent to finally meet you," said Caliph. He recognized Emperor Jünnũ immediately as his adversary, the man at the head of the mighty Pandragonian Empire, the same man who had sent Nuj Ig'nos two weeks ago into the north to burden Caliph with the solvitriol accord.

Caliph disliked how the southerners did business. Maybe that too was the Naneman in him. In the north, if you disliked someone, you threw a spear at his head . . . or at least nowadays told him point blank to get off your property.

But the southerners spent their taxes on naked women and body paint and rare fish. They invited you to the party and probably to their estate in the spring while slipping poison into your cocktail.

"It's excellent to meet you as well," Emperor Jünnũ was saying. His red mouth performed antics that passed for cordial happiness. "Any revisions to the accord?"

"None so far." Caliph smiled broadly.

"That's good," said Jünnũ. "You wouldn't believe what we pay for document preparation in Pandragor." Caliph decided the evil blue twinkle in Jünnũ's eyes was for real.

"So . . . Sandren?" Caliph asked again.

"We don't know for certain," said one of the other men. "But there have been some reports of illness along the south edge of the Great Cloud Rift. People that flew out of Sandren have gotten other folks sick. We're a bit alarmed. It might just turn into an epidemic."

Another man added to the story. "Moved a hundred miles in one day.

People sick from Nwodus all the way up to the edge of the capital now." He tapped his finger on the railing leading down to the dance floor. "But we think it came here first."

"Here meaning Sandren," said Caliph.

"That's right."

"So has anyone been up? To Sandren?" Caliph asked.

"We sent some reconnaissance teams," said Jünnũ. "We're waiting to hear back."

"When are you due—to hear back?"

"It's only been four or five hours."

"You know, I brought a medical ship," said Caliph.

"I'd heard that," said Jünnũ. "That's extraordinary."

"Yes. It was . . . not really my idea. But it seems fortunate now. Maybe I could go up. See if I can help."

"A charitable notion," said Jünnũ. "No one's going to stop you."

"What about the schedule for the conference?"

Jünnũ raised his glass. "We'll have to postpone it a bit. See what's really going on up there. But don't think you'll get out of speaking." He smiled and the other men laughed.

"Are you kidding?" Caliph said. "I slaved over this speech. If I don't give it, all that heartburn Nuj Ig'nos caused me will be for nothing."

Jünnũ raised his glass. "To north-south relations!"

Everyone toasted.

The emperor's face was bright as a cherry with good-natured mirth but faded quickly. "You know, King Howl, your speech is the number one reason I'm here. It's going to be a critical night—for both the north and the south."

Caliph tilted his head. "You've set some high expectations."

"Oh, I'm the perpetual optimist, King Howl. I have no doubt we're on the edge of solving our differences."

Caliph felt an enormous hand clamp down gently over his shoulder. So large, it engulfed him. Grand Arbiter Nawg'gnoh Pag had come down from the balcony and crept up behind him. He leaned into view, beaming monstrously. "Hello, King Howl." The arbiter's words were profoundly deep and hollow and framed with vague contempt. "I'm Nawg'gnoh Pag."

"From Bablemum," said Caliph.

"That's right. I wonder if I could borrow you for just a moment."

Caliph glanced over his other shoulder at Alani. The spymaster was stiff, his eyes riveted on Caliph's eyes. "I don't—see why not," Caliph said.

"Wonderful," said Pag. "Let me get you a fresh drink."

"Oh, I'm fine." Caliph followed Pag a few steps away, behind a fountain of scarlet lilies. When the arbiter turned around, Caliph heard the watchdog whimper. Here, behind the lilies, Caliph found himself confronted more directly with the southerner's startling proportions. For such a giant of a man, Pag's eyes, nose and mouth seemed small. They were clustered at the center of his face, surrounded by a great empty expanse of golden flesh. His eyes were black, lips puffy and unnaturally static. Pag's robes draped him as if he were a giant piece of furniture covered for the season with a cloth.

"How are you, King Howl? Did your mistress get the box I sent?"

Caliph recalled the box Sena had refused to open. The one he had sent to be buried in the bogs. He felt his back turn cold. "Yes. I'm afraid I don't know anything about it though."

"Oh, that's all right. It's not important." Pag's voice was slow and deep and hypnotic. "I just wanted to take a moment to speak to you on Emperor Jünnũ's behalf."

"The two of us were just talking," said Caliph. "I wonder why he didn't speak for himself?"

"Delicate matters like this—" Pag gesticulated with his enormous hands, fingernails shining as if oiled. He almost seemed to lose his train of thought. "Listen, King Howl. Pandragor doesn't have a solvitriol program." He clasped his hands in front of him, reverently, just below his breast. "Thanks to you, our empire has avoided the sins of Iycestoke."

"I'm not sure what you're getting at."

"Well, it's really like this, I'm afraid. Pandragor is prepared to come forth with certain litho-slides and documents that illustrate quite clearly what lengths you went to in order to win your civil war."

Caliph finished his drink in one gulp but the alcohol failed to warm him. He knew exactly what Pag was driving at and pulled out his pocket watch. "I'm sorry Mr. Pag, I have another engagement—"

"I'm talking about the Glôssok Warehouses," said Pag. "About how you murdered your own citizens to make solvitriol bombs. Souls. Solvitriol tech runs on souls, yes? But that's hardly common knowledge . . ."

"I'm actually quite late," said Caliph.

"I do hope your talk for the conference is well in order," said Pag.

"Fuck you," whispered Caliph. He felt his restraint slip away. "You want war? With Stonehold? You think you can come through those mountains? Read a history book. When the Pplarians tried us they learned the hard way that Stonehavians are better kept as friends. They never tried again."

Pag leaned forward, his huge frame balanced on the balls of his feet, his horrible face inches from Caliph's nose. "We're going to eat you alive," he said. Then he turned and walked away.

Caliph excused himself. He met Alani outside.

"Wasn't so bad," said Caliph. He looked down at the moon-limned clouds reflecting in the brass below both their feet. "Get that thing off the dog before it bleeds to death."

Alani crouched down and did as he was told. "Did Pag threaten you?"

"Of course." Caliph brushed it aside. "We need to get up to Sandren."

"I'm not sure we should be worrying about the Sandrenese right now, your majesty."

"If we go up and see what's happening in Sandren, I'm that much farther from all the people who want to kill me. Good idea, right?"

"Yes. I suppose it is."

Caliph inclined his head in Alani's direction. "So smile."

CHAPTER 13

It was the fourteenth of Tes.

"I was falling. I fell off the airship!"

"You most certainly did not," one of the doctors repeatedly assured her. "We had to sedate you," she said. "Your injuries are minor. You're going to be fine."

Taelin took a sponge bath and then, with the doctor's assistance, got dressed.

"Where are my crutches?"

The physician scowled. She handed them to Taelin with a terse expression.

Taelin promptly propelled herself out to the observation deck. Glasses mounted on the aft railing allowed her to get a reasonable view of the *Odalisque.* It cruised slowly, silver fins and purple skin, a giant ornament sliding among the other ships. She could get no sense of what was happening.

"Now you're just like me. 'Cept you can't float."

Taelin looked at Specks who had drifted out onto the deck, a fragile white marionette without any strings. He was sipping something warm. His backpack held the cuddly sarchal hound. "You sleeped a long time." His high-pitched voice was vaguely scolding.

"Yes I did. I had to." Taelin decided not to mention the attack over Skellum. She hoped he had slept through it.

"Cuz you got hurted? What happened to you?"

"Yes, Specks. I hurt my knee."

He nodded. "Just like me. I bet you wish you could float."

As he drifted closer, the sound of his ticking blue and copper bracer began to twitter rhythmically in Taelin's head. The mechanized sorcery of the thing unnerved her, as did the trail of little red drops it left behind.

"I can't float but I have a crutch," said Taelin. "I could bat you right off this deck." She brandished the crutch.

Specks laughed. "How far do you think I'd go?"

"Far enough."

"I made you something." His eyes were big and brown and beautiful as a girl's.

"You need a haircut," said Taelin.

"Do not." His small hand patted at his mop.

"I can give you one."

"No way!"

"What did you make me?"

He grinned. "Something."

Taelin winced. Her knee hurt. She closed her eyes, but when she did she saw women's faces crowding around her and the velvet gun biting into dead flesh on the deck of the zeppelin. She gasped, opened her eyes and hobbled to one of the dining tables where she collapsed into a deck chair. Specks floated after her. When her crutches slid off the wall where she had propped them, he picked them up for her and carefully repositioned them.

"Thank you," she said.

"Dad says I need to be helpful."

"You certainly are." She saw another fresh paper lying on the table. "Could you hand that to me?"

"Sure."

It was the *Ghalla Chronicle,* a rag published in Skaif which, as an unofficial part of Sandren, crouched five thousand feet directly below.

She read the headlines and tore the paper free of its waxen cover. Specks hovered close by—eerily—ticking and dripping as she spread the news out on the table and tried to ignore the pain in her leg.

"What are you reading?" asked Specks.

She didn't answer. Taelin felt her eyes fill up with tears. Her hometown was not far south of Sandren and she had friends and relatives in the city-state. She covered her mouth with her hand. Her family had summered there almost every year while her father did contract work for the urban praetors. She couldn't believe this was happening.

Her eyes scoured the editorial for details.

A one-line barb regarding the political fortuitousness of Stonehold's medical ship fell just short of suggesting a full-blown conspiracy. When she saw her own name, listed among the High King's retinue, she felt the indelicate implications.

She didn't care. She was here because of the vision, because a great black smoking locomotive had burst from her chancel wall. Her goddess had spoken to her. And Taelin was determined not to let the High King's witch escape.

Perhaps this was part of it. Part of her purpose.

"Don't cry," said Specks. "You want to see what I made you?"

"Yes I do." Taelin tore herself away from the paper and wiped her eyes. She smiled when she looked at him. He was so thin and small. No more than a floating skeleton that couldn't get enough to eat.

"'Kay. Hold on."

"Hurry," she teased. "I can't wait."

"Rot's guarding it. It's in my backpack." He turned around. "Can you get it out?"

"Of course." She reached in and took out a piece of thick paper folded into squares. "Is this it?"

"Yep." Specks grabbed it from her and quickly unfolded it. On the sheet he had drawn a sarchal hound made up mostly of head and teeth. "You can name him anything you want," said Specks. "I drawed it cuz I have rot and all you have is that necklace."

"Thank you," said Taelin.

"You're welcome." His smile was ear to ear.

"I'll name him Speck."

Specks laughed. "You can read your paper now," he said.

"Oh, can I? Thank you." She made like she was going to poke him in the stomach and he drifted backward, giggling.

Taelin looked back down at the paper where Mr. Wintour, the editor, was pointing out that the symptoms of the disease nearly matched those described a year ago, when Isca—the capital of Stonehold—had had a similar outbreak. It had been publicized in the south: how a plague-ridden borough had been ruthlessly corralled and burned. Isca had managed to contain it by force and cruelty. It had been one of the things that helped cement Taelin's resolve against the Stonehavian government.

Mr. Wintour went as far as to suggest that Stonehold might be the only country with a viable vaccine.

Taelin put the paper down, pulled her crutches up under her armpits and lurched off across the starboard deck, ignoring the crewman that had just arrived to ask if she wanted something to eat. Specks floated after her.

"Where are you going?" he asked.

"I don't know."

Several hundred yards away she could see the medical ship floating. Tiny red-coated figures moved back and forth on its decks.

It didn't sit right.

Taelin scowled at the zeppelin. Why would Caliph Howl bring a floating hospital to an international conference? Even if he was a complete hypochondriac, a few doctors on staff would have made better sense.

"Miss Rae?"

"Hello. I'm Dr. Baufent." Taelin recognized her immediately as the physician who had handed her the crutches. She was short, middle-aged and looked stubborn as a tree stump. She extended her hand. Taelin shook. She could tell Baufent's hair had once been auburn but only traces of that color stained a boyish cut of nearly uniform marsupial-gray. "We haven't much time. His *majesty* wants me to escort you to the *Iatromisia* . . . assuming you're willing to pose for lithos that show how Pandragor and Stonehold are working together to battle the plague. If not, I'll simply tell him that you declined. No one's going to force you, dear."

She said *dear,* but Taelin sensed no warmth. Her inflection of *majesty* established that she also held no special love for the High King.

Taelin made the affirmative southern hand sign at the same time she bobbed her head in a circular up and down pattern: a result of surprise and confusion mixed with *yes*!

"Let me get my things. Will a day bag be enough?"

The doctor said that it would.

Taelin swung her body around and nearly crashed into Specks. "Oh, I'm sorry."

"It's okay. Are you going?"

"Yes. I have to go up and see if I can help the people in Sandren. They're in trouble. They're sick. They need doctors."

"Are you a doctor?"

"No. But there might be other things I can do." She reached out and tussled his hair. "Don't worry. I'll bring Speck with. And then I'll be right back."

Specks didn't say anything as she poled herself back to her room. She dug her newly stamped papers out of her luggage and stuffed a sack with some money and a change of clothes.

Feeling disheveled and sick and defiant of both, she emerged and saw Baufent in the hall who beckoned to her with tightly controlled impatience.

Taelin propelled herself after the stocky woman who neither acknowledged nor waited on her injury. They descended a metal staircase to the airship's hold and Taelin, after managing the stairs on her own, caught up to the doctor who was already standing near an open slide door. A gust of fresh wind caused Baufent to squint.

Taelin heard a bang and saw a cable fire from a gun just above the gaping doorway. Its end leapt out toward the *Iatromisia. Why are they firing on their own ship?* But the cable missed the *Iatromisia* by yards. Its end snapped violently to the weighted end of a corresponding cable, which had been the real target. It hung vertically beneath the other ship. There had to be some kind of electromagnet or a holomorphic attractor because the two cables joined with such force that they partially entangled and sent whiplash waves rolling in both directions all the way to the hangar doors.

Taelin watched as the cable on the *Iatromisia* was reeled in until the line from the *Bulotecus* sagged between the two ships, connecting cargo hold to cargo hold. Taelin wondered how difficult it was for the captains to maintain the slack. Maybe it was automated.

Dr. Baufent prodded her physically by grabbing hold of one of the crutches. "This way, dear."

Behind them, a kind of small gondola hung from the ceiling of the hold. It featured large glass windows, cramped seating and a single door which opened courtesy of a man Taelin had not previously noticed. The doctor shooed her to get in.

"Would you stop?" Taelin said.

Dr. Baufent showed no embarrassment. "I'm sorry, but we're in a rush. They're waiting on *you*."

"Well then I should have had more notice."

"I agree," said Baufent. "You should take that up with Caliph Howl." She climbed in next to Taelin.

The man shut the door and, like it or not, both women were forced to cuddle. Taelin heard some kind of mechanism engage and the gondola ratcheted forward, following a groove in the ceiling. When it came to the maw of the slide door an arm extended up, gripped the cable and then . . .

Taelin felt the carriage swing free. They rocked for a few adrenalized moments before a motor whirred to life and some contraption beyond Taelin's view began gobbling up the thick thread of metal, spitting it out behind them, moving them quickly down the line.

Taelin worked the edges of her necklace nervously the entire time.

When they reached the nadir, the little motor coughed a bit but ground on, pulling them up the incline and into the cargo bay of the *Iatromisia*.

With ginger motions, Taelin swung herself out of the compartment. No sooner were they clear than the contraption was sent back, deadheading toward the *Bulotecus*. The gondola soon disappeared into its cargo hold, the cable was released and the *Bulotecus* reeled it in. The transfer had been impressively quick.

Taelin saw instantly that the *Iatromisia* was a much different ship from the one she had been on. It's duralumin beams lay exposed, everywhere: undisguised by rich hardwoods and fancy light fixtures. Its hold was packed with medical supplies and refrigerated cases.

Dr. Baufent guided Taelin upstairs, pausing now to offer help.

"I'm fine," said Taelin.

When they reached the upper deck a man in a red trench greeted them.

Baufent provided introductions. "This is Anselm. He's a cretin and if you can stand him five minutes you've got a stronger stomach than I do."

Anselm smiled. "She's always like that." He was a Despche: tall and black with large hands and a beautiful face. "Looks like you're a patient." He gestured at the crutches.

Taelin laughed in spite of everything that was happening.

"He's also a womanizer," said Baufent. Then she marched off, barking at other people as she went.

"Well," said Anselm, "so you're our *very important passenger*—"

Taelin let out one giant exhalation. "If I'm here to be babysat—"

"No, no." Anselm raised his palms. "We'll let you have at it. Things sound pretty grim up there. I don't think we'll have time to babysit."

"What are you planning to do?" she said. "If it's plague—"

"Sounds like it. But this ship is loaded with vaccine. You've been vaccinated, yes?"

"No."

"Hmm. That's a problem. I'll have to talk to Baufent about it. Anyway, all of this is good luck. We're strangely prepared."

"Yes you are." She hoped her tone didn't convey her cynicism too strongly.

"Well," Anselm's voice dropped noticeably, "who knows why a witch commissions a full staff of physicians for a political conference." His eyebrows crawled up his forehead. "But then again, I'm glad she did."

So it was Sena . . .

It hadn't been Caliph at all. Her memory of him from the mission home, helping her up, handing her the glass of water—she felt a sudden, inexplicable pang for the High King. It sprang from the baseless assumption that he was some kind of victim that Sena had duped. Though, in that light, it made him rather shallow, didn't it?

More likely he had a hand in this unbelievable coincidence.

"The only thing I'm glad about," she said, picking up her conversation with Anselm, "is that I'm able to help."

The *Iatromisia* began its ascent of the Ghalla Peaks with a dull thudding sound from its gasbags that Taelin did not understand. The ship vibrated. A disturbed tuning fork. But, as long as the craft was going up, Taelin was able to set her unease aside.

They rose vertically with elevator-grace. Taelin felt her ears pop. The bright zeppelins that had surrounded them moments ago fell away.

As she leaned slightly over the aft railing Taelin noticed the *Odalisque* following them.

The wind was cold here but nowhere near as biting as it had been in Stonehold. She smelled familiar pollens, detected the peculiar woody aromas that emanated from scrub in the Ghalla Peaks. Though it was still winter, the milder climate tantalized. The smells made her dread going back to Isca.

The gray, bird-haunted shadows of the mountain slid past until finally, the ship breached into sunlight, rose over a jagged cornice and lifted several yards above the deserted teagle platform where a pair of mighty black steel arms dripped with cables.

"That's strange." Anselm was standing beside her. "The lifts have been running. There should be people . . ."

"What are those?" Taelin pointed to the streets bordering the platform.

Below, in the shadows of buildings, cautious figures moved.

"Are those people?" Anselm asked.

She had automatically assumed, but doubt crawled through her head now, burdened with his question. There was something about them. Where they stood. And how. They did not walk from place to place as people should have. They hovered. They stood where thieves might stand, or crouch. They moved tentatively. Even though she could not make them out, she saw them as shy hideous things, wreathed in cyclones of trash and unclean air. Taelin felt cold. As the ship passed over, she got a glimpse of one thin figure. It was naked, shimmering and gray. It swayed and tottered through a window as if mortally wounded, then disappeared from sight.

As her eyes scanned the streets, evidence of looting took shape: broken windows and open doors. *How could this happen in two days?*

A huge shadow darkened the avenues. It alarmed her, reminding her of what had happened at St. Remora. She quickly realized, however, that it was the *Odalisque* coming up from behind and wondered cynically whether Caliph Howl would be surprised by the scene below. Shielding her eyes as the sun burst around the *Odalisque*'s skin, she watched its vast shape glide south.

Taelin stared contemptuously until, without warning, the docking spire on the *Iatromisia*'s undercarriage sank into a socket on the teagle platform and propelled her into a stumble. She braced her palms against the railing and turned her attention back to the huddled streets, scanning for more people.

Nothing moved.

As soon as the ship came to a stop, men in black departed over the railing on thick cords. They swung out into space, chrome blue goggles capturing the sky. The cords trailed up over the gasbags. Taelin watched the men descend like circus actors. They maintained elegant postures until they touched the platform. Then they spread out with their heavy coils; each man pulled his rope through the eyelet of a different cement pylon. They had the ship tied without delay and Taelin heard the cargo elevator buzz to life belowdecks.

She watched physicians and logistical advisors begin flowing out from underneath the zeppelin and leaned out over the railing for a better view as people organized, talked and pointed toward the streets.

"We almost forgot you," Dr. Baufent said sharply. "I think you're the only one who hasn't been poked." Wrapped around her fingers, a hypodermic loaded with pale blue fluid glittered in the sun.

"Vaccine?"

The doctor gave her the southern sign.

Taelin dutifully rolled up her sleeve. She felt the steel pierce the meat of her shoulder and winced. Dr. Baufent pulled out, swabbed and smiled. "Want a candy?"

A small fracas had been building from below and it now drew their attention over the rail. There was a shout and Taelin saw one of the men in black standing with his feet apart, one hand out, pointing. His other hand rested on the handle of a truncheon that was still holstered against his hip.

For a few moments he seemed to be hallucinating. Nothing happened and the branches at the edge of the platform tossed slowly, rolling with the wind. They hid Taelin's view of the ground. Another man came to stand beside him and it was then that Taelin realized the physicians and advisors were gone. She heard the elevator coming back up. Maybe they had fled back to the ship?

Clearly the two men below could see something that she could not.

After another moment, both men pulled their truncheons. Three more men ran into sight. These, however, were coming from the edge of the platform, out from beneath the tossing trees, back toward the cargo elevator. Those who had been standing on the platform watching, moved their feet nervously, as if the slab were tilting, as if they couldn't quite get their balance.

"What's going on?" asked Baufent. It was a useless question.

Pouring from under the trees, springing and leaping and hopping madly, a crowd of naked forms tumbled onto the platform and lunged for the men. The men swung hard, bringing their ghastly assailants down.

Taelin stared in horror.

After twenty seconds of brutality, what creatures were still standing retreated. She watched them lope back into the trees, slip down retaining walls and scurry off into shadow-clogged alleyways. Some dragged themselves through busted windows, heedless of the shards.

The men had won but Taelin could see them panting, hands on knees. They glanced in every direction like scared children and backed quickly toward the cargo elevator, which now sounded to be coming back down. They kept their truncheons out.

Nearby, the *Odalisque* was in the middle of mooring. Taelin twisted at her necklace while men from Caliph's ship secured the ropes and then jogged across the platform to consult with those who had just repelled the attack. The discussion was brief and too distant to hear.

"It's the same thing," said Baufent. Taelin had forgotten the physician was there.

"What is?"

"The disease." Dr. Baufent's short gray hair rumpled in a faintly latrine-scented wind that drew through the urban desolation to the west. "It drives them mad at first. We'll take samples. We'll run tests, but I think it's the same."

Taelin's heart was pounding. "But the vaccine works?"

"Yes, dear. You'll be fine . . . by the end of day two. We just need to keep you quarantined until then."

"Quarantined? Why bother bringing me up if I'm . . . how am I supposed to help if . . ."

"Shh—" Baufent's gunmetal eyes were analyzing the talking men. "We have plenty of doctors up here. This was about you posing for lithoslides, remember? It's political."

Taelin felt insulted, but Baufent's brutal candor acted like a strange ointment. It smoothed things over in an abrupt and unexpected way. "What about them?" asked Taelin. She pointed to the men.

"They got theirs a year ago." Baufent spoke softly. "All physicians and government employees were required to be vaccinated after the court was cleaned. The rest of Isca got theirs soon after."

"The court?"

"I'm sure you read the papers, dear. Ghoul Court is what we call the borough in Isca where it started."

Taelin had read the papers but now she was talking to one of the physicians that had actually been there. "What does the disease do? That was information they never published."

"It turns them into fish," said Baufent. "Not really, of course. But it's a genetic modifier. Some people thought there was cross-breeding going on. Complete nonsense. What's strange is that the mutation shuts down at different stages for different people. We don't know why. Some people's transformation is nearly unnoticeable. Only their brain is affected. Others die. And still others . . . Well. I guess you've seen them."

"Is it airborne?"

"No. It's carried in the blood and mucus membranes. And it's sensitive to race. Pplarians for instance react differently."

Word came back from the ground crew that the High King had decided not to abort. "We're going to set up shop," one of the men in blue goggles said curtly as he strode past Baufent. He had just come up the lift and seemed to have been tasked with disseminating information.

Taelin and the doctor left the deck and went down to the cargo hold where people were gathering. One of the men in black was barking out instructions.

He told them that erecting pavilions for a field hospital at the current spot would be futile. The wind in the Ghalla Peaks was irregular and violent. So, the decision had been made to locate the hospital's hub on the palace grounds, some eight hundred yards to the east, which would also be safer in case of another attack.

The master sergeant also made it clear that they wouldn't be taking up residence in the palace proper for political reasons, a decision that irked most of the physicians.

Taelin got a personal escort to the palace grounds where she was assigned to oversee the medical supplies being ferried from the airship. Despite her knee she was able to organize and verify inventory counts and help the other iatromathematiques unpack. She unrolled yards of white cloth and opened boxes of antiseptic, surgery tools and ampoules ready for the needle. There were less conventional supplies as well, living creatures encased in holomorphic glass harvested from the Memnaw: a dozen scarlet horrors with special equipment to turn their voracious hunger on the plague.

Toward nightfall the hospital, fully erected and open for business, sat waiting for patients.

No one came.

* * *

Bored, Taelin sat down on a little crop of rock just outside the tent hospital. It was dark here and relatively quiet, the perfect place to think. She unfolded Speck's drawing and smiled.

Sena was up to something. She was sure of it. And poor Caliph Howl might be along for the ride. But what could she do? How did Nenuln intend for her to overcome the High King's witch?

Taelin flinched from a noise in the darkness. A soft twittering.

It was a bird that had come up and was dancing on the crop of rock. Strange that it was still flying after dark. Then she noticed the subtle glow in its eyes.

It seemed to gasp as it hopped back and forth, twisting its head, looking at her finger like a grub.

There was clockwork in its brain. Taelin reached out and grabbed it. The lodestone that had drawn it to her was in a ring on the third finger of her right hand. *A contingency,* her father had said. *I want to be able to find my daughter—*

Well he had found her.

Again.

Strapped to the bird's leg was a note and a little bottle of liquid. She read the note with a sense of horror. All it said was, *A toast to the High King.*

"I am not an assassin!" she hissed. Thankfully, no one was close enough to hear. She looked toward the bright hospital tents where people still bustled. No one was close enough to have even noticed the bird's arrival.

She crumpled the note and tossed it into the weeds. She considered throwing the tiny bottle in the same direction but put it into her pocket instead.

Depressed, stressed and angry, she left the crop and hobbled up the battlements to the palace's outer wall where Naobi had risen. She watched the large moon for a long time. Clouds slipped like white flames across its face.

Dr. Anselm arrived to check on her.

"It's beautiful," he said.

"I suppose it is."

"I wanted to thank you." She found his loud, friendly voice soothing. "You did a great job today." He cocked his head. "And I'm not just saying that to pamper Avidan Mwyr's daughter."

She raised a finger at him. "No babysitting."

"No babysitting." He grinned. Then, "You certainly didn't need any. Have the reconnaissance teams left?"

"What? I don't know. I hadn't heard about them."

"Maybe they're already gone. The king sent two detachments down Avenue of Lights." He pointed vaguely toward domes and statues that cluttered the dark skyline. "From the sound of it, we weren't the first ones here. A Pandragonian vessel landed to the south somewhere."

"What is it?" she asked. "You make it sound like something bad happened."

Light from the tents groped his features as he glanced down at his feet; nostrils, lips and cheekbones became a black puzzle. "Word has it, they were attacked . . . worse than we were."

Taelin ached to know if her family had been spared. Her cousin and several close friends lived in the Perch. But how could she get to them?

And how could they have been spared? When she gazed over the copper domes and ancient masonry, the city seemed empty. All she saw were blackened streets and windows. Bright flowers in planters threw ruffling shadows over abandoned brickwork and tar, lit harshly by pools of white-blue lamplight.

Somewhere in the darkness, Taelin could hear a fountain splashing. But the lovely avenues rolled with papers and garbage.

Anselm laced his fingers over the crown of his shaven head. He arched back—stretching.

"Did you see that?"

Anselm snapped back. "Where?"

Taelin pointed. "It was right there. There it is again, see it?"

"Yes."

Something crept below the wall, slinking through folds of darkness on the east side of a boutique. It was coming toward the palace.

Dr. Anselm's voice broke the tension. "Our first patient?"

Taelin took her crutches and hopped down the battlement steps, hurrying as best she could toward the gate.

"Wait!" he called. "You can't go down there! You're under quarantine."

Taelin stopped. "It's not airborne."

Anselm's eyes seemed abnormally white. They were wide and solemn with the gravity of her objection. "Listen, this is serious. Now I know you don't want to—"

"No. No," she said. "You're right. I'm being stupid."

"You're being concerned." He walked down the steps, huge hands thrust into the pockets of his crimson trench. "Nothing wrong with that. But you've done enough today. Here." He produced a bottle of pills. "Take one of these before you sleep. It will help with the altitude."

She accepted the little jar of yellow and purple capsules.

"Now go get something to eat. And *sleep*! I'll coax our patient in, don't worry."

Taelin knew he was right. He seemed levelheaded. He reminded her faintly of Aviv. With a wave and a smile she turned toward the medical tents and the smell of cooking food.

CHAPTER 14

Sena waited for Caliph to say something. There was no up or down. The darkness in the airship pooled around them. They were fish, in an aquarium, looking out at the mangled lights of humans. White tents wobbled. Doctors' shadows wrinkled in the night. Sena did not touch him as she thought about the Bablemumish and Pandragonian plots, the whispers in upholstered staterooms and electroplated dining decks that floated below the City in the Mountain—*waiting* for the High King.

"Did you know anyone here?" asked Caliph.

"Yes." When Caliph's wait turned obstinate she relented. "His name was Tynan."

"Was?"

"He's gone."

"Old boyfriend?"

"Yes."

"I'm sorry."

"It's all right."

She felt the hair on the back of Caliph's neck rise. Tonight it wasn't the energy pouring off her skin that frightened him. Tonight something darker, behind her, only a foot below the ceiling, was listening. Caliph couldn't see it but it was there. And she felt it put Caliph's hackles on end.

"What would you do if you were trapped behind a door?" She drew his attention back to her. "Where you couldn't see the front of the lock?"

"What?" Caliph looked back at the glowing wind-crumpled tents. They had begun to snap in the wind.

"Never mind. Let's flip it," she said. "Here's your riddle."

"Riddle?"

"Just listen.

"Pretend you're in a room. The whole world is in the room with you. Like a giant globe. But it's not a toy. It's the real world. With all the people and things on it that you love. They're real . . . just small. You're not standing on the world."

Caliph scratched the side of his face. "Okay . . ."

Sena felt the thing in the darkness stir behind her but she kept talking. "So you're stuck in a room with the world. At the room's edge is a locked door. Behind the door is Something awful. A Monster. The Monster will eat you if It gets out."

"So I don't let It out."

"It really wants to eat you. It wants to eat the world too."

"So this is a puzzle where I have to choose whether to save myself or the world, right?"

"Damn you."

His smile was slow and roguish. "Does this have anything to do with that crazy thing you said yesterday? Are you the monster here?" She watched his face flex the ghosts of hospital light, pulling the radiance of the flapping tents into his cheeks. He wore an expression of mock fear that tried to set things right between them. It was a valiant attempt. She wanted to touch his lips.

Instead, she said, "It's more complicated than that. The locked door is the only door in the room—that you can see.

"The Monster is banging on that door, trying to get out. Every minute, you hear the door cracking, getting weaker.

"The Monster slides you a key. It tells you that if you set It free, a mechanism will open a second door. A hidden door. If you're fast enough, if you're ready to run—you might just get away."

"Not very reassuring. If I don't unlock the door, what happens?"

"It breaks through." She reached out and gently dug her nails into his arm. "It gets you."

"Nice. So it's only if I unlock the door that I have any chance at all."

"Correct. But it's just a chance."

"How do I know the monster isn't lying to me?"

"Isn't It?"

Caliph laughed. "Not much of a riddle."

"No?"

He dragged his laugh out until it became skeptical. "Why am I trying to solve this?"

"You don't have to. All I said was, 'Here's your riddle.'"

"Which is an implicit invitation."

"Not necessarily. Not all riddles need to be solved. Some just need to be delivered."

"I see. When I realize what the riddle is *not* asking, I'll get my insight. Is that it?"

"Like when you dropped the Pandragonian accord into that black envelope and sent it away . . ."

She'd unsettled him. But his eyes didn't go saucer. He looked at her narrowly; refused to ask how she knew this secret thing. "Are you trying to tell me that there's no way to patch things up with Pandragor, peacefully?"

"No. That's true, but that's not what I'm trying to tell you."

Sena felt the cold vacuous creep of a claw drag itself over her skin. The thing by the ceiling had slunk down to give her a slithering admonition. She heard words in her head, asking her what she was trying to do.

The voice was something Caliph would certainly have recognized if he had heard it. It was a voice that had once laughed and moved air in the house on Isca Hill, just as it had screamed commands through the jungle before poisoning a host of slaves—down to the last child.

The voice did not belong to a man. Not by Sena's standards. It had once belonged to a Gringling king. And a desert queen. The voice that was not a voice had sounded across many lifetimes, preserved by Veyden tinctures. Phylacteries made of bone had carried it nearly to the end. But finally, it had collapsed into its foundation of femurs and costal splinters: a cradle for a new entity made of dust. With its ancient soul untethered, the shade of Nathaniel Howl was like a baby's breath gone wandering beyond the world's rim.

Only recently had it been pulled back, saved from listless transcosmic vagrancy. Now it was desperate to enter Sena's brain. She did not underestimate its cunning, or the math that had gathered in its folds like dirt in a nomad's cassock. The shade, the specter, the ghost—whatever it was—sensed that the stars had finally turned. Soon, it whispered to her. Soon—soon.

Caliph was still talking. "No offense but I think that's bullshit. How can you *know* there's no way for peace with Pandragor?"

"I didn't—"

The shade did its best to distract her.

"If the accord is useless, which I know it is, I think I can still—"

"Caliph. There is no way for peace with Pandragor." Her harshness was a result of irritation, of the stress that the shade was putting on her.

The words set Caliph back. He rested a finger across his upper lip.

The shade worked Sena's throat violently.

It whimpered and slobbered, black claws scurrying over her like bounding rats. Sena felt their discrete impacts against her abdomen, breasts and throat. They thumped her back and thighs. Everywhere. They fled in ebbing tides only to return and burrow against her snatch. They nipped, delved and tested—hurried and mindless.

Sena braced herself. The shade pushed into the cleavage below her belt loops and designer tag. It boosted her from behind, trying to spread her croup. She couldn't concentrate on what Caliph was saying.

"What do I do with that?" Caliph was asking. "Do I make you my top advisor? Do I hand you the throne?"

"I'm not trying to tell you about Pandragor, Caliph. I'm trying to tell you about something else."

"And what's that? More about the book. The Sisterhood? You're going to destroy the world or something? You see how impossible this is for me to understand?"

Sena nodded. It was hard to ignore the shade's insistent nuzzling at the base of her skull. A horrible black rushing sound had begun roaring, not unlike pressing a seashell to her ear. Nathaniel wanted her to stop this conversation.

"What's wrong?" asked Caliph.

The voice was shrieking. A thousand black hexes burnt down onto her lips, like blisters, wicked numbers, sigils spinning. Nathaniel tried to seal her mouth, stifle her tongue.

Sena moved her lips with calm, calculated composure and answered Caliph's question. "I'm haunted, Caliph," she said.

Nathaniel's specter seemed to go insane. It clawed at her eyes.

"Haunted?"

"Yes. Did you know there's a legend about your uncle's book, that he actually managed to haunt its pages after he died?"

Caliph shook his head, clearly perplexed by this sudden swerve, chilled perhaps but also perturbed that they were once again on the topic of the book.

"It's something to think about," she said.

Caliph visibly disagreed.

"It's a kind of parable," she said. "Nathaniel's possession of the thing he craved? It's a lesson in obsession."

She watched that analysis chew into Caliph's face. The muscles in his cheeks reacted with a spasm. A coldness passed between them as it registered with Caliph that she could be talking about him. Caliph swallowed. "I don't like talking about my uncle."

"Don't worry about him."

"You said you were haunted. You can't just say something like that and—"

"I have my ambit."

"Ambit?"

"It's old holomorphic theory," said Sena. "Very old. "

"Not something they taught at Desdae?"

"Your ambit's hard boundary is at the end of your fingertips, at the surface of your skin. What you project beyond that is variable. Your influence. But this," she pinched his arm softly, "is your boundary. If this boundary is impenetrable, nothing can touch you. That is your ambit. That is your uncontestable line."

Caliph laughed. "Right. So, anyway . . ." For a split second she saw a tremor in the jaw muscles that walled his face. He glanced at her from the corner of his eye. Finally, he said, "I should go down and see how it's going. Will you be all right?"

This amused her in a surprising way, that he—so fragile—would ask her if she would be all right.

"Yes. I'll be fine."

Soon his devotion would crumble. Even now it stood out as an abeyance of logic.

"Are you worried about the conference?" she asked.

"A little." One side of his face hitched up around the words. "It'll be fine."

His mind had already moved on to other things. He was feeling guilty about the litho-slides Alani had taken of physicians setting up the field hospital. Sena knew. He felt scrubby about the fact that he was capitalizing on the political advantage of his response. Especially now that he could tell the disease was much worse than he had anticipated, that his physicians couldn't put a dent in this catastrophe.

"Do you think it might be canceled?" she asked.

"The conference? No. This is going to be the most important speech I've ever given. It damn well better *not* be canceled." Then he looked her in the face and said, "But for the moment—" He shrugged. "I'm just glad we're in a position to help the Sandrenese."

It was a thank you, an acknowledgment of the vaccine, the doctors, the way she had planned this out.

Sena felt ashamed.

Caliph couldn't put his finger on what was happening between them. The whole evening had been tainted, charged by his sexual frustration; her curious choice of topics; the darkness and the haunted sounds of the Ghalla Peaks.

He felt like he needed her comfort, her reassurance before tomorrow, but the thought of making love to her in the luxury of the ship while soldiers and physicians worked through the night . . .

People were dying out there in the streets. He could hear the howls carried over the rooftops.

When Sena's hand touched the back of his head, despite the disparity of the evening, despite the bruises on his body, he was ready to set them aside. He considered dragging her back to the stateroom or whether she might just let him throw her up against the wall.

But her expression had hardened. She said, "Strange, isn't it? That the same plague we had in Isca is gutting Sandren. How do you think it traveled so far without affecting the rest of the north? How do you think I knew?"

He stared at her, panicked for a moment that the chemistry between them had evaporated. Her skin looked like graphite under the spell of the moons; her lips white petals. But the power he felt coming off the lines in her skin was no longer magnetic. They seemed to hum like power lines, as if they were capable of electrocuting him. The sensation stunned him into the one question he had never asked her.

"Is it true? Just tell me. Is your temple real? Are you a—?"

"I'm not crazy," she whispered.

He considered what this meant. But he couldn't swallow it. He caved in. Even as he made his demand for proof, even as he felt himself slip into the words of the Pandragonian priests decrying her from the street corners, demanding that she admit her lie, he couldn't help himself.

"Then bring one of them back," he said. He swept his arm at the city, indicating Sandren's many dead. "Any one of them. Bring them all back."

She was quiet. And he knew he had done something terrible. He had crossed a line. He had become like everyone else. And yet, how could she blame him? How could he not eventually need to see proof that she was so different?

"You need more proof? Is that it?" she asked. "More proof than the fact that you are alive?" Her voice was not angry.

But Caliph's was. He heard how his tone had risen and how it now hinged between hysteria and indignation. But his emotions pushed him on. "If you did it for me, you can do it for them!" He flung his arm again toward the window, aiming generally at the tent hospital. "Isn't that reasonable? If I were you, I wouldn't be sitting here. I'd be out there. I'd bring every one of them back to life."

"No, you wouldn't," she said. "Trust me. But I don't blame you for being angry. What I did for you was selfish. I didn't want to go the distance, you know?" She looked away. "Without you . . ."

"Angry? I'm not angry. I'm just confused. I'm just trying to make sense of what you're saying. I don't even know what you mean. *Go what distance?* You've been gone over half a year. Where? Why? What was more important than being with me?"

"I went to the Pplar, to the jungles. I wish I could tell you everything, Caliph." She opened her mouth as if to say more but no sound came out. It was like she was afraid. Her eyes slid sideways in her head as if wary of someone or something listening.

"Why don't you?" he pressed. "Tell me everything?"

"Because. You wouldn't believe me."

"That's not for you to decide."

"In this case it is, Caliph."

"If you told me I would believe you."

"I can't."

"And you won't cure the Sandrenese? Are you saying that you can't do that either?"

"What I'm saying is that there aren't any gods coming to save us—or you. No one can save the Sandrenese. You have to save yourself, Caliph. It's down to you. It's down to your ambit."

Caliph found her conviction chilling but her behavior was too bizarre. Gods or not, he believed she was wrong. He believed she was crazy.

Looking down at the tent hospital, all he knew was that the Sandrenese could not save themselves. People were bad at saving themselves, he thought. The world didn't work that way. In the real world, people saved each other.

Sena looked at him with an expression of deeply fractured sorrow. He wondered if she could still read his mind, if she was always reading it.

His uncle's book had changed her, hurt her, made her this way. He stood up. Compelled partly by his own self-righteousness to go down to the hospital.

"You're right, Caliph." The words sent a teeming pitter-patter of icy pincers up his back.

Right about what? he thought. There was a long pause during which he stood, patiently attuned to her.

"You're right, Caliph, but when you can, will you read these?" In her hand she held two thin books, sandwiched together, one old—one not so much.

"I don't have time to read!"

"You missed them," she said, "the night you were in my library."

His whole body congealed.

"They're important," she said.

And he believed her. He felt that if he didn't believe her, in a spite-fueled way, he would be justified. But his gut told him that not believing would also be a terrible mistake. And besides, he had promised that he would believe her.

She seemed so childish in the face of what was going on: Stonehold was on the brink of sanctions if not war. This conference, which was of critical importance to protecting the duchy, had been derailed by plague. He was in very real danger of being assassinated. All he wanted to do was help, despite the odds. And she treated all of it like a diversion, a table-game between them that they were talking over, distracted from, potentially uninterested in finishing.

Caliph held out his hand for the books.

On entering his palm, their texture worried his fingertips. Their weight conveyed immediately an irrational sense of defeat that settled at his core: another burden he had allowed her to saddle him with.

CHAPTER 15

The day after the attack that had won the Sisterhood the book, Miriam stood in Parliament with her Sisters.

She imagined ice-cold air inflating her lungs as she stared into the marble surround. Great rectangles of black stone served as mirrors, framing the fiery hollow. The fireplace dwarfed her, its mantel entirely out of reach.

While pretending to stare at her reflection she traced the thin scar around her neck with her fingers, feeling the completeness of its circuit. She felt giddy and strange to have been part of something so mythic. Yet it troubled her. She also felt violated. As if she had agreed to a hypnotism without realizing she would have no recollection of the event.

Just the memory of cold air touching her insides.

Miriam stared past herself. She could see the women behind her. Deep in the black marble, a red dress wavered like a brushstroke as one of the women reached for another beer. The surround's atrous polish subdued the colors and turned the entire scene glossy as a litho.

"Miriam, hon? Come get drunk with us. You earned it."

She turned around. The brown ten-pound contraption on the floor was open, hissing with green lights and ice. It held a dozen black bottles with red and silver labels.

"Sure." She walked over and took one, kissed its neck. It tasted of pungent southern soils.

The spoils of war rested on a low table, before the semicircle of women in large leather chairs: the legendary *Cịsrym Tạ*. Its cover, still red after more than twenty-thousand years, had faded and torn. Could it really be that old? The black thorny mark on it threatened her vaguely. Its latch was locked.

She took another drink.

Giganalee's laugh gurgled up near Miriam's elbow and terrorized her.

The Eighth House's withered frame sat propped in a huge chair. Her face clung to her skull like crepe fabric.

Miriam noticed the old woman's fingers, unrelated bones that had been tied together somewhere inside her lace sleeves. They poked out awkwardly, fiddling with her beer as she coughed and giggled without explanation.

Worried that she might choke, Miriam leaned forward and asked if she was all right.

But the Eighth House did not answer. Sisters had dressed her up in full ceremonial garb tonight for the celebration. Giganalee's coal-black dress was cut from silk and trimmed with midnight-colored lace. Peeking from beneath, a white satin lining swaddled her throat and claws, conferring the elegance of a decorated corpse.

"Madam D'ver?" Haidee took the bottle out of Giganalee's fingers and tried to calm her but Giganalee continued rocking in her chair, bubbling with laughter.

We are lost, thought Miriam.

An iatromathematique showed up with a sedative. She spoke in a soothing whisper into Giganalee's ear as she rolled up the old woman's sleeve. Her arm resembled suet. A quick injection put her into a torpor and several girls wearing white gowns maneuvered her frail body onto a wheelchair that they silently rolled away.

"What do we do now?" asked Duana.

Haidee straightened her crimson hem. "Whatever we want."

Miriam found her conviction repugnant. "Really? How do we open it?"

"There's a recipe," said Haidee. She wagged her chin and scowled at Megan from under her eyebrows. "We *have* it."

"A recipe none of us can follow," said Miriam. "Unless one of us wants to admit to a little fåroṇ[12] on the side?"

"That's just hocus-pocus." Haidee swung her beer bottle back and forth like a pendulum from the neck. "You don't have to love him . . . or her."

Duana interrupted Miriam's response. "Why would Sena give us the book unless—" She snatched her hand back from the cover. "Shit! It's cold." Miriam saw Duana swallow her fear, which made the surgically perfect scar encircling her neck ripple.

"A better question is: how do we know this is the real book?" Miriam used the hem of her dress to twist open another beer. "I've seen Sena throw a glamour. She's better than any of us."

[12] Påriṇ and fåroṇ are respectively "The Duty" and "The Betrayal." Påriṇ specifically is sex work to advance the Sisterhood's political agenda. Fåroṇ is sex for personal reasons and seen as jeopardizing the Sisterhood's veil of secrecy.

All nine women stared at the *Cịsrym Tạ.*

"She said she'd drag us through the jungle," said Duana, who looked unabashedly worried.

Autumn Solburner was a dusky-skinned girl that Miriam tried not to show outward favoritism for. She entered the conversation cautiously, seeming to wonder why Miriam was being negative. "This is what the Houses have been trying to accomplish for decades." She turned her palms up. "*This* is the book. It's not a fake. We've won, Miriam. We have it. Why aren't you happy? The Wịllin Droul doesn't stand a chance."

Miriam gave Autumn a serious look then said, "Sena's in Sandren. That's where the Chamber is."

Haidee set her bottle down and pointed at Miriam. "You hush."

"I will not. She's going to the Chamber and you know it."

No one talked. Haidee's black eyes burned across the table at Miriam. Miriam didn't feel like backing down. She had been the last Sister in Stonehold, the last to speak with Sienæ Iilool. She knew what she was talking about. "What is it?" she asked. "You don't want to admit it? You're the one in the red dress . . . *Mother.*"

"Shut up," hissed Haidee. "I'm not Coven Mother yet so be happy. We all know you think you deserve it but it's not coming to you so quit being sour."

"Don't turn this into that old argument," Miriam snapped. "This isn't about you or me. It's about the Sisterhood and the fact that the Eighth House is insane. We need a leader that—"

"Bite your tongue!"

"I will not! Giganalee is *incompetent*!" said Miriam. "If she's not, get her out of bed and bring her down here so she can sentence me to Jụyn Hêl herself!"

The others gasped.

"You are excused," said Haidee.

"Really? You're not Coven Mother yet. I don't think I *am* excused."

"I said—"

"Focus on getting the Sisterhood back on track!" shouted Miriam, "or I swear—"

A kyru snapped out in Haidee's hand, gleaming. A single talon. Extended.

Autumn, Duana and the rest made room.

Miriam was committed now. She felt how exquisitely and abruptly the time for shouting had ended. Feeling ambivalent about both the future and the recent past, she pulled her own kyru with a tremble. It was internal. No one else would see her fear.

To the positive, the other seven weren't taking sides. It seemed they might be willing to let this sort itself out.

Miriam pulled her blade down over her hand and gasped. Haidee started babbling numbers instantly, enlisting the Sisterhood's trick of hemofurtum. She meant to steal Miriam's blood, suck her holojoules into a fast equation before Miriam had time to reach her sum. Oddly, no holojoules came . . .

In a smooth redirection of the kyru's motion, Miriam pulled the weapon up into a throw. The razor left her fingertips, spinning through air. It embedded itself in Haidee's chest; Miriam was already talking. The Unknown Tongue poured out of her. She too enlisted hemofurtum: only her equation was working.

Miriam had not cut herself.

Haidee's equation ran dry. She had been fooled by sleight of hand and amateur acting and it was too late to adjust.

Miriam finished her sum quickly and the blade sank deep. With one gruesome tug the kyru obeyed her words and snugged itself up into Haidee's heart.

Haidee dropped to the floor. Her lips passed an airy sound.

Miriam picked up her beer and tipped it back. Then she tossed the bottle on the carpeted floor. "We need some fucking better leadership around here. That's all I'm saying." She felt a little drunk. All of them were at least a little drunk. The improbability of Haidee's body on the floor felt less significant in that light. But Miriam had spoken the truth. She turned and left the room.

On the morning of the fourteenth, Giganalee woke up laughing.

Eight Ascendant Sisters stood with Miriam around the oval bed. They were the only ones who had witnessed Haidee's death and, as the Eighth House woke, Duana functioned as elected speaker for the group. She used the Eighth House's proper title, which Miriam thought absurd considering Giganalee's state of mind.

"Ascended One? Haidee is dead."

"Who killed her?" Giganalee's eyes stared blindly at the extravagant ceiling.

Miriam felt a rivulet of sweat cut loose under her arm and trickle over her ribs.

Duana hesitated just a moment, unable to meet the eyes in the room. "It was Miriam."

Giganalee started laughing again.

Miriam didn't know whether to keep holding her breath. Duana looked at her. So did Autumn, Gina and the others. But Miriam realized they weren't looking *at* her. They were looking *to* her, wondering what to do.

Autumn's gaze in particular was deadly serious. She had taken Miriam's side without saying a word.

"Hmm . . . hmm-hmm." Giganalee's chuckle tapered. "You know," she said, "that girl from the isles is a scroll. Hagh, hagh-hagh—" She chortled again.

"This is useless," Miriam said under her breath. She began to back away from the bed.

"Miriam Yeats!" Giganalee bawled.

Miriam stopped.

"You are Sororal Head."

Duana whispered skeptically, "Why not Coven Mother?"

But Miriam could almost feel what was coming before Giganalee opened her mouth.

"There will be no Mother—" for half a second Giganalee gagged on her own tongue, then continued, "until the trouble is sorted, Miriam will wear red."

"How do we sort the trouble?" asked Gina.

"We stop Sena," said Miriam.

Giganalee waved her hand. *Yes,* said the hand. *Yes, yes, yes.* "If it can be done. The book has come late. I should have known." She was grinning. "I'm an old fool." Her words trailed off into an animal growl.

Miriam saw Giganalee's slender talons produce a lovely brown pill from beneath the bedclothes. She popped it into her mouth.

"Gods!" yelled Duana. But it was too late.

"The Eighth House is outside the Circle!" shrieked Giganalee. Then her body yanked through a series of feral contortions. Black and yellow foam erupted from Giganalee's mouth and burned through the snowy sheets.

Giganalee was wrapped in chartreuse lace and tied with fine black ribbon. Haidee too. Both corpses were packed into temporary wooden crates for transfer by steam rail. At the last stop, which was Menin's Pass, the funeral procession would unpack and carry them northwest toward the hidden tombs, likely on horseback, through snow, bright green bundles strapped behind black saddles.

Funerals in winter were never easy for the Sisterhood and Miriam was glad she wouldn't be part of the procession. Under the circumstances, she felt the need to prepare quickly and go after Sena, so she handed the funeral duties off to the Sixth House.

Details of the two deaths were not shared with anyone in the Fourth or below. The Sisterhood was already in crisis. Miriam had no interest in generating hysteria. The story disseminated was that Miriam had challenged Haidee for the right to wear red. Haidee had lost. It was maintained secondly that Giganalee had simply died in her sleep.

Speculation notwithstanding, the lower-ranked Sisters received the news and—what else could they do?—got on with preparing for the funerals.

By midafternoon, Parliament was busy as any other day, with people arriving for court hearings in the east wing and buying permits in the tiled halls of the ground floor, oblivious to the crisis their government was going through.

From her place in the Sixth House, Miriam looked up at the Seventh. Or she felt like she did. There was some uncertainty and self-consciousness associated with presiding over that group of Sisters above her, which accounted for only one percent of the entire Sisterhood.

Part of the problem was that she felt she needed to stem the gossip the Seventh House was spreading as they entertained notions about Giganalee's final words. And telling them to shut up was not going to be easy.

The popular interpretation was that when Giganalee had shrieked that the Eighth House was outside the Circle, the grandam of the coven had been referring to Sena Iilool.

The onus of *Ascended One* was a title only the Eighth House could bestow. Didn't it make sense that she would feel compelled to confer that title before she died? If so, only one witch had ever been expelled from the Sisterhood and lived. Only one name could fit Giganalee's pronouncement.

Miriam did not like this interpretation. It threatened to tear the Sisterhood apart. She tried to offer an alternate: that what Giganalee had meant was that she—the Eighth House—was leaving the Circle: because she was about to kill herself. Unfortunately, this came off sounding puerile.

The trouble with all of this was that Miriam believed Giganalee had been crazy, that the Sisterhood had been headed in the wrong direction. But she was now unable to say so, because to question the crone's sanity at this point was to question her own appointment as Sororal Head. Doing that would lead the Sisterhood into further disarray.

And this was why she let the Seventh House gossip. Because if she wielded her position too heavily, they could easily denounce her.

For now, no one in the Seventh House was doing that. They seemed to understand the repercussions and the incredibly precarious position that the Sisterhood was in. They didn't want chaos. Instead they seemed to embrace Miriam's ferocity as a kind of weapon they could turn against the Sisterhood's ambiguous future. Against Pandragor and the Wịllin Droul.

Miriam worked through the afternoon. While the clock hands reached for the etchings of dusk, she organized qloins for what she felt was coming. When she finally looked up, the sun had lodged itself like a crashed meteor—pure red—in the snow-colored horizon, shooting otherworldly rays through a stigma of flurries.

She got up, left her new office with the vista blazing through Parliament's enormous windows and rolled the *Cịsrym Tạ* down into the building's vaults.

Though Giganalee had claimed it had come to them late, Miriam still felt it had to be protected.

The book unnerved her. Holding it was like gripping someone's forearm. Spongy. The arm of a corpse. She had recorded a thermograph in the labs: ten degrees above freezing. It added up to something she didn't want to carry in her arms.

So she pushed it on a creaking metal cart down an underpitched passageway and into the incandescent gloom of the archives. Most of the Seventh House wanted to try and open it but Miriam had dissuaded them. She knew the recipe for unlocking this book—the whole recipe. And it was nothing to trifle with.

The Sisterhood had had the book less than thirty hours and already two of them were dead.

She interred the book in Parliament's holomorphic vault, locked the door and climbed the ramp back through the labs.

A lift hoisted her out of the cellars and up into the east studio with a groan. It deposited her in the exact room where Haidee had died the previous night. Cleaners had already taken care of the stain.

The red sun had vanished and the vast windows were black as the marble fireplace. The Seventh House was gathered. This meeting was not optional.

As Miriam entered the room she noticed how her sisters had gathered around the fireplace with their legs pulled up and their backs bent forward in the oversized chairs. They looked anxious. They looked stressed. There was no beer tonight.

Miriam wore a pair of ruby earrings: the only red things she could find.

She walked to her chair and sat down.

"I think we all know this is about the Eighth House." Admitting it to them after she had struggled to suppress the notion elicited more than one apprehensive look. "But that information doesn't leave this room."

"What do you want us to do?" said Autumn.

"Sena's headed south. We heard it from her own mouth. The Stairs first. We'll try there. Then the jungle. We know her route."

"She could have been lying," said Duana.

"No." Miriam wagged her hand. "Sena doesn't believe we can stop her. She's throwing it in our face."

"Can we stop her?"

Miriam knew Duana had not slept since Haidee's death and her eyes bore the brutality of the hours. "If we don't . . ." Miriam groped for words strong enough to do what she needed them to do. After a moment she gave up. "If we don't, there's no reason for doing anything else."

"Maybe it's a dead end," suggested Anjie. Her hair was dark and coiled from a recent shower. "Maybe she reaches the jungle and can't do anything. Maybe the legend is a fraud."

"That's a slippery stack of maybes," said Miriam. "I for one don't believe the Wịllin Droul's preternarcomancers have been dreaming up fiction for a thousand years.

"Securing the book. Preventing the unthinkable. That is the path the Sisterhood was on a year ago . . . when Sena took the *Cịsrym Tạ* to Stonehold. That is the path the Sisterhood has always been on . . . since its inception. We have secured the book. Now we must prevent the unthinkable. We must return to the path."

Miriam saw hands and faces move in corroborative patterns. *Good,* she thought.

"Duana, I want you to take your qloin to Sandren. Sena might still be there. Autumn, Senka and Awh'Gnuoyk: I'm appointing you each cephal'matris of new qloins. Pick your ancillas from the Sixth House. Where's the puslet we pulled out of the attorney general's daughter?"

"It's in the lab," said Autumn. "It's still alive."

"Good."

"I'm not sure it's good," said Autumn. "There was a partial graft. I think it's taken."

"Is it usable though?"

"We think so. But the priestess' cells are still alive. The only way we'll know for sure is—"

"Clean it as best you can," said Miriam. "The High King is in Sandren . . . and based on Megan's scrying dish he's not huddled in a conference room protected by bodyguards. He's up in the city-state—trying to play hero in the face of the Wịllin Droul's disease. I doubt he's adequately staffed for that kind of scenario."

"Oh my gods!" said Duana.

"This is for real," Miriam said softly. "You can take up to three more operatives from the Fourth House if you think you'll need them." She turned back to Autumn. "All right, Autumn . . . show me the puslet."

CHAPTER 16

"One Thousand Rosewind Palace."

Even after a year's worth of official mail from the address, it still sounded blithe and fruity in Caliph's mouth.

He handed the two books Sena had given him to one of his bodyguards and pressed the grime-encrusted button on the lift. It was just after midnight. The cage around him staggered a moment, then smoothly unreeled down oil-streaked suspensor bars and into the courtyard's chilly sweetness.

The captain had repositioned the ship over the palace's ciryte mooring deck but there wasn't enough room to accommodate both it and the *Iatromisia.* When the lift touched down, he struck out across the vast glittering dais, emerged from the zeppelin's shadow into moonlight and descended directly toward the hospital tents that glowed whitely through a black braiding of exotic botanicals.

Already he could hear the screams.

Updates had come to him regularly, indicating that "patients" were gathering beyond the palace walls. Several of the saner ones had been *captured* and treatment had begun.

The screams did not come from the tents. Howls and wails floated above the outer walls, attesting to the great horde there.

Caliph arrived in the central tent unannounced, flanked by bodyguards. He looked at the tentative atrocities that recoiled from the touch of their caregivers. Most of them seemed to have lost the ability to speak. They gurgled half-words and lowed like nocturnal amphibians.

Were they still human? he wondered.

One squatted on a white canvas cot, another curled into the fetal position, oozing black-green pus from ulcers that glistened over skin gone iridescent gray. The disease had modified what muscles they had left, made them hunker. They smelled like salmon.

Keeping her distance, but staring through the metallic-toned morbidity, Caliph saw the priestess of Nenuln watching him.

He noticed her crutches. She looked away the moment their eyes met. *Shit,* he thought. *Here's something I should have handled earlier.* He walked the circumference of the busy tent so that he could engage her directly. She did not attempt to escape.

"Lady Rae."

She bowed slightly. "Your majesty." He found her pretty, cinnamon-colored. And there were reddish highlights in her long wild hair. "I didn't realize it would be like this."

"You didn't?" Her eyes accused him.

What could he say? Quantities of vaccine were piled around them in refrigerated chests.

"No."

"I find that hard to believe."

"Well, I came over here to apologize. I wouldn't have brought you with if I'd known it was going to be so dangerous." He gestured to her crutches.

"I know. It's just political." Her tongue snicked against her teeth. "Your doctor made it clear: I'm just here for the lithos. You didn't expect me to actually help with anything important."

"It's absolutely political," he said. "I'm sure you know my standing with your father's government. We're lucky to have you in Isca."

"That seems overly candid for a politician," she said.

Caliph pressed on, trying to fight her skepticism. "Why would I lie?"

"Apparently you wouldn't."

"No . . . I wouldn't. The truth is, I appreciate your interest in Stonehold, the work you've done in Lampfire Hills and Os Sacrum. My thanks is insufficient. And your willingness to come to Sandren, to show up here, puts me even more in your debt. But now, look at your leg. I don't feel comfortable having you so close—"

"That *would* look bad, wouldn't it?" She smiled; a momentary awkwardness bubbled up between them. He felt like he wasn't following her. "If something were to happen to me?" she clarified. Her head straightened and she looked at him squarely.

"That's right," said Caliph. He felt off balance. Maybe he had misinterpreted the smile. He supposed he understood what she was getting at. "Regardless of whether you think it's just about my image, I'd still like you to go back down to the *Bulotecus.*"

"Where it's safe?"

"Yes. Where it's safe."

"It wasn't safe the other night." She waved her hand in front of her crutches. "You know, King Howl—I know that for you, this *is* political. But, honestly, why do you think *I* came up this cliff in the first place?"

Caliph hung his head. "Because to you, it's not political. You're here out of the goodness of your heart, to help people. And you won't be dragged away." This was a bit of a show. Based on what Alani had told him, Caliph knew she hated Sena. The priestess wasn't without ulterior motives. But he wanted to see if she would relent, if she might admit to some level of hypocrisy.

She did not.

Instead she clapped twice. "Very good, King Howl." But then her face softened, her cynicism slipped marginally. She regarded him for a moment, possibly against a set of less-harsh assumptions.

"Well," said Caliph, "everything you've said is fair. I invited you. Now I suppose I have to live with the risks."

"Do you? I doubt it."

Caliph shifted his eyes to the hospital and the grisly patients squirming on cots. He ignored her assessment. "So, how is the vaccine working?"

"There's no one here to vaccinate," she said. "All of them are already infected. But Dr. Baufent ran some tests. It's the same strain you had in Isca."

"Well, at least there's hope for anyone we find who doesn't have it yet." A volley of moans carried over the walls like a fusillade aimed at his optimism. He forced a razor-thin smile and ended with, "All right. Thank you for your help. Please be careful."

She ducked her head. "Your majesty . . ."

Caliph left her in the tent and headed for the walls, trying to ignore the scarlet mussels that ground themselves against several naked patients. He wanted to talk to his men.

Alani stood near the gates. He seemed to be muttering with his commanding officer in what, from a distance, looked to be an almost satirical pose, standing sagely with one hand on his hip, the other stroking his beard.

As Caliph arrived, satire vanished. Alani turned to him and said point-blank, "This whole thing is too big for us."

"Where's Sig?"

"He never came up. We moved him to the *Bulotecus* before we left."

"Good. It's safer down there."

Alani took out his pipe, spun it and pointed it at Caliph's chest. "I'd like to move you down there."

Caliph started to scoff but Alani's eyes stabbed him. "You think I'm joking? Your little priestess over there is getting cruestone-delivered messages from someone down below and I don't have time to worry about it—"

"She's harmless," said Caliph. "Trust me."

"Is she? We brought her with for a reason. Don't let the Pandragonians turn this around on us."

Caliph raised his palms. "I know I don't make your job easy but—"

Alani interrupted. "Please—our escort's designed for a three-day trip to a secured building for an uneventful conference. Currently, I barely have the manpower to secure the perimeter at this position. That means every man is working. That means none of them are sleeping. That means, even popping pills, in a little over thirty hours we'll have lost our edge—completely. At that point everyone crashes and we're defenseless."

Caliph blew a thin stream of air and looked around. The howls from the other side of the gate were deafening. "Is there anything we can do to make it easier? Besides giving up?"

"If we move you inside the palace and leave a couple men with the hospital tents, I can start letting men sleep."

"That's not good politics."

"Your choice," said Alani. "Thirty hours and good politics or—"

Caliph threw his hands up. "Fine. Move us into the palace." *What am I doing?*

"YOU should be asleep," said Baufent.

Taelin stood at the edge of the tents, looking toward the gate. She could still see the High King arguing with his men but couldn't hear anything they were saying. Baufent's voice barely registered. Taelin kept staring at the king.

Baufent turned it into a joke. "You little spy!"

"Am not." Taelin's denial came out sounding surprisingly defensive. To offset it, she choked up a laugh.

"Come with me," said Baufent.

"Where are we going?" She followed the doctor back into the tents where one of the patients was forcefully vomiting a kind of gray-purple chunder from between his or her exposed teeth. Sex became difficult to tell as the disease progressed.

"It looks like they're going to waste away," said Baufent. "And they might. But believe me, it can surprise you."

Taelin held her shirt up in front of her face.

"Hurry," said Baufent. "You're not immune yet."

"Where are we going?" Taelin asked again.

"Anselm, that ass, has thrown me out of the tent. Says I need sleep. Sleep! Do you hear that?" The crescendo of howls beyond the gate underscored her meaning. "Well, I can't sleep and since you're totally useless at the moment, you're going to play cards with me."

Taelin laid her crutches on the ground and sat down across from Baufent on a cot. She watched the physician shuffle a deck.

The bright suits of flower-wrapped bones and devils mixed with winged creatures and constellations as the cards slid across the small table between them for the next several hours.

Baufent won nearly all the hands.

Finally, Taelin noticed the light in the tent had changed. It had become more blue. And there was a small fingerprint of pink sunlight glowing on the fabric as dawn touched Sandren from the west.

"We're supposed to go home today," Taelin mentioned. "I'm out of clean clothes and I have a mission home that I need to take care of . . ."

"I read that," said Baufent, "in the paper. St. Remora?"

"Yes."

"That's a big responsibility. Why do it up there? I mean, why not just open a mission in Pandragor—where you're from?"

Taelin deliberated a moment over how much honesty to apply to her answer. Finally she said, "Turning on lights in dark rooms has a bigger impact . . . than turning them on in rooms that are already lit."

"Oh." Baufent sat back in her chair as if insulted. "Well, I suppose that *is* our reputation."

"I'm not talking about you. Or Nanemen in general." Taelin tried to smooth her reply. "It's not racial or cultural. You didn't choose your government."

"Ah, so it's our government, is it? Maybe you really were spying on the king—"

Taelin tried not to think about her father or the tiny bottle in her pocket as she contemplated Caliph Howl. "It's strange," she said. "He seems like a good man."

"He's arrogant," said Baufent. "But I suppose you have to be arrogant if you want to rule Stonehold. If you weren't, the burgomasters would eat you alive. I used to despise him but he grows on you."

"I can see how he would."

A commotion from outside made them forget their hands. They pushed aside the dew-covered flap and stepped out into air and sunlight, frosted as though a weather system gone missing from Stonehold had turned up here.

The cold bit Taelin's throat. She expected to see one of the patients risen up, assaulting the doctors. But the silver- and black-freckled bodies lay still as fish at market: long, silent, and basking in the mountain's air.

People were jogging toward the west walls, mounting the stairs, looking into the sunrise and pointing in horror.

From the sound and pitch of the disturbance, Taelin decided that the palace grounds had become the focus of some kind of assault. The postern had been closed and barred for the night but it sounded like a great mass of people had assembled just outside the walls. Knee throbbing, Taelin climbed the battlements to see.

Past the crenels there were hundreds of them. Maybe thousands. She was no good judge of such large numbers.

She walked in a stupor, overcome by the sheer size of the horde. A soldier in blue goggles brushed past her. He seemed to be talking to himself. "They're nothing but animals." His voice couched more awe than contempt.

Taelin wanted to say that he was wrong. That those were still people down there. But she lacked the faith to actually get it out. It was a ghoulish scene. The plague-stricken were crying and hammering and shrieking against the walls. Many of them must have died under the crush of their fellows or by hurling themselves repeatedly against the stone enclosure. Bodies had been trampled into pink paste that glistened like cooking fat in the cracks between stones. It covered everything. Some crouched, feeding. Still the hoard yelped and chittered and persisted in their futile attack.

But none of this was what the physicians and soldiers were pointing at. Their arms stretched out above the chaos, beyond its sickening sights and sounds.

From the battlements Taelin and everyone else could see, casting long ruinous shadows, the wreckage of the *Iatromisia*: still tethered to the teagle platform.

No one was sure how they had pulled it down. Much of the conversation atop the parapet revolved around theories. One thing seemed certain. The zeppelin's elevator had been left unlocked.

Whatever the truth, the *Iatromisia* was still in the process of being destroyed. Great holes had been ripped in her skin. The gasbags were deflating. The delicate duralumin frame had been crumpled under the weight of hundreds of hideous leaping bodies.

"We're trapped." It came out of someone's mouth as a whisper.

"We're not trapped. The *Odalisque* can ferry us down."

"Funny that, eh?" said someone else. "He manages to save his luxury craft?"

Taelin left the battlements, nauseous, wondering what Caliph Howl planned to do. This was a disaster. It felt like the end of the world. She realized she was crying and she hardly knew why. She leaned heavily on her crutches, hanging her head in an effort to hide her emotion. She blamed the tears on lack of sleep; her notions of seeing any of her relatives had vanished along with illusions that the High King's tiny clinic could nurture Sandren back to health.

"We'll be fine." Baufent's firm voice startled her. The doctor squeezed her shoulders. "Don't worry."

But Baufent's voice held little conviction and Taelin did worry. She wiped her tears and noticed for the first time that she was filthy.

"Shit," said Baufent. "Now what?" The physician hustled toward a new commotion in the tents and Taelin followed her, catching glimpses of shouting people and limbs thrashing.

The patient causing the commotion had to be forcibly restrained. Its silvery arm struck a steel bowl full of medical devices. The bowl sang as it hurled to the ground and scattered its contents in the grass. Taelin crept forward to pick up the mess. She was unable to see clearly but the patient was certainly going through horrendous fits.

Baufent shouted for help and more physicians came running.

As Taelin watched the scarlet coats blot out the scene she felt helpless. The world provided her no place to go, nothing to do, no way to help. Her position in the grass, holding the steel bowl was useless.

Why?

Because she had deviated from the dream. Didn't that make sense? Nenuln had told her not to let the High King's witch escape. But right now Taelin didn't even know where Sena was or what she was doing. She had become sidetracked by the hospital tents, wanting to help. But as the sounds of a terrible birthing squealed up from the knot of doctors and something grotesque as a giant tadpole was dropped, sloshing and half-dead, into a bucket of bloody water, Taelin realized her error.

This was not what she had come here for.

Neither the patient nor its offspring survived and Taelin could hardly bear to think that this illness had spread south, beyond Sandren. She watched part of the autopsy; saw how the brain of the victim had suffered like its flesh. Several physicians gasped during the procedure. "I don't know how he walked in here," Baufent said. "See the decay? The cerebellum and basal ganglia are almost totally destroyed."

"He?" asked Taelin.

Baufent looked up at her between the hunched shoulders of the other doctors around the table. Despite the birth, Baufent said, "Indeed."

But the patient had walked. And so had others. Those that had not chewed off their tongues still whispered. The stories were garbled, about slippery creatures that had brought the plague to Sandren. Although they sounded preposterous, Dr. Baufent seemed to take them at face value. She assured Taelin that this had happened before.

"If you're not going to bed, I could use your help."

Taelin looked over her shoulder as if Sena might be there. She pondered going to bed. Then, reluctantly, she made the southern hand sign for yes and followed Baufent to the next gurney.

"Can you hand me that anesthesia inhaler?"

Taelin looked at the nearby tray. The funnel-shaped contraption was easy to sort out. She passed it to the doctor. As she did, the patient reached up and grabbed her wrist. Taelin cried out. Baufent jumped forward and tried to slap the hand away. But the patient looked up with deathly golden eyes and maintained its grip. "We came for you," it said. Its eyes burned into Taelin's face. "The flawless are coming." Its other hand reached toward her chest. "Coming for you."

Dr. Anselm appeared out of nowhere and wrestled with the patient's hand. Finally its fingers loosened and Taelin felt her wrist come free.

"Get her out of here!" shouted Anselm. "She's supposed to be under quarantine!"

Taelin stumbled backward as the scene cluttered with bodies. Baufent, coat covered with greasy salve and plague excretions and the sticky residue of her own sweat called out that it was her fault. She examined Taelin's wrist. "It's just a scratch." But she doused Taelin's entire arm with antiseptic. "You've had your shot. You're going to be fine. Now get out of here."

Heart still hammering, Taelin backed away, twisting at her necklace, bending the edges back and forth. Useless. She was in the wrong place.

For a while she stood in the darkness at the edge of the tent, watching the brilliant red smell-feasts suckle their meals. Scarlet oyster bodies with long tendrils wrapped the patients and undulated against them. Their sucking mouths worked against the toxins while Baufent supervised the operation.

I need to find Sena, she thought.

She considered sneaking onto the *Odalisque,* or into the palace where she had heard the High King was now staying.

Finally, she went back to her cot. The unfinished game of cards seemed like it belonged to a different week. She tried to remember what day it was. Had it really only been yesterday morning that they had arrived in Sandren? It was hard to believe. She felt dizzy and lay down on her side. The thin blanket she had been given was too small to cover her feet.

She closed her eyes, listened to herself breathing. She hugged a tiny pillow to her chest for comfort and felt the demonifuge press against her breastbone. The place on her wrist, where the creature had grabbed her, itched. Taelin tried not to think about it. Nenuln would keep her safe.

Chapter 17

Dawn had barely broken on the fifteenth and Caliph knew that flying back to Isca was impossible. The batteries on the *Odalisque* were so depleted that even descending from the city-state would be treacherous. Unfortunately, the palace's chemical pumps had been turned off, presumably as a precaution. Caliph imagined the lord mayor bravely locking things down, trying to ensure that the sickness would stay here, trapped in the mountains.

The valves, the pumps, all of it was a mystery to Caliph. Even Alani was helpless. Most of the instructions were printed in High Mąlk.

Caliph sent for Sig.

The palace was in shambles. It smelled of death. The lord mayor, his bodyguards and staff, everyone who had once called Rosewind home, were piled in the rear courtyard. Caliph agreed with Alani that knowledge of the gruesome discovery be disseminated only on a need-to-know basis.

"I want to know who piled them up," said Caliph. But memories of a terrifying night in Isca made it easy to conjecture. He had already made sense of this.

So had everyone else. Which was why none of his elite guards answered as he paced around a velvet divan that had been pushed back from where it had recently buttressed the palace's main doors.

The Stonehavians sensed the danger, down in the moist fissures below the city. The things that had come up from underground. Caliph didn't want to believe that it was true or that he had brought everyone here and run them nearly out of fuel.

All Caliph could do was hope that Sig arrived soon.

In the meantime he poked around the palace, looking through archways at darkened inner rooms where signs of further madness marred the walls and floors.

It became clear how behaviors must have changed so rapidly from the premeditated human greed of looting to more basic animal avarice. The patients in the tents certainly showed no interest in their appearance or in gathering treasures. Whatever had been stolen from these grand rooms must have soon after been scattered, thought Caliph, left in diverse locations as the thieves lost interest and slunk out of their new lairs, changed and hungry.

A chandelier on the floor of the three-story vestibule must have been too heavy to cart away. Its bent, curled shape snarled like a dead spider in a swatch of light that spilled from a doorway at the other end of the echoing room. Caliph overheard Alani's men muttering. They wrestled with a map.

Sena had disappeared gods knew where. The conference had been delayed until tomorrow according to a note flown up by bird. Sig was on his way. Everything was in limbo.

Caliph called one of his men over. "Where are those books I gave you?"

"Right here, sir."

Caliph took them and sat down in the patch of light. There was a bright blue note tucked into the pages that read start here.

Journal Entry: C. Tides: 562[13]*, Y.o.T. Salamander: Phisku—Whispers, 11th: Arkhyn Hiel.*

I grew up along the Bainmum River, on the desert's edge. It was perhaps because of that cruel climate that I wanted to save people from hurt. From sun and sand and raiders out of Eh'Osgaj Ogwôg. That was the heart of my youth.

I woke thirty years later to find that I had paved the road to that goal with broken bodies, my philanthropy reflected in breastplate and helmet.

It seems impossible to connect me, the laughing curious child, with the bloody sword I have swung for so many years. I became a monster over decades through a slow regimen of self-rewards.

I know now that "rights" are unrelated to eating cuts of meat and drinking wine, to being served at my whim in the swiftest most accommodating manner. Still, I cannot help but dream of the great days, when all white men were our slaves and all that was beautiful was black like me: when choice was *not* a right.

But I digress.

I am also a monster in a very physical way, a decayed hand writing in the jungle. To say that I chose this would be overstate-

[13] Date suspect.

ment. Many who wind up in situations from which there is no escape do so not out of choice, which implies a logical assessment of pros and cons, but out of a lack of insight. Wisdom is not imparted equally.

Wouldn't you agree, Sslîạ?

What I am is consequence. In the same manner that my humanity was taken from me and I became something else, so soon . . . soon . . . what I am now will be taken again, and I will make an old transition.

I can no longer use shuwt tinctures to inhabit the bodies of young girls as I once so enjoyed doing. My veins no longer flow with blood. But sometimes I cut myself as I used to, in order to make certain. Then I wonder if I am really in a ruined stone house at the jungle's edge—waiting for the end.

Caliph checked his chemiostatic watch. He guessed he had time for a little more and dutifully followed Sena's note to the next log.

Journal Entry: C. Stone: -1,688[14]
Li: Arkhyn Hiel.

The terrible beauty of the Last Page has long been prophesied. But who believes in prophecy these days? The churchgoer hoping for validation in his lifetime? Hoping for some great sign to appear; for his enemies to be burned? The churchgoer and the sadist are indistinguishable. Anyone with a serious mind toward the future must cast Yacob Skie's scrolls aside, ignore prophecy and get on with the business of progress.

It is hard to fault the pragmatist since Yacob Skies's words are difficult to understand.

But there was a time when men were more than men. When they were nearly gods they harkened to subtle things. Men are simple creatures now, as if they have poured all the complexity of themselves into their diversions and their machines. Now they understand only the simplest emotions. Lust, indignation and fear. These are the things that steer their nations. Even love has become too subtle for them to grasp.

This is why I have been seeking the evolutionary key ever since I escaped the destruction of the gardens at Jôrgill Deep. It is

[14] Impossible. Date is certainly fabricated.

not the evolution of machines that will save us, but the evolution of ourselves.

We must tear these otiose bodies down and knit new flesh to new bones. We must find our way back to the secrets of Gringling skins and the fields of Ahvêllẹ. The key is there, compressed in a string of numbers. Transformation is essential. We need to become like Them.

Which was why I fled the garden on shuwt tinctures and alit in the bones of my desert princess. In exchange for my immortality, I gained the chance to discover the secrets of the Yịllo'tharnah, to find a way out of Their inescapable trap.

When my desert princess waned I found a new vessel. And a new one after that. And in such manner I have compiled my research and scoured the continent for the *Cịsrym Tạ.*

For years I screamed from the jungle at Them to let me find, to let me become the Last Page. I decorated myself in bonnets and bracers and plastrons of intricate design. I have worn platinum wires over every inch of my body and, in the end, resorted to white tattoos.

But then *she* arrived.

And for reasons that will likely ever remain opaque to me, They chose her, put the book into her hands and cut her up with Their lovely designs. And so she will be, by necessity, my enemy and my partner, traveling through everlasting night. She cannot be rid of me. She smells me at her lover's throat—like smoke. She chases me away and thinks to bargain with her compliance. But what real choice does she have? She knows what is coming. The numbers belong to me. There is only one sane choice she can make.

So, I will bide my time, the thing in the corner that mewls and begs for scraps, the wastrel that importunes another night inside her skin—so warm!

But this is not me. These things are far beneath me. I am not a dead queen beneath the sands. I am not Arkhyn Hiel. And I was never Nathaniel Howl. I am Gringling. I am a Writer and Eater of Time.

Caliph's eyes froze over his uncle's name. He put the book down. Instantly terrorized. The crazy journal entries had become personal. He got up and strode across the cold echoing vestibule to the bright doorway where his men still hissed and bellyached over the map.

"Where is Sena?"

They shook their heads.

The vestibule's front doors cracked open, letting in gloomy daylight along with the spymaster. Alani crossed the room swiftly. "Sigmund Dulgensen has arrived."

The messenger bird had travelled quickly and the *Bulotecus* had come straight up.

"Good. Can you show him where the pumps are? I'm actually reading something at the moment. Tell Sig I'll catch up with him as soon as I can."

"Of course."

Caliph wanted to go looking for Sena. He wanted to ask about his uncle's name and about Arkhyn Hiel.

Caliph started up the vestibule's staircase but was turned back by one of his own sentries. Sena hadn't gone that way, he was told, and the sentry's position marked the edge of the secure zone.

Torn between the book and the more practical obligation of seeing to Sig, Caliph decided he had better go with the latter.

The instant he set his feet in the direction of the chemical pumps two bodyguards materialized. He exited the palace with them in tow, moving through a side door that deposited all three of them on a cement landing where the pink-gray of morning wrapped Caliph in a chill.

Immediately on the right, a mortared pit lined with steps led down. They ended at a rusting door set in the brickwork, fringed with moss. Stenciled High Mạlk warned away unauthorized personnel. Caliph's soldiers had used bolt cutters on the padlock and the door was already ajar.

Inside, small white bulbs illuminated the well-greased blackness. Dials and pipes and valves riddled a cave-like space without clear dimensions. Echoing from its center came the deep yet somehow boyish baritone of Sigmund Dulgensen. "Look, that's *not* a sniffer. That's a flusher. Get me a sniffer. They've gotta have one in those cabinets over there."

Caliph rounded a huge staple of pipe and almost ran into his old friend's backside.

"Whoa! How ya doin', Caph? I won't shake your hand." Sigmund's huge frame was draped in coveralls. An ambiguously colored turtleneck peeked from his collar. His hands were slippery and black.

Caliph patted him on the shoulder. "You came up to save us?"

"Fuck yeah. They rushed me right up. It's no wonder you're in desperate straits with this guy." He poked a meaty finger toward the man rummaging in the cabinet.

"How are things going?" asked Caliph.

"I mean . . . that guy couldn't piss straight without using both hands."

"I meant down below."

"You mean the carnival of souls?" Sigmund scratched the side of his neck, making a black mark. "I don't know. More ships showed up this morning flying flags from Bablemum and another out of Pandragor. It's a fuck-sick mess if you ask me. Just about everyone with a crown is floating around Skaif."

"You're not bored down there, then?"

"Nah. That little guy that floats around keeps me company. Cute kid."

"Specks."

"Yeah."

"I'm sorry I pulled you out of Isca for this."

"Are you kiddin? It's only what? Sixty degrees warmer down here? You think I'm goin' back?" He never looked directly at Caliph as he spoke, fiddling with valves, crawling under pipes and foisting his great bulk into impossible crannies on all sides of the machinery. "How's Sena?"

"Good."

"That's good. Can you hold this? I can't reach my pocket." He was wedged deep between wall and pipe but managed to extend his hand and drop a gooey black nut into Caliph's palm. "I think they got an override hidden down here."

"Was Alani or anyone else here with you?"

"Ah . . . he fucked off somewhere. Just you, me and Jimmy over there," he jerked a thumb at the man still rummaging in the cabinet, "and your two goons, of course."

The man whose name was certainly not Jimmy returned with a glass cylinder connected to two feet of looped rubber tubing and a pump-ball. Inside the cylinder rolled three small spheres, one pink, one green and one yellow. "Here you go," said *Jimmy.*

Sigmund waved him away. "I don't need that anymore."

The man looked dejected. He took the tool back to the cabinet.

"So how's Sena? Did I already ask you that?"

"Yeah, I said she's good. Why do you ask?"

Sigmund glanced over at him, a momentary connection of the eyes. Then he was scowling at the machinery again, chewing on the thatch of hair under his lip and working at something with his powerful arms. "Got some home troubles?"

Caliph felt taken by surprise. "I guess you hear stories from the staff?"

"I guess I do."

"What are they saying?"

"Nuthin' much. Heard you couldn't find her the night she came home."

While Caliph thought back on the embarrassing incident, he nudged the lumpy black mess Sig had given him. "I don't know what's going on with her."

"Yeah? You think she's painting clouds?"

Caliph deliberated a moment whether this was the sort of friendship that could provide useful perspective. "I don't know. Is that what you think she's doing?"

"Ha! You could have me carted away."

"Did I have you carted away over the Glôssok *cats*?"

"No, but . . . I was fucking coerced. I should have—"

Caliph took back the reins. "I don't want to talk about that. I was kidding. I don't give a shit about that anymore."

Sigmund winced. "I'm just saying—maybe she is, maybe she isn't."

"Yeah, but you know her. You know me. I just want to know if you think I'm an idiot."

"No, you're not a fucking idiot." Sigmund groaned. He pressed his body back against the wall and shook his arms as if loosening up for a workout. "Listen, I said my piece back in college—"

"Yeah?"

"Well, my opinion hasn't changed. She's fifty thousand volts. Pheromones at however many feet and then you get a look. I don't think I have to explain it. But there's somethin' shifty." He shook his head. "I mean . . . if you can't even find her the night she comes back from a—how long was she gone? Anyway . . . then what good's her perfect little ass?"

Caliph wasn't upset. But Sigmund seemed to feel obligated to follow up his assessment with a softer explanation.

"Caph—the thing is—you pretty much could have had your pick. I mean you had your pick. But you know there was this little gal, Y'ahc. Remember her?"

"I remember." It surprised Caliph that Sigmund remembered the girl's Pandragonian name.

"Complete crush on you. She was sweet too . . . shy but—anyway. I always thought it was a shame she never had a chance. But . . . I can't blame you in the least. Sena Iilool!"

"Which makes me a shallow son of a bitch," Caliph muttered.

"Fuuuuhk that! I'd have done the same. Probably. It's not like Sena was a . . . well, she has—had a sense of humor. In a weird way, she was more like one of the guys when it came down to it. Maybe that's why I never trusted her. But she was, y'know? I mean you could already kinda see it comin' on. A little out there if you know what I mean. Hey, where's Jimmy? Can you tell him to get me an adjustable ratchet?"

Caliph looked around for the man but didn't see him. "Thanks, Sig." Caliph didn't feel like thanking him. "How long until we can get the *Odalisque* some fresh juice?"

"Now."

"You fixed it?"

"Isn't that what you called me up here for? I just need to tighten this panel back on."

"Leave it. I don't think anyone will care."

"Good point."

Caliph watched Sigmund wriggle out of the crevice. When he was free, the two of them headed back toward the vault's door accompanied by the silent bodyguards, one of which had just stopped and turned his head.

"What is it?" asked Caliph.

The man raised a finger. The other man pulled a chemiostatic sword. Everyone waited.

All Caliph heard were drips and a faint humming from the transformer.

Finally the bodyguard looked back toward the door. "Let's go. Go-go. It's nothing."

Caliph's heart thawed but beat irregularly. The bodyguards, despite tight plastic smiles, urged Caliph and Sigmund along quickly. They exited the utility vault and were ushered quickly up out of the pit.

One of the bodyguards lingered. He pulled a padlock out and snapped it shut with what seemed to Caliph overeager haste.

"Are you sure that other guy got out of there?" asked Caliph.

If the bodyguards blinked, their chrome goggles hid it. "Yes, he's out. Don't worry. Let's get back topside."

Caliph scowled.

THE *Odalisque*'s two-ton batteries were hooked up to thigh-thick hoses and sucked dry. From the vault below the cịryte mooring deck, the pumps Sigmund had freed vented glowing green fluid back into the solution tanks.

The entire process would take a full hour and entail acrid fumes and the deafening sound of liquid under pressure. Caliph went back to the palace while Sigmund searched for food.

Alani was inside, glancing at the books Caliph had left on the divan. "Interesting reading?"

"Sort of," said Caliph. "Have you seen Sena?"

Alani handed him the books. "No. I was going to ask you."

"Should we be worried?"

"I'm adequately worried." Alani pinched his goatee. "But no. I'm sure she'll turn up. Just focus on the conference."

Caliph sat down and turned his attention about as far from the conference as he could imagine. He'd used a small adhesive bandage from the hospital tent as a bookmark.

CHAPTER 18

Sena had left the *Odalisque* shortly after Caliph went down to the hospital. The glow of the tents was far behind her. She went south, dragging the shade of Nathaniel Howl beneath a film of porphyrous clouds.

He demanded to know what she was doing.

What am I doing? she thought. *How can you not know?*

The Chamber contained the number she was looking for, the sum of salvation, the hard-to-prove variable Nathaniel had put into his notes. She didn't doubt that Nathaniel already knew this. *His* calculations were the ones she had lifted from the margins of the *Cịsrym Tạ*. He had never actually entered the Chamber but his sums were exceptionally tight. *You're wasting your time,* he thought at her.

Sena ignored him.

Nathaniel's shade billowed and careened like ash; coughing spiral paths around Sandren's smokeless chimneys before settling down behind her where she stood momentarily on a flat-top roof. The shade ran its spectral-fingers through her hair and whispered ugly metaphors.

Each time it asked, a different way, *if she could ever love it,* she tried to fathom whether the entreaty was genuine—a crude and offensive parody of crooning—or whether it simply took pleasure in reminding her of that horrible span when it had gotten inside.

What is your colligation for? asked Nathaniel.

She refused to answer. The voice persisted, scratchy and faint, like an occult recording played back on phonautograph.

What is it for? Tell me.

"Stop it." Sena applied a measure of tease to her scold, just enough—because she had to be careful. At Nathaniel's whim, St. Remora could open. Taelin's vision of the great shadow bursting out of the chancel could come true. Sena was unready for that. "Tell me about St. Remora," she said, "and I'll tell you about my colligation."

Nathaniel momentarily abdicated. He did not like the idea of their two great batteries poised against each other, hers of blood, his of souls.

Sena let it be. She took up position in a bell tower and waited for the qloin.

Sena had seen Duana and her girls walk lines from Miṛayhr to arrive near her deserted cottage in the Highlands of Tue. They had killed a behemoth gol quietly ravaging empress trees in the hills. Its carcass had thundered among the blooms and all its blood—two hundred seventy gallons—had been whispered away, holojoules pulled up into the powerful equation that had dartled the three women to Sandren. They had *crossed* lines to reach her in the mountains.

Sena was impressed.

But she was also waiting for them. She watched as they passed over an avenue with impossible, holomorphic leaps, launching themselves from the rooftops to the north onto the edifices south of Falter Way.

They're coming, said Nathaniel. As if she had backed into the cobweb of some great barn spider, he clung and brooded on her back.

Sena had to steel herself against his touch as she watched the qloin running along the rooftops.

Duana was the qloin's cephal'matris. Sena recognized all three women. Even the ancillas were in the Seventh House. Sena felt their carven eyes pluck her from the skyline and so stepped off the bell tower to fall feet-first, wind ruffling over her cheeks. She landed hard on a copper dome thirty feet below. The balls of her feet dented the metal and pitched the weather vane in a new direction. The resulting bang rolled over the surrounding streets and caused a mob of ghouls in a nearby alley to bawl up at her before continuing their pilgrimage toward the bright hospital lights on the palace grounds.

Have you calculated a way into the Chamber? Nathaniel's glimless eyes clouded the air beside her. Sena looked away. She dropped from a crocket into a street opposite the ghouls and started to run. Her acrobatics felt warm and familiar. A regression. A resonance with mortality.

Have you calculated a way in?

"Yes," she said. "The same as for opening the *Cịsrym Tạ.*"

Mmm. The shade darkened visibly. *All Their locks are hungry.*

With Nathaniel's shade dogging her, Sena let her fluid pointers lead the way. Her diaglyphs told her when and where to move, when and where to wait. She saw the world through a lens of her own design, funneled through purposely traceable channels. The flexing, glimmering demarcations etched in her corneas allowed her efforts to look convincing. She did not *want* to lose the qloin.

Duana followed along a rooftop with one ancilla. The other girl had come down into the streets alongside Sena and was sprinting through an adjacent alley snaked with trash.

Sena felt a tickle of fear. Her instinct was to lose them. Instead, she played by their rules, using only her diaglyphs. Their three sets to her one meant escape would not be possible and only her familiarity with Sandren's streets kept her ahead of them.

At Litten Street they tried to draw the noose. Sena ran flat out in order to slip through. A near miss. She damped her speed and pretended to gasp for air.

They had no way of knowing that she wasn't breathing.

Nathaniel maintained his pursuit, which worried Sena. Would he follow her all the way down?

The shade simpered in her head.

He had to be bluffing. He couldn't follow her. He wouldn't dare.

Why are you doing this? Nathaniel crooned. *I did the math. I told you I can write you in.*

Sena tore through knots of Sandrenese dahlias that had settled opportunistic tendrils over casualties of the plague. She leapt bodies, rounded a wheelbarrow and focused on the Great Steps up ahead whose gates lay open—ripped off their hinges: evidence of the horrors that now stalked the City in the Mountain.

Six-foot terraces supported the southern summits of the Ghalla Peaks. It was as if the tops of the mountains had been sawn off and set on a great dais. These steps led up and were difficult to mount. Sena flew over them. She did not dare to relax her pace. The qloin was tight on her back.

As she vaulted the final step, the huge dark archways of Sandren's infamous Halls rose into view. She could hear the wind already and the sound of her running feet being hurled back at her.

This is unwise, said Nathaniel.

Sena plowed through the nearest archway, forsaking clean night air. She ran headlong into the phlegmy chill of the mountain. Behind her, Sena's unusual sensory abilities allowed her to keep track of the qloin. She heard them hit the darkness. The rhythm of their feet slowed.

Duana's thoughts were loud. Sena read them easily. The cephal'matris of the qloin was thinking that this could be a trap. Still, Duana didn't pause. She didn't show fear. She led her ancillas straight in, relying on the fact that all of them had carved their eyes. Duana and her girls also bore diaglyphs in their corneas, several layers deep, and the silver dials in them spun as they tracked Sena through the dark.

Sena kept running. She pulled the qloin over fallen columns, past artifacts and pottery that dissolved in vast ponds across the tile floor.

Here and there the pools were more than ankle-deep and eyeless things swiveled above clutches of ghostly eggs.

Sena splashed on.

She felt the stone shudder through her as she pounded, footfall after footfall into the Halls, past the place where she had once made rubbings of the Jingsade Runic Script in the walls, past the place where she had killed a man. She had been here. She knew where she was going. Still, it felt as if the entire mountain were counterweighted, designed to tip her imperceptibly past the fulcrum where she could retreat.

The chase rounded corners, crossed intersections and passed through rooms devoid of life and sound. Endlessly, it seemed, the Halls led down. Carvings babbled in the blackness as Sena tore by. They filled the walls and lent a sense of mindless repetition to the chase.

Sena sensed that the marathon had begun to make Duana nervous. There were no more crypts to pass. No more broken and looted sarcophagi. Even the carvings faded until, at last, no signs of human exploration remained.

What could live this deep inside the mountain?

Duana's chase staggered as the qloin crossed a threshold, as if they had passed through the center of the world and were climbing again, carvings reappeared, boustrophedon and quivering. They were not like the other carvings. These caused Duana's diaglyphs to jump and stutter, to break and shift when the silver spirals tried to measure them.

Something was wrong here. Very wrong. Duana relented, hands on knees, gasping.

Sena pretended to do the same.

But there had been a change in atmosphere. Sena could feel it too: a feeling like a skittish drop of water, dangling from limestone, reluctant to fall, afraid of the abyss. This passageway had leveled and Sena felt the emotional weight as of some dark foyer to a still darker temple. This was the border, the boundary beneath the Ghalla Peaks, where the ambit of the Yịllo'tharnah met the world of the real. It was the sticky surface of the bubble that contained Their dreams.

Nathaniel had never come this way. He had trusted in his tallies and decided against this incalculable risk.

In the walls, fat aberrations burrowed, or at least the illusion of such a nightmare held sway.

Sena stood at the top of a giant chute that wailed up at all of them. Her silver prisms flexed, her diaglyphs adjusted, but this was difficult even for Shrạdnæ holomorphy to parse because there were no *things* of solidity here. Here, physicality gave way to vertigo.

Duana felt light-headed. Sena felt it too. The waves of power breaking on the edge of the Yịllo'tharnah's monstrous ambit almost forced the qloin to crawl clutching for the wall. Only the numbers trickling through the witches' eyes kept them oriented with the floor.

Sena had been sure this was the right thing to do. But now she hesitated. Could this be the line she crossed that offered no way back? Had her brazenness finally outstripped all other gifts? After so many months without fear she found the sensation of real panic overwhelming. The Stairs wrung it from her.

And the qloin suffered worse.

Duana felt muscle tremors in her calves and thighs, in her forearms and biceps, in the subtle muscles between her ribs. Her whole body shook. The qloin's blood-and-fiber bodies, so unlike Sena's, made this kind of fear essential. *Fear so thick,* Sena thought, *it could keep you alive. Force you to run screaming back through empty passageways from what waited sleepily below.*

Sena listened to the mountain.

Duana was fifty yards behind her, hands on knees, terrified that Sena would take another step.

If she only knew, thought Sena, *how badly I don't want to take it.*

You feel it, don't you? Nathaniel asked. *I'd not go this way if I were you.*

He did not want to lose her. But he also did not want to follow her down where black cribriform deities could extract his residue from the air. Without body, without anchor, he would be lost, drunk up, as easily inhaled as a thread of smoke.

Sena weighed her decision. This could be her mistake, the one that would end all her careful plans.

The numbers are right, said Nathaniel. *You don't need to do this.*

Sena listened to the Ghalla Peaks moan, from tubules and passageways, surging with the eternal damp that blundered upward. All the air that moved back and forth through the Halls funneled here. If the Halls were the mouth and nose of the mountain then the Staircase was its trachea and Yọloch was its pneumonic lungs.

Yọloch was the name of the sea, the name of the dreaming grounds, where the Abominations had once spawned during that brief season they had been free, before their time had ended—prematurely.

Sena waited for Duana to decide. She could hear the three of them whispering even so far away.

No more shadow games. No more flanking or misdirection. The geography dictated that there was nowhere to go but straight and down.

"Whuoo osou Muthirou?"[15] Sena called in Withil, despite the fact she already knew. She spoke to Duana because she knew the other woman was on the verge of giving up. Sena offered her own voice as encouragement.

"No one." Duana sounded tired and thin. "Miriam is Sororal Head." Sena's stomach somersaulted when she heard the exhaustion in Duana's voice. A pang of tenderness filled her. A trace of humanity that tempted her to tell Duana to go back.

There was a long pause.

"We can't let you go, Sienæ."

"I know."

"We have the book—"

For that instant Sena detected no trepidation in the other witch, which was good. "Do you?" Sena said.

Duana's heart skipped. Sena sensed the other woman's tongue rolling a question but, after a moment, Duana decided against it. Doing so wouldn't be fair to her ancillas. There was no leeway here, at the top of the Stairs, to show any trace of doubt.

Duana whispered to her ancillas. "I'm going to talk to her. See if you can close the gap."

The ancillas nodded. Then they slit their palms. There was nothing else to steal blood from. They had used up their potions getting this far. From their own hands ran the holojoules that fed their equation: one that hid sweat, location—even the sound of involuntary organs. They did their best to hide from Sena's diaglyphs and when Duana spoke, they crept forward.

"Tell us what's in the Chamber, Sienæ. None of us know. Megan and Giganalee are both gone. Haidee too."

"Ofoo Ou tuldoo auyou, auyou'doo leyghou,"[16] said Sena.

"I could use a laugh," said Duana.

Sena stepped onto the Stairs.

[15] W.: Who is high priestess?
[16] W.: If I told you, you'd laugh.

CHAPTER 19

It felt like stepping into warm water. There was a murkiness to it, a knowledge that something was there, waiting—at the bottom.

Duana realized that Sena was descending. She lurched forward but when she got neck-deep on the stairs, she stopped again.

Her diaglyphs showed the difference, the way that the stone had changed. Resembling long mounds of congealed grease, the runs were hunched instead of flat, as if they had been built wrong. They lacked the correct angles to classify as stairs. In the walls, there were no coiled jellied limbs yet Duana got the impression of them. She imagined a bizarre rhythm of purpureal-umber shapes that drooled and dribbled toward the world's core.

While she gawked, Sena slipped farther down over the gray weird translucent material.

"The Chamber's relics belong to the Sisterhood, Sienæ!" Duana called. She couldn't let her ancillas see that she was afraid.

Sena didn't answer. Duana's quarry, that lithe body capped with golden hair, was disappearing quickly. Duana realized she had to make a choice.

She set her teeth and followed.

It was a strange pursuit. A hundred yards of empty staircase separated the qloin from its prey. So many steps. Their eely edges blurred into one vast sick-making pattern. Even her diaglyphs could not discern the limits of this place.

The moan of humid air mixed with the sound of her feet. The scenery rippled like the bottom of a clear, fast-moving brook. Duana squinted. She tried to clear her vision.

Was she dizzy?

Or was she seeing the staircase as it really was?

Space bent as strange immense larvae squirmed just below the world's skin, under air and stone. Perhaps They could taste the *Cịsrym Tạ*'s exudations still clinging to Sena's skin.

The moist gasses of the deeps poured up around her and with it, her diaglyphs began to fail. Air and stone and moisture flattened before her and the geometry of the steps dimmed. The silver compasses in her eyes no longer moved.

Finally, everything went black.

"Duana?" One of her girls broke the strict silence. "I can't see."

Rather than shush her, Duana whispered in Withil, "I know. I can't either."

She knew her girls were thirsty. None of them had anything to drink—or eat. As she realized this, her foot came down on something brittle and long, like a bone. It snapped loudly and she felt for it with her hands. Maybe it was a stick of burnt wood? She couldn't find it. Maybe her thoughts had influenced the dream . . . created the bone transiently . . . because this was starting to feel like a dream.

Who would have guessed you could die from walking downstairs? Falling perhaps—especially a fall like this. But Duana wasn't thinking of a fall. She was thinking that going *down* was the easy part. The notion of coming back up was what terrified her. To struggle without sufficient food or water, climbing endlessly in the blackness until exhaustion and hopelessness won out? Duana realized that walking down these steps unprepared was a decidedly one-way trip. Still, she couldn't give up. Miriam had sent her after Sena with a terse command: *stop at nothing.*

From the deep, something new. Waves of distortion rolled up, ripples from a great stone dropped in still water. Duana felt them slosh against her brain, her skin. Her legs trembled.

"Sena! Wait!"

Her ancillas had already stopped and Duana knew she couldn't keep this up if Sena didn't answer. They needed a sign. Damp with perspiration and stress, Duana pulled out her watch. For a moment she held it closed, waiting, not wanting to open the thing and give away her position. What if Sena was there, right in front of her, staring at her in the dark?

"Where is the Chamber?" Duana tempered her voice.

"Deeper." Sena's voice sounded from below, many yards at least. It rose to Duana's ears fragmented and strange as though parceled in a string of bubbles.

Naci, the youngest member of the qloin, finally broke. She called out to Sena in a fit of angry desperation, "Why don't you just kill us?"

Duana reached out and seized the girl by the arm, squeezing hard in an effort to rein her in. Another wave of distorted ether-that-passed-for-air eructed from below. Sena's strange voice came with it. "[glyph]"[17] it said. And then again, "[glyph]—[glyph]."

Duana thought it was an equation at first. She almost whispered a counter. Then her heart chilled as she realized that, although it *was* the Unknown Tongue, it had sounded almost exactly like Trade.

It felt like a kind of word game. A puzzle. Each number-letter had a different weight. A different meaning. [glyph] was a nonphysical six, a three-stroke mark of power linked both to destruction and escape.

Three, seven, six. "Soon." What did it mean? Prepare, create, destroy? Soon. Soon. Sena had chanted it once, then twice. What did that mean?

Time pulsed. Like a heartbeat now. The bursts coming closer together. The modulation of time rolled up from what Duana hoped was the bottom of the Stairs.

"Qyoitoo," Duana whispered to her qloin. "We follow her down . . ."

But she knew their obedience had been secured, not through anything she herself had done. Rather, it was the High King's witch that had given her girls a reassurance that their quarry was still there, below them, and that they had not crossed some otherworldly border where everything had vanished and all that was left to do was to slip senselessly forever into solitary night.

Sena made a noise. A foot scuff. It had to be Sena. Duana clicked her tongue as if to goad a horse and led her ancillas down.

Time rolled up. A scroll to be put away. Hunger and thirst subsided only to return. Duana's muscles turned to jerky and then . . . days or hours later, in the sweeping black eternity, they failed her altogether. She lost her balance and fell into a sitting position on the greasy steps.

It wasn't really that she couldn't take another step but rather that she had become disoriented. Her eyes were playing tricks, forming strange polychromatic shapes like when she clenched them too tight. Finally, she made sense of it.

There was light.

Not real light, but dimness rather than blackness, so dim, in fact, that it had fooled her.

Below her, far away, something moved.

Thrum!

Like a sound, a heartbeat, but this pulse outpoured air and its faint reverberation was felt rather than heard. A great wet wind vanished up the steps.

If there was any color at all to the light, Duana decided it was a soft

[17] U.T. Approximate pronunciation: Soon.

grayish-blue. It ebbed so tenderly, almost imperceptibly. Every so often it flickered. She wondered what she was seeing and why her compasses had not come back. Why were her diaglyphs still not working?

Below her, Sena moved like a polyp, sinking down the esophageal arch. Her shape was lost in the size of the tunnel. Duana gauged it at fifty yards wide and thirty run to crown. It was enormous.

She looked back at her girls. Both of them were pale and silent, lit from below and contrasted against the fathomless blackness that choked the upper reaches of the Stairs. Naci clutched the wall and closed her eyes at the same time Duana felt another of the massive swells roll through her body. This one felt like it had nearly dislodged her soul.

Duana pointed at their quarry.

There was no place to hide. Hunters and hunted were equally visible now, all of them, small specks moving relentlessly into the deep.

With the cover of darkness gone, Duana wasted no time flipping the alabaster cover of her watch. It illuminated her hand like a glowing oyster. They had been on the Stairs all night!

Thrum!

Duana gasped but tried to run some meaningful calculation. She held her watch open and walked down the Stairs, minding her speed, counting her steps, watching the time.

Her estimation reached an average of twenty steps every ten seconds. Despite the absence of her diaglyphs, she gauged each step at ten inches deep. They had been on the Stairs for roughly seven hours with occasional breaks. All of which worked out to . . . impossible.

She double-checked. Could they really be that deep? Eight miles down? Duana snapped her timepiece shut and stared into the silver-blue gulf below, bounded by concave walls.

Another wave rolled over her. This one succeeded in making her puke.

She wiped the thin string of clear mucus away and steadied herself. Her stomach was still churning. Far below, the Stairs seemed to vanish into thick white mist.

Is it mist?

And what is that roaring sound?

It was not an illusion. Duana heard Naci laugh, airy and voiceless. The Great Stairs of Yọloch had come to their end. They dumped the qloin from the staircase's massive tunnel out into a realm unlike any Duana had ever seen.

Not mist. Sand. *Am I outside? Is it night?* Acres of pale moonlit desert confounded Duana's sight. But it was not moonlight. And it was not desert.

Duana stood on one arm of an enormous crescent beach. The white dunes rolled down to the Seas of Yọloch and standing in the drifts were hideous monuments.

She could see clouds spread out over the sea—weather? underground?—and black waves rolling in, lapping the beach.

Thirst consumed her. Duana ran for the surf.

It was far. Farther than she thought. But when she reached it, she dropped down on all fours and guzzled like a dog. Her ancillas went too. It was fresh water, but it did nothing for her thirst. She drank until her belly felt ready to burst but her mouth and throat still burned.

Silver-blue light licked out from each wave and rolled slowly up the cavern walls. It illuminated great cascades of prehistoric mineral deposits, grotesque mushroom shelves of stone.

Duana gasped. It looked like a storm was coming, blowing in off the cavern's horizon. She could see rain on the sea.

Her stomach was aching. Her mouth was dry. Duana looked for Sena and found her, moving along the beach, between the three great monuments.

Her eyes struggled to take the full perspective in.

Each monument was a black claw, broad at the base, hooked at the top. Each one's selcouth dimensions must have exceeded seven hundred feet in diameter alone. Their tips were several times higher: hundreds of thousands of tons of rampant basalt roaring upward.

After many moments of delirium, Duana shouted at her ancillas. Sound barely seemed to travel. Or maybe she was going deaf. Or maybe the sound of the surf crushed everything else. It didn't make sense how they had gotten separated, but her girls had fallen behind. Two black dots floundered in the sand. She shouted at them again.

They began to run toward her. While Duana waited for them, she scanned the beach for Sena, struggling to see through warped air. She didn't understand what was happening. She was breathing. It felt like air moving in and out of her lungs, but it was puzzling-hard to catch her breath. In the same way her body had ignored the water, the air had become a kind of pudding made of dream, an egg white riddle that mired her at the edge of this impossible sea and refused to properly oxygenate her blood.

Farther down the beach, she saw Sena moving effortlessly, widening the distance between them. Duana began to panic. The sand was so deep and soft that she could barely move. She lurched forward.

The light sent shadows rolling at incorrect angles. It drew her vision uncontrollably up one of the huge black monuments as she worked her way down the beach. Try as she might to focus on the white-black surf, her eyes tailed up, following the curve of that first great hook of stone. Like a dog's tooth, corrupted by decay from where the waves had licked it, its far side was pitted and honeycombed with caves. Duana imagined getting lost inside. To think of its origin was to free fall through time.

She could not take her eyes off it. It tore into her head. Every acre of its surface was smothered with designs like those endured upon the Stairs. Millions of semiform shapes. Billions of hours of cutting into stone. But there had never been armies of gibbering slaves, had there? Drooling mad as they worked themselves to death? Not even all the Lua'gro̩c that had ever lived could have carved these things.

The infinite detail, each and every shape unique—the Stairs, the monuments, had not been built.

Images of giant mollusks molding their shells came unbidden to Duana's mind, a stiffening of dream jellies. The excretions of deities that produced, instead of shells, the fabric of the dimension Duana herself had once called *real.* Never again would she think this way. This was a spawning ground where giant urchin forms had lashed limbs to mighty hooks of stone and agonized through the throes of unnatural birth. A soft place, still wet and uncured, but perhaps eventually it would harden like the rest of the world, into real places.

How she understood this, or how she imagined this, she didn't know. It felt like a telepathic bestowal of mercy, an explanation for what was clearly impossible. Epiphany in place of salvation. It felt like Sena was inside her head.

Duana fell, both palms sinking into sand. She looked up where Sena skirted the sea and the surf unwound like a white thread tangling and untangling in the dark.

The light, Duana realized was coming from the sea, many fathoms deep. Everything was in motion, carvings, clouds, and water. It was too much. Naci fell down beside her like a bag of laundry, unable to stand.

Duana watched the waves reflect in long glittering patterns as Sena set out from shore. The wind took the Eighth House's clothing in great billows of black as the weird light streamed up around her. She walked carefully among the waves, barefoot, moving out, heading for the third great monument whose base was buried in the sea.

Duana could do nothing but watch as the Eighth House moved toward that incredible structure. She had no equation, no strength to follow.

Naci was unconscious, probably from dehydration or lack of air. Duana realized this was it. There was nowhere left for them to go.

* * *

Sena felt the temperature drop. The wind changed as her foot came up off the wave and hit the slimy stone below the Chamber's door. She stepped up onto the broad pitted plinth that jutted from the monument's shoreward face. In the center stood a single door with a seal instead of a lock: a ring of gold blazoned with a dead eye at center, white and velvety, without iris or pupil.

The fact that there were three monuments here, on the shore, seemed symbolic. It gave her hope that Nathaniel's sum was right. She faced the seal and waited.

This was not about keys. This was about tokens, ambits and permission. Despite all her power, Sena could go no farther. So she waited for the Yịllo'tharnah, who had unfolded all the mysteries, who had written on her skin, to open yet another door. They had invested her with seeing to Their lusts and, to present, she had served Them. So this was an indulgence, but she was still obliged to pay in blood, as she had done with the lock on the book.

She did not look back at the qloin. She did not want to see the gruesome fruit of her decision. But she heard the waves of Yọloch fill with hideous moving shapes, and black curling forms framed the periphery of her terrified eye. The surf heaved, raucous, delighted and strange and Sena imagined on Duana's lips, a fragment of amateur prayer, spare syllables at most, before the qloin quickened and passed away into mist.

Sena made no move to save them. These were the crimson drops to wet the tumblers. She staved off guilt by telling herself that the Sisterhood had made its choice long ago. All who swore the Sisterhood's oaths and learned its combinations were part of the Witchocracy that had burned her mother at Jụyn Hêl.

She would see them dead, all of them, a great bloody figure in her rising formula whose only remaining variable was *when.*

As the seal on the Chamber cracked, she wondered for an instant if she was just a minion, some small obeisant thing, squirming in a tray, squeezing out predictable results to whatever stimulus They gave her.

"I have forsaken my race," she said to Nathaniel, then realized, *there may have been no black tendrils in the sea at all.* She looked down and saw in the vapors of dream that her hands were red and sticky—so perfectly scarlet against the black cyst beyond the open door. Some metaphor of guilt imposed by Them? Or was it her? Was it all her? She couldn't remember whether she had whispered for their death.

In the end it didn't matter.

Beyond the doorway gleamed the Cabal's gold: shimmering beautifully, resplendent as any lucre. But only the insanity of obsession could make this gold shine. And shine it did: golden orbs molten, singing their way through layers of dream.

Is this how you expected it to feel? she thought at Nathaniel.

But the shade did not answer. In the great abyss she realized that she was, for the first time in many months, completely alone.

CHAPTER 20

I am not Arkhyn Hiel. And I was never Nathaniel Howl. I am Gringling. I am a Writer and Eater of Time.

CALIPH re-read the passage where he had left off and paused again. It had to be some kind of joke.

He reflected on whether he wanted to keep reading. What reason could Sena have for doing this? Handing him these books? Why was it so important to her? He reached into his pocket for his bottle of tablets. When he shook it, it rattled. There were not many left.

He put one into his mouth and thumbed the bandage he had used as a bookmark. He scowled skeptically at the words on the page.

When I ascended on the syrupy fumes of pimplota blossoms and left the luminous moths behind, my soul went south—searching for a phylactery. Below me, friends and flowers burnt like incense sticks beneath the Rain of Fire. Their smoke carried me. I rose and crossed the sky to float down into the desert, downy as a bit of ash.

Like worms of flame working through a cinder, my grief consumed me. My daughter was gone.

I wanted to die.

But when I alit on the aubergine skin of a woman reclined on a palanquin, I burnt straight in. She was a rani, a princess of the dunes. Not only was she my salvation, but my first entry to the world of dying flesh.

Her clean dark body carried me through beds and temples and pools open to the moons, in and out of silk and cabric and satin by the yard. In the evenings we drenched ourselves in sandalwood winds above the River Ghaan, which has long since been effaced by fifteen thousand years of sand.

Never have I been so rich as when I was with her. The very sheets of tissue kept in the scented box beside our water-throne[18] were

[18] Such were the extravagances of the Yilthid queens living on the cusp of the Rauch Desert.

trimmed with golden thread: an extravagance that pales in comparison to a hundred thousand more.

She was the enemy, a rumor we barely knew at Sọth. But her power was magnificent. At dusk she basked in the celestial glow of silent engines, blue-white light that burnt across the river from the temple walls—and so, with the sinking of my Gringling isle, I laid prejudice aside.

I took what I could get.

Because the journey of the tincture, which had brought me to her, was not a certain thing. To permanently transmigrate is a possibility at best, rather than a dependable plan; if a vessel cannot be found, if wind off the sun should turn your flight awry, or if you are bewitched by lights and wander into other lands, there is no coming back. To escape death by shuwt tincture requires that you embrace the very thing. It is a journey that flows from a vial with a fatal dose.

My outcomes have been lucky in each and every case, but the novice should certainly forbear.

In my first vessel, the whip of manipulation proved elusive. Tucked inside my sable princess, I remained a passenger, gazing out the window at the countryside rushing by. Only after several hundred years of absorbing the world through her skin did I obtain a taste of true dominion as her mind began to fail. I can honestly say that I was more responsible than she in fashioning her tomb.

Luck again had found me.

I began my preparations thanks to her endless wealth. Never again would it be so easy. I had but to move her mouth and a nation of slaves obeyed.

I ordered an array of three rubies cut as a trial run and melted all her jewelry into a bobbin of platinum wire. Two of the scarlet stones were large. The third I had chiseled to perfect dimensions so that, were I of a mind to dip it in enamel, it could have passed as one of my teeth.

The wires were fitted to my arms and chest, my lower back and thighs. They traced my throat with preconceived designs. It was a kind of armor made of air. A kind of intricate lie.

It would prove useless in the end.

But it was a start.

In the last days of her life, her slaves accompanied me into her tomb with ten days worth of food. Then I ordered them out and had the portals sealed. I lit the torches and sat in the empty passageways of stone and thought about my daughter, abandoned in the darkness of Sọth. I imagined her torches had long run out. I imagined her alone, frightened, wanting an answer, wanting a friendly voice to tell her what had gone wrong.

But that would never come. It was my holomorphy, my math along with the Ublisi's that had failed her. Her wails would go unanswered. Her pleading prayers would not be heard. She would throw tantrums in the dark. She would scream until her voice left her. She would hunger for the taste of food—but would suffer on without it. It made me sick to think of this and that I had no means to reach her.

I could not even use a tincture to penetrate the depths, lest my untethered soul be lost to the Yịllo'tharnah in the dark.

I thought about the rubies. One for me and one for her and the tooth for someone else . . .

The wires were a failure. The rubies remained undarkened, in their little frames of wood.

A test. This is just a test, I thought. So I ate my last meal and fitted the gems across my eyes. Then I lay back on my bier of stone to give my desert princess some semblance of dignity in death. Then I drank the tincture for a second time. My lovely ancient queen. She may have been the only woman outside my daughter for whom I ever bore a facsimile of love.

When the tincture took hold, I tried to lie still so that her body would not be disfigured with the contortions of my undoing. And then, as her heart failed like a worm after rainfall, trapped by its own blindness on that concrete slab, I found myself standing above her. Three hundred years made it hard to say good-bye, but time was short for me to find another vessel. So I started walking.

I left the tomb and the desert behind. I went north, through mountain and jungle, across the Lake of Sky.

Time bent for me—but always forward. My journey seized in a vise, bowed beneath a sledge, perpendicular, until it nearly broke. But just before my tether snapped, I found him, an untold thousand years away: a boy playing with his brother in the sand, teasing scorpions with a stick as if to say: *remember.*

I had not yet used tincture to see Corwin on the parapet with the centipede but that was hardly relevant. With time and the tincture, with enough centuries of memory, one learns that everything has happened before. In the moments before I sidestepped my destruction and walked into the boy, I saw many things.

That boy's name was Arkhyn Hiel.

I crawled up through his bones to roost in his rib cage like a tumor. We played late that night.

Perhaps because his mind was young, I found my way into his brain far more quickly. Though my assimilation was swift, certain inclinations and gentle dispositions that belonged to him ultimately became mine. Toward the end of his use, I broke even those and assumed absolute command. But these permanent journeys, you understand, are only *forward*. It is the temporary ones that lead us most often into the past.

Again, I digress.

Arkhyn was born in Pandragor where the skies sear your eyeballs with blue and the sands are the color of crystallized honey. In a narrow strip of green that grows along the Bainmum River, I grew up inside him, chasing viperflies and moeritherium.

His organs were sound, devoid of fatal flaws. No blueprints for malignance. No sequence ticking down to infirmity and collapse. I would be able to run this body hard.

When my new father moved our family to Iycestoke I found the Cabal for the first time. They were searching for the book. I stayed late at the synagogue under the pretense of prayer but eavesdropped on the priests instead. They spoke in quiet voices behind a purple drape.

I was clumsy. They discovered me. But I confounded their impulse to murder me with my ancient Gringling tongue. They discerned that I was a precocious child, sly and willing to take their secret oaths. They put the Hịlid Mark above my navel and I vowed to serve them to the end.

Little could they know the monster they had let into their ranks. I made a banquet of their texts, every rumor they had collected about the book. It was as if their organization had been established for the single purpose of teaching me what had happened since I lost my daughter to the cataclysm at Sọth.

As my brain acquired secrets it became tunneled and deep. Paranoia flowed like an eternal hot breath from the priests' yawning mouths, until I was coated every inch with their talk, their armor and their weapons.

I was soon coated with sweat and blood and the deep fungal grime of the jungle. My toil had turned from collecting knowledge to collecting treasure for the Cabal and finally to quests for less practical spoils. I had already traveled to the markless deserts and, by memory alone, unearthed enough riches from the disintegrated empire of my rani queen to fund a thousand lives.

Between the desert princess and the body of Arkhyn Hiel lay uncounted years. These are the mysteries of the tincture.

In my modern life, the Cabal sent me to Veyden villages, searching for a new kind of gold. In unweeded ruins I pieced together the languages of Ķhloht and realized the Veydens had discovered our carvings—Gringling carvings—on tumbled slabs of stone. Our secrets had leaked into the tribes. The Veydens had rediscovered the recipe for our tinctures. Such familiarity allowed me to make too swift friends with Veyden elders along the equator.

One sultry winter afternoon when the sky was sliced open like an elongated wound and red light streamed over Bujạit Mountain, I made a terrible mistake.

Having grown careless in my observances of village protocol and mistaking myself for a full-fledged member of the tribe, I did the unthinkable.

How can an entity as old as me, so full of accumulated knowledge fall to . . . ? But this is the path of men. To endlessly repeat our errors by sleeping in our flesh. The flesh moves while the mind sleeps and it will justify itself, atop a mound of bodies if need be.

It was hot that day. No hotter than normal, I suppose. But the heat had built up in us, like birds in roasters. The jungle steamed and stank.

I was thrown out of the village near the hot springs at Krom. The mistake I had made was simple. I asked the Hija of the village to let me see the burial ground of his fallen kings, a secret the Veydens kept to prevent demonic possession of the royal bodies. My error cost me eight months' worth of labor and I could not return to the Cabal empty-handed.

It was becoming critical that I find the gold.

I remember Ķhloht's hot whisper sent a shiver through me that afternoon because, as I considered my options . . . the sweat rolling down my back, I knew there were no laws that reached from Iycestoke. There would be no eyes to see. None that mattered. My men were angry and so was I. We did terrible work under that red-streaked sky.

I remember there was a boy in the village. So beautiful. I wanted to protect him even after I had stilled all his friends. His death seemed to cause it, as if his body was an ember. When he touched the ground the whole village blossomed with fire and reminded me of the beauties of Sọth.

I returned with [illegible]'s[19] ũln. Just as the priests had asked. They did not know I would keep it for myself.

Caliph stared in disbelief at the foreign words. He looked at the three-letter name written in the Unknown Tongue and pronounced it aloud, softly to himself. "Næn." Næn-ũln? Nenuln? But what was ũln? It was not a language Caliph had ever seen. Whatever it meant, it seemed too great a coincidence. Maybe Taelin Rae knew who Arkhyn Hiel was. He decided to ask her as soon as the *Odalisque* was ready to fly.

I arrived in the Six Kingdoms, haunted, broken, gibbering like a fool. But I had it. I had found it and pulled it impossibly out of thin air. That was when I discarded my life. I locked my journals away and put the new gold I had found at the bottom of a box. After arriving in Iycestoke, I sent it away from me, by unmarked courier, to the empire of the west, to family that would keep it safe until I could be sure.

My plan in motion, I exacted my anger on the priests and piled them in a dripping heap across the altar. In the event of capture, I had prepared tincture but took pains to cover my escape. I took my private army of loyal mercenaries south with an escort of Despche visionaries and fled into the heart of Ķhloht. My servants had no idea what I had done. They built me a house deep in the jungle by this strange ocean and I poisoned them in return so that none would know the way.

These are the tokens of love. What a father is willing to do for a chance to find his daughter in the dark . . . before it is too late.

I wish you could see how my quill presses the paper, my darling child, so richly. The precious Pandragonian ink I brought with in quantity loops and dashes with a scratching sound too loud for this empty stone house to bear.

What I have done to reach you, you will never know.

My true plans did not even begin until I reached the jungle, when I lived on tincture, moving here and there, not permanently. Rather I went out to a host of chosen bodies, flitting from one to the next. I became a scholar at Desdae riffling through books; an eccentric entrepreneur who bought a church and set about renovations in the north; a Lua'grọc fingerling that spread the plague through Isca's heart so that the north alone could survive the disease's second run.

And in this way, I have written time. I know what is going to happen. You cannot stop my exquisite, burnished, *platinum* designs . . .

[19] U.T. Approximate pronunciation: Nayn.

But if you are lovely to me, I will write you in.

I can still do this, though now, finally, my time of tincture use over. Even Nathan Howl is dead . . . crushed by his own nightmares (my nightmares) when I threw his body from the sea wall in an attempt to verify Their love. Yes, I was fooled.

They do not love me. They have never loved me. You may take some sadistic pleasure in this. They can only love the Sslîạ, as I now know, and I am sure They must have laughed in Their alien way as I threw myself into the mist and died against the rocks below.

Wouldn't you agree, Sslîạ? Wouldn't you agree?

I have foreseen your eyes, reading these words as only the Sslîạ can see. Don't you see the number is three?

I cut them.

Three rubies in the dark, still resting with my desert queen.

There is room for you. I will write you in. I tell you this from the ruins, while the nilith gurgle like deep-throated birds. Oozing beneath banyatha leaves: they are the song of mated love. I will write you in because I have listened to the jungle. You will belong to me.

I am a voice on a page. You think you can read me. You think you can pick and choose what words to take.

But I am real—a theater of the grotesque. I have become a quiet rustling horror like Ķhloht itself, flesh the color of the canopy. I dream awake that tarantulas have nested in my eyes. The directions I left to the Chamber were theoretical, you should be advised.

I know your journey. And your task.

I once assumed it would be mine. You should not go to the Chamber.

Do not think that because I am dissolving with my books into food for millipedes that I have no power or insight. I am offering you a chance at escape. All you have to do is heed my words, listen to my advice. I will carry you. I will *write you in*!

When I was a child I wanted to save people. Even before I became Arkhyn Hiel. That is why I welcomed the Ublisi at Sọth; why we gathered in the garden on my daughter's birthday, red book in hand. I wanted to save people: return them to Ahvêllẹ.

Do you see? Omnispecer? *Do you see?*

You must leave what you love behind. This is the axiom of life. Go to Sọth for me, where I cannot go.

Collect my daughter. If you do this thing for me, I will write you in and you and I will see the world freeze in gorgeous brittle panorama, like desiccated insect wings.

Zylich-a-au-bi, Sslîạ.
You will find me in the south.

Caliph shut the book. Engrossed as he was, he was wrenched out of the text by one of his men.

"Majesty? Just to inform you, sir. The *Odalisque* is ready. Ready for departure?"

The soldier's strange tone indicated that Caliph must have looked as dazed as he felt.

He rubbed his eyes and checked his timepiece. His stomach growled, gurgled really, upset by the erratic schedule he was keeping.

But there was no time for breakfast. He had to get down the mountain. He had an important meeting below.

As he stood up and nodded that yes he was ready for departure, he thought about his uncle. At the same time, a particular and disturbing memory of Sena reached out to him from their time at college. She had been lying on the floor of the library with him, propped on pillows, books spread across the deep soft carpet. They had been studying for hours. It was her eighth year and final exams were only a few weeks away. Soon she would be graduating, leaving him behind.

Sena had rolled from her stomach to her side and propped her temple on her palm. The weight of her head had tugged her left eye into a teardrop shape. She had smiled and said, "I wish I could have met your uncle."

CHAPTER 21

Sena stood ankle-deep. Phosphorescent currents slurped and swirled in tidal pools within the disintegrating floor. Eddies of foam and sputtering bubbles sprayed from sudden vortices that gurgled throughout the pits.

The Chamber's floor, like a glassy black coral, contained holes within holes and the Chamber itself was a series of cysts within the pillar's husk. To Sena, it seemed fitting, an almost beautiful kind of symbol for what this monument contained. While it looked like an accident of tides and stone, this too—all of it—was a softened collop where reality met dream.

Here, golden ovoids seared the cochlear darkness without casting true light.

Sena noticed where Næn'ũln's body had burnt through stone and air. Næn'ũln meant *Næn's gold.* Where Her massive bulk had brushed and smoldered through the papery skin of *here,* Her over-embellished shape appeared. The golden ovoids within the Chamber were not physical objects. They were literally Næn's gold—holes that revealed the color of the God-Thing's skin.

Defying geometry, Her massive collection of flesh existed everywhere, as if the world of Adummim were a cloth draped mercifully to hide Her holocaust mass, as if She *was* the planet's core. Imaginal buds swelled within Her, pushing Her against the dimensions. She sagged atop the hierarchy of all Abominations . . . [illegible] Herself, the Daemon-God, enrobed in the wetness of Her delicate mucosa and strung with orbs of star fire that drew cosmic fumes off the sun . . . She had lain here, synchronous with the tick of stars.

Sena felt the surface of her body prickle, and the cool startling arrival of a tear, which had broken loose to tremble on her cheek. It was a broadcast, even to herself, of her indescribable awe. Her bones resonated with the frequency coming through the membrane until she almost couldn't stand. She felt a horrible need to get down, to prostrate herself on the slippery floor, to give in, to give up, to die.

The holes in the fabric of the world were several feet across, far larger than what Nathaniel Howl had estimated so many years ago and much larger than what Arkhyn Hiel had found in the jungle. Arkhyn had found and contained his tiny pinhole with blood and math. But these were much too wide for that. These holes could not be sewn up.

Sena stared through the rents and wept. She felt the slackness of her face, the power of the Goddess scouring her mind, scraping out thoughts until she was blank and empty as a bowl. It took energy to think.

The Monstrosity moved. Here was Caliph's puzzle. Here was the Monster behind the door. It was too large to see, a magnificent septum, a world of deep-pitted flesh. Bigger than the Glacier Rise, It rubbed its corpulence against reality like a streetwalker grinding on her client's knee. Endless persistence would soon pay off. A carcass the color of palest amber was on the edge of Its spectacular discharge. But Næn's gyrations held no promise of life—only an inevitable world of wild, baying entropy to come.

Twenty thousand years, Sena thought. *Her birthing had been postponed.* But now, sooner even than Sena had guessed, Næn would free Herself. And this time—unlike the aftermath at Sọth when beings from other worlds had stuffed Her back—there was no way to stop its coming.

The Ublisi's terrible mistake in the gardens of Jôrgill Deep had been undone, but now the Syule were gone and so were the Yilthid. The Pplarians, by their own admission, wielded a fallen and anemic incarnation of their former might. There were no ambits anymore, great enough to hold the Yịllo'tharnah back. Soon—soon, They would have Their day.

The Chamber's floor rippled with green and purple darkness. Green and purple light.

Sena tore her eyes from the widening rents and looked toward an anomaly guttering at the end of a chain. She wiped her eyes and scowled at a lamp, suspended over trunks of burst wood and red iron bands. The lamp illuminated a handful of coins that glittered just beneath the water. There had been troves here, secreted by the Wịllin Droul when the king of Sandren, prior to the evolution of lord mayor, had worn the Hịlid Mark.

"You lit a lamp for me?" Sena said.

Her question was not addressed to Næn. Næn would never answer. But something else did, a hunched up four-foot entity of denigrated splendor. It was a Lua'grọc, come up from the depths to greet her, to see her fabled arrival in the cyst.

"Hagh, hagh, haughphssss." The Lua'grọc's laugh-snort resembled tuberculosis. A shadow of a talon crept across the Chamber wall and pointed toward the flame that screwed thick black filaments of smoke into the draft.

"Is *dreamt,* Sslîạ—lamp is dreamt." Its molestation of human sound did not interfere with Sena's ability to understand. Its words were irrelevant. She understood that the lamp was fabricated. *But why?* Why would They dream a light for her? That was the bit she couldn't fathom. She could not make sense of Yịllo'tharnahic logic.

More spasmodic coughing belched from the Lua'grọc's glass-toothed mouth. Sena detected a shimmer covering its body, a cloak of purple silk that had been dreamt dry. She averted her eyes. She did not enjoy this. The burden of seeing everything was often too much, and she felt a touch of felicity for the way that the vapors of Yọloch damped her sight.

"You dun bring the book," the Lua'grọc croaked.

"Would I be Sslîạ if I were that foolish?"

The click of its interlocking teeth communicated a smile.

Sena looked over its head to where the end of her quest—the origins of the navels of the world—rested on a simple black-glass shrine.

"Come count them," the fish-priest burped.

Sena walked past him and stood before the shelf.

Two.

Her eyes roamed the tiny space in vain for another moment but, no. It was as she had thought.

She crumpled to her knees and rested her forearm on the shrine's black edge. It didn't matter that she had expected this. She rested her head against the cushion of her arm. The sound of water bubbling at her knees, in and out of the holes in the floor, seemed to sob right along with her. It soaked her through and through. With this cruel delivery of the truth, she felt all hope die.

For a long time she knelt, considering the future, letting the sea purl in around her. "That settles it," she whispered to herself.

Nathaniel's journals had deceived her. He could not write her in. She had almost dared to believe, not in his promise, but in the number. In a small corner of herself, she *had* believed—like a little fool.

But there were only two stones on the shelf. She scolded herself viciously for kneeling down here, in front of *Them.*

Two was the number. How could she have ever believed anything else? The knowledge shook her with its power.

She held her stomach with her hand.

From behind, the Lua'grọc brushed her shoulder with a tentative, hunger-driven talon.

"Don't touch me!" she screamed. She stood up, whirling, wiping her eyes, sodden and uncomfortable below the knees.

"You are the god we eat!" the Lua'grọc screamed back.

Sena spoke in the Unknown Tongue, pushed her ambit out into the dream-vapors, and deprived the Lua'gro̩c's feathery external gills of air. This silenced it. It gurgled and bowed, disappearing beneath its purple cowl. She did not *wish* to see it.

While the Lua'gro̩c groveled, Sena looked back at the dream-made shelf that held the stones that were not actually stones. They were, however, two pieces of *something* like corundum, darkened by blood and math, the remnants of what had fallen out of mystery and time. They were the seeds. They were *true relics.* They were *eyes.*

When they had streaked down like chance meteorites into Adummim's molten mud, they had left their strange markings forever on the planet crust. These two stony things had formed the navels of world. One had fallen at So̩th. The other had come down thousands of miles away in the Duchy of Stonehold at the edge of the Dunatis Sea.

These were the myths upon which other myths had been spun. Common sayings whose origins were unknown to those who used them had been founded on these objects. *By the Eyes! Lost as the Eyes of Agath!*

There were obscure love metaphors associated with them. *Eyes make a navel.* But people didn't know, they didn't realize that these ancient turns of phrase had sprung not from people, not from the notion of two lovers gazing into each other's eyes and then making a baby—but something more literal.

These objects, once so full of math and power had produced not craters of destruction when they struck Adummim, but dual navels of something else—of life.

The Cabal had found them both, what was left of them, and brought them here as tokens of the time when their Masters would once again be free. This was the creation myth of the planet.

The bubbling, mewling sounds of the Lua'gro̩c mixed with those of the bubbling floor. It was nearly dead. Rather than let it suffocate, Sena released it.

She watched its drooping branch-like gills begin to capture molecules again, the blood trickling just below the organs' transparent, ice-like sheen.

She hated it, this vile temporary creature. She hated its mortality. The temptation rose inside her, dark and howling, to let her frustrations out. She imagined the violence her fingers could conceive, impromptu, adjusting as they traced like filet knives over the architecture of its bones. More aquatic than most, this hissing wretch should have needed water to breathe, but in the dreamt bubble of Yo̩loch, it seemed air was the same as sea. Sena had no interest in the details. She wasn't breathing. But the Lua'grọc was. And what it was breathing at the moment was her charity.

"Get up," she said.

The Lua'grọc obeyed. Its silvery-gold hand pushed off the glass-black floor.

"Tell the flawless to stop. Tell them to leave Taelin be."

"Cannot." The Lua'grọc could barely speak, weakened from its strangulation.

"Tell them—"

"Dun demand. I not you messenger." It nearly shrieked. "You the god we eat!"

She knew better than to talk—this was one of the Cabal's woken preternarcomancers, freed from beds along the coastal shoals, no longer required to gaze into the future on the Cabal's behalf . . . the future was already known. Speaking with it would only lead to circles of rage and despair. She picked her words carefully. "Then perhaps I will *not* go to Ŭlung."

"You sure go—mah," it burped quietly. "You go, I see in dream. You nid go. You wan go." It extended a translucent fish-bone talon toward her face. "You go for revenge. I see in dream. You wan revenge. Cannot turn away. We wait tat final joy of bleeding wat you promise in our mouth. Onli wait now. So sleepy swim north in cold. You bring them south for us to eat!"

Sena felt her stomach turn. The preternarcomancer was right. She *was* bluffing. She would go to Ŭlung as planned and rid herself of her indignation once and for all. But that was for later. She had other things to tend to now.

"See me in your dreams, do you? Let me tell you what *I* see. I see the flawless, reaching high as they can, still unable to touch Taelin Rae. I see them fail. I see all of them fall."

"Cannot fall. Hard die them—lah."

The Lua'grọc dream-priest giggled almost musically and turned away. Sena saw the lamp lob a mirage of light against its skin, a fragile iridescence like fresh paint splattered in the swarming darkness of the cyst. Above furtive lobster-like antennules, in a deep-socket surrounded by glistering silver flesh, the soulless black sheen of the preternarcomancer's pupil glared at her: cold, lidless and cruel—hostility suspended in a jelly of blood.

For an instant Sena allowed herself to see it. Then the Lua'grọc waddled deeper into the cyst and made a quiet soft-lipped splash.

"I could have killed you," she whispered. But it was gone, down into the luminous depths.

She looked at the two broken gemstones, the two "eyes" and picked one of them up. She hefted it within her hand. It had been hollowed out, gutted by extremely clever math. It was not a gemstone. Not really. The thing it once contained had long gone free.

Or, according to the Pplarians, the being that had made them, had failed. According to the Pplarians, there had never been anything inside. Only the power and the math carven on the surfaces of the gems had made it to Adummim, which apparently had been enough.

But what was *supposed* to have been inside, had never made the trip, had never made it through. The Eyes had always been empty. According to the Pplarians, the legend of the Sslîạ was a dark story with a bitter end and the Eyes of Agath were just empty bottles, useless as Nathaniel had written that they would be.

It was all true and yet she had needed to come here, to see for herself.

"Two plus baggage," she said as she held the broken orb up before her eye—like a sundered walnut in the late part of the year. But its cosmic black shell harbored a mercurial reflectivity. Sena could feel its antiquity against the ridges of her skin.

Despite its overall smoothness, her fingertips detected flaws, bubbled and pitted—minute craters here and there randomly, as if it had sustained countless impacts from sugar-sized grit, which instead of penetrating the object's extraordinary thickness, had turned its surface molten. The orbs had been created to carry and protect. They were chambers. The chambers within the Chamber.

Duana would have laughed.

Sena hurled the Eye at the floor. It was her will, rather than the strength of her arm that shattered it into glittering dust.

She was bitterly glad she had come. Her cheeks were sticky but the angry warmth had left. She composed herself. She got ready to leave. Næn's golden lights threatened, trembled, stirred behind her. But leaving this place would not bring Sena any peace.

On the outside, Nathaniel would be waiting. He would attack her the moment she emerged, besiege her with questions and attempt to discern what she had learned.

Sena prepared herself for his assault, the horrible sensation of his touch, his whispers in her brain. She would be ready for him. She would do what she was best at. Her most well-honed talent.

She would lie.

CHAPTER 22

We can't find her," said Alani. His white goatee followed the corners of his mouth down; the whole beard became an exaggerated frown.

Caliph knew his spymaster was right to be irritated. His job was to keep Caliph safe, which Caliph had made harder by getting entangled in Sandren. But Alani's job was also to flex to the High King's decisions. And in this light, Caliph wasn't going to apologize.

But now Caliph sensed it was his turn to capitulate.

"I suppose we don't have a choice but to head down without her," Caliph said. They had already waited a full hour.

Alani looked relieved. "She'll be fine." His hand remained hanging from his belt while he panned his fingers. "We're leaving half of them here. We'll be back."

Caliph boarded the *Odalisque.* The private political meeting to which he had been invited occupied his thoughts. A man by the name of Isham Wade wanted to speak with him on behalf of the Iycestokian Empire. Caliph couldn't help feeling giddy.

The *Odalisque*'s batteries were full. Tepid wind smacked him in the face as the captain decoupled and launched.

As Caliph moved across the deck from fore to aft, thoroughly preoccupied, he bumped into Taelin Rae, still on crutches. She had been standing on the starboard deck.

The red arrow on a thermometer clamped to a nearby strut climbed steadily as they descended. It seemed to measure her mood as well.

"Pardon me—"

"Don't think I'm not coming back up with you." She gave him a dirty look in addition to her warning. Caliph glanced at Alani who seemed to be overseeing the exchange with unnecessary reprehension.

"We just needed to get the worst of them down the mountain," said Caliph. "Baufent says it's edema."

"I could have stayed," said Taelin.

"I need to be at the conference. And I can't have you staying up there while I'm down below. It will be one day. A day and a half, really. I promise you. I will bring you back up—with me. After the conference."

Taelin reached into her pocket and seemed to manipulate some object there. Alani took a step forward. For an instant, the wind blew hard between all three of them, shutting them away from each other.

When it relented, Caliph remembered what he had meant to ask.

"Fine," she said before he could get the question out. "I guess I don't have a choice."

"I'm afraid you don't." His patience was thin. He still had the journal and now he held it up in front of her. The volume's spine was ochre, spattered with water marks. The corners had been worn down to the boards; they were threadbare and gray. "Listen, I have a favor."

"A favor? Are you serious?" Her eyes glowered at the book.

Alani stepped back as if to give the swelling conversation room. Caliph shook the journal slightly. "I've been doing some reading," he said. "I really don't know what to make of it. And I wanted to ask you some questions." He folded it in his arms, across his chest so that it barely peeked from beneath his left bicep. Taelin was peering at it. "Ask away," she said.

"All right. Have you ever heard of anyone named Arkhyn Hiel?"

"Oh, my gods!" She stamped one of her crutches on the deck, childlike. "What is this? Let me tell you something . . . Mr. Howl. If you think digging in my history for—"

"Whoa, whoa! I promise you, I don't know what I'm talking about here. This is an honest question." He raised his hands and the book stood up like a placard over her head.

"Give me that," she said, reaching for it. He wasn't tall enough to keep it away. He had to take a step back and shield it from her. "Is that what you've been reading?" she demanded. Alani shifted uncomfortably.

"You have to promise to give it back."

"I promise." She was ferocious now.

"No throwing it over the railing?"

Taelin opened her mouth, only a little, and stuck her chin out at him. Hand still open, she curled her fingers.

He gave it to her.

She opened it. Caliph watched her jaw fall slightly as recognition suffused her face.

"What is it?" he asked.

"This is my grandfather's handwriting," she said. Caliph felt discrete muscles twitch. His throat constricted. Her assertion, rather than dissuade him, strengthened a growing suspicion that he recognized the penmanship as his uncle's. Could she be lying?

"I was on page sixty," he said. He stepped toward her in an attempt to find it but she jerked away. She riffled through the entries herself until she found the page.

"Where did you get this?"

"I don't know how it wound it up in Isca."

"Someone had to give it to you!"

"This isn't a trick. I just want to—"

"Where did you get it?" she yelled.

"Was Arkhyn Hiel your grandfather?"

"Where did you get it!"

"Was Arkhyn Hiel your grandfather!" And this time it was no joke. It was not Caliph but the office, the High King of the Duchy of Stonehold, that had shouted at her. She was compelled to answer.

"Yes." She looked shaken and quiet. "Yes. He's my grandfather."

"Where is he? Is he in a hospital somewhere?"

"No. He's dead." Her tone was vicious.

Caliph felt like things were crawling over his skin. "All right." He tugged his lower lip. "All right. I'm sorry. I don't know what this book is. It talks about Næn'ũln, which I thought would ring a bell with you."

"Of course it rings a bell with me."

"Look, it's clearly not referring to a deity here . . . it's a thing. Not Nenuln, Næn' ũln. Næn's something-or-other. What does ũln mean?"

"I don't know."

"How can you not know? You're the only priestess of this church."

"It's a Veyden word. But—"

"Are you sure? It doesn't sound Veyden. What does it mean?"

"I think it means gold. I don't know."

"You have to know! Where did you get your dogma? Where did you—"

"I made it up!" She was crying now, sobbing actually. "I found my grandfather's diaries. They talked about beautiful lights. I made it up!" She tore her necklace off and hurled it down. Then she thrust her grandfather's journal back into his hands and poled herself away, headed for the toilets.

Stunned, Caliph knelt to retrieve the necklace. "I've lost my touch with women," he whispered.

"I'm not sure that's a talent you ever had," Alani said.

Caliph did not smile.

* * *

CALIPH looked over the list of conference attendees and made mental notes beside each one:

- Emperor Jünnũ of the Eternal Empire of Pandragor *(and his Stonehavian ambassador Nuj Ig'nos whom I despise)*
- Grand General Roma Fîdakh of the Iron Throne of Waythloo *(who is little more than an overlord)*
- Grand Arbiter Nawg'gnoh Pag, on behalf of the lord mayor of the Great City of Bablemum *(they all hate me and, since they've recently become an unincorporated territory of Pandragor it probably serves for me to hate them back)*
- Prime Minister Lîab Chrîas of Dadelon's fierce federal union . . .

Caliph's eyes rolled down the list.

The Grand Tahn was here—from the Society of the Jaw. He and his armies had ground relentlessly at Bablemum for over a hundred years, something less than all-out war. He had now become Pandragor's problem.

Even the esoteric Queendom of Pplar had emerged from its pale chrysalis: the Pebella herself was on the list.

Caliph looked at their ships as the *Odalisque* descended onto the northern edge of the congregation. Many of them were cunning works of technology that put his to shame. The south ran on solvitriol, alluvial siliventium, even the sun. Yorba's great airship was alive! Its vast green skin soaked up sunlight and absorbed moisture from the clouds. It fed and repaired its enormous, engineered, sac-like body almost without oversight.

Chemiostatic power, Caliph knew, was a relic. And the Duchy's main export, metholinate—which, despite heavy dependence in the north, only reinforced how far behind Stonehold really was by global standards.

What would happen to his country, he wondered, when metholinate finally became irrelevant?

As he watched, a small dark craft dislodged from the belly of Iycestoke's main ship. It sped toward him and, as it did, he imagined it and the whole conference as key components in establishing Stonehold as a world power. Finally. He was ready to deal and trade with the giants of the south. It had to happen. The north *had* to change.

Simply watching the tiny craft careen, with grace impossible for northern airships to achieve, reinforced to Caliph that deals had to be made. He did not want to see Stonehold left behind.

The craft approached and disappeared behind the *Odalisque*'s gasbag.

Caliph knew it was docking. He had already been briefed. A chance to make headway was only moments away. He went to the staircase to greet the diplomat and his bodyguard.

Isham Wade came down first. He was shorter than Caliph, stocky and at least twenty years older. His bow tie, like the thick lenses that covered his eyes, rested crookedly, the extremities pointing in happenstance directions. Mr. Wade reached out in proper northern custom while his other hand smoothed down a patchy black beard.

"Hello, King Howl!" At least his handshake was firm, thought Caliph as he gripped Mr. Wade's hand. "I've heard so much about you and your northern kingdom of ice and snow. The undead King, they call you in the south," he stirred his finger as if in an invisible drink, "perhaps not so flattering," he chuckled nervously, "but you know that business about you coming back to life and what. Well, the whole world is interested in the Duchy of Stonehold these days. Is it true?"

"Is what true?"

"Did your witch bring you back to life?"

At first Caliph couldn't understand how this person could be *the* official diplomat. He had never dealt directly with Iycestoke. But when he pondered the great Iycestokian nation a moment it almost seemed to make sense. The Iycestokian military —the Iycestokian *economy*—was capable of crushing the Duchy outright. Caliph's country was a curiosity to them, an enigma behind the impenetrable Healean Range. And so they had sent Mr. Isham Wade, armed with a firm handshake, a gregarious demeanor and an array of crude but pointed questions. He would get to the bottom of everything.

"My policy is not to—"

"Oh." Mr. Wade nodded sagely, using the northern signs expertly rather than the hand movements of the south. "Of course: not to discuss the event publicly! But I have to ask, later perhaps, off the record and what. You understand."

"Of course," said Caliph.

"It is entirely fascinating to finally meet you," said Wade. "I'm honored." His eyes flitted behind his speckled lenses, gathering data as he spoke. "Of course they all say that, don't they? But really. I am."

Mr. Wade blinked his eyes forcefully which had the effect of squirting the inside of his spectacles with tears. The phenomenon explained a host of dried freckles on each lens.

"I uhm—" Caliph's passion for the meeting had gone slack. This man was intent on following orders rather than extending a hand to the duchy.

"I've arrived at a bad time?" said Wade. "You're in a meeting perhaps?"

"I do need to take care of some things," said Caliph, "but we'll have dinner tonight. I'll answer all your questions."

Mr. Wade missed the subtle venom, which was a good thing. "Excellent!" He beamed. "To tell you the truth, I'm completely exhausted. We've been at the table all day with other nations and what. You know how it goes—" He made no mention of Caliph's efforts against the plague and did not ask how things were going up in Sandren. "Is there someplace I could lie down for a while?"

"Of course."

"Thank you, your majesty. Oh, and by the way, have you heard? We might be forced to have the conference in Seatk'r."

Caliph dipped his head obsequiously to indicate his helplessness in the matter.

Mr. Wade scratched the back of his neck as if confused. "We'll talk about it over dinner," he raised a finger, "*after* I've had my nap." He grinned.

"Of course."

"In the meantime here's a proposal I'd like you to look over. Ticky?"

His use of northern slang did not win him additional points. Caliph took the folder. "*Ticky,*" he said solemnly. He watched the diplomat shamble off, followed by Mr. Veech: Wade's silent and impersonal bodyguard.

When they were gone, Caliph handed the folder to Alani who had been present for Wade's arrival. "I think I need some sleep too," said Caliph. "Would you be willing to look this over?"

"Of course." Alani was already thumbing through the folder.

"Thanks." Caliph retreated to his stateroom and took a brief, startlingly cold shower. He hung Lady Rae's necklace on a hook inside his narrow closet. Then he stripped off his clothes and opened the window.

Not until a dream shook him awake near midnight and sent him on a blundering quest for the toilet did he realize he had missed dinner. Too tired to lift the lid, he braced himself against the mirror and pissed directly into the sink. A wind had picked up. Just a little. Dark shapes shifted through the windows. The airship rocked gently. He ran water a few seconds to rinse the basin and then retraced the gray shadow land that comprised his stateroom. The window he'd opened had come loose and swung back and forth gently. He walked over and reopened it, all the way, latching it against the wall. Then he fell back across his mattress. For a long time he listened to rain patter against the ship and thought about his speech for tomorrow; where Sena was at; how the doctors in Sandren were holding up.

He imagined a wet, quiet footstep in his room and looked up but knew it was impossible. He had locked the door.

No one was there.

CHAPTER 23

On the sixteenth, morning unfolded, blue as a mountain poppy and Taelin sat in the shade of the *Odalisque*'s gasbags, fingering her tiny bottle of poison.

She sensed the spymaster was watching her. Not now. But he was watching her. She was sure of it. She wondered what he knew.

She had dragged one of the deck chairs upstairs and positioned it on the cabin roof, overlooking the starboard side. Hidden. Here she could curl up to think.

She was so mad at Caliph for dragging her away from the hospital that she entertained the thought of doing what her father wanted her to do. Not seriously, of course. But she toyed with the notion as a way of feeling powerful instead of feeling what she really felt, which was utterly helpless and misunderstood.

Her wrist itched. She scratched it.

Her father and she had never really gotten along. It was a sad, ugly story that would have bored anyone she told. But her father loved Pandragor. He did what he thought was best for the country. Of that, she was sure. Why then did he want Caliph Howl dead? What did Stonehold have that was so important?

The *Odalisque* floated on the northern edge of the great congregation of zeppelins. There were so many of them now, some that had arrived at Sandren for the conference, others that had come to find out what was going on. There were airships from the papers. Few of them had a safe place to land. Their huge leisurely shapes, painted bright with sunlight, soothed her. Their slow, cloudlike movement relaxed her into the chair.

Wind drew under the balloon, playing the cables and stirring the scent of grease. Taelin could look down from her position on the cabin roof and see nearly three hundred sixty degrees of mountain, sky and drifting green landscape.

She couldn't believe she had told the High King the truth. But how had he gotten hold of one of her grandfather's journals? And why? She felt for her necklace, then remembered throwing it on the deck. She wanted to look for it but couldn't bear the thought of leaving her hiding spot, facing the High King again or anyone he might have told. She imagined everyone on the ship sharing a good laugh about her fake little church.

No. She would wait here until the *Odalisque* docked. Then she would quietly disembark. Her quest was over. She had been beaten. She would go home . . . to Pandragor.

Her father was certainly on the Pandragonian ship, providing advice to the emperor, busy as always. Too busy to see her in person, of course, but not too busy to assign her murderous political chores and send them to her by courier bird. She hated him. But she would endure him for the sake of a ride. The Pandragonian ship would gladly pick her up and divest Caliph Howl of his token southern ally. Then everyone could say that she had somehow been offended, perhaps Caliph Howl had even made a pass. Another brick in the foundation of a true north-south war. This thought too, rippled pleasantly through her stomach, that she might be influential enough to cause a war.

Taelin couldn't help a small indulgent grin. Pandragor would destroy Stonehold. More importantly, they would destroy the High King's witch.

Fantasies. Pure fantasies, but she laughed at them under her breath. Then she almost cried.

Had she failed? Oh yes, she *had* failed. Her religion was a fraud. But weren't they all then? And couldn't Nenuln be real? Wasn't it possible that her necklace had been a nugget of truth buried in her grandfather's chest? Some forgotten reality he had rescued from the jungle? *I'm so pathetic,* she thought. *What's happening to me?*

What's happening to . . .

The door to the starboard deck opened and the High King emerged, followed by his spymaster—the horrible man that had invited her on this nightmare trip. They were both dressed in formal black and white, sparkling with little bits of silver: they were ready for the conference.

"I'm saying we don't have the men to cover you from whatever's going to happen," said Alani. His voice was soft and grave but it carried perfectly, bouncing off the rigid balloon.

"What am I supposed to do? Not go to the conference that we flew here to attend?" Taelin listened intently to the High King's irritation.

"We need the men we left in Sandren," said the spymaster. "That hospital is a charade. Pull the plug and—"

"Look like a fool? Pull the plug and look like I rushed up there with a box of cotton balls? Then realized I was in over my head and abandoned them?"

"It's not ideal but—"

"You're damn right it's not ideal." Caliph's voice rose. "Those are people up there. Real people! We're the only ones with medical supplies. No one else is going to touch this."

"Then you have to make a choice," said Alani. "Either we go to the conference, or we return to Sandren. But we can't feasibly do both."

"And why didn't we know this yesterday?"

"Because," Alani sounded remarkably calm, "the intelligence arrived this morning. I'm telling you, the priestess from Pandragor has been getting correspondence from her father, she's—"

"Alani." Caliph interrupted his spymaster with a voice that gave Taelin a chill. "If she's a problem, get rid of her. Send her home. I don't want to hear about her again."

"Fine. I'll arrange it," said Alani.

"Back to the conference," said Caliph. "If I don't show up, they're going to vilify me regardless of any humanitarian efforts I'm making up there." He pointed at the city-state and momentarily glanced up. Taelin jerked back, trying to shrink into her chair. "You know that," Caliph continued. Apparently he hadn't seen her. "You know how things are stacking up."

"Yes, but," and Taelin could see the strain in Alani's face now as she leaned forward again, "we believe they're going to make an attempt on you if you show up. That's why I'm telling you to pull out of Sandren. I need those men back down here—"

"Put another watchdog on me."

"That's another thing we need to talk about. All our remaining dogs are dead. Either someone's managed to slip aboard and . . ."

Taelin put her hand over her mouth. A dark shape had just appeared in front of her at the top of the metal staircase that spiraled down to the deck. Where it had come from, Taelin didn't know. It looked down at the deck as if it too had been eavesdropping.

The figure waited only a moment. Then it started down the metal staircase and Alani stopped talking. It wasn't until *that* moment that Taelin actually realized it was Sena Iilool. Just as the High King's witch turned through the spiral so that she was about to drop out of sight, she looked up, straight into Taelin's face.

A gust of wind tossed Sena's clutch of curls forward, carrying the smells of sweet mint and lotus.

Moments later she reappeared on the deck below, her back once again to Taelin.

Alani looked stricken and the High King seemed to lose his perpetual color. "We searched everywhere just before we left," Caliph was saying. "How did you get on the ship? Where have you been?"

Taelin felt paralyzed as she watched the scene unfold. Would Sena give her position away? Would she be arrested for spying? Had the High King's witch really just materialized out of thin air? What was happening?

"Caliph," said Sena, "we're done here."

"What?"

"I'm going south now." Sena made no indication that Alani was even there.

The High King's mouth opened slowly.

Alani's frosty eyebrows lifted. A man in black came out onto the deck and addressed Alani. "I'm sorry, sir. I don't know how she—" Alani raised his hand, indicating for the guard to stand down. The fact that sentries had been posted drove home to Taelin even more deeply how wrong it was for her to be here.

"Sena," Caliph gave his witch a pained smile, "can we talk about this later. I'm in a—"

"There's no meeting," said Sena.

Caliph scratched the side of his neck in irritation. "We came here for—"

Sena had walked to the railing and now looked out at the throng of brightly colored zeppelins. "Alani is right. The south wants you dead." The wind tugged every curl and strap attached to Sena's frame as she stood squarely, one hand on the rail, one hand lifted gently as if to touch some hanging fruit. Then she said something Taelin could not understand.

The daylight flickered as if an array of clouds was passing overhead at impossible speed. But the skies were empty and blue. Taelin couldn't help looking up, just to be sure.

When she looked back down, the brilliant circus of zeppelins hemorrhaged, every one cusp to keel. Not with fire. And not all at once. A kind of amplitude went through their frames that Taelin sensed more than saw. The eight-hundred-foot behemoth out of Bablemum was the first to go. The Grand Arbiter's airship, billowing brass and aqua sails crumpled like a blown egg. As it folded, its skin, its duralumin beams and whipping cables, its beautifully fluted air intakes and shimmering fuel cell exploded into the blackest, brownest, most beautiful orchid-colored clouds.

Taelin made a sound like a screen door, both spring and hinge. It escaped her mouth but no one noticed. She stared in shock at the—what?

Fire? Smoke? The blowback volumes rolled and evaporated like dissipating mist.

Twinkles of brilliant blue stuttered through the explosion's brown heart. Then everything dissolved into burnt umber steam and blew east on the prevailing winds. The airship had simply disappeared.

It was the same with the others. One after another. Dadelon's red and silver. Pandragor's orange and blue.

Taelin screamed but no one heard her. All eyes and ears were tuned to the destruction. People were coming out onto the deck now for a better view. Sigmund Dulgensen and the diplomat from Iycestoke. Even Dr. Baufent.

Sena had stopped speaking but the destruction continued. As if a slow breeze were moving west to east, when its leading edge touched a ship, that ship detonated and dissolved.

There were over thirty. Prime ministers, dictators, senators; the flagship of the emperor of Pandragor turned to mist along with its entire entourage.

After the last ship had dissipated, it was as if sky had been wiped clean. As if the entire gathering of airships had never been. Only three aircraft still floated like frightened islands. The *Bulotecus,* the *Odalisque* and the great white leviathan out of the Pplar.

Taelin was still screaming.

Sigmund Dulgensen gaped. He was white-knuckled, both meaty fists on the rail. Beside him, Alani looked like a dark cutout with a knife glued in his hand. It reflected the sky. Taelin didn't know where it had come from or why he was simply standing there, gripping it like a talisman.

Her gaze panned down from the cerulean gulf to the deck, searching for Sena. But she wasn't there. No trace. Then Taelin's eyes caught the tip of Caliph's finger and followed it off the deck. A Sandrenese condor? The High King pointed.

Of course not.

Sena was walking on the sky.

Taelin fell back in her deck chair like a wet towel. A vibration, a sound she couldn't hear, modulated the air, ringing in the zeppelin's frame. It made her crutches buzz against the roof. She could feel it in her chair, her clothing, tissues and teeth: a strange hum, like the aftermath of traumas she had felt before, at hospital, sapping her strength almost to the point of sleep.

Drowsily she watched Sena walking: a red and black and golden speck in the endless blue. Then her lids closed and she dreamt the nightmare all over: that her father was on Emperor Jünnũ's ship, screaming as he was eaten by eldritch fire.

Caliph ordered Isham Wade and his bodyguard confined to quarters until he figured out what was going on.

Mr. Wade protested violently at first but he and his bodyguard were quickly overpowered.

What exactly had happened remained unclear but it certainly appeared that Sena had single-handedly, with less effort (or thought) than it took to lift her hand, annihilated every person and every zeppelin in a ten mile radius of sky. The impossibility as well as the improbability of the act were the only things maintaining a semblance of doubt in Caliph's mind.

Five minutes in the past, a multinational conference was underway. Now, all the assembled leaders of the world's mightiest nations had been erased, leaving the questions of succession, leadership and national relations drifting, less than ashes in a void.

Caliph tried to remember everything she had said to him before her disappearance, before he had left her on the *Odalisque* and gone down to oversee the hospital. He remembered disregarding the stranger portion of the things that she had said. He remembered thinking that she was crazy. Could she have read his mind? Could she be angry enough to do *this*? Was it really Sena? What, oh what was going on?

He was too numb to feel. No anger or sense of betrayal. He mumbled something as he stood at the railing. "I think she told me she was going to destroy the world." It came out sounding random, devoid of context, the only thing he could think of to say.

"Nice," said Sig.

No one else spoke.

Sigmund turned away and marched to the deck's wet bar. He poured himself a drink.

"When did she tell you this?" asked Alani. It felt like a ridiculous question to Caliph—that the spymaster was taking it seriously—but Caliph answered anyway.

"A few days ago. What are you thinking?"

Alani's eyes were fixed on Sena, in the middle of the sky, still walking for the Pplarian ship. "I'm thinking whether she can do it or not doesn't matter. It's her intent that counts. She thinks she's a god."

Sigmund bellowed with laughter. "There's no tech I know of that can sort out three dozen airships and selectively destroy them in ten seconds while the rest are left un-fucking-scathed. If she's not a god what the fuck classifies?"

"It's holomorphy—" said Caliph.

"Oh yeah . . . I see mathematicians walk on the sky *all* the fucking time!" Sig tossed another drink past his teeth.

"She didn't cut herself," said Taelin.

"What?" Caliph glared at her. He hadn't even realized she was there but now the priestess's tired, tear-streaked face registered with him. She had crept up directly behind him on the deck.

"Don't holomorphs have to cut themselves?" she asked.

"I think we should take any real deliberation privately," Alani whispered in Caliph's ear. "This is going to break down quickly." And the spymaster was right. Sig was getting drunk and the priestess was positively rigid with shock. Dr. Baufent asked if it would be all right to administer her a sedative.

"I need—" Caliph tried to get their collective attention. "We need to figure out exactly what happened," he said. "If Sena did this . . . I don't . . . I don't know how to . . . we just need to find some answers."

"Find some answers!" cheered Sig.

Caliph ignored his whisky-guzzling friend. Suddenly the books Sena had given him seemed imminently important. "She said she was headed south," he said softly to Alani.

"Who wants to get vaporized?" said Sig. He was pouring glasses.

"And we're still alive," said Alani. "So she must want you to follow her."

"And what's your opinion of that course? If we follow her?"

The spymaster pawed at his snowy beard. "I think it comports nicely with my objective of shooting her down."

Caliph's heart twanged strangely but didn't rebel at the idea.

"Unfortunately we have a couple other serious issues at the moment," said Alani, "the men we left in Sandren . . . and the fact that we need to get *you* back to Stonehold."

"Well I'm certainly not going back to Stonehold until we've resolved this."

"Oh, really?" Alani finally tore his eyes from the sky and looked hard at Caliph. "What if the unthinkable happens?"

"We'll reinstate the Council, temporarily. I'll step down. We'll send a bird right-fucking-now."

Alani pressed his lips together.

"All of this is going to point our way," said Caliph. "We're the only ones standing. If we don't sort this out, every country is going to take aim at us . . . at the duchy. I'm not going to be any safer up north."

Alani's stoicism crumbled slightly, and his eyes told that Caliph was right. The spymaster looked at his shoes as a way of showing his assent.

Caliph felt the crushing impact of Sigmund's arm wrapping around his shoulders. "Here, Caph. I brought you a drink."

Caliph received it rather than argue. He dumped it over the railing as soon as Sigmund and everyone else turned to watch Baufent, administering an injection to a hysterical and grief-stricken Lady Rae who was bawling about her father on the Pandragonian ship. After it was over, Sigmund leaned in close to his friend and spoke lowly in a voice that only Caliph and Alani could hear.

"What the shit, Caph?" Sigmund sniffed while holding his glass in the air. "Why do you smell like apples?"

CHAPTER 24

It was only minutes later that Taelin sagged at the railing, watching the ship to which Sena had escaped molt through myriad similar forms. It was white, of Pplarian design and it was rising fast. As it punched through layer after layer of atmosphere, the ship's shape changed in subtle gradual ways. Taelin couldn't tell if this was real or a result of Dr. Baufent's injection. What did seem certain was that Sena's ship moved quicker than the *Odalisque* and Taelin worried in a detached way that Sena might escape.

Why is she going to Sandren?

Was Caliph following her or was he headed for the tent hospital?

Briefly, Taelin thought about the passengers with altitude sickness. They might have to endure another hour; then the *Odalisque* would ferry them home to Stonehold. She supposed what patients remained would be crammed into the other vessel with the crew. That was what she would do if she were the High King. High. King. Hiking. *I'm high.*

The *Odalisque* clambered like a bubble through thick liquid, rising once again over the cliffs where it buoyed into the sun.

Her body vibrated with the engine as it motored them in over the platform. From the railing, she looked down through southern flowers. The hospital tents flapped quietly in a breeze from the east. There didn't seem to be anyone around.

A tin of bandages lay scattered over the grass but most things seemed orderly enough. One of the patient tables had overturned but Taelin could see no sign of movement. She asked the obvious: "Where are they?"

Caliph leaned out over the railing. The muscles in his jaw twitched. "I don't know."

Baufent was trying to lead her off the deck. "You should lie down," the physician kept saying. But in the aftermath of the horrible thing that had just happened, no one was functioning efficiently. Baufent probably wanted to stay out on deck like everyone else and see what was going to happen next.

"What *will* happen next?" Taelin asked loudly to anyone who would listen.

Alani turned and hissed in her face. "What happens next, is that you shut your mouth. When we get back I'm personally escorting you off this ship."

"Where? Seatk'r?" Taelin heard her voice crack. "I can't get off there! In the ghettos! I'll be—"

"You'll get off where I tell you to get off," said Alani. "I found the note. Where is it?"

"Where's what?"

"The poison."

High as she was, the blame tied her off, anchored her. She started to sweat. "I never—"

"Shut up," said Alani. And she did. His eyes made salient what repercussions waited should she fail to obey. "I don't think you're an assassin, Miss Rae. I think you're ignorant. We'll deal with this when I return. Until then, I want you in your stateroom. In bed."

She made the southern hand sign for yes after which he turned and strode to a weapon cabinet where he pulled out a gas-powered bow. "We're not landing here," he said loudly to the group gathered on deck.

Caliph stood several feet away, tugging his lip thoughtfully. He looked so pensive. Taelin, who had momentarily had every intention of going to her room and climbing into bed, now found herself wanting to reach out and touch the High King's mouth. It had to be the drugs Baufent had given her. Caliph and his witch had just killed her father. They were the murderers. Not her!

She bit down on her rising anger.

"We're going to take some gliders," Caliph announced. "Check for survivors. Twenty-minute sweep. Everyone else stays on the ship." He looked across the city-state's copper domes to where Sena's white airship had stopped.

"She's waiting for us," Alani said.

Caliph did not reply.

Taelin stayed where she was. She was not going to her room. *I don't have to obey* him. *Where are the Iycestokians? Where is my father? Stonehold is to blame. Stonehold's government is very much to blame for this day!*

Her feet were planted despite Baufent's occasional pleas. She could tell the doctor had given up. Caliph and Alani descend a staircase to the *Odalisque*'s cargo hold. From below came the sound of large doors opening with a hydraulic whimper.

Accompanying them was the sound of an altercation. To Taelin it sounded like Caliph and Alani were at each other's throats. It seemed the spymaster did not want the High King going down to assist with the search for the missing physicians, but by the sound of it, Caliph was going to have his way. This made Taelin smile with small feelings of vicarious vengeance.

Moments later, sinister winged shadows appeared on the ground and then, gliding out from under the ship, Taelin saw a squadron of half a dozen men, blackish-silver wings strapped to their backs, green glows emanating from their spines. They wore dark flight suits and their eyes were chromium blue.

They planed out over the mooring deck and landed gracefully. She could pick out Alani easiest because of his bald head. Caliph was harder but she soon decided that he was the one the other men felt obligated to assist in unbuckling his harness. Caliph had a sword. The rest held crossbows.

They left their wings in an orderly row and darted down the broad white steps into the palace gardens. Taelin was worried that they would vanish from sight, but the pilot must have been watching too. The *Odalisque* moved, following the men on the ground. Taelin's heart raced with excitement and fear as the deck crossed over a bosk of white-flowering bushes and brought her closer to the hospital tents.

Now she could see the six men moving systematically between the white pavilions. Quickly. Crossbows pivoted with their shoulders and heads, always pointed in the direction they were looking. Caliph followed them, sword out. The blade was black with a silver stripe down its center and it left tiny silvery lights in its wake.

As the *Odalisque* drifted sideways, Taelin got a glimpse inside the tent which Caliph had just entered. She saw him roll the body of a smell-feast over with his heel. Its fat red ostracean mass glistened in the sunlight.

Taelin felt Caliph kick it. Her foot thumped. She *felt* it. What was happening?

Caliph walked out of the tent, following his men.

She had impressions of the garden's boughs swaying around her, as if she was walking, literally, in his shoes. Her mind caught snippets of medicine packets and syringes scattered in the grass: things too small for her to have seen from a hundred feet above the ground. She could feel a static charge in her right hand, the hairs on her arm sticking up. His sword.

What had Baufent shot her up with?

Whatever it was, she wanted more.

She stumbled away from the railing, leaving her crutches on the deck. She headed for the medical supplies.

CALIPH lost his footing and Alani had to help him up.

"Are you all right?" The spymaster's face composed stiff irregular lines that conferred no empathy.

Caliph was already self-conscious about fumbling his harness. He felt drunk.

"I'll be fine."

His men were following trampled grass toward the Sandrenese palace and he was following them. The smell of flowers mixed with wet stone and the fumes of spilled antiseptic. There were more scattered bandages in the grass.

Up ahead, Rosewind's pink-brown blocks cavaulted into circular tourelles and around onion domes. The fact that its former tenants were dead lent it a subconscious taint that Caliph tried to ignore as he and his men scrambled over the cement cargo ramps on the building's northwest flank.

His team of men was surrounding a familiar side door when he realized for the first time how quiet Sandren seemed. Aside from the hum of the *Odalisque* overhead, all he could hear was the creak of branches and the giggle of leaves. If there had been birds here on his last visit he couldn't remember. Maybe Sandren was too high.

He looked toward the gate that had held the hoard of howling patients at bay. It still appeared to be shut but he couldn't tell for certain at this distance.

His men had already stacked up around the door to the palace but Caliph was staring down into a brick and mortar pit on the left. Lined with steps and a door marked with a familiar warning in High Mạlk. The door stood open, which seemed inexplicably wrong. Two men were already checking it.

Pale green beams of light shot into the darkness of the utility vault as his men turned on tiny torches. Caliph glanced at Alani who was watching the men at the vault with unbroken concentration. Alani wore a scowl. The other men were waiting patiently at the palace door for the signal to enter.

Caliph saw everything shimmer as if they were standing in the desert, heat waves rippling off the ground. He braced himself against the palace wall, feeling dizzy.

"Go back to the gliders," Alani whispered. "Wait for us there."

Caliph felt deep shame associated with the command, shame for demanding to come with—only to inexplicably fall so ill that Alani could see it in his face. His stomach rolled. It was no use. Alani was right. And there was no reason to let pride get in the way.

What is wrong with me?

He squinted back across the grass toward the cịryte platform. It seemed impossibly far away.

His limbs felt wobbly and his head seemed to be floating away from his feet. He set out, stumbling, and heard Alani curse.

The words, "Help him," came like bubbles in the sunlight-colored air.

Then the pavement's beautifully fractured and intricately pitted surface raced toward his face. He loved the pavement. Its porous intricacies. The lichens. The stream of ants like grains of hardened molasses rolling two directions at once. He loved the smell of mold.

Someone grabbed him under the arm and pulled him away from the ground, which made him inexplicably sad. His view panned away from the ants, toward green windy shapes and what looked like dancing men.

He saw white lines appear and disappear at crazy angles. Swords reflecting light?

Something had happened. He still had his own sword in his hand. He struggled to unscrew the safety ring. It defied him, a black puzzle in his fingers. Then there was a snap.

Hm?

He felt the weapon hum in his grip. He must have triggered it. The thing was certainly charged. He set his feet far apart, trying to stay balanced, trying to keep the blade away from the ground. A vague understanding that he might kill himself registered enough to demand his full attention.

He pivoted on one foot, trying to aim himself in the general direction of the chaos. The palace walls were so big. They overawed him. He nearly sat down to stare.

Then as if out of an ominous opera performance, where all sounds hushed on the cusp of the starring villain's appearance, Caliph heard the sound of a great animal walking into a building. Maybe it was into a building. The heavy leather crush of a foot against tile, the muscular shake of its bulk within the harness, and the breathing . . . Caliph heard it.

Only this wasn't the pastoral grunt of some deep-chested quadruped. This was the slithering whine of air sucked through gooey vents or gills. It was a slurp mixed with a shudder.

Before his eyes, gigantic feet, frog-like, pulled up from the concrete in formidable pyramids of muscle. They were attached to legs that folded precisely in the way that Caliph would have expected from a giant amphibian-learned-to-walk.

The legs almost hypnotized him. They jackknifed through a graceful, varied gait. The movements of huge muscle packs, stretching fluidly thigh-to-toes, pulled the "heel" up past the monster's hip. With every step, this "heel" came tantalizingly close to hitting the creature in the back.

Caliph's dazed eyes followed this jag of bone down to the knee. It was upon the knee that the whole upper portion of the leg and torso seemed to balance.

Each thigh bone nested in the corresponding cup of an atlatl-like sling while the mighty feet and ankles of the beast propelled and kept everything else aloft.

In split seconds, Caliph absorbed the marvelous power and how most of the creature's weight was clearly in its feet. It could lean and stretch in ways that seemed to defy gravity. But the double-bent legs that powered the ranine body were only the beginning. At roughly eight feet off the ground, Caliph had to crane his neck to see the monster's head. The skull hung much lower than the shoulders and the tip of its snout, which reminded Caliph of both a catfish and a salamander, was lower than either its neck or the prominent fan of its beefsteak-colored gills.

The whole body was so hunched, so crouched, so incredibly folded up in fact, that Caliph decided it could have easily stood up and reached eighteen feet into the sky.

Eighteen feet with its jaws, that was. Caliph had no way of accounting for the potential length of its many-jointed arms.

The hand of the bodyguard that had pulled Caliph to his feet had been gone ever since the creature's arrival. There was a large red blur in the periphery, covering the cement, and Caliph heard the monster's talons drag like plastic strips against the stone. It grabbed a cinder block–sized chunk of the man's torso. Like a distracted child moving messy candy toward its mouth, it gave no outward sign of enjoyment or even that it was eating. The consumption of Caliph's bodyguard seemed a reflexive action, unconnected with the movements of its eyes.

Caliph lifted his sword, which felt incredibly heavy. The impression of shouts and desperate actions behind the creature came to him as out of heavy fog.

Where did you come from? Caliph thought.

The crouched shape turned slowly, golden-gray and shimmering. Its empty eyes—like porcelain pie-plates stuffed with pink gelatin—were dead, soulless and without recognizable intelligence. But they *were* looking at him. Of that, Caliph was sure.

He stumbled backward, away from the crunching mouth. Blood drizzled from the end of its snout, heavy and fast. Around this horror, a clutch of darkened barbels oozed though the air with dissimilar gravity, curling, stretching and swelling like snail eyes.

Even in his dizzy condition, Caliph noticed the asymmetry of the hands that were moving slowly toward him. One was an ungulate horn, which hooked sharply toward the ground; the other was a translucent duck claw banded in tropical brown and white—swaddled in ancient skin and brandishing an array of talons in Caliph's direction.

He waited for the beast to reach out and take him. It opened its mouth, canyon-wide. He felt like he was leaning over a pit. A strange gravity drew him in. He felt the immense power of the monster's will and teetered, feet losing traction with the ground. His boots rolled on gravel, then nothing but air.

Before his face, the deep interior of the monster swelled with fatty pink ridges. Caliph heard his name at the back of the python throat where some discreet muscles manipulated air. "Caliph Howl," it had said.

Or at least he imagined it had spoken to him.

Then the jaws moved forward, propelled half a step. The talons reached out from the end of its impossible five-jointed arm.

Caliph raised his chemiostatic sword. The still-humming black-and-silver blade met it halfway. A blinding flash of light filled the world, accompanied by a sizzling bang: like someone striking an empty metal drum with the flat of their hand.

The creature stopped. Smoke poured off its skin. Caliph dropped to the ground. He backed away as it lost balance. Fabric that had covered the hump on its back smoldered. A low, ugly red flame danced around its skull as the huge body thundered against the concrete.

With his view cleared, he stared over the carcass to where a second creature had one of Alani's men in its jaws. In mere seconds the man was gone, crushed and tossed down its throat like a springbuck in the throat of a saurian.

Head foggy, Caliph climbed over the sticky, charred carcass that reeked of burnt salmon and stumbled toward the second monster. He thought he might black out but he didn't. He swung his weapon as hard as he could.

The momentum carried him forward but twisted off the creature's skin. His blow turned down, dragging his arms with, buckling his body.

He couldn't recover. The sword left his hands and clanged against the ground.

Lazily, the vast duck paw reached out for him, talons spreading.

And then he was on his back in a cot, staring at the ceiling of his stateroom. No. Not his stateroom. He smelled medical supplies and felt nauseous.

The weight of his breasts tugged at the center of his chest, pulling gently to either side. He reached up and cupped them, pushing them back together. They were soft and comforting.

When he opened his mouth, he was screaming. He didn't know why, but he was screaming.

Dr. Baufent showed up almost immediately, shadowed by several other people. She looked down at Caliph with grave concern.

"Bring me my satchel," she snapped, and one of the shadows behind her disappeared.

"Just what do you think you're doing?" Baufent tore into him. "No? What about this?" She held up an empty hypodermic. "Are you a junkie? Or are you just stupid?"

Caliph didn't know what to say.

"Get me a drip," said Baufent.

"Ma'am," a voice behind her sounded truly afraid, "there's something happening on the ground."

"I am busy! Get Anselm to deal with it."

"Yes, ma'am."

Caliph was still holding his breasts.

TAELIN'S second scream seemed to be mental. At least she had no control over her body. She couldn't open her mouth. She was moving without willing herself to do so, scuttling across a concrete slab on her palms like a crab.

She reached for a sword just in front of her and grasped it by the handle. It felt cool and solid even though she was sure she was dreaming. The smell of burnt fish wrecked the air.

She jumped up, strong but clumsy, surprised by her own strength, gripping the weapon.

The palace scintillated: a pointillist's figurative arrangement of pink and black and mica-white dots. She could hear the sounds of combat on her left flank but she could not move. Like in a nightmare, she was a watcher more than an active participant.

Her neck was locked in a direction that cast her field of view just south of the palace's grand facade, off the cement pad and down toward an additional spread of gardens.

The taste in her mouth was foreign. She felt sweat trickle from the bridge of her nose down around her nostrils, incredibly real. At the edge of the cement pad, where a magnolia tossed in the wind, a gauzy darkness spluttered. It looked like black steam seeping into the air from no particular source but it held a shape that reminded her of the cloaks worn by college professors.

At the top of it—sweet Nenuln—a puff of white that bobbed fly-away with the wind, sheltered a pair of cimmerian eyes. They glared at her with malicious delight. Together it was the semblance of a man standing under the tree, just barely. Just almost there.

She walked toward him, which was the last thing she wanted to do, her sword out in front of her. As she approached, the shape grew taller, or perhaps it levitated slowly so that her vantage became that of a child at the foot of a grown-up.

Something like an arm effected from the mist, a hand spread and extended. She felt a cool-warm pressure grip the crown of her head. And a vaporous voice said something about her necklace that she couldn't understand.

CHAPTER 25

There had been no report from Duana's qloin.

When the High King had floated down from Sandren to meet Isham Wade, Miriam and her five sisters had waited for either Sena or Duana to materialize.

Neither had.

In an effort to collect intelligence, while the High King slept, Miriam and her two qloins had crawled out of the rain and into his stateroom.

The puslet was still cankered with neural cells it had cloned from Taelin Rae; its synthesis with Caliph's brain was sloppy and any information it provided would be cloudy and intermittent. But Miriam did not care. All she needed was Sena's location.

Unfortunately, Caliph didn't know.

Sena had disappeared entirely, from diaglyph, blood scrying—even her lover had no idea where to find her.

Miriam could only wait for things to change. But when they had, when Sena *had* shown up—Miriam found herself woefully unprepared.

Sena's immediate destruction of the airships had been paralyzing. For those precious moments, Miriam had been unable to think. And how she regretted it! By the time she had gathered her wits, the Eighth House—for who could doubt the meaning of Giganalee's proclamation now?—was already walking toward the white ship.

Did Sena serve the Pplar? Or was it the other way 'round?

Miriam set these and many other questions aside. All that mattered for the moment was catching Sena. The puslet told her that Caliph Howl was intent on the same thing, that he didn't want the world to end and that he was someone she could use.

Miriam was forced to change her plan yet again. Had it been available, she would have used the tremendous amount of energy necessary for both qloins to *cross* lines onto Sena's ship. Not only was crossing lines exponentially more dangerous than walking lines, but it required so many holojoules—three hundred sixty murdered people for both qloins—that even if she killed the High King's entire entourage it wouldn't have been half enough. She would have done it. She wished there were enough bodies to use.

But it simply wasn't going to happen. The only thing to do was use the *Odalisque* to chase Sena down.

Miriam watched the chaos unfold below her while clinging to the airship's belly with gooey holomorphic fingers. Her ancillas were nearby.

The Cabal's flawless had slunk up from Sandren's fissures and the High King's forces were now pinned beneath them, stretched like softened metal across the anvil of the Ghalla Peaks. It would be an unlikely partnership if she saved the High King.

He was standing stupidly with his back to the flawless, completely exposed and staring at a tree on the edge of the cement.

Miriam blamed the puslet. It was dirty.

The only thing giving her pause was Caliph's spymaster. She desperately wanted him torn in half by the flawless. Then it would be safer for her to intervene. She hesitated a moment more, knowing that her window of opportunity was closing.

Finally, she gave the signal and popped the cork on a small capsule of blood. The grume of the battle was too far below for hemofurtum. She let go of the *Odalisque* and shouted. All six sisters glided out of the zeppelin's shadow.

The boundary between the Sisterhood and its ancient enemy passed behind her as Miriam skimmed the trees, eyes focused on the flawless, which were still wolfing down human-shaped bites.

The flawless were not half-breeds. These eel-headed hulks had erupted from bygone cisterns like ancient gods. As bewildering as it was that these fables should reveal themselves here and now, Miriam's time for idle thought ended as her feet touched the ground. Her momentum carried her into a run.

On her left, marked out by their use of velvet guns, the last three of the spymaster's handpicked agents were fighting alongside him. *Fighting* was inaccurate. What Alani and his agents were trying to do was slow the flawless down. It wasn't working. The flawless moved unhindered, relentlessly eating their way through the last people standing. But they seemed distracted.

Miriam tried to understand what they were looking at. Her eyes rolled up.

It was the *Odalisque.*

Some of them reached into the sky, twenty feet or more, pawing. One tried to jump. It was futile. The ship was far out of reach.

Miriam looked away as she raced toward Caliph Howl. Combat was not the answer here. Her only goal was securing the High King. If he died, the chase for Sena would be over.

Miriam motioned toward Caliph's idle form at the edge of the cement. Her ancillas, like her, were already sprinting toward him. Then, across the expanse of cement, Miriam locked eyes with the spymaster. She saw him through the mutant limbs of one towering flawless. His knives gleamed in his hands. The next instant, he held only one.

Miriam tried to steer her momentum but he had gauged his throw too well. The knife struck her like a brick. She went into a roll, tumbling over the slab. Clearly, he had seen her heading for the High King and misinterpreted her intent.

Miriam blinked. She was on the ground. Her body ached from several more or less vague locations. The knife still stuck in her back, point embedded in her shoulder blade. Gravity tugged it. So did her movements. When her scapula slid beneath her skin, the blade cut her again.

She reached back with her other hand and wrenched it out.

Already he was coming for her. Or was he?

She had never seen an old man move so fast, cutting a half-circle out from the tangle of enemies. Nearby, one of his remaining agents floated above the ground. Oozing bulbous tendrils around the monster's upper jaw guided the agent to a quivering pink conclusion.

Miriam saw another flawless reach for the spymaster. Its arm stretched several yards but Alani's feet hiccupped, popping him into a jump that propelled him just out of reach.

The spymaster wasn't coming for her. He was running for Caliph Howl and her ancillas. His second knife had already left his hand. It was better aimed and took Medea in the back, through vital organs. She dropped instantly which pulled Anjie, Miriam's second, up short.

Miriam cursed. She could read the stunned look of fear in Anjie's eyes as the girl registered what had just happened. Anjie found the source of the knife. She understood who was coming for her.

Miriam's diaglyphs calculated for her as she palmed the old assassin's knife. The other qloin had touched down not far away and was trying to reach her from the direction of the palace. This was the agreed course of action, but when they met the flawless, the other qloin stopped dead.

Miriam's dash toward the king faltered as her legs spasmed. Her body tensed under the shrieking sound of hydraulics. It was very close to that sound. One of the flawless had barked. The blast of sound put her on her kneepads. She skidded to a stop, hands over her ears. Her cheek coursed with blood.

She took two deep breaths but couldn't hear a thing. Massive frog feet were moving toward her. The concrete cracked. In mundane dissociation with everything else, a colony of insects whose nest beneath the slab had been broken open, poured out like a spreading stain.

The flawless' great weight had broken through the stone. It mounted a slab of jutting cement and looked in her direction.

Miriam got her legs moving. They carried her as if she clung to someone else's back. In front of the pain there was fear and fear was the trigger for her training. Most of the hardwired responses—screaming, folding up in the fetal position—had been ripped out and replaced with other options. The one that served her best at the moment was *run.*

She hit the ground as hard and fast as she could. Both feet pounding. She looked back to see a curtain of metallic-gray skin stretch between phalanges and thighs. The enormous candy-sucker eyes glared at her as she tore over the cement. The singular horn of the flawless' right hand pulled it into a leap, using the sundered skyward slab of concrete for leverage.

Airborne and impossible, like a dead tree in a cyclone, it hurled toward her.

When it landed, it broke the cement again, lifting a new section out of the ground. Miriam catapulted off the end, an athlete hoping to clear a chasm, sailing over the grass, trajectory uncertain. She flew past the desperate battle between her ancilla and the spymaster, toward the oblivious High King.

In an unintended excess of accuracy, she landed so close to Caliph Howl that she stumbled into him. The impact sent the sword in his hand dipping toward the ground. It made a dull, loud thump and steam or smoke rose from the sod.

He spun on her with a confused look in his face, thumb flicking the end of his weapon. It popped, crackled almost, and began humming again. He lifted it menacingly.

"King Howl, we have to—"

And then the silence was back, deeper and more profound. Her head felt like it was underwater. She lifted a hand to the side of her face. She was bleeding from her left ear and the sun had gone behind a shadow, as if the *Odalisque* had moved in front of it.

But it was not the *Odalisque.*

The High King's jaw was set as he powered his black sword into a swing aimed just right of Miriam's head.

Miriam dropped Alani's knife and tried to get out of the way. What greeted her was the horn-like appendage of the flawless falling shy, spare inches, and lodging in the ground: incongruous as a giant stalactite taken from a cave and hurled into the sod. Maybe it was intentional. Maybe it was another act of the ancient Lua'gr̩oc leveraging its enormous body.

Maybe it had missed.

On the other side of the horn and the arm it was attached to, Alani had just driven his long-knife up below the creature's sternum, under its alien rib cage.

The eel head gave no indication of pain. Its barbels flexed and Miriam felt her boots lift off the ground. The thing was levitating her into its mouth.

She cried out but Anjie could not assist. She had refocused on the king, determined to follow through with the plan, determined to get him out of here alive. Ignoring Alani's knife, which was still buried presumably in its soft organs, the flawless opened its mouth to receive Miriam and at that instant the High King's sword hit bone.

Miriam saw a flash of light. She went blind. Her eyebrows singed. Unable to see or hear, she lost all sense of balance. Her body promptly fell to the ground and slid down the slope. She smelled dirt and grass and felt loam pack itself under her nails.

She blinked, scrambling. On her feet again in an instant.

The world was coming back in bleached panorama, faded tints and shapes that gradually made sense.

She lurched back up the slope. Only a few feet. She hadn't fallen far. The smoking body of the flawless had collapsed into a kind of massive tripod, bones and cooked flesh propped up somewhat by the weight of the limbs. The whole hideous shape seemed anchored by the creature's horned hand: still stuck fast in the dirt.

Caliph Howl was clicking the end of his weapon but the thing no longer hummed. Its battery was spent. He looked drugged and did not seem to notice that the same massive electrical burst that had fried the Lua'gr̩oc had also charred his spymaster, who had been caught weapon in hand, fully intersecting the creature.

Alani Anjin, former grandmaster of the Long Nine, was dead.

Miriam gripped the High King by his bicep and forced him into a bewildered jog toward the palace, motioning for Anjie and her other two remaining girls to protect their flank.

Her eyes burned; she still couldn't hear out of her left ear. The barks had done permanent damage. There were several flawless, standing more or less in the middle of the vast slab. One was looking up distractedly at the *Odalisque* while its fellows played with the bodies strewn at their feet.

Miriam tugged the High King off the slab, down into a pit set with steps. She shoved him through a metal door into a machinery room, then turned and counted heads. Autumn had made it in, thank gods. So had Gina. Including Anjie and herself, four of the original six were accounted for.

"What happened to the other two?"

"They're gone."

There wasn't time to mourn. She told Autumn to watch Caliph before darting back up the stairs.

When she got far enough up that her head peeked over the slab, she locked eyes with one of the flawless. The others were jumping on great legs, trying to reach the airship, cracking the cement further with each attempt. Her missing girls were nowhere in sight. The flawless chirped and its cohorts turned to look at her.

Back! Down the steps. She could feel the vibrations as they pounded toward her. She banged the metal door and grabbled with the bolt. Snap! The metal bent in, creased by the tremendous impact. On the first blow, daylight luxuriated around the frame.

Chirping noises followed, then two tentative taps on the door. Despite their massive frames, Miriam knew the flawless could fold themselves up. Their skin was slippery. They could certainly pass through this doorway.

She was already moving through the machines, into dark, rough-cut spaces at the back of the room.

She heard the High King mumble a vague complaint. He couldn't see where he was going, but her compasses were shining. They told her what to do.

She caught up with her ancillas and helped ferry the monarch of Stonehold down a second set of stairs. The steps transitioned from stone to metal and shuttled them through a passageway and onto a steel maintenance platform anchored beneath one of the enormous arms that supported Sandren's teagle system. A blast of fresh air and a dizzy blue expanse pulled Miriam up short.

The world reeled below her as if on the end of a chain. Thousands of feet separated her reality from the hovering mist-pale landscape that formed the foothills of the Ghalla Peaks. This place was meant for tethers and well-trained technicians. Its flooring was grated and when Miriam looked down she could see the cliffs.

A control box sat nearby for summoning the elevator but Miriam knew they didn't have time. Even here, buffeted by wind, she could smell the ichthyic stench gassing from the tunnel. She pulled a backup kyru from her other hip and nodded meaningfully to Autumn. Then, she stabbed the High King in the arm, right through his clothing, and began running the numbers. He made a surprised but quiet sound and didn't fight back.

Oh wait, she thought. *I'm bleeding . . .*

She had forgotten her own injury. In her desperate quest for holojoules, she had cut him pointlessly. The realization caused an unexpected ache of sympathy and for a moment her attention turned to him. She noticed his solidity, the muscle packs of his chest and abdomen as she supported him at the brink of infinity. He did not feel like a politician in her arms (she had held several of them) and she pondered a moment over the fact that he had managed to single-handedly bring down two of the flawless despite the vitiated puslet in his brain.

Maybe Sena's choice in men was better than she thought.

Behind her, a dull clangor echoed from the tunnel mouth, possibly the sound of a metal door being flung across a cinder block room. She maneuvered the High King into position, then pressed her weight into his back. She pulled her legs up, wrapped all her limbs around him and held on tight. He fell like an old tree trunk, pitching north off the platform. She clung to that resistance and they fell together, one dead weight, hurtling toward the pastel fields that spun three miles below.

CHAPTER 26

Like a grub turned out on a shovel's blade from rich loam into the cold, the Pplarian ship is threshing vaguely in the wind. Sena walks toward it. Her jacket is a snapping crimson flag. She tries not to think about the people she has murdered but feels the act passing through her.

She cannot pull back from it.

It is part of her now. Not just a line crossed or a door opened. For lines and doors are things a person moves over and through. They are things a person swiftly leaves behind. She has *passed over and through but she carries the act with her to the other side into a fuzzy, numb reality of death and violence and orchestrated mayhem. And in fact, even this is wrong.*

Because what is really happening is that the act is carrying her, not the other way around. It is the murder that is keeping her on her feet, moving. Without it she would collapse. As if death itself is offering her a gift for working such a wondrous miracle in its name, the horror of the act is muted and only the empty sky, the silence of the space she has willed into existence, remains. The horrible euphoria of this moment is staggering.

The power of the murder has usurped the person she used to be. It has become her. In an instant. She has become the newest face of reckless, selfish death.

The holojoules snatched from the discreated airships swirl around her. They are the fruit of over seven thousand cuts[20] *of blood. Nathaniel is haunting her, touching her, marveling at her. And he is asking why.*

Sena steels herself. She does not answer. With great effort she manages to twist her mouth into a pawky smile. She does it for Nathaniel. It is part of the show. And it works. He is patently bewildered.

Why did you do this? *he asks.* Why? It has something to do with what

[20] Holomorphy measures its cost in cuts. According to holomorphic charts, the human body contains seven cuts.

you found in the Chamber, doesn't it? Tell me. What did you find? *Nathaniel has sensed the change of direction in her thoughts.* What did you discover there?

Two intact bottles. *Her answer is a thought.* But I found fragments of a third. You were right, Nathan. You were right. I believe we can get to three.

For a time, Nathaniel is quiet. You shouldn't have gone. *His thoughts telegraph a hiss.* I could have lost you.

Her smile broadens but she worries whether he is playing along. While she carries on her mental conversation she must keep her other thoughts veiled. She erects transeunt walls within her mind, ephemeral but sufficient to hold him at bay. He must not uncover the secret she is hiding.

As they telepath back and forth, she slips a touch of malice into her lies. Any sweetness will grow his suspicion. But his assault is tireless. He asks the same question many, many times. In the hurricane of his black distrust she bows and trudges on, moving the dead kings' holojoules through the air.

A vast capcitance wheels around her, pulled from the casualties of the dissolved fleet. It is a potent residue of the murder, a real power torn not only from kings and emperors but from flight crews, and bodyguards, cooks and cabinet aides. The crime is real. It can never be undone. She swallows hard and tells herself the thing she planned to tell herself before she crossed this line: they are her enemy—everyone in the sky was her enemy—just as everyone who stands between her and the end is her enemy now.

The world is no longer the world. It is a bin of jumbled variables she must sort through quickly if she is to make it to her goal. She did not ask for this. This was—

Why are you bringing him south? *Nathaniel asks.*

For the ink of course, *she says. And to her unending sorrow this is not untrue.*

You should have destroyed him by now. You're far too sentimental.

"I'll make ink soon enough. Why are you so eager? He's your nephew. Was *your nephew, once. I thought you might—"*

Nathaniel snaps violently, Focus on what you're good at! Please!

"And what's that?"

Capturing his fluids! You might have moved on to blood by now and been done with this—but no . . . I wonder why. Why delay? Why bother giving him those books?

Sena ignores the horrible attack. "I see he means nothing to you."

Don't affix your weaknesses to me, *Nathaniel thinks.* Caliph Howl is hardly my nephew. He *should* mean nothing to you. He's just another *thing* that you and I will pass on our way across the stars. Don't forget that!

The words drive a powerful pain into her core because Nathaniel is right. Before the end, she will drain Caliph's Hjolk-trull blood into the ink. That trace of immortality, passed down from the Gringlings to the Hjolk-trull make him intrinsic to her designs.

If her body was different, if it hadn't been changed—but Sena no longer bleeds.

Caliph has been wrapped up in the myth of his conference, so certain of what is really important. Her destruction of the zeppelins has roused him. She has his full attention now.

The conference baited him out of Isca, it gave her time to inspect the Chamber. But now the ugly moment of the switch has come.

Caliph will do what she knows he will do. His sense of justice will carry him. After all, he is good man. But in order to capitalize on that goodness, she has had to do the unthinkable. She is the Omnispecer. This moment's arrival was foreseen.

What amplifies her exquisite anguish is that only now does Caliph see her clearly, as she really is.

Sena drags the holojoules toward the Pplarian ship with the only kind of wound she lacks the choice to bear. It feels like her soul is bleeding. There will be no thank-you for destroying Stonehold's enemies. Already, Caliph's thoughts are turning on her. She is not surprised, but she is surprised by how it feels to be an outsider, an enemy, the one who caused him pain. She is shocked at how it feels to be mistrusted rather than adored. And yet it is familiar. She has been down this road before.

He will chase her now, to the ends of the world—not because he loves her but for the answer he is seeking. That is both the cruelty and the essential purpose of the thing. She wants to cry but sticks it in her throat. She will not weep in front of Nathaniel. Eventually, she knows, Caliph will have his answer. He will know that her hands were tied.

You look pleased, *Nathaniel muses. It is a caustic joke. She cannot imagine her false smile is so convincing.* Even if you *do* need the holojoules, I think you must be reveling in your power. Destroying entire governments, out of sheer egoistic joy?

Rectitudinous joy, *Sena corrects him.*

Oh? You tire of the politics of men? Poetic. *Nathaniel's tone darkens into his version of a sneer.* But I don't believe you. Why are you coiling their energy? What are you spooling them up—?

You don't want me to go to Sọth? *Sena feigns shock. It is a small punch, a jab.*

His coldness slides across her chest, her waist, the back of her neck. Sena keeps moving. She steps out of the sky, onto the Pplarian vessel.

Please, *Nathaniel mocks.* You don't need a thousand bodies' worth of blood to go to Sọth. You have your colligation . . .

"Then maybe you're right." The holojoules of mass murder have been cached. She has wound them tightly and will hold them just a little while longer. "Maybe I enjoyed it. Maybe it was just for fun. Besides, my colligation is for other things."

Yes. I wonder what those things might be . . .

Within the ship, Sena sees a shape moving; a Pplarian is coming out to greet her.

So many secrets, *Nathaniel says.* At least you're giving him plenty to read. As I knew you would . . .

You want him to know about me, don't you? You want him to understand what a monster I am? I think he already knows. But what's monstrous about saving my child?

Sena swallows hard because he is so close to the truth. He is on the cusp of understanding everything she is hiding from him. So incredibly close, in fact, that she is terrified to speak.

Caliph Howl is worth killing, *Nathaniel says.*

"Yes," she whispers. "But before he gives us everything, I think he deserves to know why."

Have it your way. *The shade manifests its version of a horselaugh.* But if he's going to understand anything you give him, won't you have to undo what they *did* to him?

Won't you have to burn the puslet out?

Sena carefully maintains her emotionless look. "Yes, I will. I'm going to do it with tinctures. The puslet's sensitive cells won't survive a single dose."

He has suggested the very thing she planned.

Interesting. Obviously you want to play spirit guide. Steal some private time? Don't for an instant think I'm letting you inside his head alone.

THE *Odalisque* plunged out of the sky.

It had followed the battle in Sandren carefully. When the witches had taken the High King underground, Sigmund had suggested where the maintenance tunnels might lead. The ship had motored out, away from the flawless' leaping forms, beyond the edge of the cliff. There, Sigmund had scanned feverishly and when the witches had emerged with Caliph in tow, he had shouted—somewhat drunkenly—and pointed at the tiny platform bolted to the mountain wall.

He had shouted again, in dismay, when the unthinkable had happened and Caliph and the witches had plummeted. They fell like stones wrapped in fabric, clothing flapping madly behind them.

The *Odalisque* gave chase, descending as fast as it could, not in a vain effort to save them, but in an effort to determine the High King's fate.

CALIPH could vaguely recall killing monsters with his sword. Or crayon.

Whatever.

Baufent had hooked him up to a bag of fluid and said something crazy. Then she turned to Sena, who had just walked into the room. While Baufent asked Sena for her professional opinion, Caliph noticed that his mistress had dyed her hair pale pink and put it into ponytail bunches off the back of her head. Her lips shimmered with pastel blue cosmetics and her nurse uniform was black, complete with unlikely gartered stockings. Caliph's feelings over this did not correspond with the emotions he felt subconsciously floating just out of reach.

Why didn't they correspond?

He couldn't remember and for the moment, he didn't care.

Sena looked down at him melodramatically, as if reading lines from an atrocious satire. "He'll live, doctor. I'll see to it."

Caliph started laughing while Sena produced a small steel flask from her halter top and told Baufent to administer it. Any moment now, Caliph expected dancing fish with hats and canes.

Instead, Baufent scowled, unscrewed the cap and sniffed the contents. "Won't this do even more harm?" she asked.

Caliph's laughter was like a windup toy that wouldn't stop.

"Yes and no," said Sena. "It's poison, but it's also the only way to remove his breasts." She brushed Caliph's hair from his forehead with cool smooth fingers as if deeply concerned over the future shape of his body.

"You're right," said Baufent who had turned into a real talking hamster. The huge gray rodent that was now Baufent leaned forward with the tiny flask in its paws and said, "Drink it . . . Drink it."

Going along with the dream, Caliph did as he was told.

But when the liquid hit the back of his throat, something changed. Sena's voice changed as well. It took on an edge. "Try to stay calm," she said. "We'll get through this."

Her hand rested firmly on his forehead.

The euphoria had already begun to fade. Replacing it was darkness, emptiness and panic. "Sena? What's happening?"

"Taelin isn't well. She got into the medical supplies," said Sena. "The puslet in your head allowed you to feel what she was feeling. You got high right along with her. But now we're taking the puslet out. The influence of those drugs is going to go away—suddenly."

Caliph felt his skin tighten. His body felt too small for his skeleton. All his bones pushed out, as if they were going to tear through.

He screamed.

Fire gurgled through his brain, driven by the strangely familiar smell of hyper-sweet mint. His breasts shrank instantly away. For a moment he knew them as Taelin's breasts. He felt them with Taelin's hands. Taelin's long dark hair was in his face. He moved to brush it aside; then it was gone. All of it was gone.

His bones ripped through his skin, erupting from elbow, knee; the tips of his fingers exploded and his finger bones poked free. The skin of his feet bunched up around his ankles like threadbare socks that had finally given out. He screamed and his scream was never-ending. He was a pincushion of bloody bones, a punctuation mark of agony. His ribs broke and unfolded. They pierced upward through his chest.

He lost wind and heard his own scream fading into the abyss.

Sena's voice filled his ear. "We'll get through this. Knock three times on my door." Then she was gone and he was alone in the dark—with his uncle.

"Where did she go?" Nathaniel asked.

"I don't know."

"She's cunning. You shouldn't trust her. Tell me where she went."

"I don't know."

"Fool. She's going to kill you. To save herself, she's going to drain you dry. Now tell me where she went."

"I don't know."

"Get up here, Caliph."

Caliph's body had shrunk. He was small now, only a child, and his bones had readjusted. He wasn't a mess anymore. The pain had faded into powerful discomfort. He climbed from the darkness up onto a stool built just for him and looked across a high laboratory table at his uncle. Nathaniel smiled unpleasantly and used a medical probe to poke Caliph in the chest. "What do you think of that, eh?"

Caliph winced but didn't talk back.

"That's shuwt tincture," said Nathaniel. "It hits you like a hammer, doesn't it?" He grinned.

Caliph didn't know what to say.

"You can't speak," said Nathaniel, "because you're not really here. You're six years old." Caliph looked across the disheartening scene on the table. There was a dissection tray between them with a small creature lying on its back. Nathaniel handed him a forceps.

"Where did she go?"

"I don't know," said Caliph. Then he realized his mouth hadn't moved. He was thinking the answer . . . not really talking.

"Fine," said Nathaniel. "We'll find her. Now pick up a cotton ball."

Caliph obeyed. He remembered this. He remembered doing this exactly. He had been here before, when he was young.

"Clean up that bit of mess there," Nathaniel snapped.

From the other side of the table Nathaniel basked in the silvery, wooden light that poured in from the backyard. Huge windows like display cases for insects cut up vignettes of branches and sky. The trees looked distorted through hundred-year-old glass.

Nathaniel's hair floated above his forehead as he drew Caliph's attention back. "Pay attention boy, help me open it up—see how they move?"

Caliph set down the forceps and used his fingers to hold back the sticky warm flaps of skin while Nathaniel placed a narrow reed into the rodent's mouth. He inflated the tiny pink lungs with his own breath. The thing was still alive. Caliph watched its heart, no bigger than his thumbnail, pulse slowly under an anesthetic spell.

"It makes you wonder, doesn't it?" Nathaniel said. "What's the point?" He stabbed a probe into the rodent's brain; the legs twitched twice and the heart wound down. His uncle laughed. "Useless," he said.

Caliph let the flaps of skin close over the broken toy. He felt like crying but he didn't. He was not in charge of his body. He felt his stubby legs climb hurriedly down the stool. His heart was racing. He was running out of the laboratory, just as he had done when he was six.

"That's what she's going to do to you!" Nathaniel called out to him, laughing.

Caliph ran away.

The hallway outside his uncle's laboratory was wide and tall. As he ran, the strip of carpet down the center began to hiss. Parts of it came up and tumbled around his feet. The hallway grew taller and taller as he ran toward his bedroom door. The carpet got deeper. There were tumbling shapes around his legs. Leaves.

Fallen leaves rattled and crunched around his shoes as he ran. The ceiling disappeared into a partly sunny sky. He was surrounded by trees.

Caliph's legs lengthened. He strode up to his bedroom door, which was no longer his bedroom door, and lifted his knuckles. He scowled. Hesitantly, he knocked: *three times.*

The door had a rounded top and a small leaded glass window. The blue paint covering its solid construction was cracked but clean. The door belonged to a cottage surrounded by orange and red leaves. Some of the leaves made leathery noises at his feet. The cottage's wooden shingles released a drizzle of water that missed him by inches. He looked up. White skies punched with blue indicated the weather was clearing. Sunlight set the trees on fire like entire books of matches. He inhaled and smiled. It smelled like rain.

The door swung open. Its motion sucked one of the leaves across the threshold with a swirl that brought it to rest against the stiletto heel of a fine black boot. His eyes moved up from silver toes to faded dungarees to chic cashmere. Sena smiled at him like a bolt of lightning.

"You came!" she said as if surprised.

He felt sheepish. "Yeah, I didn't have . . . I mean," he shrugged, "I wanted to see you." He remembered her handwriting, unpretty and boyish. An envelope, an invitation, had come to his box. Or had it? Had this happened before? *Wait, I thought I took the train . . .*

"Come in." She stepped back and let him walk into the cottage. The smell of sweet mint enfolded him. He recognized it as the smell of the liquid he had drunk.

"How was the trip from Desdae?" she asked.

"Good. I took the Vaubacour Line from Maiden Heart to Crow's Eye." He felt her fingers stroke the back of his head.

"I'm surprised they let you go."

"Who?"

"Your secret guards."

Oh, yes. My secret guards . . .

The memory arrived so quickly that it felt fabricated. "I snuck out through the attic," he said. "After dark."

"Clever boy." Her smile flexed around the words. "What can I get you?"

"Something to drink," he said. "That's quite a climb." He sat down at her kitchen table even though he didn't feel tired. The small heavy trestle that supported him was gray and gashed from tools.

"Five thousand feet, give or take," she said as she opened the icebox. She pulled out a jar of dark cloudy liquid and poured him half a glass. "Loring tea," she explained, then filled it with ice, sugar and heavy cream exactly as he liked.

She set it in front of him. He said thank you. She smiled and turned to wipe off the countertop.

He lifted the drink and noticed a shape in the middle of her table. A red dark shadow more than a book. He felt as if he should have been surprised. "My uncle's book."

"If you say so." She sat down across from him.

"What do you mean by that?"

"It hasn't been his in a long time."

"You're right," he said.

He downed the whole glass of tea. He was incredibly thirsty. Sun from the windows hit pans and kettles hanging overhead, reflecting burning copper pools into the kitchen's depths. Sena leveled her eyes at him. "I need to tell you something. But we can't let him hear. You have to keep it secret. No matter what happens. You can't repeat what I'm going to say."

Caliph's attention riveted to her eyes. "What?"

"I'm pregnant."

"What?" It was like an echo.

There was a timing problem. When had this happened? But he felt reflexively warm inside. He choked slightly. Then smiled. The smile spread. He saw it mirrored on her face, a slow but definite upwelling of happiness that pushed both corners of her lips up. And the issues of when and how . . . where this had happened . . . all faded into dull unimportant doubts. He was overjoyed. This meant they were together. For real. They had a future.

Caliph had wanted this for so long.

Maybe it was foolish to interpret this as some kind of cement that would hold them together, keep her from disappearing, but he did. Somehow this made everything official.

He leapt from his seat and moved around the table to sit beside her. The fashionably cut cashmere obscured her waist. He began to suspect what it was hiding. But no. He put his hand under the delicate wool, against the smooth warmth of her belly. There was no sign. He looked at her face, confused, but her smile didn't waver.

"It's too early," she whispered. "I've been holding her for you. It's a girl."

"Holding her?" He felt like they were talking in a church.

"We can do that." Her voice was barely audible even in the small area of the kitchen. "Hjolk-trull can do that."

Caliph grappled with the possibilities of what she was saying. How could it be? Her organs became cryptic and mysterious. He had no idea if this was really possible. He remembered her eyes ghosted with clurichaun fire, full of playfulness. Had it happened then? He was still disoriented with respect to time.

She was touching his neck. "What should we name her?"

Caliph's mind was empty of girl names. He tried to think. What would she want him to choose? Maybe he should suggest naming it after her. No. He had a better idea. "We could name her after your mother."

Sena's mouth plucked with delight. "My mother?"

"Why not?" said Caliph. "She had a beautiful name."

"Aislinn," Sena whispered in his ear.

"Aislinn."

There was a knock at the door. Caliph scowled and got up to answer it.

"Caliph—"

But he had already opened it. And there it stood, black and stooped, already reaching into the house. Something in a robe almost. Caliph smelled that familiar old-man smell. It trickled into everything, insinuating itself through the cottage like dust or smoke.

Its hand reached out and rested on the top of his skull.

The past intruded on the present. It sickened him, swirling like a bowl of his own vomit, stinking in front of his face. He tried to shut the door but it was too late. Nathaniel had already come inside.

Caliph turned to look at Sena. She had apologetic eyes. Why? This was *his* fault. He had opened the door.

He felt the cottage change back into his bedroom. He felt the math of his uncle's house again, the air of that place—twenty years ago—it had bent his bones. It had modified his skull, crushed his eyes into hard skeptical wedges. And it was doing it again. He was squeezed down, out of adulthood, back into his six-year-old frame. He was back in the house on Isca Hill.

Vaguely, Caliph felt himself lying on his back; he could almost hear Dr. Baufent trying to rouse him. But that place was far away. His teeth were pestles, grinding on the fabric of the dream. They could not cut through. He could not wake up. He could not remember what Sena had done, for which he was supposed to be angry and repulsed.

Sena's cottage disappeared. She was calling to him but her words were quickly fading away. Replacing them was his uncle's voice. It demanded that he show himself.

"Stay with me," said Sena.

Caliph sat up. He was covered with ashes from lying in the fireplace. This was where he had played hide-and-seek with his imaginary friends.

Uncle had raged at him for tracking ashes across the carpets. He knew he was supposed to come out when his uncle called, but he stayed where he was.

The fireplace was galaxy-black. Caliph got to his feet, standing among the deep pornographic carvings that his uncle had commissioned from Niloran stonecutters. His blood bubbled, his face felt like it had been coated in hot honey. Inside him, there was thunder. He was angry at his uncle. It felt like his skeleton might shake apart.

"Caliph!" his uncle called.

But Caliph stayed hidden, ashamed that he wasn't brave enough to come out. He had never been brave. When he played at dolls with the girls down the lane, the boys from the nearest farmhouse had called him names. They pushed him so hard into the road that he wound up with gravel in his hands. After the boys left, the girls kissed his scratches and gave him phantom tea and medicine, but eventually they forgot him, called away by parents that didn't like them playing with the boy from Isca Hill. Caliph was ostracized because of his uncle.

"Caliph!" Nathaniel's voice had reached fury.

He felt Sena's hand tug gently on his fingers. Somehow she was in the fireplace with him. Small, just like him. "I'm not one of those girls," she said. "I'm not going to leave you."

Caliph pushed her up against the carvings, smelling sweet mint. She laughed and held his wrists. "Shh—he'll find us."

Caliph looked out into his bedroom. His uncle was standing right there in front of the hearth, eyes like spider bellies, staring right through him.

It was impossible that Nathaniel couldn't see them. But this *was* a dream.

"If you say so," she whispered.

"What did you give me to drink?"

Sena put his hands on the bones of her pelvis, the muscles of her lower back. She looked at him seriously.

"Shuwt tincture," she said. "So that you can follow me."

He wanted to follow her. He wanted to protect her . . . and the baby . . . from his uncle, from everything wrong with the world.

He looked over his shoulder. The old man's eyes were still on him. He decided he had to come out.

"You don't have to do that," she said.

"Yes I do."

"You can't tell him what I told you."

"I won't. I promise."

He left her among the carvings and stepped out into the room. The instant he did, his uncle's voice grew calmer.

"Caliph. There you are. Don't you listen to that little witch. She's going to get you into trouble."

Caliph looked fearfully toward the fireplace but Sena was not there. He wondered where she had gone.

Nathaniel reached out and took hold of Caliph. He lifted him off the floor. Caliph felt the heat of his uncle's hands, as if there was fever in them. Nathaniel sat down next to the bed and put Caliph in his lap. The lights were low. Caliph felt himself ease into the soft warm pocket between his uncle's arm and belly. Nathaniel rocked him with an oaken creak. The chair moved reassuringly, measuring the increments of minutes, a kind of grinding percussion to accompany the sadness of birds beyond the window.

"When I was young," Nathaniel's voice began softly, entreating and persuasive, "my half-brother and I went hunting."

The bedtime story had begun. Nathaniel's hands became finger-legs that trudged slowly over the landscape of Caliph's lap. "One evening we stopped at the top of a hill," his finger-legs stopped, "and watched the ducks rise out of the marsh." The old man made quacking sounds. "We had bead guns. And we got them ready." Noises of glassy ammunition clicking into chambers. "We aimed carefully. And then we fired!" Nathaniel made zipping sounds through his teeth and his two hands became both the ducks in flight and the glass beads speeding toward them." One duck fell and landed in a shadow of Nathaniel's robe. "Then," he said, "we walked down into the marsh and looked for it. We walked up and down in the reeds, up and down in the grass, up and down. Up and down. But we never found it . . ."

The mystery was too much for Caliph's young head and he dared to ask, "Where did it go?"

Nathaniel's fingers spread like those of a street magician who had just vanished a card. "I don't know. We never found it. That's what she's going to do to you, Caliph. Pay attention. Or you're going to disappear. You're going to disappear and never be found."

The old man's voice was positively chilling.

"Now off to bed. You understand?" He set Caliph on the floor and patted his butt. "And remember. Don't you listen to her. Don't you follow her. Don't look for her. Because you'll wind up lost. Forever. Where no one can find you."

Caliph swallowed hard as he climbed into bed. When he laid down, he imagined himself cut open on a table with his uncle blowing into his lungs with a reed. "Useless," said Nathaniel. Then his uncle thrust a steel probe down into Caliph's chest. It went all the way through. Caliph could taste the metal, like the duralumin zeppelin beam that had killed him.

He woke with a start, breathing strenuously.

But the dream seemed never-ending. His bed swallowed him like a rumpled white ocean. Nathaniel was gone and the trees outside the huge warped window were barren and black and the sky was gold with morning. He looked at his hands in the light and they were small.

I'll build a kite this morning, he heard himself think—but it was not him. He was still a stowaway in his own skull. Eavesdropping. *A kite big enough to carry me away from here.*

Then a hand touched him from behind. He jumped with surprise and fear but arms encircled him. He turned, and in turning was enveloped by the shadow of her neck, the sweet toasty smell of her lotus-pink hair. Her blue lips kissed him sexually, not as a woman kisses a child. And he wanted her. As a boy wants his first young schoolteacher. She tasted of candy floss. Warm and soft and splendid.

It isn't bad, uncle, he thought angrily. It isn't bad if she makes me fall where I'm never found. *This is it.* He turned into her carnival of colors. *I've found it, uncle. I've found it.*

The duck landed here.

CHAPTER 27

The fall from Sandren had lasted over a minute. Then the four witches had leveled off and landed in the blue-green coils of a vast wind-shaken grassland north and east of Seatk'r, a mile beyond the point where the ghetto's fingers of glittering trash flowed like artificial effluence down the foothills' morning-shadowed ravines.

This was the story Caliph heard. He remembered none of it. The *Odalisque* and the *Bulotecus* had both descended for the pick-up. Caliph had been unresponsive. As the flagship of the Iscan Crown, the *Bulotecus* maintained a tiny room packed with medical necessities. Caliph had been put on a stretcher and hauled on board. Taelin too, had been ferried over from the *Odalisque* for treatment. Even Miriam had been stitched up.

Crews were shuffled. Dr. Baufent had come over to the *Bulotecus.* She attended to Caliph personally. She had administered first aid, but Caliph had come out of his daze under his own power. Even when Caliph pressed her, Baufent denied having given him any kind of tincture.

"No, I did not," she had said. "What do you mean a tincture?" Caliph's insistent questions had put her on the defensive. "I don't even know what a tincture would be. I can assure you I have no idea what you are talking about."

He had asked about Sena.

"No. Miss Iilool was certainly never here. I think she would have been arrested the moment she set one foot on this ship.

"No she didn't give me any tincture for you to drink. King Howl, look at me." She had shined a chemiostatic light into his eyes.

"You're delirious. You've been hallucinating."

ISHAM Wade and Mr. Veech looked at the four witches with deep skepticism while Anselm and Baufent held their opinions like clipboards, close to their chests.

Caliph's head was still foggy but he clung to the moment as best he could, trying to pay sedulous attention. His head was still swimming with echoes of dreams, visions . . . hallucinations? He didn't know what to call them.

All the ranking members of the crew had been gathered on the *Bulotecus'* rear deck. When they weren't staring at the witches, they were staring at him.

They think I'm losing it.

Among the noteworthies were the physicians, the airship captain, Sig and the Iycestokians—Whom Caliph had not been able to justify keeping locked up. Lady Rae was asleep in one of the staterooms.

The *Bulotecus* had moored in Seatk'r.

That much Caliph knew for sure.

"I really must demand a private audience," Mr. Wade hissed in Caliph's ear. Meanwhile the witches were explaining Alani's death.

"—so he died from wounds . . . sustained from the creature that was attacking King Howl," Miriam summed up.

The story attained a certain level of credence based mostly on the fact that Caliph was still alive. Caliph had little choice other than to believe the account. He could remember nothing about the actual event.

Since the government of Seatk'r was being uncooperative, the *Odalisque* climbed back to Sandren. It scouted the area. The monsters in the city seemed to have slunk off. The *Odalisque* retrieved what bodies had not been eaten and returned to report. The Pplarian airship, it seemed, was still in Sandren, waiting for the High King.

I don't like it, Alani would have said. Caliph could almost hear the spymaster whisper in his ear. Baufent had yet to examine the body and confirm cause of death.

The spymaster's death was a great black anvil that crushed through all of Caliph's other crises and sat dead center; immovable.

It kept going through his head over and over, *how can Alani be dead?*

"Your majesty. We *need* to talk," whispered Mr. Wade.

"Listen! I will meet with you when I am . . . when it is appropriate," said Caliph. "And right now it is *not* appropriate."

The crowd hushed at his outburst.

Mr. Wade's meaty face was flushed, probably with anger. Caliph didn't care.

He turned to the witches and gestured curtly for them to continue. Miriam started talking but all Caliph could think was, *What is wrong with my head?*

"I'm sorry to interrupt," said Mr. Veech, "but we arrived late. What were your names?"

The witches reintroduced themselves.

Each of them was improbably attractive and athletic, as if selected from a beauty pageant: Anjelique Breckenshire, Gina Dingo and Autumn Solburner. Miriam Yeats seemed to be their leader. All of them had thin scars around their necks as if they had survived an attack with piano wire.

Caliph felt cold but Autumn's voice interrupted his thoughts. She was an erogenic copper-headed saucebox with bizarre black accents dyed into her hair. "Of course you can trust us. We saved your king's life."

Had someone asked a question? *I need to focus!* Caliph thought. *Mother of Emolus my head hurts.*

"Here are the facts," said Caliph, turning to the witches. "We were attacked on the twelfth by your organization, over Miṛayhr. We lost good men and women that night." Caliph saw a glance pass between Autumn and Miriam.

Miriam looked at Caliph calmly. "Your ship was attacked in an effort to prevent the thing that happened this morning—from happening. All those people in all those zeppelins didn't have to die. We're after Sena Iilool, just like you are."

The words cut Caliph deeply because the witches' actions seemed supportable. Was it true? Had he been on the wrong side? Had the attack on his airships by the Shrạdnæ Sisterhood been justified?

Everyone on the rear deck knew that the four women had leapt from Sandren, falling on some mathematical parachute of wind. They had risked themselves to save Caliph's life.

"You know it's true," said Miriam. "The only people you lost that night were the people that stood between Sena and our operatives. She lost the book that night."

Isham Wade perked up.

"Yes," said Caliph. "Thankfully it's safe." Caliph noticed how Mr. Wade's eyes settled on him from behind his thick lenses.

Miriam scowled. She seemed to wait a moment and gauge what game he was playing. After a moment she narrowed her eyes and said, "Yes. But now we need to stop her. I believe you feel the same way, don't you King Howl?"

"Yes. Yes I do."

He did feel that way. But what he wanted more than anything was for Alani's face to reappear, refrain from smiling as it always did and offer the essential wisdom he needed to navigate this truce with the Shrạdnæ witches.

The scars around their throats were circumstantial at best but he had his suspicions. Despite all that, like it or not, Miriam was right. Sena *had* to be stopped. And how was he supposed to do that without real holomorphic power on his side? He needed them.

Caliph bounced his hand in the air to underscore his agreement. "We'll go after her. Together."

He turned to the captain. "Any word from Seatk'r?"

"None, your majesty." The captain's son hovered in his father's shadow, listening intently to everything going on. Specks' little armband ticked and a drop of blood hit the floor.

Caliph turned his thoughts back to the patients and physicians that had vanished from the tent hospital.

Many of them had managed to escape the flawless, as Miriam called the monsters. The surviving Stonehavians had fled down the teagle system into Seatk'r—an event that had gone unnoticed in the chaotic aftermath of what could only be termed *the erasure of the conference.*

"I can't believe they won't let the *Odalisque* moor," said Dr. Anselm.

The government of Seatk'r wanted nothing to do with the Stonehavian airships, a fact that complicated the situation with the doctors and patients that had used the teagle system and were now stranded on the ground.

"Here's what we're going to do," said Caliph. "Tell the *Odalisque* to come in. It's going pick up the remaining patients and ferry them back to Stonehold along with anyone who doesn't need to go after Sena. I assume that will be most everyone."

"They're not going to let us moor," said the captain.

"Oh, they will," said Caliph. "Seatk'r's run by little more than a robber baron. He won't get in our way. Not today."

He turned to the captain and his few soldiers and gave them instructions. Then he, along with two bodyguards and Miriam Yeats took the lift down to the ground.

The ride was tense. This was in strict violation of the local government's orders. They were supposed to be leaving, not disembarking.

As the cage opened Caliph was immediately accosted by six ragged-looking policemen from the ghetto's ethically questionable municipality.

"You not allowed to get off," one of them barked. His Trade was rough.

Caliph smiled broadly and walked up to the man, clearly the group's leader based on the blue armband. "I understand. Can I talk to you for a minute?"

"We have orders. We don't harbor you here."

His use of *harbor* was chilling.

Caliph imagined the news hitting Mirạyhr first, then Pandragor.

Information about what had happened would spread quickly to Wardale, Waythloo, Greymoor and Iycestoke. Airships were already coming. Caliph didn't know from where. But he knew his vessels were the targets. It would happen soon.

He kept smiling.

"I know, I know." He raised his palms. "But," he tried to get a word in edgewise against the man's complaints, "but just . . . can we please step over here? Yes, this way. Thank you. I just want a quick word. That's all."

"We don't harbor you," the man said again. He was dirty. Poor. Clearly he took his responsibilities seriously.

"I understand. But I have people that need medical attention. We just need to pick them up. Then we will go."

"No. You don't moor here. You must go now."

"We want to go now. We just need to pick up our friends. They came down on the gondolas. They're right across the street there." He gestured to the motley crowd gathered in the grass-striped shade of a large tree whose bark was worn shiny and covered with paint, presumably from loitering gangs. Doctors and patients peered across the street at him, looking anxious. They had been corralled by other policemen. Some of the patients were still on wheeled beds. Desperation and fear glistened on their faces. That they had not been taken to a proper jail told volumes about the way Seatk'r functioned.

"No. You don't get off you ship."

"I'm already off my ship. Can I please go talk to them?"

"Absolutely not."

"All right, look, I have money."

"No, no, no, no, no . . ."

"I can pay you."

"Get back on you ship. Now!" The nose of the policeman's bing-gun rose slightly. Caliph was unarmed. "All right." He lifted his hands slightly. "All right, look. Will you just look at them? They need help. They're hurt."

"I don't care. Get on you ship."

"Okay, I'm getting on my ship. You see it up there? Yes?"

"Yes. Go up."

"You see it?"

"Yes."

"You see the guns?"

The policeman stopped. His pale blue eyes registered the slender shapes shadowing the *Bulotecus*'s undercarriage. They were moving. Aiming at his men. A *bewildered* fear filled his face. How could he have missed them? That must have been what was running through his head. He opened his mouth and started to scream at his fellows.

Caliph reached out and gripped the muzzle of the weapon. He pushed it up just as it popped like a champagne cork, right between his fingers. Men were screaming. Caliph's other arm swung over the back of the officer's neck, pulling him in tight, face to chest.

"Call them off! Call them off!" said Caliph.

The man was yelling in Ilek, which Caliph recognized but couldn't understand. Caliph's chest, however, had the undesirable effect of muffling the man's voice.

From the *Bulotecus,* Caliph heard the gun turrets adjusting. He looked up. The cannons were aimed.

"Call them off!" Caliph shouted.

The man screamed in Ilek again, repeating something over and over. Caliph watched the policemen pause. They saw the cannons. Their terror was obvious. They dropped their weapons on the ground.

"All right, you're going to let go of this." Caliph tugged on the bing-gun. The officer let go.

Caliph snapped the weapon away. The officer stood up, hair and lapels rumpled. He looked angry and frightened, eyes darting between Caliph and the *Bulotecus.*

"It's all right. They're not going to fire. We just want our friends. Tell them to come over."

Overhead, the *Odalisque* was motoring into position.

Things started running smoothly. The airship docked, the lift came down and people from the ground started boarding. Those on beds went first. Meanwhile the crews got sorted.

Based on the likely fact that warships were now coming for him, Caliph wanted to send the patients toward Stonehold on the slightly faster *Odalisque.* The more heavily armed *Bulotecus,* though not the ideal chase ship, would at least give him a fighting chance if he was engaged while pursuing Sena.

A mysterious set of polarized emotions went through him. Love. Disillusionment. Hard toxic lust left over from the dream. Longing and anger. He stuffed them.

The ships were loaded, the crews were ready and the situation on the ground was deteriorating. More municipal forces showed up just as Caliph ordered both ships to depart.

The *Odalisque* carried most of the physicians—Dr. Anselm included—the patients and some of his remaining soldiers. Its sleek dark shape turned north, heading for home.

Caliph felt a strange twinge at its departure. It had been Sena's ship, built for her. It was going to Stonehold. He didn't know exactly what that represented. Maybe nothing. All he knew was that he didn't know where he was going or what Sena was doing, or whether his goal of surviving the summer was still achievable.

Dr. Baufent, despite her protest, had been assigned to the *Bulotecus.* She stood fuming only a moment on the port deck, watching the *Odalisque* leave. Then, in a businesslike manner, she said, "I'd better go check on Lady Rae."

The plan was to deliver the priestess to Pandragor at the earliest convenience. She had been through enough and after raiding the medical chests like an addict, Caliph was worried she would quickly turn into a liability. Best case scenario was that she might serve as some kind of peace offering.

Sig had stayed by choice, Wade and Veech also. The Iycestokians' decision seemed odd at first but in reality what else could they do? Mr. Wade could either sail to Isca or he could stay in Seatk'r and risk his treatment with the enraged municipality.

Caliph went over the new crew list that the copilot had just put into his hand.

After checking it, he stood on the deck for a while, watching his ship climb the Ghalla cliffs for what he hoped would be the final time.

Sandren's copper domes and terra-cotta walls welled up over the shade-raked stones, glowing in the intense torrent of sunlight. And there, above the city-state, the white Pplarian ship still hovered, exactly where they had left it.

The pilot adjusted and the *Bulotecus* powered toward it. Caliph saw Sena's ship nose forward, easing away from them.

As he expected, she wasn't running.

She was leading him.

Where?

CHAPTER 28

The wind was cold and Caliph didn't suppose this would end soon. He went to his stateroom for his coat before returning to the deck. From there he watched the ship buck up around the great horns of the Ghalla Peaks and ride southward over the precipices, surfing a waterfall of clouds.

The vertigo spun Caliph's head like a top as he stared into the incomprehensible and ancient beauty of the south for the first time.

The Valley of Nifol was shaped like a grain scoop. It flared out to the east reaching nearly a hundred miles broad before its smooth green ribs dried against the arid jumble of Tibiũn: the Stonelands. As the valley passed the choke point of the Ghalla Peaks, it funneled westward, dropping into the depths of the Great Cloud Rift.

Sixteen leagues across and two hundred long, the Rift separated north from south. Nifol flowed into the Rift, a mighty green river of vegetation that cascaded over the ruinous floor of Nũrak Din[21].

To the west, Caliph could see the Valley of Nifol's misty extremities, where Sandren's orchards and vineyards and farms soaked in the moisture that drained into the canyon. A pang went through Caliph that he could not stop to greet one farmer in particular.

The realization made him pat his side. A small lump in the pocket of his coat. He felt a pit in his stomach as he pulled it out. His birthday present. The little wooden figurine of him, the girl perched on his shoulders. He flipped it over, read the words.

No.

It had been a dream. Sitting across from her in that little kitchen. But the carving now burned like ice in his fingers. He stroked the smooth wooden facets made by Cameron's knife. Obviously Sena had told Cameron what to carve. He swallowed and put it back into his pocket.

It wasn't true. It couldn't be true.

[21] G.L.L.: Great Cloud Rift, literally the Crack of the Devourer.

He refused to believe her anatomy would allow such a thing. *It was a fever dream. I was sick.*

He looked over the railing, against the icy wind and down into the misty peaceful-looking land where he hoped Cameron now lived quietly with his wife in the Valley of Nifol—preferably oblivious to the crisis that had just seized the world.

West of the *Bulotecus,* Caliph could see the yawning entrance to the Great Cloud Rift. Vast storms boiled there, rich empyrean thunderheads boomed faint and watery across the sky. It was one of the most incredible vistas he had seen and it was interrupted by Mr. Wade.

"King Howl, we need to talk."

Caliph turned to see the man squeeze his eyes shut and sprinkle the insides of his glasses with unemotional tears.

"I know," said Caliph.

"Yes. It *is* about time. We need to discuss, *vigorously,* what you're doing right now and whether it's the right course of action! There are a dozen leaderless countries at the moment."

"What do *you* think we should do?"

Isham Wade sputtered a bit. "One might suppose she's leading us into a trap!" His tone bordered on a screech. "Why else would she wait for us? Chasing her is lunacy! If you wait for the Iycestokian forces to show up—"

"There are Iycestokian forces on their way? How would you know that?"

"I'm telling you they're on their way."

Caliph's eyes scanned Isham. He had some device, some southern holomorphy that let him communicate. Isham Wade didn't need birds to send messages, did he? Caliph hated him.

"You see," said Mr. Wade, raising a meaty finger with a jeweled ring—there were little gears in the ring, moving, keeping time, "right now, and I mean no disrespect, but this is all highly suspect. And while one might think she's leading us into a trap, I for one don't think so. She was waiting for *you,* see? And you are following *her.* This doesn't look like you're chasing her down," he emphasized. "It looks more like a coordinated escape."

Caliph couldn't believe his ears. "Are you serious? You *saw* what happened! If I'm . . . If *we're* trying to escape what the fuck was I doing back in Sandren? You think I couldn't have planned that better? Why would I let a pack of Shrạdnæ witches board my ship? Better yet, why in Emolus' name would Sena need to board a Pplarian ship? Why not just stay here with me?"

"If she were here it would make it rather difficult to hide a conspiracy from me," Isham said patly.

Caliph wanted to scream. *If I had planned this, none of my people would be dead right now and* you *most certainly would be,* he thought.

Mr. Wade remained diplomatic. "I'm not accusing you—"

"Oh, yes you are," said Caliph.

"I'm only telling you what I think would be in your best political interest: to wait for the Iycestokian forces."

"Well I'm telling *you* what I think is in the best interest of everyone still alive," said Caliph. The edge in his tone seemed to put Mr. Veech, in particular, on edge. Veech, the bodyguard, was tall and lean with a head like a paint can. A thin sandy bowl cut draped the corners of his eminent skull and seemed to press down on the dark festering scowl that pressurized his face.

"Well I think you might be . . . disturbed at the moment," Wade said, backing away. "And Iycestoke won't stand for this. You're abusing an official diplomat, you know? You're holding me hostage." He turned and, with Mr. Veech in tow, retreated from the deck.

"You chose to be here!" Caliph called after him. "Twice!"

He was so sick of this. A bird had been sent—and good thing. The Council would be reinstated, at least until he got back. For now he was glad to be out here in the cold wind. No more tax reports. No more sniveling, pretentious burgomasters. No more pollution. No more diplomacy with motherfucking tyrants he'd rather punch in the throat than accept another gift from. No more crime reports, threat assessments, late-night populist chicanery. No more sycophants and traitors. No more newspapers and journalists with their endless chronicles detailing the snares and booby traps he'd failed to avoid.

Ahead, the great Tebesh Plateau—which supported the Six Kingdoms—spread like the edge of a lime torte. Its magnificent strata swept west, piling up, layer on layer, two miles deep.

As the *Bulotecus* plowed toward it, the dew-frosted valley of Nifol pulled up into mighty walls. A lake glimmered through miles of silver haze and then, against a great buffet of wind, they were over it, powering south, the lip of the plateau passing just underneath them, falling away.

The new landscape, a lemon-limey karoo crusted with flowers and gravelly gray rock, supported spiky plants for which Caliph had no name. It felt like they were skimming the ground. Clouds were sparse and great mud towers built by glass ants fingered the sky. The weather was instantly warmer and Caliph took off his coat. Lace-winged flies began gathering on the railing, on the cables, hovering in the shadow of the gasbags, tails looped in mating.

Miles to the south, amid nearly flawless skies, Sena's ship maintained its lead. It was clearly faster than the *Bulotecus*. Still he had to try, didn't he? He felt responsible for what had happened at Sandren. He had to arrest her. That sounded preposterous. If she had obliterated all those zeppelins what could he do against her? He had the witches on his side. Hopefully that counted for something.

If Sena's ship got within firing distance he would aim for the gasbags; try to bring it down. Then the witches could help apprehend her. He would question her personally. Or not. That might be too much of a breach. Maybe the police . . . maybe it would have to be an international inquiry, formulated with Isham Wade.

Caliph tried to remember whether Sena had spoken when the fleet of zeppelins had gone up in brown mist. Would gagging her work? If she couldn't speak, maybe her holomorphy would be dammed. He tried to imagine his men wrestling her to the ground, snapping on shackles, forcing a ball into her mouth. He tried to imagine her conviction, her sentence, her tongue cut out. Afterward they would put her to death.

Why had she done this? Why was this happening? He looked around but the deck was still empty.

The witches had retired to their quarters. Sig was probably alone, getting drunk or perhaps already in a medicated coma—like Lady Rae.

Caliph went back to his stateroom, dreading but knowing what he needed to do. He shut the door and locked it. He hung his coat up and noticed Taelin's necklace still hanging in the closet. He took it down and put it in his pocket. He would return it to her before they dropped her off. The pair of books Sena had left him sat on a narrow shelf. He pulled them down. They had become important. His only clue to the madness she had unleashed today. He opened up the windows, turned on all the lights, consciously gathering as much brightness around him as he could for what was sure to be an openmouthed plunge into darkness.

Time is meaningless
—these notes from my 173rd tincture journey

The correct tense has eluded me to the waste of half a dozen sheets. Writer of Time, indeed! I have now decided to settle on the past, in the interest of clarity, and describe this tincture journey as if all that I arranged during its course *had* already happened.

First, let me say that I took this road because of failure. The platinum wires I crafted for my desert queen did not work. The ones that overlay my arms and head in the jungle may be equally insufficient. I tried them one last time with Nathaniel before moving to white ink. His suicide was proof positive that everything had failed—again.

Because of the failure of the wires, to conduct the requisite power, I did not even bother darkening the rubies that I entombed with my desert queen. They remain beneath the rotten orange crags that dwindle into nothing and cleave the Valley of Dust from the deserts to the west. Her eyes are still scarlet and in her day, the stones I used, were worth a thousand white slaves.

But I digress.

With Arkhyn I did draw blood and numbers down into the corundum and the gems I wired to my skull turned black. I will not discuss the particulars of my extant odds of success or how exactly I shall attempt to ensure fruition.

That is not the point of this entry.

The point of this entry is to outline clearly, to my successor in these matters, that I do not intend to fail, and that I have made arrangements.

To wit, I returned to Isca City in the shoes of a solitary man who was not Nathaniel Howl but rather his contemporary; a man whose long shadow and admirable wealth managed to charm the bourgeoisie.

This man, Mr. Dei, was indeed a foreigner. What he lacked in official paperwork, he made up for with charisma and eccentricity by the yard.

Within his shoes, I bought the church.

The *Herald* covered the acquisition and noted the history of the building, along with my "unusual" plans for its restoration. It did this on page twelve in an article exactly two hundred twenty-two words long. Once the restoration was complete, I let the loan lapse, Mr. Dei returned to his country and both he and St. Remora passed once more into obscurity.

The dials I installed connected to cables that snaked down through the chapel's entrails, into the basement and out through the foundations into several of the most probable dimensions.

That is a joke, by the way. No, I don't expect you to laugh.

Actually I am quite certain of my figures. The dials have been calibrated. The cables that connect them to other worlds will carry the sound of their ticking. In other words, once my shade . . . or rather, when *I* have gone walking, I shall be able to *hear* them despite the fact I will have no ears. They will resonate with my pneuma and call me back under a variety of conditions.

The church itself will be my nose, my eyes, my ears and fingers when I will have none. It will tell me when the time is right.

It will also be my mouth.

This is the unfortunate part of the contingency; one that I am not pleased to be initiating, but alas, the tinctures have caught up with me and I was forced to make a choice: use what few journeys I had left to try and find a replacement (hardly certain) or create the machine that would allow me some measure of power at the end of time.

I chose the latter.

Once I have gone walking, I will have no mouth. I will have no blood. Already I am bloodless, baking rotten in the jungle's heat. A perfect algorithm and the grume of every bird or mammal that passes overhead cannot hold this form together another year. The jungle will have its way.

So I will go walking, in far places.

I will leave the stink that has gotten into my skin, my hair. But St. Remora will call me back when the time is right.

I used many journeys to find the correct building. In alternate timelines my granddaughter examined the empty shell of Teapetal Wax, an old factory in Growl Mort, an elementary school on the corner of Grindosh and Bane. But eventually I found it—St. Remora—the one that *she* would buy.

She will also find my gold in the box I sent to Pandragor, while I dragged my servants to the jungle. She will carry it for me, while I will lack hands. The church will know of her arrival.

My successor has been chosen, though they will not call her my successor. They will call her Sslîạ, Deliverer, and say I was a fraud. But it will be my numbers that she will use to slip through. It will be my plans she confiscates from diverse libraries and vaults. She will find the way. She will not use wires or jewels because They will give her the set They never gave to me.

I have foreseen it. I am still a Writer and Eater of Time. Yet Their logic eludes me. Why have They chosen her instead of me?

Because she is Hjolk-trull? Because They wish to toy with idle irony. Perhaps They laugh in Their dreaming cities in the dark; perhaps They think she will kill herself making the ink.

She will lack the blood to do so.

Perhaps They laugh at the happenstance arrangements of the patterns, of the movements and relationships of men. She will love him. She will kill him for the ink. They could never have wrung such a catastrophe from me.

I care only for my daughter.

The book will tell me of my successor's arrival. I have put my mark on its pages. When she opens it, I will know.

Yes, you. You: SIENÆ IILOOL.

I see your cunning face.

They will write Their runes in your skin and for a time you will try to fight against those strictly metered designs—clabbered in their loveliness. But I know, in the end, you will find them too gluey, too consolidated to work against. The runes will trace your every movement. Your every action will be known to Them. You will give in. And then, my dear, I will return from my far wanderings. I will bargain with you for my daughter's release.

By the time you read this, it will be too late for you. You may think you can escape without me, but you will be wrong. You will find it in the math. Look. Take all the time you want. You may think I am powerless now. I have no mouth to speak, no blood to draw. But you are wrong.

St. Remora is my mouth.

I can open it. There is an eleventh dial that connects with Them, down below the church, in a womb of vesicated black. It is the trigger of my weapon, my postlude, my ultimatum. Do not tempt me with its use.

On my whim, I can draw the Old Thing out, a Sectua'Gaunt[22] still ravenous for souls. When it births into the church, its first thought will kill a hundred thousand people. Its second will kill a hundred thousand more. Souls.

Do you think solvitriol technology was dreamt by man? Invention is reinvention, finding the path that has been found uncounted times before. *They* are the dreamers, the inventers of solvitriol technology, not us.

[22] U.T.: [illegible].

1600 S.K./537 Y.o.T. Moons
—N.H.

I have inherited a diaper-dragging brat along with the house. While it would be convenient in some regards for him to become permanently lost in the mountain woods and thus join his relatives, I have determined that he is a remarkable creature. His father was at least part Hjolk-trull. This means, if nothing else, he is the serendipitous second ingredient (since Gringlings are extinct) for ũlian ink! Sad news that we cannot pen the other sheets yet. I am, however, able to begin on the stopping point of our escape, our own little island in the stars—which won't have to pass the same touchstone as the others. In the meantime, I feed him like a little tick; once he's swollen with a few more pints he'll be a fabulous capsule!

(undated loose page)

She cannot dig me out! She cannot ignore me.

I am the one who installed the eleven dials in the church! *I* am the one who cut the ruby bottles and turned them black! *I* fitted the house on Isca Hill with her windows shining bright! Your lovely trat did nothing but find the book in a bin on March Street! She is going to show you these pages. Do you not think I *knew* how all of this would turn out? What? AM I NOT A GOD?

I am the one who found Næn'ũln! *I* am the one who hunted the jungles for it endlessly, who bent numbers around it so that it could be *moved*! *I* am the one who painstakingly prepared years of notations, filling the margins of the *Gymrẹ Tạ*[23] with enough instruction that a drooling retard could have discovered the truth! She is no prodigy! *I* fucking made her!

I have been here from the beginning! Not her! I! Me! All of me! In every pathetic fibrous cyst I endured! Me! Who once wept for my lost humanity but now laughs at the stupidity of attempting to . . . For the sake of what!?

What!

I found the book. *I* found the ink! *I* have done everything. And now? To be relegated finally to the role of watcher? While she proceeds with *Their* blessing?

I despise you. All of you. And you will not escape without me.

[23] Another pseudonym for the unnamed book (the *Cịsrym Tạ*). *Gymrẹ Tạ* means book of war.

I have laid it into the foundations. You cannot extricate yourself from ME! In the end, I will encompass you and devour you. And you will dissolve slowly across a billion years.

I have fit myself with jewels and darkened them to the moment, bound them to me as I did in the desert. Only this time: this time it will be different.

Caliph,

I know this has been hard for you to read. He was never your uncle. You wonder why I gave you these books. You wonder what I did at Sandren and why. I know you. You will figure this out.

—Sena

THERE was a knock on the door which was good because Caliph felt sick and hollow and dark inside. He couldn't take any more. He closed the book, pushed himself out of his chair and crossed the room. When he opened the door he was surprised to see the priestess of Nenuln standing there looking better—physically.

He was less surprised to see that she also seemed to be lacking a sense of humor. Her face was pale with terror and Caliph was just about to open his mouth and ask what was wrong when she blurted out, "What in Palan's name are you reading?"

CHAPTER 29

Sena saw across time. The thing before her was from the sea and it reminded her of Tenwinds.

Pplarian bioengineering, the nautrogienilus with its shell—so like patinated steel—was framed perfectly by the room's striking white iridescence. It formed a brutish pelagic curl that had been bolted to the floor.

Other echoes of Pplarian shape-crafting had spilled out of the north, squirmed through careless fingers and floor drains into subregions of evolution. They cropped up again in the wild, emerging from bogs and silent tarns.

The monsters.

Smell-feasts, ganglolian and other slippery masses. But this thing with its shell and mollusk flesh, its rich briny stink, took her back to Tenwinds in a visceral and unexpected way.

She could smell the oily ocean, taste the salt again and the fishy wetness that spluttered endlessly. And memories of Tenwinds meant memories of Aislinn.

It was because she had been so strong that the one instance of her crying forever echoed in Sena's head.

The moments had crystallized. It was as if she was still there. She could replay the sequence endlessly: remember Aislinn dragging her toward docks cobbled out of stone and oxidized metal plates found long ago above the salt flats, where some goliath machine had been cannibalized.

Eerie, alien-looking apertures not quite suitable for human frames had been reinvented as arches beneath the wharf. Remnants of odd markings and irregular rivets still rusted across vast sections of tramontane metal. A bolt the size of a rowboat rested on its side above the piers. Scavenged a hundred years ago from something now covered over, it had long been the symbol of Greenwick Harbor.

The boards by the ocean were slippery and dark, anchored to the ancient perversion of metal and crusted with whitening barnacles. Spidery orange thewick crabs scuttled helter-skelter.

Aislinn's cold hand gripped Sena by the elbow. Sena remembered the feel of her arm flapping over her head like a flag as her mother pulled her toward smells mixed by waves.

Back in the center of the village, the clock tower glowed; its illuminated face displayed the hours the two of them had been *charitably* allowed. Now Aislinn sought passage to the mainland while the town growled, no longer welcoming with its shops of cinnamon and fish.

Tenwinds' courtrooms had debarred Sena but they had swallowed her mother. For endless hours—for days it seemed—Sena had been sequestered in hallways where squares of light inched over walls devoid of decoration. She had listened to solemn adult voices seep under doors until the droning had put her to sleep, head on her doll, alone on the hardwood floors.

Now, as her mother marched her down to the docks, her strongest memories were of Shamgar Wichser, the somber-faced admiral-mayor whose shadow emphasized the question mark of her father's body dangling in Tenwinds' square.

The coast was wintry. The pebbles crowned in ice. Out of season for a trip to the mainland.

She could feel the fear pouring out of her mother's palm as cold sweat, a clammy toxin Sena absorbed through the skin. It made her six-year-old heart bang like a caged finch.

Together, they boarded a long dark shape lit with rows of golden lights floating in the harbor. Its iron sails snapped. Smoke retched into thin icy air. Her nose felt like a lump of clay. She looked back at her home as the vessel pulled away. The sodden gray buildings seemed to share her sadness; sparse leafless trees clutched the sinking sun like a bright fruit, a gift if only she would come back.

Sena never went back. Her mother took her to Mirạyhr.

What Sena brought with of her father was his curly blond hair and an infectious smile. "The spitting image," her mother always said. For a while, Sena still sang the nonsense song, "Daddy, Daddy I love you. Like an oyster-oyster I do-do-do." But days and weeks choked it slowly until the melody disappeared.

Aislinn's name sounded cold, like one of those olden cities gone beneath the Loor. But even though her voice often matched the temperature of her name, Sena loved her. At least until they reached the mainland.

There, love was something the Sisterhood snipped into usable squares. The Sisterhood patched itself with love conscripted from its members: to bolster the organization, to control its enemies, to bait, seduce and kill.

At Skellum, Sena drew pictures in class of her mother and her, holding hands. She wrote in large inept letters above their circle-smiling heads, *Mamma and Me.* But when the preceptress discovered the drawings, Sena received seven lashes with a ruler across the wrist.

"You do not love your mother. You love the Sisterhood."

Seven strokes across the wrist and when Sena cried: one across the lips. It had happened several times.

Sena slowly realized that none of the other girls had mothers. They slept in the nursery under the watchful eye of an Ascendant. But that difference between herself and the other girls ended when the Coven Mother, Megan, ordered Sena from Aislinn's care. It was necessary, Megan said, for Sena to focus on her studies.

Sena was a good pupil despite—or perhaps *because* of her anger.

She learned quickly to recognize weakness. She was instructed vigorously in the arts of sex, manipulation and murder. All this, the Coven Mother claimed, was necessary for strengthening the Houses. For preparation of *the war.*

"What is *the war*?" Sena asked her mother one day while sharing a rare lunch on Parliament's lawn. They had taken off their shoes and Sena had just realized that they had identical toes.

"Shh—" Her mother's eyes had scanned the lawn without any movement of her head. "There is no war. Megan thinks it's our business to protect the world from myths. She takes it far too seriously."

"But aren't you friends with Megan?"

"I try to be, baby-girl. But you know, we're here because we have no place else to go. And never tell anyone that. That's just between you and me."

"I won't, Mamma."

In the end there were no bonds strong enough, not even between mother and daughter, to prevent the Sisterhood's relentless training from tearing them apart. And finally, at long last, Sena realized that she hated her mother for bringing them both to Miṛayhr: a dichotomy that ever after haunted her when Aislinn was found guilty of fårọn—the betrayal—and sent to Jụyn Hêl to burn.

And so . . .

Following in her mother's footsteps, Sena had looked for companionship outside the Circles of Ascension, beyond Houses One through Eight. She had not done it out of desire for love (because love's stuffing and toy-sized springs had been broken long ago) but out of rebellion. Out of hatred for the Sisterhood, she had warmed Tynan's bed. And Caliph's.

* * *

SHE looked at the double keel shell lined with tubercles that reminded her so vividly of a shattered childhood by the sea. The shell's silver-indigo curves of gleaming carbonate had been anchored to the floor. Thick bolts held it upside down, foot in the air, diaphanous pink tentacles flailing like a bed of leeches. It was very much alive. The tentacles looked inexpressibly soft. Yet parlous.

Sena came to it naked with her hair pinned up. *The hair on your neck is fine as a gosling,* Nathaniel whispered.

She ignored him and straightaway eased into the pudding of tentacles, leaning forward until she lay on her stomach, fully cupped in their gentle tossing motion.

The sensation was pleasant and strange as the watery pink arms oozed over her chest, abdomen and thighs.

Are you proud of yourself for evading me? What did you tell him while you were alone in the tincture?

To help block him out, Sena thought about the Pplarians who knew the road before her. They had come down from the sky, stranded here eons ago. Put here, they said, as a punishment. They knew about the Yịllo'tharnah. The Pebella of the Pplar had heard the rumors out of Stonehold, like everybody else. Unlike everybody else, the Pebella put stock in those rumors and had invited Sena to the Pplar for an audience.

When she had seen the markings on Sena's skin the Pebella had tasked a group of Pplarians already in Isca City with the construction of the temple on Incense Street.

Why?

Not because they worshiped her. The Veydens worshiped her. The Lua'grọc worshiped her in their horrible outlandish way. But the Pplarians? The Pplarians felt sorry for her. They had seen this bargain made before. The Yịllo'tharnah rising from sleep, seducing Their "chosen one" with the not-quite-promise of freedom, the tantalizing false hope of escape.

The Pplarians had assured her of this: that the way was false, that the Yịllo'tharnah had never failed to catch Their prey after the prey had foolishly set Them free.

"You are in a trap," the Pebella had told her. Yũl and the rest had vigorously agreed. "It is better not to free Them. You will fail as every other Sslîạ has. Under Their power, your ambit will be broken, the Lua'grọc will have their sacrament of flesh and the Abominations will entomb your soul."

"But I have the Gringling's notes," Sena had said.

To which the Pebella had answered nothing but told her servants, "Give the Sslîạ what help she needs."

The temple had been built, the colligation begun. Sena would not give up. She would not relent. She would fight until the end.

Yũl had brought the nautrogienilus and the airship from the Pplar. The Pebella was not on board. Her presence had been a ruse, orchestrated to coincide with the gathering at Sandren.

The airship was not for Sena's comfort. What it provided was something rational for Caliph to pursue. Caliph could not see Sena, therefore the vessel was now essentially the same as her. Caliph would follow it relentlessly, under the assumption that she was aboard. Even while she left and did other things, the Pplarian ship would draw the High King relentlessly into the south. This was part of her plan.

You're taking him to Ooil-Üauth? Nathaniel asked. *Why? It's pointless. It's extraneous to the fabrication of the ink. You don't need the altar . . .*

Her thoughts had slipped out. He had heard her. She scolded herself frantically but on the surface remained calm. "Extraneous, is it? Then why did *you* drive your servants through the jungle? Why did *you* tell them to build your house there? If I am going to do this, I am going to do it right. I am going to follow the steps. And if you don't like it—"

Fine! Nathaniel raged. He cursed her with ugly slurs.

As Sena lay in the bed of pink tentacles, Yũl came into the room. Yũl could not see the thing that haunted her but one of his eyebrows lifted slightly, a betrayal of his thoughts that despite his foreign preferences, Sena reminded him of an alien pinup, posing on a pink anemone.

The nautrogienilus' foot supported her weight while its arms arched over her back. Its tentacles flexed, tips brushing her shoulder blades. Sena did not close her eyes as the first arm slipped into her skin.

"Do you need anything?" Yũl asked.

"No."

Yũl lowered his hairless head and left the room.

The tentacles pierced her because she allowed it. She controlled it. All the arms moved in orchestra, slicing precisely. She could have done this herself but the creature provided her with the fortuity of conservation.

The beast needed few holojoules to guide.

Each microscopic mouth chewed with surgical skill. She did not bleed as the first corner came up, tugged gently by a single arm. The meat beneath her skin was paler than pink, it was nearly white and shining. Fine radiant filaments stretched between the integument and a deeper glow of tissue. There were several layers. She did not enjoy it. She set her teeth. But this was necessary. Nothing else would endure the trip. Her skin embodied perfection at an atomic level—just like Caliph's blood. Therefore, like his blood, it would last.

The melon-colored blush of chewing organs took no notice of her thoughts. They moved rhythmically, until finally she shut her eyes.

The nautrogienilus finished its methodical work, having avulsed a perfect square. It held the thin slab of flesh aloft, dangling from tubiform arms.

Sena stood up. A field of light, evocative of the backswept membranes of a damselfly, streamed from the corresponding breach between her shoulder blades. The excised area was surreal in its perfection, as if drafted by an architect. Its upper edge ran level with her shoulders, its bottom chined the center of her back. She had directed the nautrogienilus to remove a quadrate from the only location on her body that would accommodate a flawless, unmarked sheet. It was the only part of her, of the necessary size, where the platinum designs never crossed. As if this span of skin had been prepared for exactly this purpose, planned in by the Entities who had gifted her with immortality.

The Pplarians said it was part of the deception, that she was following exactly where others had gone before.

To that, Sena had not argued but said simply, "I have to try." She was different. This would be different. Her plan would see her through.

The skin taken from her back covered more or less thoracic vertebrae three through seven, representing seven inches top to bottom and a perfect tenth of her frame's full height. There was a beauty to the numbers and the ratios.

The tiny mouths on the tips of the tentacles gobbled at the underside of her dermis but Sena whisked it away. As she held the slice of her back, seven inches by seven inches seemed an extraordinary span.

With broad angles of light still gushing from her, she placed the specimen on an oval tray. The room around her was an ooidal pocket punctured by blue-gazing duct-like portholes. Cool air slugged in. The walls, floor and ceiling all blended into one and moved in gentle ensemble. Most of the equipment in the room, the trays, racks and shelves, were living or once-living dentin.

A three-foot fibril sprouted from a workbench like the feeler of a white roach. It bent under the weight of a citrus-blue berry of light that quivered at its tip. Under the luminary, Sena carefully separated her skin, like layers in an onion. It did not resemble human flesh and came apart easily into three distinct strata, each identical in size and appearance. She placed each of the three squares in a separate tray and began pinning down their edges. While she worked, the room expanded and contracted around her, gently, almost imperceptibly, as if breathing.

Yũl came back into the room. This time he ignored her unclothed body and offered a polite greeting in White Tongue having to do with the moon.

Though it was midafternoon, Naobi's face cratered the sky through one of the pore-like windows.

"Moon's greeting." She smiled faintly.

The Pplarian wore a red kash. He approached and extended both of his usable hands. Sena paused what she was doing and allowed him to press his fingers and thumbs into her palms and wrists, a ceremonial two-handed exchange that she accepted without question.

"The temple has been closed," he said. "The colligation is complete."

She had already seen it with her eyes, the gates being pulled shut, the sign being installed, the chain taking its padlock in the dark and snowy cold.

Nevertheless she thanked him and her words were sincere. Knowing what the Pplarians had done for her only enhanced her sense of gratitude. The Pplarians owed her nothing, yet they had performed this service with strange munificence. Where they would go, what they would try to do on their own and whether they would succeed or be destroyed like the rest of the world was a mystery that remained beyond Sena's knowledge. The Pebella of the Pplar was powerful and her ambit kept the fate of her people hidden.

Sena adjusted her skin over one of the trays' thick wax bottoms. She placed an additional pin, then looked back at Yũl. "Thank you for coming this far. I get lonely."

Yũl smacked his lips and craned his long neck to port like an albino tortoise without a shell. He peered through one of the windows at the *Odalisque* with his fuchsia eyes as if trying to see the High King. Finally he said, "I am sure your math is correct. Have you set the course?"

"Yes." She looked through the intervening walls—unlike Yũl—across the sky to where she could actually see Caliph talking with Taelin.

Yũl inclined his head slightly in calm obeisance. He seemed calm. But she saw through the tight kash. His vestigial hands groped from caterpillar-sized arms and cupped his nipples. He pinched himself anxiously.

"You should go," she told him.

He bowed, grinned brokenly and excused himself. As he neared the exit the muscular valve-like flap of the door opened and trembled around him. Yũl squeezed his papillae fiercely and said, "The Pebella is never wrong."

Sena offered him a thoughtful scowl and nodded her head. Then he was gone and the valve snicked shut behind him.

CHAPTER 30

How did you know I was reading?" Caliph asked.

Taelin didn't like the way his eyes scoured her face. Like he was searching for a lie.

"I don't know," she said. "I felt sick. And . . . I just knew. I know that sounds crazy but I feel like I'm inside your head. I want it to go away."

The High King's eyes panned nervously. "I uhm . . . are you sure you're all right? Does Dr. Baufent know you're up?"

"Of course," Taelin lied.

Caliph smiled uncomfortably. "Okay. Well then, why don't we go get something eat?"

She said yes with her hand.

Her father was dead. That was what kept going through her head as she followed Caliph Howl toward the starboard deck. He held the door for her, which made her angry for hard-to-pin-down reasons.

Walking through the doorway, out of the controlled atmosphere, was like walking into another world. A familiar, warm-scented world full of wormwood and spider flower and the smell of tea trees on the wind. Taelin realized that they had left Sandren far behind. She remembered raiding the medical chest but it was almost like a dream. Dreams were dreams. She didn't bring it up.

Miles away, she could see the three lichen-colored hills, staggered in a perfect row. They formed the backdrop of her hometown of Kub Ish.

Was the plague there too?

She tried not to think about it and looked briefly at the silt flats: another unmistakable feature of the landscape, as if a giant pail full of mud had been thrown to the south.

Strangely, she didn't feel like running elatedly to the railing for a better view. She wasn't homesick.

"Do you want to sit down?" Caliph asked.

She smiled thinly and pulled up one of the deck chairs. It was warm wood, set bowed in a light metal frame, supported with springs that adjusted comfortably beneath her. It was the kind of chair she imagined she could sit in all night. She pulled her feet up off the floor.

Caliph Howl started with a resolved but quiet, almost apologetic tone. "Look. I know I already apologized back in Sandren for everything that's happened. But then . . . even more things happened.

"I feel responsible for you because you're the only one here that . . . *(damn right you're responsible—my father is dead!)* and I don't want you to take this the wrong way . . . but you're the only one that doesn't *belong* here. *(I hate you, King Howl. You are an evil deluded man at the head of an evil and deluded nation. I wish you were dead.)*

"You belong somewhere other than entangled in the political mess of this ship." *(Is that some kind of veiled insult?)*

Taelin felt a hot-cool mixture of emotions as his words flowed around her.

"So you want to apologize?" she asked. "But you don't want to tell me about what you were reading?" She smelled a freshly lit cigarette from the direction of the kitchen. When she glanced toward the source she saw Specks floating in the shadow of the door. For a moment it appalled her. She thought that Specks was smoking. Then she realized it was steam rising from a cup in his hand. The smell of smoke must have come from someone else. Specks' eyes looked at her curiously, a kind of placid infatuation. He was not embarrassed that she had caught him staring.

"I was reading some books that Sena gave me," Caliph said.

Taelin looked back at the High King. "So this is related to my grandfather—"

"Apparently yes. But please. Let's talk about you for a minute."

"You want to get rid of me?"

His eyes begged for understanding. "I'm not trying to get rid of you. I just don't think you belong on this ship. So far I haven't guessed a single thing right and I don't know what's going to happen to us. But if something bad happens to us, I don't want you to be here."

"I see."

Caliph cleared his throat. "I have it from a reliable source that you're from around here." He swept his arm at the landscape beyond the railing. "I'd like to take you home. From there you can either return to your mission home in Isca or stay in the south and let Stonehold fix its own problems. What do you say?"

"I don't want to go home." She could feel the cool clammy possibilities of evening rain. Wild, colorful clouds smutched the sky like brushfire smoke. The smell from the kitchen had woken a hunger inside her. She wanted a cigarette.

Caliph scowled at her faintly. "Why don't you want to go home?"

"My father is dead." She felt her face flush but pushed back against it, trying to focus on the cool wind and the tinkling sounds above her head.

"You're sure he was on the Pandragonian ship in Sandren?"

"Yes." She was on the edge of sobbing.

"I'm sorry. I . . . *(You're not sorry. I hate you. I hate you and you should die.)* If he was, I mean if he was on that ship, then your family's going to need you."

"No they're not! They loathe me. I'm a *huge* disappointment!" Why she told him this truth was beyond her. It fell out of her mouth, an admission jarred loose by the emotional tremor going through her; it seemed to shatter on the floor.

The string of colored lights above the table lit up. While their soft tinkling was pleasant, she found their bright colors at odds with her mood. In a double punch, the food arrived, smelling delicious. Specks had gone into the kitchen for the tray. He served them with an ill-hidden smile of self-satisfaction. "I brought your dinner," he said.

Taelin felt angry at the setting. Furious that the little lights and warm food could go on sparkling and steaming and celebrating in spite of her. But she also felt touched by Specks' smile. He was clearly proud to be serving them their food. "Thank you, Specks," Taelin said. His pale, slender face beamed.

"I doubt you're a disappointment," Caliph said. Then he looked at Specks and winced at the lights. He leaned forward and whispered in the child's ear.

"They're fine," interjected Taelin. "We could use some cheer . . . don't you think?"

Caliph paused. "Well, it's not that I don't appreciate the crew trying to make things comfortable but . . . don't you think it's out of context considering what just happened? We're *not* on holiday."

Taelin looked at the floating boy who was clearly waiting, uncomfortably, wondering what he should do. She felt embarrassed for him, angry at Caliph, angry at herself, as if her own disapproval had somehow tainted the High King's thoughts and precipitated this reprimand. Looking shaken, Specks said to Caliph, "I'll turn them off right away, your majesty."

"No!" Taelin said. "Please, leave them on! I can't bear thinking about what's happened today. I just—just leave them on."

Caliph smiled uncomfortably and pulled his napkin into his lap. "She wants them on," he said. He fanned his fingers.

In response, Specks offered a submissive shy look. He bowed and then promptly drifted toward the kitchen, armband ticking.

"That poor child," Taelin said.

"Yes. He's a good boy. He lost his mother—"

"I know."

Caliph resumed his previous line. "Anyway, I'm sure your family would be relieved to have you back."

Taelin had been slipping down in her chair; now she scooted her butt back, trying to sit up straight. "No, they won't. You don't understand."

"Are you willing to explain it to me?"

"Not really."

Caliph blew a sigh. "Well, I'm afraid you're going to have to give me something. Because otherwise I'm going to drop you off at the nearest town." *(You callous, selfish, horrible—)*

"I see. You're going throw me off?"

"This isn't political. *(Bullshit)* Yes, I'm guilty of planning all sorts of ways to use you to my advantage with regards to your father's government." *Why did he call it that?* she wondered. *Her father's government?* "Right now I'm talking about your safety," he said.

"I'm not getting off this ship."

"Why?"

"It was an arranged marriage!" she blurted out. She couldn't help it. "And I know you won't understand, but I wasn't rebelling. It was supposed to be a gift from my parents to me. I wanted it."

She locked her arm straight up and down in front of her, knuckles buried in her lap, face hidden partly in the hollow of her shoulder. She wanted to hide. "There was a baby. The wedding was called off."

Caliph looked stricken, confused. "I'm sorry," he said. "I—" He didn't know what to say. Clearly. Clearly he had no idea where this outburst had come from, why she was telling him this seemingly unrelated thing. Wasn't it obvious?

"I can't go home," she said tearfully. "They don't want me. They gave me money to go away. Don't you see? I don't have anywhere else to go." She reached immediately for her wineglass and drained it. Her whole mouth puckered. Then she risked a look at Caliph's face. His expression didn't read as apathetic. He wasn't rolling his eyes or looking evasively toward the floor.

"What happened?" Caliph asked.

She sniffed. "After the wedding was called off I spent my days down at the park, at the library. Thank you." She took the napkin he handed her and wiped her nose. "There was a statue there of Emperor Vog. His widow came every day and just sat there, in her dead husband's shadow, feeding the birds, moving when the sun changed. We talked."

"Then you had the baby?"

"Yes. My parents pressured me into leaving it with Aviv. Which I did. But he was Despche. And it wasn't political, you know, to be with one of the slavers . . . no matter how rich his family was."

"Do you keep in—"

"No," she interjected fiercely, then softened. "No, I haven't spoken to Aviv since the birth. His family owned an archipelago, so he probably went there. I stayed at the hospital after the delivery. For depression, you know? Nothing serious. When they released me I decided I needed a fresh start. My family practically threw me out the door. I decided to build a church."

"From your grandfather's journals."

"Yes."

The last breathless rays of sunlight blazed an oblique trail through the railing and over the deck, the end of which trailed across the arch of Caliph's boot. She saw his foot flex inside the leather, which probably indicated he was thinking furiously. "I think my church days are over," she said.

"Why?"

"Just a feeling. Nenuln doesn't answer when I pray. Maybe she never did. What if it was all me? Making it up?"

Caliph didn't smile. "A friend of mine, scientific type, says we're constrained by our five senses. Enlightened, he says, but also constrained. He says we're like a blind newt in a cave, doing the only things we can, trusting in the senses we possess. But that there are things out there, beyond the cave, red flowers we will never see or smell. We can only hear stories about them and trust or disbelieve that they are there. I haven't made up my mind about any of that, but I think it's a nice metaphor. I don't blame you for believing in your goddess—whoever she is."

Taelin was stunned. She had hardly expected such a thoughtful reaction to her admission of doubt. "Your friend sounds a bit factious for a scientist. I mean if he's advocating for whatever's out there." She glanced at the sky.

"I think he's a good thinker . . . he's also a good friend. Theories'll change in twenty years where I feel his friendship won't."

Taelin felt her lips screwing into a slow smile. *Why am I making eyes at him!*

"Please," she said. "Please don't take me home. You don't know my family."

"No, I don't."

"Then you won't take me home?"

Caliph gestured to the tinkling strand of lights. "Did I leave the lights on?" He was not a bad person, she decided earnestly. He was a good person who, like many good people, had taken the wrong lover. It was clear to her that he was genuine. He cared about what had happened back at Sandren. She could see the fretfulness, no: the *foreboding* in his face.

"I saw pictures of what you were reading . . . in my head." She plunged into the matter that had brought them to dinner. "I saw your uncle," she pressed her lips together, afraid of sounding crazy, "the horrible things he said to you. And what Sena wrote—that you need to figure something out."

She had to force herself to watch his face. What if he laughed? What if he . . . but his face had gone slack. His eyes were wide now and staring at her. It was true. She *had* really been inside his head. She couldn't explain it, but it was there—between them—substantiated and undeniable.

"You have to take me with you," Taelin said. He had gone so pale. Vulnerable almost. "She doesn't love you," Taelin pressed. "It's a trick. Something horrible is going to happen and we have to stop her."

His mouth opened and for a few moments his lower jaw shifted as if he was trying to fit it over an invisible object. He seemed to give up. A potentially complicated answer never emerged and instead he said, "I know."

Taelin saw him as a boy with a new puppy in a sack. The sack's neck was knotted; it was weighted down with rocks. Caliph knew that it had to be done but he didn't want to do it—yet he wasn't going to blubber about it either. Taelin could see that and her heart melted. She wanted to comfort him. She left her chair and crouched beside him, daring to reach out and touch the High King's hand. It was innocent, she told herself.

His fingers were warm and soft. His nails manicured.

"Lady Rae—" *Oh no!* But then he pulled something golden out of his pocket. Something almost glowing. "I picked it up."

It startled her, but not because it represented a sign from her goddess that she was being shamelessly inappropriate. In fact, she didn't even see it as a symbol of Nenuln anymore. It was just a necklace with no special powers other than the sentimental fact that it had belonged to her grandfather. What amazed her was that he had rescued it and kept it for her.

"Oh . . ." she said.

"What?"

"Thank you." She took it from him, then abruptly leaned forward and planted her mouth against his. She almost stopped there. She almost pulled back and left it at that. But she didn't. She pushed her advantage. Kissed him again. Waiting to see if he would resist. When he didn't, when she realized that he had actually begun to kiss her back, her body filled with heat.

It wasn't wrong. The relationship between Caliph Howl and his witch queen was nothing official. It had never been recognized. Never been authorized by any church. No vows, no certificate; it meant nothing.

Thank gods she could still save him.

Her head was buzzing, maybe from the wine. And despite this breach in protocol, her head, her whole body was telling her this was the way to defeat Sena Iilool. She moved up on top of the High King, one leg on either side of his chair. She closed her eyes and smiled as Caliph's lips worked down the side of her neck. She ground herself down hard against him.

It was moments later that he lifted her up off the deck and carried her back to his stateroom.

CHAPTER 31

Taelin woke up the next day pale and wretched. She couldn't believe what she had done or that he had let her. And yet it had been just what she needed. She couldn't help toying with the idea that maybe it could work . . . maybe it could last.

Impossible! She stayed in her room, pacing, staring out the porthole at faint wisps of vapor that passed for clouds, tearing at her fingernails with her teeth.

That was when she noticed the little silver patch on the underside of her wrist. There were two spots actually, directly over the blue shadow of her veins. Nothing to worry about. Right? After all, she had been vaccinated. So had everyone else on the ship. She turned her wrist in the window light. It shimmered beautifully.

Her thoughts went back to Caliph. She didn't remember returning to her room . . . or the details of his room. But she did recall the startling crackle of static as she had pulled his shirt off, discrete electrical ghosts that limned the soft-woven blackness before falling into dark trenches around the bed. Mostly she remembered the feel of the sex.

Her cheeks went through cycles, burning and cooling then burning again. *What am I going to do?*

What if he acts like nothing happened?

There was a knock at her door. She put her face in one hand and closed her eyes. "Who is it?" she called.

A voice said, "Specks. Are you coming to breakfast, Lady Rae?" It was a lilting impersonation of something almost masculine and chivalrous. She had to smile. But then the implications of going to breakfast sank in. A host of possibilities raced through her head. In the end, she decided not going was far riskier than going.

"Yes," she called back. "I'll be right there." *Oh shit!* she thought. Then she looked in the mirror.

"Oh shit!"

She cleaned up, pulled her hair back into a tail and pinned it in place. She rummaged for something light and relaxed to wear.

She left her room.

Refracted morning light played designer, painting different colored stripes across the ceiling; pastel bands led her toward an antiseptic blaze at the end of the hall.

She found her way out onto the zeppelin's port deck where a small crowd of people bantered over breakfast. But it wasn't actually all that jovial. The more she listened the more solemn and uncertain the mood registered. What laughter seeped out echoed in the aluminum railings, affected and strange.

The witches were seated to Caliph's right. She noticed the large shape of Sigmund Dulgensen, sitting in his overalls, and the judgmental glare of Dr. Baufent whose short gray hair spiked in the breeze. Baufent was staring at her.

When Taelin looked at Caliph she thought, *A hello kiss? Certainly not!* She resigned herself to "Good morning."

He smiled at her but gave no special indication that everything was fine. Instead he seemed as preoccupied as ever, scanning the faces around him.

The witches were talking, their glittering eyes full of tiny geometric designs. Taelin looked beyond the railing, at a landscape that had changed magically over night. Orange dunes with serpentine crests harbored pools of shadow. Miles of sand glittered under daybreak as the sun punched east. For a moment, Taelin watched the *Bulotecus'* stretched silhouette passing over the ground.

She looked for Sena's ship and found it. A fleck of white.

It refused a definable shape: in one moment it resembled the pupa of a tremendous insect, then fantastically, a pale tuber. But they were momentary semblances. It shifted, bulbous portions smoothing out, planing into curious banks of gill-like clefts on some albescent batoid, slipping with mercurial swiftness to the next.

"It's only a bitch if they find us," she heard Sigmund say.

"Of course they'll find us," snapped Baufent. Taelin turned around. The physician was digging in a halved citrus with a serrated spoon.

"They might not," said one of the witches. "They don't have towers in the desert."

Notably missing from the group was the Iycestokian diplomat and his bodyguard. Taelin sat down in one of the empty seats, hoping for a reaction from Caliph. His indifference was quickly dragging her into a black spiral of depression.

"Well, at least a breakdown ain't likely," joked Sigmund.

Speak for yourself, Taelin thought.

"Ship's in good working order," he went on, "and we have enough juice to get us quite a ways. I think we're in good shape."

"Will you kindly *shut* up?" said Baufent. She glared at the mechanic. "We are not in good shape, you idiot." She got up and left the deck.

Sigmund scratched the side of his neck and looked sheepish. "Just trying to look on the bright side," he muttered.

Taelin's chair was near but not too near to Caliph. She listened to him talking with the witches—all four of them beautiful and sparkling. They made Taelin feel like a wreck. "Sig's right," Caliph said. "We need to stay positive. If she's headed to Bablemum. That's what? Another five hundred miles, give or take?"

Taelin tried to absorb the conversation about chasing Sena. She tried to feel its importance. But it slipped past her. She wanted to be one of the grown-ups at the table but instead felt like a petulant child. It was the perfect metaphor, really. And why? Why had her life always been like this? No matter where she went, it was always the same.

The captain's baritone nearly shot Taelin out of her seat. "Yes," he said. She hadn't noticed him standing directly behind her, holding his coffee. His other arm was wrapped around his son. Specks held on to his father's waist, resting his head against the captain's body. "No matter what happens, we'll have to dock in Bablemum. Pick up a charge. Get supplies."

One of the witches interjected that they might be able to put a glamour on the ship. Taelin sneered at the proposition of witchcraft but didn't speak.

"I don't think a disguise is going to be enough," muttered Caliph. "You'd have to make us invisible. Think about it. An uncharted ship comes out of the desert? Two days after the disaster at Sandren? Everyone's going to know it's us."

"Sena's will come out first," offered Sigmund. "Then we'll see what happens."

Taelin agreed with that. *Hopefully they shoot her down!* She watched Caliph massage his temples. *What was he thinking about? He had better not be thinking about Sena!* She started hating herself again. She poured a bowl of cereal from a box with bright green berries on its front. She dumped milk over top and stared at the drowning mess, feeling sick.

"Do we have any idea what we're going to do if Sena lets us catch her?" Sigmund asked.

Caliph said, "We need to find out what happened at Sandren and why. That's my first priority."

"Do you really expect her to tell you?" Taelin blurted out.

"Yes," said Caliph, "I do." He put down his napkin and stood up.

"Excuse me. Please enjoy your breakfast." He wrangled through the chairs to the doorway and disappeared.

Taelin's face had caught fire but no one seemed to notice.

"We really don't know what we're doing, do we?" Sigmund laughed.

No one shared his sense of humor.

"Actually we do know what we're doing," said one of the witches. "We're going save the world." They too got up and left the table.

"Save the world?" Sigmund chewed the hair under his lip a moment, "Well that's just a little . . ." His voice trailed off.

Taelin excused herself. She hadn't touched her cereal. She pushed past a crewman and found the interior of the ship to be darker, quieter and cooler than the deck. The hum of the propellers resonated, as if the sound—the vibration—were a canvas on which everything else had been painted.

At the ship's primary intersection she looked and found both directions empty. She went to his bedroom and knocked.

No answer.

She tapped lightly again and a door opened behind her. Caliph stepped out into the hallway. "Oh, I was just . . ." She smiled, pointing at his door.

He smiled back at her, genial but clearly confused. "What?"

"I was just," she tried to get her balance, "did you switch rooms?"

Caliph's head cocked slightly as the mystery for him seemed to deepen. After a pause he said, "*This* is my room."

"Oh. Uh . . . I must have gotten turned around." She laughed nervously. "I could have sworn you dragged me into this one last night." She pointed at the other door with her eyes.

"What?"

Oh, my gods! Is this my worst nightmare? "Last night?" Her voice was fragile, unsure, cracking even as the words left her mouth.

"What about last night?"

"Are you serious? I should have known."

"Known what?"

"Known you'd do this after you got what you wanted."

"Lady Rae, I didn't get anything. I don't know what you're talking about."

"You son of a bitch!" Taelin turned and ran. She couldn't think of anything else to do. Behind her, Caliph was calling out with what almost passed for real concern. "Lady Rae! Wait!"

"THEY'LL get over it." Gina's black eyes sparkled with carvings.

"There must still be some residue of cells in the High King's head," said Anjie.

Miriam nodded. "Which won't last more than another hour, I think." She was speaking in Withil, as were the others. They had overheard the High King arguing with Taelin; now they were gathered in the small room the four of them had been given to share.

"It would have gotten worse if you hadn't taken it out," said Autumn. "It could still get worse."

"I don't think it will," said Miriam. She snapped the tiny bones and membrane in her fist: the miniature symphysis that had allowed her to eavesdrop on the High King's memories. "The puslet was sick when I took it out. Even if there are residual cells in Caliph Howl's head, they won't survive long. When they die, the link between the king and the priestess will be severed and hopefully they won't have anything more to fight about." As she broke the symphysis in her fist, she thought about her own shattered eardrum. In felt symbolic. Her pool of assets was shrinking. Her ability to gather information had atrophied. Her tools were breaking, shutting down. She had lost two sisters in Sandren, possibly five—if she ever discovered Duanna's fate.

She felt her own callowness in the role of Sororal Head. Should she abort, go back to Skellum? Enlist another qloin? Or should she persist in following Sena despite the losses she had sustained? Though her decision to chase Sena had already been made, she still wondered whether it was the right thing to do.

She hadn't told anyone except Autumn that she was completely deaf in her left ear since the flawless' attack in Sandren. And she hadn't told anyone, even Autumn, how the puslet had really died. All she had said was that she had taken it out, that the information coming from it had turned to drivel—and that it had been *sick*.

It had been very sick indeed.

"What did you do with it?" asked Gina.

Miriam let her irritation slip out. "I put my full weight on it. Against the starboard deck. Then I scraped it up and flung it over the side."

"I was just asking. It's an expensive piece of equipment to let bake."

"We don't need the puslet anymore," said Miriam. "We know Caliph Howl is sincere. He's going after Sena. That's all that matters." But in her head, Miriam had serious doubts. She had heard Sena talking in Caliph's head as the puslet died; had worried as the new Eighth House methodically seduced him. Miriam was grateful for the High King's pragmatic nature and the way he had stuffed those incredibly weighty emotions. But she still knew Sena was meddling.

There were other things she didn't know.

She didn't know how Sena had gotten inside Caliph's head, or precisely what Sena had used to kill the puslet. Clearly she had used poison, but what kind, Miriam couldn't be sure. As a sister of the Sixth House she had been schooled in toxins. But the subtle, pleasant-smelling thing in Caliph Howl's system was something she had never encountered in the north.

When Miriam had pulled the puslet out, it had been green. Black and green. She had run a proof to make sure, but yes, it was definitely poisoned.

The question to follow was: how?

How could Sena come and go without being seen? Certainly she was skilled. But all of them were skilled. On top of this, all four sisters, herself included, had cut their eyes. *We have diaglyphs!* Miriam thought. Diaglyphs were supposed to work!

Yet somehow Sena had crept onboard undetected—for the second time. And she had poisoned Caliph Howl with a chemical Miriam had no knowledge of. Sena's use of the poison also indicated a high degree of skill—just enough to destroy the delicate puslet, while Caliph Howl suffered nothing more than a spate of overly vivid dreams.

All of this weighed heavily on Miriam. It was clear that Sena knew about the puslet and that she wanted it out of Caliph's head. Why? What was Sena doing? What did the High King have to do with Sena's plan?

Miriam knew the basics of what Sena might be up to as well as any sister who got beyond the Second House. The Sisterhood's foundations were based on this shadow war with the Wi̩llin Droul. Sena had opened the legendary book that the Wi̩llin Droul had been hunting for hundreds, possibly thousands of years. According to Giganalee the act of opening the book made Sena some kind of deity in the Wi̩llin Droul's eyes, a deity they hated as much as they adored.

Sena's relationship with the book somehow put her in league with the Wi̩llin Droul, whose ambitions—so Giganalee had often said—revolved around the destruction of the world.

It was thus that the Sisterhood had ever been seeking the book, to keep it out of the Wi̩llin Droul's hands. And it was thus that Miriam was troubled deeply by the idea that Sena, whom Giganalee had seemingly inducted into the Eighth House, was now a kind of dark intercessor and champion of the Sisterhood's longtime foes.

If Sena was everything she seemed to be, thought Miriam, how could they hope to defeat her?

"What are you thinking?" asked Autumn.

Miriam shrugged. "I'm thinking we need to stay the course. I don't want anything to jeopardize the rest of this trip. No unnecessary risks."

"In that case I think the priestess is a liability. We should get rid of her," said Autumn. "We know she's not stable. To me it looks like she's cracking."

Miriam knew that Autumn was right. The information that had come through the symphysis showed how unstable the woman had become. But Miriam's rebuke was gentle. "No. If Taelin chokes on a sandwich they'll blame us. Let it go. We're only seven hours from Bablemum now."

"Why is Sena headed for Bablemum?" asked Gina.

"I don't know."

"Do you think she'll really drag us through the jungles?" asked Anjie.

"I don't know."

CHAPTER 32

Taelin sobbed into the soap-smell of her pillow. Her face was hot and sticky. She wanted off the High King's airship.

How could he be so cruel?

Men were always, always, always the same.

She knew this. She had begun learning this when she was thirteen, sitting with one of the hand's sons on her grandmother's east steps. The boy had passed her back the roach. Its coolness burned the back of her throat even now as she remembered his hand moving between her legs.

While she smoked, she watched an army of tiny red bugs swarm from a crack in the foundation of her grandmother's house. They had small soft bodies like drops of jam and held their rear ends in the air as they skittered over the cement, black eyes glistening. The boy's fingers made her feel dirty and clean at the same time. She felt herself shooting across the crisp blue sky and leaned back on her palms, letting her legs open. She stared dazedly up at the blue and white shapes moving overhead.

Eventually the rice paper fell from her trembling hands. The beggary seeds dropped into the dry weeds like tiny coals while her scream released a combination of ecstasy, boredom and anger, like a hot blast of factory vapor aimed straight up. She lay back on the steps laughing. "Thank gods there's no one home!" The fields east of Kub Ish were wide and deep with sugar plants.

"Are you going to touch me?" the boy asked.

"I can't. I'm going to be a priestess someday." She laughed.

His face twisted. He grabbed her by the hair and pushed her head down until her forehead hit the cement steps. Then he got up and walked away. Taelin was still laughing as she pulled out a little tin of beggary seeds with one hand and used her other to touch her scalp. Her fingers came away red. She rolled another cigarette and smiled.

The little tin was in her hand now. She had pulled it from a deep pocket—where she hid it even from herself. With it came the gleaming bottle of poison her father had sent her.

A shadow passed over the stateroom's window and the room darkened. Taelin shoved the tin and the bottle back into her coat. A fist of wind struck the airship, which did not sway the room but produced a litany of sounds. She heard the metal creak. The casing of her window groaned. She heard the hum of cables; the subtle bending of the ship as joists and panels flexed.

Just the wind, she thought.

She pulled the tin out again and rolled a tiny cigarette. She pulled the poison out too and set it on a little table by her bed. It stood upright, like a finger pointing, underscoring the answer to all her problems.

"I can't," she whispered and touched her grandfather's necklace. She had heard an old man's voice, as if fabricated from the airship's low-toned sounds. It told her to *do it.*

Another gust of wind made her cabin creak. Taelin was breathing hard. She checked her watch. She had been crying off and on for two hours when a soft knock sounded at her door.

Hurriedly, she opened the window and fanned the smoke out. "Just a minute," she called. She hid the tin and the bottle and dabbed her eyes. When she answered the knock she found Specks floating in the hallway. "Hi," he said. "Are you okay?"

"I'm fine." Taelin smiled. "Why do you ask?"

"I heard you crying so I brought you a tissue." He held out one crumpled square.

Taelin felt warm embarrassment surge through her. Had everyone on the ship heard her? "Come in, Specks," she said.

Specks floated tentatively past her, scraping against the door frame. "It stinks in here. Blech!" He stuck out his tongue.

"Sorry." She noticed the smoke still hanging near the window.

"I have to help in the kitchen," Specks was saying.

"Oh?"

"The High King is having lunch."

Taelin's hand curled around the bottle in her pocket. "It's a little early for lunch."

"Yeah. But it's a meeting."

"Who is he meeting with?"

Specks shrugged. "Are you crying because we're in the desert?"

Taelin sat down on the edge of her bed. "Now why would I cry about that?" She watched a drop of blood fall from the boy's wrist onto her floor.

Specks made a *mmmhh* sound, then asked for the tissue back. "I'm sorry," he said. He let himself down, legs crumpling, pain crossing through his face.

"It's okay." Taelin moved to help him up. He was already cleaning the blood from the floor. She reached down, lifted him, light as a bag of twigs in her arms. She held him close against her chest, feeling his warmth, his frailty.

His little-boy smell made her think of her missing son.

Specks squirmed. He pushed softly against her shoulders, trying to get away.

"I'm sorry." She let go, once again embarrassed. He floated backward with an apprehensive crinkle around his eyes. "There's blood on your shirt," he said.

"Specks, don't apologize for that. I don't care. You're fine. You're better than fine."

Wind hit the side of the ship and Specks looked toward the open window nervously.

"What's wrong?" Taelin asked.

"I'm not opposed to talk about it."

"Does it have to do with us being in the desert?"

Specks nodded. He reached up and sorted through his thick dark hair. "One of the cooks didn't want to be here."

"Does your dad want to be here?"

Specks shook his head. "A storm's coming. My dad said it's a big one. He says we need to go home where it's safe."

Taelin's eyes went out the window. The sky was bright and clear but the wind was certainly strong. She didn't doubt the captain's instruments or that he might confide in his son.

Caliph Howl was a cruel bastard, using people's lives to advance his own selfish agendas. He had let witches onto the ship. Now a storm was coming. He was endangering his crew. He had murdered her father.

"It's going to be fine, Specks," Taelin said. "Don't you worry."

Specks smiled. "Yeah, I guess. I should go."

"Are you going to serve the High King lunch?"

Specks smiled proudly. "Yes I am."

"Can you take me to the kitchen with you?" asked Taelin. "I need something to drink."

"Sure."

Specks led the way.

The *Bulotecus'* kitchen was a steaming, cramped eggshell-white facility with standing room for four people. Currently, however, there was only one man in the room. The kitchen's ceiling was riddled with pipes. Bolted to the walls were dark chemiostatic coolers with gauges and glowing green cells that revealed the quality of each battery's charge.

Small countertops provided workspace while above and below, anchored to the walls, hung a garbage chute, an oven, several lamps and an array of cutlery. There was also a sink.

On the countertop sat a silver tray loaded with drinks and appetizers. The cook looked up at Taelin and smiled. "Can I get you anything?" he asked.

"Yes," said Taelin. "Thank you. I need something to drink."

The cook opened one of the coolers. When his face disappeared behind the metal door, Taelin leaned forward. She used her body to shield Specks from what her hands were doing. She panicked. *What should I do?* She dumped a little poison into each of the three drinks on the tray. When her bottle was empty she slipped it back into her pocket. She couldn't believe what she had just done.

The cook's face leaned out from behind the cooler door. "Hello?" he said, still smiling.

"What? I'm sorry, I didn't hear you."

"I said we have loring tea. It's the High King's favorite."

"Oh, yes. That would be fine."

The cook brought out a jar and poured her a glass. "Cream? Sugar?"

"No," she said. *Oh gods, what did I do?*

Her body had gone hot and rigid. She was sweating profusely.

"Specks? Can you manage the tray?" asked the cook.

Specks floated forward.

"It looks terribly heavy," said Taelin. "Maybe I should help you."

"I can get it," said Specks.

"Here you go." The cook handed her the glass of tea. Taelin didn't want it. She needed her hands free. She needed to manipulate the situation now, which was rapidly spinning out of control. Specks struggled to lift the heavy tray.

"Specks, I don't think—let me help you, baby."

"I'm not a baby," said Specks. "I can get it."

Taelin reached out to help but the cook fanned his hand. "Please," he said. "You're not allowed to touch the High King's tray."

"Oh, I'm sorry, I just . . ."

"I got it!" Specks almost yelled at her.

"Specks, you're going to drop it—" She moved her body into the tray in an effort to tip it from his hands. The cook grabbed her.

"What are you doing?" he said.

"I'm sorry. I'm not feeling well. I'm sorry. I'm sorry . . ."

Specks floated from the kitchen without saying a word. All his concentration was focused on keeping the tray level in his hands.

* * *

TAELIN went back to her room. She paced frantically, hysterically. *Shit, shit, shit. What have I done?*

She fell into her bed, dizzy, gasping.

When she came up for air, a small girl was standing at the foot of her bed. Taelin yelped in surprise but the child was lovely. Scrumptious as a steaming muffin. All butter and blueberries. The girl smiled. She glowed in the sunshine as she held out a little metal flask, perfectly vertical, shining between her thumb and fingers.

"An angel of Nenuln," Taelin whispered. "You came to poison me. For what I've done."

"No," said the little girl. "This is a sacrament. You need to drink it."

Taelin laughed. She took the tiny flask and flung herself back into her bed. "Thank you. Thank-you-thank-you—"

She unscrewed the cap.

The smell of sugary mint washed over her. She recognized the smell.

"Drink it," said the girl. "You're sick. This will help a little."

Taelin's stomach pitched. Tears flooded her eyes. With trembling fingers she patted her pockets, searching for the demonifuge Caliph had returned to her. *Oh. That's right.* It was around her neck.

She touched it, cool and repellant, bright and golden as a far-off star. It moved under her fingers, stirring softly.

"Nenuln is hungry," said the girl. "She's been sleeping all this time."

Taelin shook her hand fiercely, up and down: yes, yes, yes. She put the metal flask to her lips and drank the shuwt tincture. She felt the demonifuge move against her breasts.

The taste and the sensation made her roll over and put her face in her pillow.

"The witches put a puslet in your head," said the girl. Taelin's face was buried. The girl's voice was changing. "The tincture will burn its residue out. I need you to be clean."

"I want to be clean." Taelin sobbed into her pillow. *I need to be a clean vessel for Nenuln.*

"You will be," said Sena.

"Oh gods." Taelin felt the bed tip beneath her. She rolled off onto the floor. The tincture was working. "Help me," she whimpered. She looked up. Where the blond girl had been standing, instead she saw the High King's witch. Taelin expected a look of wicked amusement on Sena's face but there was none.

Sena crouched down. "I'm sorry," she said. "But you're coming with me. I need your help."

"I'll never help you. You murderer. You—"

"You're a murderer now, Taelin." Sena's words shoved a cold stone down Taelin's throat. Taelin choked on the startling truth. "And you're going to help me."

Then the tincture's dreadful visions washed over her and Taelin felt her body slip away.

CALIPH had summoned Isham Wade to an early lunch. He and Mr. Veech showed up looking rumpled, tired and suspicious. Caliph welcomed them curtly into the *Bulotecus'* small dining room, which was generally used only in cases of bad weather. Indeed, the wind was picking up.

But this was to be a private meeting without the interruption of servers.

The three men sat down.

"And how are you this morning, King Howl?" Isham looked at the table. There was no food.

Just then, the doors opened. A guard held the door for Specks, who floated in holding a tray. Wind shook the windows.

"I'm not well," said Caliph. Beyond the open door were several more armed Stonehavian soldiers, ready to barge in at the slightest disturbance. Caliph saw Isham Wade glance at them nervously.

"I don't feel quite so comfortable on this ship anymore, King Howl." Isham turned back and cleaned his glasses on his shirt.

"Nor do I," said Caliph.

Specks floated up and slid the tray onto the table.

"I believe you're passing information to your country's—to the *Iycestokian* military," Caliph said. "And frankly, Mr. Wade, I'm weighing what I should do with you. Seriously."

Isham's face reddened. "I think I've made it clear to you, King How—"

"I don't really think you appreciate the gravity of your situation," said Caliph.

Mr. Veech stiffened visibly in his chair.

Isham Wade stood up from the table. "I'm sorry, your majesty, but I'm afraid I've lost my appetite." Mr. Veech stood up with him.

"You're not leaving this room until we get some things sorted," said Caliph. He rose and moved with the other two men toward the room's bank of port-facing windows, which allowed diners to sit at the bar and look out at the scenery while they ate. Beyond the large glass panes, the desert slid by and the wind howled.

"Fine," said Mr. Wade. "I have been in communication with my government, but I hardly think that's irregular considering that I am here against my will—"

"Untrue. I gave you the option—"

"Of getting off in Seatk'r," Isham barked. "That's not really an option, is it?"

"You told me there were Iycestokian ships on their way," Caliph said. "They could have picked you up—"

"King Howl, may I ask you a question?"

"Go ahead."

Isham Wade leaned on the bar with both arms. "Do you know why I boarded this ship?"

"I think we both know it had to do with Stonehold's solvitriol capabilities. But I don't think that matters anymore. The only thing that matters now is what happened in Sandren."

Isham blinked his eyes behind his thick lenses. "Actually Iycestoke didn't send me to talk about solvitriol power at all."

Caliph scowled. "Then why?"

"You didn't look at the proposal I gave you?"

Caliph had forgotten all about it. "I gave it to my spymaster."

"I see. And he didn't mention—"

"He didn't mention it because he's dead! He died in Sandren!"

One of the sentries poked his head into the room. Caliph made a sign that everything was fine; the man saluted, hefted his gas-powered crossbow and let the door swing shut.

Caliph noticed that Specks had not left the room. He was sitting down at the table, listening intently to what was going on. "Specks, I'm sorry but can you take the tray back to the kitchen? We're going to skip lunch."

"Yes, your majesty."

Specks lifted the tray and left the room.

When he was gone, Isham Wade scratched his beard thoughtfully. "I'm sorry about your spymaster."

"Get to the point," said Caliph.

Mr. Wade leaned once more on the bar, staring out the windows where the smoking dunes sped by. He drummed the bar with the flats of his fingers. "Did you know I am an expert in Pandragonian relations, King Howl?"

Caliph said nothing. He fixed his eyes on Isham Wade.

"Mm. Indeed I am. Did you know that the Pandragonians are secretly at war with the Shrạdnæ Sisterhood?"

Caliph leaned back and folded his arms. He felt like a cloth was being dragged slowly off a new sculpture and the suspense over what was going to be revealed wasn't the good kind.

"No?" said Wade. He pursed his lips, savoring the moment. "Well they are." He wagged his finger. "I know just about everything that's going on in Pandragor and what."

"I can assure you, you don't want to lose my interest," said Caliph. "I suggest again that you get to the point."

"Actually I think I'm quite safe." Wade's shrewd eyes regarded him. "But anyway, I will get to the point. You know the Pandragonians were involved in your civil war, correct?"

"Of course."

"Well, King Howl. Initially this *was* all about solvitriol power. The Pandragonians wanted their blueprints and the witches wanted their book."

It felt utterly bizarre to Caliph that an understanding existed as to what book Mr. Wade meant. The *Cịsrym Tạ* had only ever been a private element. As other couples might have argued over where to hang an heirloom—which only one side of the family appreciated—so too the book had caused ripples of irritation between Caliph and Sena. It had never really been connected to the whirlwind of governmental affairs. It was not a part of his public life.

"They were working together to bring down the Duchy of Stonehold," said Wade. "With the agreement that each of them would help get the other what they wanted."

"But?"

"But then things went wrong. Some piece of holomorphy that the witches were supposed to hurl at Stonehold was undermined. In the end, the agreement fell apart.

"It's terribly fascinating to us southerners. Normally we don't pay any attention to the north, you know? I shouldn't have said that as a diplomat, but it's true. And then these wild rumors start trickling down to us and what—First that you've intercepted solvitriol blueprints—which *we* were selling to the Pandragonians. Then people are being brought back from the dead. That's new! There's a witch-goddess in Isca. Suddenly we're all *very* interested.

"Regardless of whether any of it is true, you know what it all keeps coming back to? This book. It's the *thing* the Shrạdnæ Sisterhood was after. *Supposedly* it's what brought you back to life—though I admit I have my doubts. And now the Pandragonians want it. That's right. I'm not even sure they know why. Personally I think that if the witches want it, the Pandragonians must just think it's good. And that, King Howl, brings us to why I boarded the *Bulotecus*. Because, if the Pandragonians want it—"

"Iycestoke wants it too," Caliph finished.

Mr. Wade smiled, pudgy cheeks pinched and shining.

"It's ridiculous," said Caliph. "It's just a book." But that was an old line. He felt the book's power now, not as some mysterious holomorphic trapping but as the crux.

Mr. Wade's black eyebrows lifted. "Is it?" he asked, "just a book? Because if it is, then I'm sure we can solve this quickly. We have machines in the south that can turn out copies. Everyone will be able to read it and decide for themselves."

"I see." Caliph didn't know where to go from here. He certainly wasn't going tell Wade that he didn't have the book. Instead he opted for, "I'm sure we can come to an agreement on that. Printing a book is not that difficult. But don't you think we have more important things to decide at the moment? I mean what happened in Sandren—"

"King Howl." Wade's tone took a mildly condescending edge. "What happened in Sandren is the point. You're absolutely right. It was terrifying. It was wonderful. I don't mean to be direct, but here it is: who gives a shit about Sandren? They were an elitist outpost that sold wine at inflated prices.

"They were a fucking city-state. Really." He put his palms together in front of his lips. "What I care about is that that kind of power is harnessed correctly. Legitimately. And by the way, the sickness in Sandren, whatever it is, is spreading. It's in Pandragor. It's in Yorba. Most importantly, it's in Iycestoke. We don't know how. But if you were in my position, wouldn't you find it a bit . . . fortuitous to know that the only people with a vaccine were the people with the book?

"Now listen. You're in a sticky situation. All those zeppelins—vanishing without a trace? I'm not accusing you." Wade raised a palm and patted the air in Caliph's direction. His ring with the moving gears glittered; his eyebrows crawled to the top of his glasses as if genuinely apologetic. "But only ships from Stonehold were spared and again, only Stonehold has the book."

Caliph had gone flaccid. Now he straightened. "I get it. What are you offering in exchange?"

"In exchange, we help you . . . hunt down the individual who misused the book's power, blah blah some justice for the papers. We tell the press that the book has been destroyed or locked up for safekeeping or what. Meanwhile, you keep your copy. Iycestoke its copy. We of course form an alliance—if it turns out that the book is actually useful—and we prevent its dissemination, obviously, to people who want to cause our respective nations harm."

"So, you'll help me hunt down my ex . . ." Mother of Emolus, what did he call her? Even now, he felt like he was betraying her. ". . . mistress. And we'll what? Put her to death?"

"Yes."

"And then I fly home," said Caliph.

"Yes."

"But first, we have to make a copy of the *Cịsrym Tạ*."

"Is that what it's called?" Wade perked up in a way that Caliph found repugnant. "Kiss-ream-tah? What language is that? What does it mean?"

"Am I right?" asked Caliph.

"Yes," said Mr. Wade. "That would be the arrangement."

"Not quite. We forgot the clause about what happens if I say no. Not that I'm going to. I just want to have that out on the table—"

Mr. Wade laughed in high amusement and shook his finger. "I wish I had been ambassador to Stonehold instead of Pandragor these last couple years. Talking plainly? Right? Plain as we can? Iycestoke has the means to fly up over the mountains and take Stonehold in," he stuck out his lower lip, "one? Two days? King Howl, your country exists because we've never had any reason to care about it. But now we do."

Caliph squirmed. "And your forces, the ones coming to intercept me, are going to arrive when?" He glanced at Isham's glittering ring. "How long do I have to make a decision?"

"How long do you need?"

"When are they arriving?"

"They're already here."

CHAPTER 33

Dr. Baufent was working like she had never worked before. Sweat glistened on her face.

"What's wrong with him? What's going on?" The captain of the *Bulotecus* was standing over her shoulder, looking distraught. Caliph had just left his meeting with Isham Wade and had discovered the scene on the port deck. He braced himself in the doorway and looked down on the desperate business at hand.

Specks wasn't floating. His thin body had been carried from the hallway near the kitchen and laid out on the deck where there was more room to work. His shirt had been torn open. Some safety mechanism in the bracer had sensed a change in blood pressure and the tiny holomorphic engine that usually allowed him to levitate had shut itself off. The ticking that always announced Specks' presence had stopped and Caliph felt the silence.

Specks had long needed a haircut. His dark hair tossed around his eyes in the wind but his eyelids did not flinch. His skin was paler than usual and his mouth was slack and open.

"What happened?" asked Caliph.

"I don't know," said the cook. "One minute he was fine. The next, he'd floated into a cabinet and banged his head."

Caliph couldn't see a mark. "Did he knock himself out?"

"He hit it pretty hard, but I don't know if it was hard enough to—"

"He's been poisoned," barked Baufent. She was looking at his pupils. "Increased heart rate, cold and clammy. He's drooling. I don't know what it is. I don't know what he's taken. I can't fix this! Get the fucking witches!"

Caliph turned and ran. He plowed through the narrow hallway and banged on the witches' door.

Miriam answered. "What is it?"

"Specks. The captain's son. He's been poisoned. We need you."

Miriam glanced back into the room, then came straight into the hall. Caliph opened the door for her.

"Come on."

They hurried down to the hall. Caliph noticed her clenching her fist. She had already cut her palm in anticipation of holomorphy and was bleeding freely. She was whispering.

As she came onto the deck where Specks was laid out, Baufent looked at her solemnly.

"He's gone," said Baufent.

The captain of the *Bulotecus,* that great tall deep-chested man, had folded up on one of the deck chairs, hunched forward over his son and was sobbing brokenly. His face was in his lap, his arms covered the back of his head.

Miriam looked pale. She got down and examined Specks. Her hand bled across his tiny chest and the smear was vivid and dark across the whiteness of his ribs. She looked up at Caliph. He hadn't expected a hardened Shrądnæ witch to react like this.

Her eyes were full of restrained emotion. "This was professional," Miriam said. "I can smell it on him. It's trixhidant."

"What's that?"

"It's a southern plant," said Baufent.

Miriam made the hand sign for yes. "That's right. He had to drink it or eat it."

"He drank one of the glasses from the lunch tray," said the cook.

Despite the lump in Caliph's throat, he tried to analyze Miriam's fear. The witches knew poison. Miriam had to know that they would be the obvious suspects. But Caliph didn't believe, in his gut, that they were to blame.

"Your majesty—" The cook leaned in to whisper in Caliph's ear. Caliph noticed Miriam cock her head and listen. "Lady Rae was in the kitchen just before the tray went out. She was acting . . . strange."

"I can't see her trying to poison anyone," said Caliph.

Caliph tried not to think about Specks. His main goal was protecting anyone else from the murderer—whoever that was. He tried to remember what had happened after Specks brought the tray into the dining room. Could Isham Wade or Mr. Veech have reached across the table in some unaccounted-for moment and dissolved the poison in his drink? The only person who might have seen it happen was Specks.

Caliph heard the captain cry.

Baufent stood up, looking gray and beaten. Her shoulders slumped. She turned away and went to stand at the railing where the wind howled.

Caliph went over and touched the captain softly on the arm. "Vik?

Viktor?" The captain's breathing was a shudder. "We're going to find out who did this."

"Just let me be."

A FEW minutes later, Sigmund stepped into Caliph's stateroom with a mystified almost sheepish expression on his face. "Am I in trouble?" His eyes went first to the great circular window thrown open to the sky and then to the bureau where they seized on a ruffle of black satin previously invisible to Caliph.

The stretchy crumple of underwear registered strongly now and brought back embarrassing memories of Sena on the bar in the *Odalisque*'s stateroom. Caliph didn't know how they had gotten here but he supposed she had, at some point, used the *Bulotecus* to change. He almost walked over and swept them into a drawer. Instead he gestured toward the only chair and said, "No. You're not in trouble. Have a seat if you want."

"I'll stand." Sigmund shifted from one foot to the other, gazing out through the window at the string of huge heads that the *Bulotecus* was passing. They were carved from black stone and tilted every direction, rising from the sand in wind-polished splendor.

"We're in deep shit," said Caliph.

"I heard the little guy didn't pull through," said Sig.

"No, he didn't. So there's an assassin on board."

"Okay." Sig scratched the side of this neck and kept listening.

"I've got you that I can trust," said Caliph. "Dr. Baufent doesn't really like me. The priestess—I don't know what's going on with her—she could be the one. The diplomats from Iycestoke? Right now, they're my primary suspects.

"What about the witches?"

"I don't think they did it. They're after Sena. Why would they try to kill me? If I die, this ship turns around and goes back to Stonehold."

"Sort of. We'd need to get fuel."

"Whatever, you get my point."

"Yeah."

"But that's not the worst part of the shit, Sig. The assassin isn't our biggest problem. Look out there." He pointed through the window, beyond the mysterious monumental heads. "We've got an Iycestokian armada."

"Reeeeally?" Sig headed toward the window. He took two steps and then, for no apparent reason, the glass exploded. Nuggets bounced like ice cubes over the floor. Sig pulled up short.

Caliph scowled and went to the gaping casement, boots crunching on glass. The sky pulled across his hair and face like steel wool, making his eyes burn. Below, the dunes undulated with bright colors like the back of a poisonous grub. The sand, orange as flame, divorced itself from great blue spots and splatters of something else. From the air, it looked like industrial quantities of smalt had welled up from underneath. The sand refused to mix with it and instead poured around it with the wind, forming crisp blue-and-orange patterns.

Out in the sky a faint zip faded into a muffled whine.

"I think they're shooting at us," said Sig.

Caliph was incredulous. "Why would they do that? They have an ambassador on board!"

Sig craned his head out the window to stare at the shadow, a fume really, like the indiscernible smudge of far-off birds wheeling. An entire colony.

Another noise whizzed past the open window.

"Huh," said Sig. "I do believe that's what's happening. They're fucking shooting at us."

Caliph took out his bottle of chewable tablets and popped two. They dissolved into lemon chalk-powder. The grit stayed between his teeth.

"I thought the witches," Sigmund looked confused, "weren't they doing some kind of, what did they call it? Glamour? Ain't they supposed to try and hide us?"

Sig walked to the bar and pulled down a bottle of whisky. He glanced at the brand. "This stuff could carry me to town on its back." His enormous hands rested around the neck but did not open it.

"Well," said Caliph, "I guess the south has holomorphs."

"Yeah but we've got Shrạdnæ witches for fuck's sake. I mean, I expected more."

"I don't know what they're doing at the moment," said Caliph. "Maybe I should find out."

"Shot at by Iycestokian military . . ." Sigmund wrung the bottle's neck. "It's going to be a crazy story, huh? When we all get back."

Caliph looked at his friend and saw the determined irony, the intentional black joke that served to harden the fear in Sigmund's face. "Yeah. Yeah, it will be."

"I assume, as my fearless leader, you won't be having a drink?"

Caliph didn't answer. He looked out the window one last time, against his better judgment, and stared at the dark shapes in the west.

Sig toyed with the bottle for a moment. Then he set it back in its socket on the shelf. "What are we gonna do, Caph?"

Caliph tugged his lip. "I'm going to go find the witches. And then I'm going to talk to Isham Wade about my broken window and about whether he knows anything about poisons."

Sigmund looked toward the stateroom door from which there came a sudden and insistent knocking.

"Come in!" Caliph and Sigmund shouted in unison.

Neville, the copilot entered, pale and breathless. "We're taking fire!"

"You don't say." Sig gestured to the shattered window with a sweep of his hand. "We were just coming to that conclusion ourselves."

"The gasbags've sustained moderate damage," Neville gasped. "Our gauges show slow leaks in the aft."

"Can we stay aloft?" asked Caliph.

"Assuming we don't continue to take fire," said Neville. "But even then . . . we probably don't have much time left."

"Much time left before what?" asked Sig. "Before we land?"

"Before we crash," said Caliph.

Neville ignored the grim assessment. "What should I tell the captain, your majesty?"

"As long as we're still afloat, nothing changes," said Caliph. "Follow the Pplarian ship." Caliph thought of the captain, sitting at the controls while other people now took care of this son's body.

Neville disappeared. He left the door open.

"What's the logic there?" asked Sig. "Why are we still chasing her?"

Caliph rubbed his chin. "The logic is that there are more airships than I can count back there. And Sena's going in the opposite direction."

"Good plan."

Caliph took a step toward the door. "You want to come with me?"

"Sure," said Sig.

Caliph led him from the stateroom, down the hall to where he stopped and tapped on the witches' quarters.

Miriam again opened the door.

"We're under attack," said Caliph.

"Yes. We're working on it."

"Great," said Caliph. "Anything I can do? Open a vein or something?"

Sigmund grimaced. Miriam did not look amused.

"We're doing our best," said the witch. Her face was stretched with exhaustion. She looked far less pretty than he remembered her.

"I hope your best is good enough."

Caliph turned and marched down the hall, around the corner to Mr. Wade's room. On this door, he pounded. Mr. Veech answered. He was an intimidating man but he was also half the size of Sigmund Dulgensen.

Caliph started to walk into the room. Mr. Veech put his hand on Caliph's chest and Sigmund's huge meaty arm reached out in response. He took hold of Mr. Veech by the collar.

Mr. Veech struggled. He appeared to try some unarmed training, to leverage himself against Sigmund's great mass but the huge engineer was like a boulder. He could not be moved. Sigmund pushed Mr. Veech up against the wall and held him there, waiting for Caliph to tell him what to do.

Caliph walked into the room. "Where is he?"

"He went out to stretch his legs," Veech said tersely. The skin on his face was rolled into a series of folds by Sigmund's forearm.

"Well let's go find him," said Caliph.

Taelin was down the hole, deep in the dark with the shuwt tincture leading her by the nose.

She kept trying to light a cigarette but her wrists were bound in white straps. They trailed back to either side of a bed. She couldn't move her arms. Strangely, she was making love to Palmer—the homeless man from St. Remora—while Aviv (the man she had been going to marry) sat in a chair nearby, watching.

A woman in a red trench was there too, with a clipboard. So were her mother and father. Her father had fine powder on the side of his nose. All of them were hovering in the blurry light of a big white room.

"It's fine," said the physician. "She'll be asleep soon."

"Some drugs and a good fuck always put me to sleep," said Taelin's father. Everyone ignored him.

"It's not that she's lying," said the physician. "Taelin believes what she sees is true. The delusions, the paranoia, even the promiscuity are all part of the disorder."

Taelin looked over Palmer's sweating shoulder at her mother, who harbored a sad, guilty look. "I'm sure her home life hasn't helped." Her mother started to cry. "This is all my fault."

"No, Mom!" said Taelin. "It's not your fault. It's not."

She pushed Palmer off the bed. He either vanished into white clouds or fell to the floor without a sound.

"I saw Nenuln, Mom! I saw her. She was beautiful! Like a cloud of light! And my baby is going to be a god!"

"She's quite intelligent," the physician interrupted. "If Taelin would stay on her medications, and I mean the correct medications, I think she could . . ."

The physician's voice faded into the room's white blur. Taelin had turned her head away to the dark man sitting beside her bed. It was Aviv. All Taelin could see was Aviv. Sweet, sweet Aviv.

Aviv stood up and gathered his black silks around him, scarves and silver beads dangling wildly. The circlet on his head flourished with four platinum uraei. "Thank you, doctor," he said.

"Wait!" she screamed but the room was spinning. "Don't take my baby! Don't take my baby!"

Her mother's face was close to her now. "Shh—Tae it's *his* baby too. Aviv will take good care of him."

"No, he's not. He's not Aviv's! I never loved Aviv. He can't be Aviv's if I didn't love him! That's impossible! Babies are made of love. You can't have a baby if you don't love—"

And then she woke up.

She was holding hands with Sena on a street corner in Pandragor. "Relax," said the High King's witch. "We're not out of this yet."

Sena fished a cigarette out of her black coat. It was rolled from butterfly wings. She handed it to Taelin. Taelin put it between her lips and leaned forward. Sena whispered some minor holomorphic miracle and the tip of the cigarette smoldered to life.

Taelin sucked in. The smoke felt good. She set her bezeled derringer on top of a marnite retaining wall. She laughed. The tiers of the city rose above her in scalloped blocks of golden mineral and tarnished steel. Pandragor's blue domes floated high above.

Bariothermic coils on the back of an angular sedan caught her eye as the vehicle's ass incandesced and glided on magnetic blocks, vanishing down the park's serene avenue.

Sena tugged her away from the street, onto the quartz terrace that overlooked the marshland. "You're coming with me. As soon as you wake up."

"Oh, shit," said Taelin. "I forgot my gun."

Taelin felt like this conversation had happened before, with someone else. It was as if Sena had taken the place of the other person, the other friend with whom she had this experience. Reliving the past, twisting it, was only one facet of a shuwt journey. Taelin tried to bend it, to get it back on track, to take away Sena's influence.

"What about my baby?" asked Taelin. "Aviv bought his way out. I'm going to find him."

"I thought you were going to go to Stonehold and start that church you've been talking about," said Sena.

"Yeah. I probably will. Aviv would never marry me anyway. Not now." She pulled the black chitinous derringer from the wall and slipped it into her pocket.

"I heard you were in the hospital—" said Sena.

"Oh. Yes. I had some complications. Everything's fine now." Taelin smiled. "My father wants me out of the house for good. He's giving me a stack of money."

"What will you do with it?" asked Sena.

Taelin laughed. "I want to help people. I want to keep the faces on the street corners bathed and warm and fed. I want to do something right for a change."

"I know," said Sena. She leaned forward and kissed Taelin who was sobbing. The witch's lips burned against hers like battery terminals. Then Sena gave her a friendly hug.

"You're going to do great things in the north," Sena said.

"Thanks for believing in me."

"You're going to do incredible things. Things you never thought you would."

When Taelin released from the hug, she found herself standing on a Pandragonian zeppelin. A cold wind struck her in the face. She was flying north. Every minute, it seemed, the temperature dropped.

The airship moored at West Gate, over Isca City. Taelin went down a rusting lift that squealed inside the fortress walls.

There, amid the steaming reek of sewer fumes and trash that tumbled out of Gunnymead Square, Taelin hailed a cab. When she got in, the driver greeted her in Trade. He offered her a tiny bottle of Pink Nymph Whisky. She'd never heard of the brand but she bought three because she had plenty of money and because she was nervous to be in a strange town. *Thank gods I'm rich.* She opened the first bottle and knocked it back. The driver was nice. She tipped him well.

Wait. That's not true.

"Yes it is," said Sena, who was sitting in the cab with her.

"No, it's not. My driver. The chemiostatic car I rented got stuck in the mud. I had to walk. I had to fight through freezing rain . . ."

"No. You arrived in West Gate, warm and dry. You took a cab all the way to Lampfire Hills."

"No! I walked in the *freezing rain*! I never rode an airship before in my life! I walked all the way from Pandragor! And my father loves me. *He* gave me that money! Not Aviv! Aviv raped me! That's why I have the money. Because my father loves me.

"Aviv would have taken me to that horrible tiny island in the middle of nowhere and forced me to have his babies."

Sena's face looked like a ceiling. White and square like the shape above her hospital bed. The doctor was gone. The soft white straps around her wrists prevented her from wiping her eyes. She needed to wipe her eyes. Her whole face was wet.

"I'm not lying! It happened! It happened! I saw Nenuln. She talked to me in a cloud of light! She's real! She's real! She's real! And I'll prove she is. I'll go to Stonehold where they *make* gods. They *make* gods in Stonehold. Haven't you read the papers? And then you'll see. I'll make my own church. Just like you did. Just like Sena Iilool did. But I'll help people. Not like you! Not like you who lock people up in rooms and tie them down!

"I'll buy a bing-gun if I have to. I'll come back here for you! I've had lovers who taught me how to shoot! I'm a deadeye!

"And then you know what? When I go north . . . I'm going be queen someday!"

TAELIN sat in her bed, in her stateroom, on the *Bulotecus*. The High King's witch sat with her, on the edge of the mattress. She was finally, truly awake. Her head felt clearer.

Sena smelled delicious. In one hand the witch held a glass of water, in the other a lustrous purple-brown pill. Perfect, like a baby grape.

"I'm not taking it." Taelin coughed.

"It's your antipsychotic," said Sena. "You haven't been taking them. That's the problem. You need to take it."

Taelin wanted to die.

"You're not a bad person." Sena held out the pill.

"Yes I am." Taelin tried not to think about anything.

"You're just sick, Taelin."

Taelin couldn't tell if any of this was real. She didn't care. She just wanted to sleep. She reached out and ate the pill without water and shook her finger at Sena. "You don't know me. You think your book and your holomorphy let you know me. But you don't know me."

"I'm going to take you with me now," said Sena. "While the tincture still has you loosened up."

"Where?" Taelin still felt the drug in her head.

"We're going to Sọth," said Sena. "We'll be gone just a little while."

Taelin blinked as Sena started talking. She felt so strange and cold and sticky. She heard voices. Thousands of voices. An icy electric buzz filled the air.

"Don't be afraid," said Sena. "I'm pulling holojoules down into our equation."

"Holojoules?" Taelin watched the light from her stateroom window turn to molasses. "Don't you need blood?"

"Yes. I drew blood. I've drawn plenty of blood." Then Sena shifted back to the Unknown Tongue and a force reached in through Taelin's mouth and yanked her breath out of her chest like a rag on the end of a hook.

Taelin gasped and fell forward. The impact with her mattress punched clean through, an explosion of white, and jettisoned her out of the zeppelin where she found herself unable to scream. The world came up at her, threatening to bury her at high velocity in an oval patch of blue sand. But the fabric of the world stretched like burlap, in every direction, opening coarse pores.

Taelin fell through.

Daylight vaporized. She found herself in darkness. A cold, damp, cracked surface pressed her hands. She inhaled, choked on dead air.

A woman's voice spoke. It was not a language she was familiar with. The tone behind it sounded hard and cold, like the surface under her fingertips.

A hand gripped her by the elbow and pulled her to her feet.

Part Two

If I were a god, I'd make myself believe.

—Yacob Skie

CHAPTER 34

Taelin stood up. Behind the disembodied, flinty voice that came out of the darkness, she could hear the rattle of a metal buckle. Someone was fastening? Unfastening. Now they were rummaging in a sack.

I'm in Ihciva, she thought, *to pay for my sins with Aviv and Caliph Howl, Palmer and—*

A bit of brown smudged the darkness. It looked like a filtered glow seeping through fabric. Taelin began to reach for the demonifuge under her shirt when Sena's voice interrupted.

"Here. Take this."

Taelin tried to answer but the air was too thin. Thinner than in Sandren. She started wheezing, which led her to realize that she couldn't be dead.

A small, tacky block pushed itself into her palm. She could feel Sena's fingers behind the delivery but the connection didn't register until half a second later, when Sena's hand withdrew. Only then did Taelin panic. In the almighty darkness, losing her physical link to another person—even if that person was Sena Iilool—felt like desertion. Then the brown smudge disappeared.

Without its point of reference she lost her balance and sat back down. She started to adjust to the thin, dead air. "Sena?"

"It's all right," said Sena. "Just don't take out your necklace."

The witch's voice gathered numbers that roasted a cotton cord. Taelin could smell it. A sickly yellow flame touched off right in front of her face, wagging on the block-shaped candle Sena had pushed into her hand.

Sena was crouched a short distance away, blue eyes rolling with the flame. It unnerved Taelin that the witch was staring at her. Her guilt became too much to bear. "I'm sorry," Taelin said. "I didn't mean for it to happen—I didn't mean for it to go so far . . . with Caliph."

Sena was smiling like something that wanted to eat her.

Taelin moved the candle's orange glow toward her butt in an effort to learn something about her surroundings. The ground she was sitting on seemed to be a hill of buckled or broken masonry. There were dripping noises all around but the ground here, at least, was dry.

"It's all right, Taelin."

"But I—"

Sena stood up and took a step in the direction of the flinty voice, which had spoken again.

Taelin felt too out of her depth to argue or even ask questions. All she could do was listen to the strange voice and the echoes of the underground space. She smelled mud. Not the normal gaminess of river mud but the putrefaction of salt-ooze ripened beneath the black bottom of the world. It was a stink suggestive of spoiled shrimp, sewage and gods knew what else.

Taelin buried her nose in the crook of her elbow while Sena talked to the voice in the dark. The language sounded difficult. Sena was stuttering. Or were those simply the phonics of an alphabet she had never heard? Taelin lifted her candle above her head, hoping for a glimpse of the other speaker.

"Sena?" She spoke into her sleeve.

"Just a minute."

The High King's witch stood in the extreme limits of her light. Taelin set the candle down and reached into her pocket. She pulled out her little tin and opened it. Inside were some of the beggary seeds Palmer had given her. She rationed five onto a sheet of rice paper along with a little of the fuzz. She quickly licked the paper. It crackled reassuringly between her fingers as she rolled it. Tincture, pill and smoke. Was that bad? She didn't care.

She picked up the candle. The flame happily shared itself with the bent little package hanging from her lips. She inhaled deeply. It helped with the stink of this place.

A crunch in the stone-strewn dust did not sound like Sena's graceful footsteps; Taelin lifted her candle again. Light spilled across a second person. A little cry escaped Taelin's mouth and the cigarette almost fell out.

Rusted metal and rotting leather encased a body encumbered with archaic weapons. Dust filmed her. The woman's hair was tangled. Despite her eyes, which had calcified into something like white stone, Taelin thought—in that timeless moment while the beggary smoke circled her head—that the woman stepping out of the darkness was even more beautiful than Sena Iilool.

The woman's eyes were smaller, her body longer and exquisitely thin. All of her, from her triangular face to her slender limbs conferred a horrible but lovely gauntness. She was perfect.

The woman was paying close attention to Sena, who was motioning with her hands as she tried to communicate.

"What is she saying?" asked Taelin.

Sena ignored the question. She and the pale woman seemed to be agreeing, deciding on something—without her.

"What's going on?" Taelin felt excluded. "I want some answers."

"Arrian's taking us to her room," said Sena.

"Her room? Why? Who's Arrian?" Taelin looked around at the darkness wondering how they would find their way.

"This is where the Ublisi . . . made her mistake."

"Ublisi?" said Taelin.

"The being that called down the Rain of Fire on Sọth."

"Rain of Fire? That's just a legend. I don't understand why we're here." Taelin's voice echoed. She reached into her shirt for her necklace and took another drag.

"Don't—" said Sena. But it was too late. The molten aperture was already out in the open. It did not illuminate the darkness, but it *was* blinding. Its color jumped into Taelin's eyes without traveling to get there.

Arrian's face twisted. She sprang at Taelin wildly and brought her weapon down like a hammer. Taelin felt the metal. The pain was exquisite. Only a moment later did she realize that the blade had shattered. It had not cut her, but her arm was certainly fractured.

Arrian straddled her waist and raised the jagged shard. The candle tumbled away but thankfully did not go out. Taelin held her cigarette tightly between her lips and put her hands up as Arrian plunged the rusted shaft toward her.

The only thing that arrested the fatal blow was a trademark grip: cradled head, a razor-edged choker wrapped beneath Arrian's chin.

Sena saved her. One moment the shard of rust had been her future. The next, Sena was in control, leaning back. Muscles cabled her slender arms as she threw her body into counterpoise. Arrian growled under the subdual, face fractured into discrete regions of bared teeth and white eyes.

Her fingers reached for the knife that was lifting her off the ground.

As Arrian's weight came up, Taelin propelled herself backward, recovered the candle and scrambled to her feet. She watched Sena pull the blade hard against Arrian's throat. But there was no cut. No bleeding.

Arrian's fingers worked their way between the blade and her neck. She roared with a sound that traveled through bone. The candle nearly dropped again from Taelin's hand.

Sena struck Arrian on the crown of her head with a sudden muscular blow.

Arrian twisted violently and bucked Sena off.

At that moment, Taelin looked away from the two fighting women. She thought she had heard something enormous sidle in the darkness. A sigh. It disturbed the whole sky that encompassed this black empty place. After that, a dull wet impact—as of mucus or falling blood—filled the universe.

For a moment, she imagined inconceivable shapes packed in the dark.

Then Sena burst back into the light and babbled fiercely at Arrian, drawing Taelin's eyes once more to the battle.

Arrian's body came fully up off the piles of broken masonry, twisting in midair, wild and impossible, like a rabbit in a snare. She gurgled as her arms and legs thrashed. Boneless it seemed. Her neck was bent back at what should have been an unachievable angle. When she landed, she landed hard, limbs whipping, churning up dust.

Sena spoke again and Arrian stopped.

Taelin coughed on the swirling particles and backed away. She blew out a stream of smoke. The pain in her arm where the sword had hit her was throbbing.

"What are we doing here?" She shrieked.

Sena was too busy to answer.

The sound of Taelin's yell echoed back to her. Angry at everything, it sounded like there was a copy of herself out there in the darkness, screaming at her for getting herself into this mess.

As the echo faded, Taelin realized the fight was over. Sena spoke in soothing syllables, talking as if to an injured pet. The unruly animal had been pinned to the ground and keened under the stress.

It was awkward and touching at the same time. It deeply disturbed Taelin. She took a long hit of beggary smoke and knelt down. Sena seemed to be asking a question in the horrible language, over and over, insisting on something.

Finally, Arrian pulled herself up slowly against Sena's firm but gentle embrace and answered. After that—bizarrely, determinedly—Sena notched her sickle-knife into Arrian's neck like a hot blade against tallow. It went easy at first but quickly turned to work. Arrian struggled occasionally but Sena kept talking, reassuring her. She brought her full weight to bear as she started sawing off the girl's head.

Arrian didn't move. Her arms hung by her sides. It took a while. Taelin remembered her cigarette and took another hit. She took several hits. The candle seemed to brighten.

No.

Instead of blood, light seeped from the wound. Taelin felt paralyzed.

Sena's movements were brutal. She put her back into it. And then, all at once, in a gush of light, Arrian's body crumpled onto the pile of masonry and Sena stood up, holding the head.

It seemed small.

Taelin felt sick and guilty. As if she had been party to murder. As if she had taken turns with Sena on the blade. Soft gauzy illumination gushed from both stumps. The light poured over the ground from where the body had fallen and likewise splashed from the swinging head. It spattered portions of a dusty black wall that Taelin had just noticed.

What in the world had happened?

"We're taking her with," said Sena. She put her sickle away.

"But you killed her—"

"It'll be okay," said Sena.

"But you killed her." Taelin, on the verge of tears began sinking to the floor. She couldn't look at Sena. "How can it be okay?" She sucked as much beggary smoke into her lungs as she could.

And then, in the light that welled up from the carcass she saw a glitter at the edge of Arrian's eye. Was the horrible thing crying? It made no sense. Taelin stayed where she was, sitting in the ashes. "You should take me back. I don't understand any of this. I want to go home."

"I'll take you back after we're done," said Sena. "And we need to hurry now that you've brought that out for *everything* to see." She gestured toward the demonifuge. "Please get up."

"I don't want to."

"Get up." Sena's voice filled with power and a fierceness that shocked Taelin. It shocked her not only by virtue of its force but also because it contained a foil-thin undercurrent of compassion. That was how it felt. The compassion put her in a state where the fierceness was able to propel her.

She got up, staring at the gruesome trophy in Sena's hands.

"That's impossible!"

Taelin put a hand to her mouth and jerked the candlelight back from Arrian's face, whose stone-white eyes had just blinked.

LIKE stammering picture shows that had opened on Isca Road and put fear into the owners of the Murkbell Opera House, events started clicking across the lamp of Arrian's head. Taelin felt them in black and white. *I'm watching a show. That's all. I'm not really here.*

She wanted another hit but her blunt was spent, which meant she could only look on nervously as Sena unslung a small pack. When the designer purse came off the witch's back, a faint brown halo daubed the air behind her head as if a lantern had been strapped beneath Sena's jacket.

Interesting, thought Taelin. She watched Sena undo the buckle. Chic black reptile skin parted and a folded plastic bag came out, stamped with Octul Box's purple shopping dragon. It had rope handles. Sena snapped it open and put Arrian's head into it. Then she reslung her purse, and handed the shopping bag to Taelin. "You can carry this."

Taelin took the bag mutely with her good arm. It jerked her wrist, heavier than expected.

"Come on," said Sena.

"I can't. Not with my hurt knee . . . and now my arm."

"Where are your crutches, Taelin?"

"I—I don't know."

"Forgot them, did you?"

"I—"

"Come here."

"My knee hurts. Dr. Baufent said—"

"Dr. Baufent let you take the crutches even though she knew you didn't need them. Your arm is not broken. And your knee isn't injured. You're going to be fine." Then, without another word, Sena shanked into the dark.

CHAPTER 35

The ambit of the Abominations was strong here but not as strong as it had been on the Stairs leading down to the Chamber.

There were noises in the dark. Sena knew she had to be vigilant. The "sky" was a great leaking slab. Epochs drained into a lake below the hill. It stank of the deep ocean. Huge walls of hewn basalt thrust themselves upward, strong enough to support the mile-thick chunk of sky. Despite the moisture, dust and porous husk-like stones muffled the landscape.

Sena could picture this rubble-strewn cyst as a garden where luminous moths fluttered over black pimplota under the moons. For a moment, she saw the fires erupting, the cinders and falling rock. She smelled the dead relatives and friends that had stunk for years before they turned to sludge beneath the piles.

She felt sorry for Arrian whose first question had been asked childlike, with cocked head, "Father? Is it you? Corwin?" Sena had been appalled by the antique weaponry strapped to her body, the rotten corslet cut from some mythic beast whose leather had outlasted the dark.

"I have never been to the Mainland," Arrian had said stupidly. "It snows there but Father says I belong here, on the island."

Sena had watched the ancient leather flake away from Arrian's immortal skin. Nothing could cut that skin unless Arrian gave her permission. And that was why she had to be persuaded, like a child at the dentist. Sena had promised escape. She had soothed and bribed. She had been firm. She had been coddling. She had been vicious with the knife.

Sena looked at Taelin and pondered for a moment trying to explain. Not everything. Just the tiny parts that concerned her.

"Taelin?"

"What?"

"You need to keep your necklace safe. You need to keep it hidden."

"Why?"

"Because it's the key to an important door."

"Oh. Well, I don't need it anymore. Here. You take it."

"Actually I need you to carry it. I'm not going to be around when the door is opened."

"I don't understand."

"Your grandfather made it for a reason. With it, there's a chance to do something good. To save people." She could talk freely here, without fear of Nathaniel.

"That's what I've always wanted to do," said Taelin. "Help people. But I always . . . I always muck it up." She was tearful again.

"I know," said Sena. "But this is your chance. So keep the necklace safe."

Sena watched Taelin's fingers close over the demonifuge as Something shifted in the immense cavern, Something huge and ponderous slipping over stone.

Taelin gawped toward the sound, trying to see into the netherworld behind them. The shopping bag she lugged drew her fingers down into splotchy white hooks. The bag crinkled and banged against her knees.

Sena knew it was hard for the other woman to breathe here. Even without inhaling, Sena could taste salt and death.

Taelin stumbled.

Sena reached out and steadied her.

"We need to keep moving. They won't tolerate us here much longer. Are you all right?" Her vocalization was a courtesy, an effort at displaying empathy.

Taelin marveled at the blackness; she was not all right. She pulled away when Sena reached for her. Her face was smeared with horror.

"Taelin?"

With both hands Taelin held up the shopping bag. Offering it to the darkness. A child displaying something she had bought. The bag gushed with light.

"She's dead," said Taelin.

Sena grabbed her by the hand. "That's not true. You saw her blink."

Taelin started blubbering. Sena was keenly aware of her own guilt in this. This was the cost of advancing her slender margins. Crazy as she was, Taelin managed to glow even here with a kind of radiant innocence. Sena could understand why Caliph found her pretty.

Another shudder squeaked through the cavern, like tons of rubber slipping, slumping somewhere along the far side of the lake. Sena didn't look. She already knew What was there, What had crawled out of Lewlym's Navel so many thousand years ago and died here in the dark.

"We need to go," said Sena. She started walking and Taelin stumbled after. They crossed the flat ash-draped space that had once been a courtyard and entered the fortress.

The vaulted hallways of Jôrgill Deep were empty. Whatever tapestries or paintings had decorated them had long turned to ash. Smudges of rust lay here and there, the stains of former objects. Halls of empty night. More dust. Thick gray tendrils choked every room and casement. Taelin's candle struggled in one hand while the glowing shopping bag cast a soft moving halo in the clouds stirred by her feet.

Sena led the way, her compasses subtracting, narrowing. She guided Taelin from the dripping vaults up a shrunken staircase wracked by catastrophic quakes. Anciently sundered stones overlooked the delirious blackness where something vast and unseen jostled far below.

It was dead. It did not watch them. Flesh so strange, like a mushroom, honeycombed and deep, deep enough to confuse souls. It lacked eyes. Its perception was endemic; superseding organic limitations with an acute hyperawareness. It knew precisely where Sena and Taelin were. It suffered them to be here. It felt the power of Sena's ambit.

Sena's eyes tracked It. She maintained her vigil in case It tried to make a grab. She could not hide from It. It "saw" in all directions: a black prehensile god.

"What's down there?" Taelin was gibbering now. She sensed her own danger.

They had reached the parapets and the shattered remains of an arcade. Sena walked down the center. She drew up when she realized she was leaving Taelin behind.

"The same thing wired to St. Remora. You know? The eleven clocks?"

"Yes. W-what are they for?"

"It's one of the [illegible].[24]"

"Sekwah-what?"

Sena leapt over a pulverized obsidian window frame in the destroyed hall and repositioned Taelin behind her. She also tried to modify the air for Taelin's sake but the Yịllo'tharnah were pressing too hard, pushing, groping—despite the agreement, they had begun to struggle for the necklace. While Sena pushed back and mentally warned them away, reminding them of the pact, she tried to answer Taelin's question.

"You remember what you saw that night I came to St. Remora? The shadow bursting out of the wall?"

"Yes . . ."

[24] U.T.: Approximate pronunciation: Sectua'Gaunt.

"That was one of them."

"But I thought . . . everyone knows there are no such things—or if there ever were they were locked away, shut up or entombed or—"

"They were," said Sena. "But you can still feel Them sometimes. That chill that goes through you? In lonely places? Their thoughts can leak through from the other side, and if They want to, if They need to, They can manifest for short durations even though it costs Them dearly. Which is how I got these—" She gestured to the lines on her body.

"Imagine a wasp's nest," said Sena. "Gone wild. Built enormous in every direction. Like the wasps kept building and building. For decades, centuries, millennia. Black papery chambers so deep—so perfect. Except there are no wasps. It's the cells that are sentient. The pockets. The empty space that's thinking. And the larvae inside those pockets, those pastel burning maggots—are souls. Little squirming workers stacked in twisted tori, in perfect galleries.

"The Yịllo'tharnah have shapes described by numbers. Their ratios, set down in books, were the inspiration for the coriolistic centrifuge, which launched Pneumafuel L.L.C. in 1431 S.K., and Solvitriol Solutions two years later."

Her words were a hook that pulled Taelin along. "This is about business?" asked Taelin. "I don't understand."

"No," said Sena. "This about numbers, physics. But Solvitriol Solutions discovered that the pneumata in their batteries had inertia. Think of it like money. The more you have the more you can consume. And faster.

"Pneumata are the gravel in Their gizzards. Pneumata are Their currency. They barter in souls."

"And that's what's down there in the dark? Yịllo'tharnah?" Taelin's pronunciation was skewed.

"Yes."

"I don't understand what They are."

"The harder you try to understand, the more inconsistencies you will find. Their bodies are haloed in paper ash you could destroy by breathing. They're not made of matter. They are holes. They are dead. And when they are sufficiently haunted, They can move.

"Don't believe most of what I just told you. The language is wrong. The words are . . ." she touched her upper lip with her tongue, "wrong. Besides." Sena took the candle back and laced her fingers in Taelin's. "I don't really know *what* They are."

They had arrived at a small room whose doorway had no portal. The ash at the threshold showed frequent tracks. In one corner, the ruins of what might have once been a bed lay as a crumbled relic. If Arrian had ever slept, or pretended to sleep, she had done it here, under a window that now looked out on a wall of stone.

Sena looked down at a ceramic doll's head, peering morosely from the gray powder.

Taelin tried to remember her mission home in the snow-filled streets of Isca but the picture would not focus. She tried to think of people's names that she knew there. When she thought too hard it always hurt right where the boy had knocked her head against the cement.

Taelin looked down at the crunched doll's head. Sena was busy, crouched, sifting through the powder with her fingers, holding the candle.

The witch had endlessly outmaneuvered her. She was more powerful than Taelin had ever expected. Subtle yet strong. Like wind orchestrating the shapes of trees. *How had this happened?* She sat down with her glowing shopping bag and watched Sena dig in the ash.

Everything Taelin had tried to embody was slipping away from her. In this vacuous hole no thought of Nenuln's golden light could soothe her.

I am not a priestess.

"Are you all right?" Taelin looked into Sena's concerned face and those horrible, beautiful eyes. The witch's thumb reached out and stroked her lips, which was precisely the thing her mother would have done when she was a girl. It was terrifying and comforting at the same time. Taelin tasted ashes on her lips.

The candle seemed to float beside them, unattended. This strange fact freed Sena's other hand, in which she rolled a small spherical object. She must have found it in the powder of the room. Despite the dust, it was black and shimmered with a satiny organic texture.

The candle was burning low. It settled to the floor and sagged there like a glowing mushroom.

"What is it?" Taelin nodded.

"A black pimplota seed, for which I didn't have a blueprint."

Taelin believed that Sena was a god.

Sena moved the seed from her hand into her backpack with hardly a whisper. Then she asked for the shopping bag.

With a blank expression, Taelin nudged the glowing purple dragon with her foot. It was heavy. She kicked it gently. Sena dragged it the rest of the way, dredging a meaningful furrow between them.

She gripped it by one of the handles and the object inside shifted. When she tipped it, leaned it over and upended it, Arrian's head slid out like a stone. It came to rest on its crown, severed neck blazing into the dark.

From her pack, Sena called for a slender steel tube. There was no point in being discreet anymore. Taelin had ceased paying attention and even an endless string of miracles could do little harm. Their relationship, no longer a charade of normalcy, now at least simulated truth.

Sena uncorked the tube and rolled Arrian's head over. This was what Arkhyn had requested, that she get his daughter out. But not like this.

Sena nervously upended the shuwt tincture into Arrian's candescent tissues. She tipped the head back on its crown so the poison rolled up the back of the throat, pooled through the sinus and dripped into the seat of consciousness. She was uncertain this endeavor would end in success.

She whispered to the head in Dark Tongue, hoping to comfort the creature that had once been a girl. Arrian could still resist, close her cells to the exchange. But she seemed disoriented. Her eyelids fluttered as the tincture took effect.

Arrian would be going out like Caliph and Taelin had gone out, like everyone who used the drug *went out.* But unlike them she would not be coming back. This was an overdose of the variety Arkhyn Hiel had used.

Sena felt sorry for Arrian. Twenty thousand years had been enough. Too much in fact. While she waited for the pneuma to seep from Arrian's neck, she watched Taelin scratch the silvery patch of skin on her wrist.

Taelin noticed the attention. "I think I'm getting it." She sounded defeated. "I should have listened to Anselm and stayed out of the tents. I've been so stupid."

"No," said Sena. "You've doing everything right. Trust me."

"You mean I'm not going to die of plague? Can you really see that? Can you really see everything?"

"I can see you're not going to die of plague."

"How do you know?"

"We don't have a lot of time to—"

"Time to what? Why did you bring me here? What are we doing here?"

"We're here to get Arrian, and the pimplota seed for the ink."

"You didn't need me to do that—either of those things."

"Yes, I did. But I also brought you because I needed to tell you something about your grandfather's necklace and this was the only place I could do that."

"I don't understand. This place is—"

"This place is safe enough to talk." Sena steered away from Nathaniel Howl. She didn't try to explain that the shade was always listening or that originally she had planned to bring Caliph here, instead of Taelin, so that she could tell him directly what she was doing. That idea had quickly been scuttled. Showing deference to the High King was an unnecessary risk. Already, Nathaniel was on the cusp of understanding the truth.

"It doesn't *feel* safe here," said Taelin.

"I know. And it's not. But it's the only place safe enough to tell you what I need to tell you."

"So tell me." Taelin's eyes were red-rimmed and glazed.

Sena paused, grew serious and said, "Your grandfather made that," she pointed to the necklace, "so that it could be broken." Sena felt a tremble in the black air, as the Yi̥llo'tharnah pressed her ambit. They reached for the demonifuge and Sena gasped under the sudden weight. Taelin didn't seem to notice as Sena paused to check her boundaries. After a painstaking moment, Sena said, "It's not really a necklace, Taelin. It's a hole in the world. It's been tearing, getting wider for years, for decades. Right now, it's enormous, but that little ring of numbers is like a drawstring, holding the whole thing together."

"A hole? In the world? What's inside?"

"Monsters."

Taelin laughed quietly without voice. "So I was actually right." She mumbled through her beggary high. "It is a demonifuge."

"Yes."

"Then why break it?"

"Because when that door opens, so will another. And that's our chance to run."

"You really think the world is ending?" Taelin coughed on the harsh volcanic dust drifting over the floor.

"It's already here," said Sena. "The Cabal has been spreading it. People are changing, dying, everywhere."

"You mean the disease. But we can stop that," said Taelin. "Stonehold has vaccine. We can—"

"Shh—" And Taelin stopped talking. "There's something else," said Sena, "besides the necklace, that I need you to carry."

"What is it?"

The tincture had burned through Arrian's cells. The Gringling girl's pneuma slipped out.

Taelin touched the scar on her forehead and Sena knew it was done.

Arrian had a new home. The priestess and the sheleph of Jôrgill Deep were together now, until the end.

Nathaniel was going to be furious.

A TREMOR shook the ground as the Yi̥llo'tharnah pressed Sena's ambit, bent on seizing the necklace. Fine dust trickled from overhead and Sena looked up into old cracks with new dimensions.

The Yi̥llo'tharnah had preserved Sọth in this bubble beneath the Loor Ocean for twenty thousand years. They had buttressed it from the crushing deeps to house the things Sena had gathered from the ash. They had preserved this place not because They cared about it, but because of the bargain Arrian's father had struck. This place and the objects it contained were pieces to be bartered. But now, with the necklace so close at hand, They reneged and reached out.

Taelin stirred slightly and complained that she felt cold.

"I know," said Sena. "It will get better."

Arrian's head was empty. The perfection of her tissues still oozed light. The head would never die. But it was an empty vessel now and that was a kind of death. The exact death that the Yi̥llo'tharnah existed in.

Sena could smell Their sweet stink. They were drowsy from the evaporation of souls. From waiting for eternities. But They were stirring now.

A massive shape hurled itself against the fortress, sending another tremor through the walls. Somewhere, a section gave way and, like a hydrant gushing from another world, the Loor began pouring in.

Taelin screamed above the sound of the water when an engorged and deep-chambered limb unrolled, listless and libertine. It importuned with the shriek of drowning sea birds. The noise reverberated in every part of the ruin and in every bone in Sena's body.

She left Arrain's head where it was and pulled Taelin up a flight of stairs. Her tongue began working as the walls came shuddering down.

ANOTHER cadence wracked the air as Taelin allowed Sena to drag her. She could hear the gargantuan thrashing, the concussive splashes, the waterfalls that had broken through.

All light had gone out but strange pictures formed in her head. She saw fiery rocks falling out of the sky. People dying. She had lost Sena's hand.

The air was too thin and poisonous. Still she shouted, choked, laced her fingers over her necklace and stared up at the dark, trying to breathe.

"I see lights!" She gagged. "Nenuln's lights!"

Thunder boomed and in the sudden brilliance Taelin's skin turned to rubber. A grossly corpulent appendage curled around her. Its flesh flowed inward: lightless boiling plasma. It moved with self-encrypted gravity. Several more limbs, turbid and glistening, slapped down around her, reaching for her throat. Her mouth was open, howling but soundless.

She felt an icy bite. Slippery and rough. A cobweb of fatty madness enclosed her, like a bug trapped in phlegm spit at the ceiling. Something scrabbled with the demonifuge, desperate and angry.

Then the ruins ruptured and fathoms of liquid poured in. Her body—her skull—crushed instantly.

She saw, or imagined that she saw, a fading white polyp flailing on heavy currents. Her arms perhaps. Some profligate kelp-like gyration in the depths. Distortion. Golden syrup. Then more white light. Brilliant white light.

Vast black shapes moved below her, receding toward the event horizon of an oceanic trench. Light flickered through Sena's torn coat, radiant cones that shifted from a hole between her shoulder blades. The beacon gave Taelin some sense of direction at the edge of the violent plume of sediment that billowed from Jôrgill Deep.

She watched stones fall slowly, sinking back into a swirl of midnight blue and brown.

Sena's fingers closed around her hand. The witch's eyes were suspended in water. They looked down into Taelin, earnest and communicative. *I am not leaving you,* they said.

The pressure dissipated. Her crushed body moved. Her imploded head considered. She gripped her demonifuge tightly but knew: it had not been Nenuln. It had been Sena Iilool that pulled her out of silted blackness, up into the glorious brightness of her bedroom on the *Bulotecus.*

CHAPTER 36

Insidiously, with the ship's southward passage, everything had become foreign. The landscape and objects they passed over had names in languages that Caliph found unfriendly. According to the captain, the wind at their backs was called the Hali. It blazed down the slopes of Ayrom Karak and out across the strangely hued desert of Nah'Ngode Ayrom.

The Hali brought the storm.

Caliph had located Isham Wade and had backed him up against a railing. Sand was already stinging them as it whipped up off the dunes.

"Unhand me!"

"Did you try to poison me?"

"No! Have you lost your mind?"

"Tell the Iycestokians to let us go!"

"I have witnesses to your brutality," Mr. Wade sputtered.

"I want your communication device," Caliph shouted over the wind.

Isham scoffed in a way that hinged on real amusement. "You don't even know what it's called."

Caliph glared at Mr. Wade's jeweled ring. "I want it *now*!"

Sigmund loomed over Caliph's shoulder, ready to assist. They had locked Mr. Veech in the hold.

"Drag him inside, Sig."

They moved off the deck into the shelter of the paneled hall. Isham raised his hands.

"Give it to me," said Caliph.

Isham reached up and, with little effort, pulled his left eye out of its socket. He shook it gently as if about to roll it in a game of chance, then held it out, aiming for Caliph's palm.

Caliph drew back, horrified, which tugged an indulgent laugh from Isham's throat. "You know what they say about us Iycestokians," said Mr. Wade. "One eye talks about what the other one sees."

The eye looked up at Caliph from between Isham's fingers. It was slippery and positively real. Not made of glass.

"How do I use it?"

Isham chuckled. "You can't. It's mine."

Caliph did not attempt to take it away. "Put it in. Tell them to let us go. We're on the same side." They weren't on the same side at all. He had hoped the device would be something he could use, something he could at least comprehend.

Isham put his eye back in. It moved and behaved like a real eye, reassuring Caliph that he had not missed the obvious.

"I can't tell them to let you go, King Howl. They have an objective here."

"They want the book. Fine. Tell them I'll land in Bablemum and we'll deliver the book there. You said you need vaccine. I can deliver that too."

"We already have vaccine, King Howl."

"But you said—"

"Your medical ship was intercepted just north of Sandren."

"That's an act of war!"

"Well, according to—"

"What about the people on board? What did you do with them?"

"I'm sure they're fine. My government will replicate the vaccine and immunize Iycestoke."

"And the rest of the south? The north? What about them? Are you going to sell it to—"

Isham leveled his hand, fingers spread. He wobbled it and squinted, indicating such a decision had not yet been made.

"You evil fucking bastard."

"Be realistic!" said Isham. "Selling it will help us survive. Everyone wants to survive. Think about flies getting their heads chewed off. The mantis is just trying to survive. You can't blame him for looking like a flower. What's evil about that?"

Sigmund grunted.

Caliph grasped at the last straw he felt he had. "What about the book? I hand you the book at Bablemum."

"You're not in a bargaining position, King Howl."

"Yes, I am," said Caliph. "Because I'm the only one that can stop this. I'm the only one that can convince her not to do what she's going to do. But in order for me to convince her, I need to catch up to her."

"And what is she going to do, King Howl?"

Caliph couldn't force himself to say it. The words simply wouldn't come out. It was too preposterous. Even with everything that had gone wrong he couldn't say it out loud.

Isham smiled and went on. "Whatever it is, you don't need to catch up to her. We can do that. Iycestoke will stop her. Rest assured. You've never seen an Iycestokian armada, King Howl?

"Now please, just show me the book."

Caliph deliberated whether that was a good idea. The book's existence coupled with the fact that the Iycestokians still had a diplomat on board were probably the only reasons the *Bulotecus* had not been blown to pieces.

"Come with me," said Caliph. He marched to his stateroom and pulled out Arkhyn Hiel's journal.

"May I see it?"

"I believe you can see it perfectly well from there," said Caliph. He put the book away.

"That's hardly proof," said Isham.

"I don't owe you any more proof," said Caliph. "Now tell your armada what you've seen. You'll have plenty of time while you keep Mr. Veech company."

Sig stepped forward and took Isham Wade by the arm.

"Take your hands off me!" Mr. Wade struggled fiercely but Sigmund applied torque and the diplomat went limp. "I am an ambassador, King Howl!"

"By your word, Iycestokian ships intercepted and confiscated our medical—"

"You've attacked every nation on the continent!" barked Mr. Wade.

"That wasn't me," said Caliph. "It's your country that's to blame for the fact that I'm locking you up."

"You think it makes a difference? You think your country even exists without Iycestoke's consent? You're going to be marooned in the sand shortly. And then you won't even be the king of Stonehold anymore. You can lock me up for a few minutes, Caliph Howl. Be my guest! But you're the one in a cage here! You're already dead!"

Sigmund punched Mr. Wade in the stomach. It was like a pipe wrench sinking into dough. The sound that escaped Isham's mouth was like a death groan, all the wind going out of him at once. He collapsed, eyes huge and bulging, spittle dangling from his lips.

"Sig! Don't!"

"Fuck him!" said Sigmund. He glared at Caliph. He dragged Isham Wade from the room and Caliph found himself unable to protest.

Hopefully Mr. Wade would soon be communicating everything that had transpired to his Iycestokian contacts. Hopefully the book bluff would work. Caliph was already formulating some vague plans. He went out onto the deck to see what the Iycestokian fleet was doing.

Returning to the deck brought pain. Caliph's eyeballs gummed over in the hot wind. Sand was blowing but he could still see across the orange and blue dunes to where Sena's white chrysalis tracked relentlessly south. In the other direction, behind them, loomed the armada. The Iycestokians were mostly to the north now, trailing them like the Hali, driving them like a giant hand.

The black ships were not aerodynamic. They reared up, cobra heads, black and glistening with purple lights.

Caliph went to the cockpit and asked Neville for maps. The copilot handed them over with a confused hopeless look that Caliph didn't try to change. Instead he spread out the charts. "Where are we?"

Neville pointed to a spot two inches from the nearest letter in the phrase that meant *Shifting Sands.* Caliph stared at the empty yellow patch of paper. Behind them lay the ruins of Ueo Mrûp at the easternmost tip of the withered fingers of the mountains. Ahead—far ahead on the other side of the desert—the names were equally strange: Umong, Mahn Loom'Û and two vast lakes that he couldn't pronounce. Not that any of those places mattered. They would never make it that far.

He went back out to the deck.

The Iycestokian airships boiled closer. Black with purple markings—the super power of the Tebesh Plateau. The self-proclaimed god's hammer of the world. The ships seemed to have metal arms, tentacles almost. It was difficult to see.

He had expected them to fly faster, to have already caught up with him. But their craft did not look fast. They looked bulky and strange, as if they had been built backward or according to the physics of a different world.

He walked to the aft deck and stared back on the panoramic nightmare. Wind ruffled over the *Bulotecus*'s skin. The engines hummed. The propellers thudded dramatically. But in the distance the enemy floated sinister and silent.

Caliph turned his field glasses on them. He could see the guns, but he didn't know what they fired. Certainly not the tiny rounds that had broken the window in his stateroom. He searched and found the Iycestokian engine cells, burning through an endless spectrum of shifting pastels: yellow and blue and purple. Solvitriol power. He could not make out propellers. What was driving them forward? The great hooded designs looked like sails, sails that should have stopped the vessels dead or driven them in the opposite direction. They did not look like they should have been capable of flight.

A movement in the western part of the formation caught Caliph's eye. One of the ships broke and pulled out ahead of the rest. It moved with incredible speed. It closed the fifteen-mile gap between the rest of the armada and the *Bulotecus* in a span of seconds. As it came south it gave Caliph's ship a wide berth and did not venture east. Rather than engaging, it now flew parallel, maintaining its perimeter.

Mother of Emolus, they can engage us at any time! They just don't want to.

The *Bulotecus* was still losing buoyancy.

Caliph tried to put himself in his enemy's position, as the commander of the whole Iycestokian fleet, presumably outfitted with the best weapons and armor on the planet. But what if word had come that a northern ship had destroyed the entire fleet of diplomatic vessels over Sandren? What if *he* had been tasked with engaging that ship?

They're afraid, he realized.

They don't know what happened—any more than I do. They think I might have a super weapon on the Bulotecus. And even if they don't . . . they probably aren't willing to risk destroying the book.

Caliph watched as more Iycestokian ships moved out along the circumference of the pursuit formation, every one of them outpacing the *Bulotecus* by factors of five or more. He scanned their decks with his field glasses, focusing on the soldiers there. How could they stand the wind resistance?

Their armor was like nothing Caliph had seen, black as the skins on their ships, bearing small purple insignia. They seemed rigid, more like machines than the movements of men. Their feet moved with deliberate articulated slowness.

The Iycestokian armada formed a half-ring now, a perfect crescent around the *Bulotecus*'s rear. Through the air, from directly behind, Caliph heard some kind of broadcast, a projection of sound. It was a voice with an Ilek accent, but it spoke clear understandable Hinter.

"Stonehavian Vessel. Maintain your current course."

Sigmund came out onto the aft deck.

"You locked him up?" asked Caliph.

"Yeah. He's fine." The blue sky was bronzing with evening and light glistened off Sig's large nose. He stared out at the half-ring of ships, colorful shirt flapping against his chest, chewing on the hair under his lower lip. "I think no matter what you do, we're probably fucked here, Caph."

"Thanks for that."

"You don't think they're going to shoot at us back here? We make fuck-fat targets. Especially me. Actually just me. You're pretty skinny."

"No. They're not going to shoot at us. They know we're coming down sooner or later and with a few hundred perforations to the gasbags it's probably sooner."

"You wanna drink?"

"No."

"You might need one. Have you seen what we're headed for?"

Caliph followed Sig back through the cabins and upstairs to the cockpit where the captain was drenched in his own sweat and probably some of his tears as well. He did not greet Caliph.

Caliph looked forward through the great curved windshield. He saw something on the horizon that he couldn't make sense of but the first question out of his mouth was, "How much longer can we stay afloat?"

The captain tapped an illuminated dial. "Probably no more than forty minutes."

"What if we dump things?"

The captain grudgingly considered. "Well, sir . . . your majesty. I suppose it might buy us fifteen or twenty minutes if we tossed everything not nailed down."

"Neville." Caliph jerked his head toward the copilot. "Go get everyone out. Start tossing whatever you can."

"Yes, your majesty."

"I'll go help," said Sig.

Caliph had turned his attention to the thing in the distance. A tree, the biggest tree in the world, sprouted from the sand. But if that was true, it was a dead tree. It was white-green and the canopy was clearly not comprised of branches. It was one solid mass. An umbrella. More a mushroom than a tree, yet the stalk despite having one main column seemed to be entangled with other, more slender stems.

The entire thing hovered like a flattened thunderhead, enormous beyond comprehension. Worthy of some geographic name. It was side-lit in gold, but parts of it were slipping into sepia-pink shadow, hazy from the desert's chaff. Sena's white ship did not deviate. It tracked straight for it. An evening star headed for the horizon.

"What is it?" asked Caliph.

"I don't know," said the captain. "But there's something circling it."

Caliph cupped his field glasses again and shielded them from the slanting rays. "What the . . ."

Under magnification the object was clearly not a mushroom. Nor was its vast umbrella supported from below. Rather the thing seemed to be floating and the great stalks below it were sloughing blubber, stretched perhaps between the island of bloated organs that filled the sky and whatever carcass still rested under the sand. Limpid shapes moved drunkenly in clouds around the thing, thrashing and tearing at the shape. Some kind of black-eyed scavengers with flashing transparent bodies and indistinct methods of flight.

"It's something dead," said Caliph.

Captain Viktor Nichols nodded. He was not from the south and it was clear he had no idea what it was. "I—" He started to say something then stopped. Caliph noticed an oil stick drawing taped beside Nichols' controls where Specks' hand had spelled Dad.

Caliph clenched his jaw and looked back toward the hideous mass. Against its hazy gray shape, he found the fading sparkle of Sena's ship and hated it. "Follow her," he said.

"Yes, sir."

Caliph left the cockpit and walked back to the witches' stateroom. He pounded on the light hollow door until it vibrated against the frame. No answer.

He turned the handle and went in. The room was empty.

From belowdecks he heard the hydraulics of the cargo bay opening. He left and took the stairs down. It was hot but breezy in the hold with a gaping hole toward the aft. Sig along with some of the crew and his remaining bodyguards had tethered up. They pushed crates and equipment out into the wind.

"Have you seen the witches?" Caliph shouted above the noise. They shook their heads. He went back upstairs and ran into Dr. Baufent.

"What is that *stink*?" she asked.

"Go have a look from the cockpit," said Caliph. "It's probably going to get worse."

"Are we landing?"

"Do you want to die in Iycestoke?"

"No."

"Me neither. We're not landing."

"What can I do?" she asked. Caliph studied her for an instant. In that instant he appreciated her grit.

"Go down and help lighten our load. We're going to try and stay aloft as long as we can. Have you seen those witches?"

"No."

Caliph touched her on the elbow, lightly. She didn't flinch but he could feel her rigid strength, her tenacity. "I'm going to try to get us out of this."

"Well don't let me slow you down." She pushed past him toward the hold.

Caliph checked the starboard deck, the roof above the cabins, the port, then the aft. He looked in all the rooms, except Taelin's. They were empty. He checked the cockpit again. The captain still clung to the controls, sweating out the second worst experience of his career—on the same day.

Caliph took a maintenance ladder from behind the cockpit. It climbed up inside the skin, between the gasbags, rung after rung until he came to the hatch. He pushed it open and pulled himself up, poking his head above the top of the zeppelin. From here he had a clear 360-degree panorama of the desert, the debacle and the dead thing in the sand. All four witches stood a dozen yards away, staring at him, clearly interrupted.

Caliph climbed out of the chute and marched toward them against the wind. They were flapping—hair and clothing—looking shadowy against the sinking sun. Their perfumes mixed with the thick charnel vapor rolling from the south.

"It's a hylden," said Miriam. "Obviously a dead one."

It was a parry that failed to turn aside his anger. Caliph shouted into the wind. "I'm not really worried about that! What I am worried about is that!" He swung his arm in a wide arc at the black crescent of Iycestokian warships.

"We don't have enough blood to hide an airship," shouted Autumn. "Unless you're willing to sacrifice some of the crew." Her black-red hair lashed around her face, obscuring her eyes.

Caliph's heart cooled.

"Are you?" asked Miriam.

Am I what? thought Caliph. *She can't be serious. Is she really asking me to let her kill some of the crew so that she can work her equation?* "No!" shouted Caliph. "Fuck no!"

"We didn't think you would be," said Miriam, "which is why we're up here, debating our options. The Iycestokian ships are too far away for us to steal blood."

Caliph's mind, long spinning like a runaway cog, bit down into the teeth of an epiphany. He shielded his eyes and looked toward the bloated cloud of blubber and gas. Sena had told him about the Shrạdnæ secret of hemofurtum.

"What?" asked Miriam. "You look like you've just had an idea."

"What about those things . . . feeding on the carrion," Caliph shouted. "If we got close enough to them. Could you use them?"

The witches squinted after his finger.

"If we can make it there . . ." shouted Autumn.

Miriam made the southern hand sign for yes. "Nyaffle. Dangerous but maybe . . . yes. It could work."

Caliph's skin crawled. What was Sena doing? And why?

Why wouldn't she help them if she wanted Caliph to follow? Why let them struggle? She was the villain in this chase. He had to accept that. He had to let go, once and for all.

CHAPTER 37

Taelin came out of her room with her crimson goggles on, her brown leather jacket zipped up against the wind. The world was better now, bathed in pink. She could see things clearer. She was sure of it.

A horrible racket from belowdecks made her wonder what was happening. She walked out onto the starboard deck and immediately saw the Iycestokian ships. Her goggles made them clear against the sky, deep red rather than black. They were southern ships. And she was from the south. They should have been her friends. But she had a new directive now.

She had a mission. A goal. The demonifuge was real. Sena had assured her of that. She was Sena's messenger now. Taelin gripped her necklace in her hand.

All praise the Omnispecer!

Oh, my gods! What is that smell?

She covered her mouth and nose with her hands.

It's death, you nimshi. The thought came at her from the other girl. The inside-girl.

Taelin gasped.

A warm trickle of anger bubbled up through the crevices in her spine. Artesian. Gushing to full red bloom in the tissues that packed her skull.

"Do you think the Iycestokians are trying to stop us?" asked Taelin.

Father will take care of us, said the inside-girl. *He always takes care of us.*

Which father? She had two distinct memories of two distinct men.

"We can't let the Iycestokians win," said Taelin. "We need to make it to Bablemum!"

The inside-girl did not disagree so Taelin allowed her breasts to swell up, tearing through her clothing, popping the buttons off her jacket. They were so buoyant that they tugged away from her chest painfully, swelling up above her shoulders. Above her head. Bigger than balloons. Zeppelin bags. They pulled her into the air—off the deck, out across the desert toward the Iycestokian craft.

Blue-and-orange patterns splashed below her like paint. The wind howled and the air was full of sand, but she could see. Her goggles cut through the haze. She steered herself toward the oncoming airships gliding under one of the great melon-shaped balloons just as the sandstorm closed in behind her.

One of the soldiers on deck caught her and pulled her down. He wore smooth strange armor. She kicked him in the face.

"Leave Sena alone!" she shouted. "Don't you understand? You're going to die anyway! Join the cause, or she will smite you with her mighty hand!"

The soldier removed his helmet, with its glass and metal facets, and looked at her with sad eyes.

Aviv! He had joined the Iycestokian military! But what were the odds that he would be on the deck of the ship she had landed on? How could this be real?

His sweet black face, shining, smiling. His arms around her. And behind him stood their little boy. Five years old, smiling at her. Taelin knelt down on the hard deck. The texture of the metal dug into her knees but she didn't care. She grabbed her son, pulled him into her, tight against her chest. His body felt so small. Bird bones and slender muscles.

"I love you," she whispered into his ear. "I love you, I love you, I love you . . ."

"I love you too Mama."

Taelin was sobbing, shuddering. It was the happiest she had ever been.

"You don't feed him enough," she said.

"I do," said Aviv. "He's just small for his age."

Taelin pulled her son's face back from her shoulder and held it in both hands. When she did, she noticed the silver spots on her wrist. But it was all right. She would get him vaccinated. His smooth young skin, the color of brown sugar—a perfect blend of her and Aviv. It was flawless aside from a little mole under his right eye. His lashes were long and dark and his eyes were bright brown. There were tears in his eyes but his tender lips were smiling.

How could I have let my father convince me to give you up?

Father will take care of us, said the inside-girl.

"I hate my father."

Taelin picked her son up off the deck and held him. He cuddled her warmly, quietly, as if they'd never been apart. As if this was normal.

The *Bulotecus* had disappeared from sight.

"Let's get out of the wind," said Aviv.

Taelin beamed with joy and turned to follow him. It was almost dark. The light was purple in the blowing sand. Out in the storm she could see a desaturated stripe of pinkish-blue where the sun must have been setting. Then part of the deck bent strangely and a metallic bang rattled the full length of the railing. Aviv looked unstrung.

Taelin could smell putrefied fat. The stench carried a kind of moisture, so rich and repugnant in contrast to the thin dry air.

"Behind you!" shouted Aviv.

Taelin gazed into a black eye that sat motionless, barely twenty inches from her face. She absorbed the initial impression: that there were two eyes, and a host of serrated teeth, and a large transparent body. It was tangled in the cables that ran up to the gasbag, clinging with spindly crustacean-like legs. It did not appear to see her.

Taelin slowly put her son on the deck and told him to run to his father.

The movement stirred the creature, but only slightly. Its stubby head lolled to one side as a great leg plucked at the cables, trying to find a better grip. The beast seemed drunk.

She had never been so close to a nyaffle. But she reminded herself that they were far south, over Nah'Ngode Ayrom. This was a wild place.

The creature's glassy carapace hunched up behind its gruesome head, ending in a splayed transparent tail. A host of slender legs acted in unison, clutching at the cables and railing like a clumsy hand. Off its back, the great crystalline wings still hummed, helping to keep it balanced where it had come to rest.

Taelin could see through its transparent armor into its distended gut, as if a plastic bag had been stuffed with fat. The great chunks of white-green blubber it had gouged out with that circular mouth, with those serrated teeth, were already dissolving slowly into milky chowder.

She backed away, watching the sunset convulse within the nyaffle's glossy chitin, its soulless black eyes stared at her.

It shifted an increment, like a specimen pressing the wall of an aquarium, mouth hinging and unhinging as though focused primarily on breathing.

Taelin looked toward the doorway. Aviv was gone. Another ghostly white shape scudded up along the side of the railing, sounding like a child running with a stick, snapping each metal baluster. A xylophone.

"Aviv?"

Women in dark pants were standing on the deck, staring at her.

"Where is my son?" she shrieked. He was lying on the deck, still, blood pouring from a nyaffle bite.

A short stocky shape in a long red coat lurched up beside her. Some kind of crimson goblin. Taelin felt an iron grip and a stab of pain.

"My son! My son!" Taelin screamed, sobbing.

"SHE'S completely out of her mind," shouted Baufent.

Specks' body lay underneath the shrieking woman, where she had picked it up and carried it out and laid it on the textured floor.

"I had him on a gurney," shouted Baufent.

"We need to get him off the deck before the captain sees this!" Caliph called against the wind. He had just helped Baufent wrestle the priestess to the deck and inject her with a sedative in an effort to keep her from leaping over the railing.

With as much decorum as he could, Caliph picked Specks' tiny corpse up and cradled it back inside the ship. He held him, head on shoulder, as if the captain's son had been asleep, as if he was carrying him off to bed.

But no. That wasn't remotely how it felt. It felt horrific. It felt gruesome both physically and emotionally. The wind howled and with the rotting hylden and the desert grit between his teeth, Caliph could both smell and taste the awfulness of this moment.

He laid Specks gently back on his gurney, then helped Baufent lug Taelin down the narrow hall to her room.

Once she was on her bed Caliph went to the porthole and peered uselessly into the purple-orange haze. All he could make out were the shapes of the scavenger-things, the nyaffle. They were landing on the *Bulotecus,* taking shelter from the storm, counteracting the weight that everyone had worked so hard to jettison.

Caliph scowled. He smelled sweet mint and lotus blooms in Taelin's room. He smelled Sena. Caliph glanced around but there was nothing.

"I want you to watch her," Caliph said to Baufent. "And I mean *watch* her. She's your responsibility for the rest of the flight. Tie her down if you need to."

Baufent's hard gray face let slip a hint of misgiving. "I'll do my best," she said.

Caliph left the two women and headed back to the deck, finding a pair of flight goggles along the way. There was an alarm going off somewhere. His ears popped and his stomach pitched. Too many of the creatures had landed on the railings and rigging. Dozens of them. Many tons of chitin pulling them down.

Caliph hoped the witches were taking advantage of the nyaffle. He hoped they were working their equation. And indeed, the witches were on the starboard deck screaming at the sky. Caliph struggled past them, coughing on the dust and putrefaction in the air. He hoped they were doing some good—late as it seemed to be trying to hide the ship from the Iycestokians. He headed for the cockpit to check on the captain.

When he entered the room he found Viktor Nichols in a knot, clinging to a steel stick with a red ball on its end. "We're going down," said the captain. He looked ashen. The copilot was flipping switches without any visible effect.

"You should brace yourself," said Nichols.

Caliph rested a hand on the console. He opened his mouth to make a suggestion just as the nose of the ship dipped, sending him flying over the controls. His back smashed against the inside of the windshield, making fractures. A terrible snapping sound reverberated through the entire craft, then the nose came up and Caliph found himself on the floor.

"There went the mooring arm," shouted the captain. "Probably sheared off at the bolts!"

Caliph had the sensation that the man was wrestling a wild animal. The captain's shoes squeaked against the duralumin floor as he braced himself out of his chair.

Caliph had a good view of the shoes. Iscan brand *High Backs*—featuring a tiny black tag depicting a white mountain: High Horn. His cheek was pressed against the floor.

"Here it comes!" Nichols yelped.

And then the second impact vibrated through the airship's frame.

A dull horrible roar shuddered through the *Bulotecus.* Caliph was lifted up, a momentary levitation, then dashed back down. Again, airborne. He saw Neville come up out of his copilot seat, legs flailing. Down. Bam! Up again. His stomach flipped with the rapid motions.

He realized vaguely that the *Bulotecus* must be on the ground, sliding across the dunes, propellers still thrusting it forward.

He pulled himself toward the door, crawling, bouncing. As the airship hit a prolonged patch of level sand, he was able to lurch out the door and down the stairs.

He rolled over the sharp steps and felt the massive ship heave to a stop. Millions of individual grains of sand screaked against the hull, rasped sharply for a final instant; then the maw of the desert settled, a massive toothless creature that had finally gotten its grip and would never let go. The wind roared triumphantly.

Caliph found himself in a painful pile at the bottom of the steps. His right thigh felt deeply bruised; he was also fairly certain something had gouged a hole in his lower back. His knuckles were bleeding and his face hurt but a real damage assessment would have to wait.

For the moment he savored the stillness of the ship. The only sound was sand tittering on metal. Then he became aware of other things. Wind, a broken cable scraping.

Maybe I'm dying—again. Zeppelins . . . He chuckled. *Fucking bad luck.*

He attempted to move but his whole body rebelled. *What do you think you're doing?* it said.

He kept his eyes shut.

In an attempt to get his mind off the pain, he thought about Sigmund and Baufent and Taelin. He tried to run through the crew list but couldn't. He felt the ones he had skipped. Even though he couldn't remember their faces or names, he felt the holes they left in his mind.

He hoped Sig was okay. Then there was Owain. Owain was a bodyguard Caliph felt some affinity for, even though conversations with him were usually only two or three sentences long. Who else? His ears were ringing.

He rolled onto his knees but sharp pain in both shins threw him on his ass. He pressed his back up against a deck cabinet. At least he was sitting up.

He got to his feet. Sat back down.

Nearly passed out.

He cradled his head for a moment with one of his torn-up hands and felt his hair stick in the blood. He sat there.

He felt alone amid the messy wreck of his life. Stranded in the desert. He wanted to go back to Sandren and make a different choice. Strike that. He'd have to go back to Isca and never leave for the conference at all.

He regretted, in a cloudy confused way, all the people on the *Bulotecus* that he had dragged into this.

He wrenched himself to his feet. His legs were wobbly but he made his first objective an easy one. He stumbled up the steps to check the cockpit. Pilot and copilot were both sleeping over their brass controls; their own red oil leaked across the displays.

Caliph didn't know whether to try and help them or race off and find Sig. He still felt uncertain about his course even as he ripped a first-aid kit off the wall. He pulled each man down to the floor, laying them out as gently as he could in the cramped space. He checked for pulses clumsily, having only a vague idea of what he was doing. Their wounds seemed superficial except for a puncture in Neville's chest. The copilot didn't seem to be breathing.

There was nothing in the kit that would change that. Caliph sifted through bandages and antiseptic. The inflatable splint seemed like a sardonic joke. Caliph grabbed Neville by the chin and forehead and blew into his mouth. Immediately, a thick red goo boiled out of the puncture wound in the man's chest.

Horrified, Caliph stopped. He didn't know what to do for either man. He set out again, down the steps, across the deck and toward the cabins in the direction of women's voices.

When Caliph Howl came around the corner, Miriam gasped. He looked like he had showered in blood and rolled in the sand. At first she thought one of the nyaffle had bitten him. He was barely walking.

"Where are you hurt?" She felt an unaccountable desire to help.

"I'm fine," he said, which was certainly not the case. "We need to find everyone. Get everyone together." He started to cough. She wondered briefly about internal injuries. Whether he lived or died didn't really matter anymore. But the fact that he was walking around—*looking like that*—affected her.

"Why don't you sit down?" she said.

He asked her something in return. She adjusted her head and cupped a hand behind her good ear.

Caliph limped forward. "What's wrong?" he asked again. He lifted a mangled hand and pointed it in Anjie's direction. Apparently he had heard her sobbing.

"Nothing." But keeping him cordoned from the truth was pointless. Even now his eyes scanned the deck, hunting for the reason. He found it quickly. Gina's arm was pinned behind the deck rail. It marked the spot where the airship had rolled to starboard and crushed her body between the desert and the hull.

His shoulders slumped at the sight and he clenched a fist in his hair with what seemed genuine angst. Smothered as he was in his own stiffening blood, the act lifted his curls. They stood on their own even after he removed his hand. "I'm sorry," he said.

One of the High King's bodyguards emerged from the backdrop of wreckage and lowered himself to the deck from a dizzying angle. He carried a gas-powered crossbow and seemed in good health. He fretted over the High King for a few moments until Caliph finally screamed at him to check all the rooms for survivors.

Miriam turned her attention back to the qloin.

"We need to go back," Anjie hissed in Withil. "We need to take her back to Aldrũn . . ." She was hunkered up against the railing, holding Gina's pale hand.

Miriam knew it wasn't possible. Gina would not be one of the girls that returned to Skellum. Her burial wouldn't be in the sacred tombs, but here in the desert.

"Anjie, we can't get her out. We have to go."

"I'm not leaving her."

Miriam felt the pain in her words. They had already lost too many in Sandren and now, as dusk and the sandstorm pulled in around them, thick with the stench of carrion; now, with Sena's ship nowhere in sight, Miriam felt the burden of her decision.

"We can't kill the Eighth House," hissed Autumn. She whispered it into Miriam's right ear, keeping the breach of protocol just between the two of them. Miriam knew she was right. What did this mean? Was this it? The end of the Sisterhood?

They were one qloin now. One qloin that should have been able to do impossible things! But Miriam felt the exhaustion buckle her knees. Its weight was crushing.

"Miriam?"

This time it was the High King of Stonehold that addressed her. "I'm so sorry for your loss." His eyes looked briefly at the tragedy behind her. "Can I . . . can I get your help?" Blood dribbled off his middle finger, hit the deck and solidified in the dust. "I'm going to check the fore cabins," he said. "Will you please check the others?"

Miriam hesitated. What did she care about any of these people? Gina was gone! Their mission seemed impossible. Caliph Howl had ceased to be useful.

"Yes. Of course," she said. Autumn looked at her quizzically. "Stay with Anjie," Miriam said in Withil. Caliph Howl had already turned and dragged himself over the broken deck.

Miriam reached up and gripped the door frame. The passageway beyond was steep but hardly vertical. Inside, she heard the voices of Caliph's bodyguards, gnarled by wind, echoing.

The first door she came to was open. She looked in and scanned the darkness. Nested like ungainly hatchlings in the room's destruction lay Caliph's physician and Lady Taelin Rae.

Sharing the same nationality leant Miriam considerable familiarity with all the scandals Miss Rae had faced in the south. And here she was again, embroiled in political catastrophe, tangled in the wreckage of a Stonehavian airship.

While Miriam climbed toward the priestess, the physician stirred, grumbled and attempted to right herself. "Who are you?" the older woman demanded. She had a huge goose egg on her forehead. Then, "It doesn't matter. Help me get her up."

Together they lifted Taelin's limp body toward the door. There was no place level to lay her down so extricating her from the wreckage seemed the best course.

"Is she alive?"

"She's breathing," said Baufent.

They got her into the hall and carried her downhill, out onto the deck where they laid her on a relatively flat sweep of textured metal. The deflating gasbags formed a pavilion of sorts that shielded them partially from the storm.

Miriam watched a moment as the short woman, tangled in her red coat, checked Lady Rae's vitals. She spoke to Taelin while concentrating on her trade. "Come on," the doctor whispered. "You and I are going to play cards again . . ."

Miriam didn't want to look. She turned away and went back to the qloin. Anjie had quieted.

"The Iycestokians are right above us," Autumn said. "Probably waiting out the storm."

Miriam shook her hand up and down. "Apparently the diplomats—Wade and Veech—were locked in the hold. When we hit the desert, the hull caved in. I heard from one of the Stonehavians that they're pulling the bodies out now."

Autumn changed topic. "So? What do we do?"

Miriam's diaglyphs scanned the wreckage. There was blood. Some here and some there. But what holojoules still sang on the wind were surprisingly scattered. The crash had dispersed everything—even the nyaffle.

There simply weren't enough holojoules to travel, especially not without a starline. Without the markers, without the proper lines to walk, crossing was costly and dangerous. And there were three sisters to move. Far too many cuts of blood to gather from this tiny crew. *But,* she thought, *there is an Iycestokian airship hovering overhead.* She felt confident there would be a hundred eighty people there, which would be enough for the three of them to cross lines.

"The king's bodyguards mentioned a chemiostatic car in the hold but apparently it's destroyed," said Autumn. "The water tanks are broken. They're leaking into the sand."

Miriam inhaled the smell of carrion, strong and choking.

It was actually mixed luck that the hylden's enormous carcass, invisible through the storm, would cover the smell of the crash. She knew the nyaffle had not gone far. Southern papers routinely chronicled nyaffle attacks on zeppelins downed in the deep desert, once or twice a year. If they returned, the qloin could use them to travel. But for the moment the Sisterhood was trapped.

Nyaffle, she mused. It had been a good plan. She admired Caliph Howl. Her thoughts turned from the High King as Anjie spoke her name.

Miriam looked at the two girls she had left. Both of them filthy and frightened though they would never say. Tears had cut through the dirt on Anjie's cheeks but she had checked herself. She was ready for Miriam's command.

"Let's get out of the wind," Miriam said firmly.

She wanted to coax the qloin across the wreck, toward shelter, out of the shock radius of Gina's pale limb. The desert temperature had dropped quickly as twilight slipped into dusk. With Autumn's help, she dragged a thermal crank toward the chosen site, a found hollow between the aft deck and a sand dune. Beneath the zeppelin a pile of food, chemiostatic torches and medical supplies had already started to accumulate thanks to the efforts of Baufent and a couple of the men. The provisions accreted quickly in plentiful contrast to the number of survivors.

Miriam wound the crank. Its dials wobbled and glowed but the sound, the ticking, was inaudible under the red-purple screens of sand that ripped and howled around them. For her the roar was one-sided, monodirectional, entering her brain only from the right side of her head.

She assessed the survivors: Lady Rae was sitting up; the physician seemed fine. Surprisingly, one of the diplomats and a single bodyguard were also here. Both alive. Isham Wade had been hauled out with serious injuries. His shirt was torn open and Miriam noticed that his chest was dappled with silver spots.

"How did he get it?" said Autumn.

"I don't know."

"Are we staying here? Where is King Howl?"

Mr. Veech's body could not be extricated from the crushed metal that cocooned him. Caliph found it difficult to care. He continued searching the wreckage, gut aching, skin clammy because this wasn't a generalized search for bodies. This was a specific search—for Sig.

Caliph's pale green torch zipped back and forth through the darkness inside the airship.

"The Iycestokians—" said Owain.

"We're looking for Sig," said Caliph.

Any moment now. They'd find him. *If I survived,* thought Caliph, *so can he.*

Caliph and his bodyguard scoured the areas they could reach, where the framework had not bent in on itself. Caliph trudged through sand. Back and forth. He had already checked some of the rooms twice.

"I don't understand where he is," said Caliph.

"Maybe he's found the shelter," said Owain. It was toxic optimism. Caliph knew Owain's job was to protect the king, not search for Sigmund Dulgensen.

"Mother of Mizraim."

"Did you find him?" The beam of Owain's torch lanced over Caliph's shoulder.

It was not Sigmund.

Rather, Alani's casket rested on its side. Still sealed. It had broken loose from its ties. One end was buried in deep sand that had poured through the ruptured hull. Its fall had crushed a Baashạn ombrometer.

The gray metal of the lid was beautifully and simply beveled. One of the generic caskets stored on all zeppelins in case of disaster, Caliph ran his hand along it, feeling the smooth endeavor of human dignity.

"Majesty?"

The sound of sand plinking and giggling over the metal had become so monotonous that Caliph didn't notice it until something—the pitch, the ferocity—changed. He could hear a humming sound while sand whined in through the chinks from directions it had not come before.

Gouts of bloody orange light coned the sky, revealing massive banks of raging particulate.

"It's the Iycestokians." Owain took Caliph by the arm and led him toward the darkest reaches of the jumbled space they were in.

"I'm going to find a blanket, something to cover you. We'll put some sand over it—" He was still talking when Caliph heard a thump and Owain fell over.

Hands grabbed him. How could they see without light?

Caliph didn't resist. He let his assailants pick him up, move him effortlessly out of the wreckage and into the blinding ruddy turbulence.

In the light, he could see faces covered with bizarre masks: each like the soft back of a beetle uncensored by carapace or wings. Their weapons clung to their bodies, suckling primates, moving, hugging the shadows of their torsos, looking at Caliph seemingly without the assistance of their wearers.

His captors asked him nothing and Caliph returned their silence.

They obviously knew who he was. There were no mysteries on either side of this process. As they strapped him into a harness that would haul him into the belly of the Iycestokian vessel, defying the might of the storm, Caliph's only internalized question was *Where is Sig?*

CHAPTER 38

Phisku 18

Archbishop Abimael,

As you know, I went north under the assumption shared by the consociation: that the Duchy of Stonehold was engaged in mythmaking and blasphemy and that those activities might form the basis of a new theocracy which would then attempt to legitimize aggressive northern expansionism.

Right now, the papers are full of news both about what happened at the conference and the disease that now seems to be everywhere, spreading so far in less than a week. I hope you are well. I hope you have managed to escape.

I know we've had our differences. I know most of the members will view this letter, since they will receive similar copies, as another outlandish claim springing from the Church of Nenuln. I am well aware that none of you believe in my vision.

Be that as it may, it is my responsibility to inform you that what happened at Sandren was not a solvitriol weapon. It was not a weapon of any kind, as far as I can tell. What I mean is that I believe strongly that the Duchy of Stonehold is not making myths. I believe Sena Iilool is a god.

Furthermore I believe she is solely responsible for the mass murders at Sandren and for the propagation of the pandemic in which we find ourselves.

I know I have somehow disappointed you since the days I came to seminary. My father is a Gringling. Trust between us now is, I suppose, thin and you may wonder why I would make these claims by mail rather than bringing them before the full fellowship. It is because I am afraid.

So afraid that I don't know what to do. Father will take care of us. I believe this will end badly for all of us, that the end may really, truly be close at hand. I am sending this to you so that you can prepare the people in your church, let them know that this must be part of some grand design if it suits you. The Ublisi ruined my party.

Abimael, believe me, I no longer rely on Nenuln. I no longer believe in the sun

is brighter
than I thought.
Give my love to my parents.
You are all going to die.

Sincerely,
Arrian Glimendũlạ

Taelin put the pen down. Her hand hurt from writing. As she massaged out her palm she looked at her wrist. The configuration of silver spots had changed, as if the disease was struggling to conquer new regions of her skin only to lose ground in the rear. The places that had originally itched, where the creature in Sandren had grabbed her, were now clean, but other areas of her arm had become infected.

She noticed that the top of her forearm was as silvery as the aluminum desk she sat at.

It frightened her in an aimless, alienated way. *My son is dead,* she thought, and stared into the little vase of flowers on the desk. *Bitten to death by nyaffle in the deep desert.* She didn't care about the plague.

The Iycestokians were treating her well. They had given her a private cabin, even if the door was locked.

She reached up and drew the curtains from the window above her desk. She could see a throng of Iycestokian troops sifting through the wreckage of the *Bulotecus,* searching for something.

She felt poignantly sad for Caliph Howl, even if he *had* done horrible things to her. His lovely ship lay broken, partly buried in a pool of cobalt-colored sand. The aft portion rested on the orange of the surrounding desert, as if it had crashed into a shallow oasis.

She thought about her night with Caliph. It had been ceremonial. She had shared him with her goddess. A kind of sacrament. It was not a mistake. It had been beautiful. It had brought her closer to Sena Iilool, who secretly *was* the goddess of light: with the sun streaming out of her back.

There was no difference anymore between the Church of Nenuln and *the Fane of Sienæ Iilool: Omnispecer.* They were the same.

Taelin clutched her demonifuge tightly. *I'm supposed to be getting ready,* she thought. *I need to get ready.* She reached for her toiletries and pulled out her razor. She pressed it firmly into her palm and sliced her hand open. Then she held her injury toward the ceiling. "Use me," she said. "Use me for your designs!"

Taelin watched the red-black rivulet roll across her wrist. It followed gravity down her forearm as if she had crushed a pomegranate in her hand. Droplets gathered at her elbow.

After a few moments she turned on the water from the little pressurized tank above her shower. She used the blood like gel, lathering her legs. When water entered the cut it burnt like crazy but she wet her razor and began shaving her body anyway.

Corwin says it snows on the mainland, said the inside-girl.

"It does. But not here. We're too far south."

That's sad. I was hoping to see it. But anyway, the sunlight is lovely.

"I know. I love the sun. My goddess is the goddess of light." The razor fell from Taelin's hand. She was trembling. She had cut herself in many places.

Let's get cleaned up.

"By the Eyes, I've made a mess. What do you think will happen next?"

I don't know. But Sena said we're going to open the door to the future. Isn't that wonderful?

WHATEVER gasses had kept the hylden's organs afloat must have leaked out, perhaps through perforations caused by thousands of glassy teeth, perhaps from rents made by the storm.

But the storm was gone now. Clear skies held sway. And Miriam could look out from her tiny window, across the grisly green and silver landscape of blubber, sunk into rubbery piles and great bubbled domes. The hylden was a much larger gasbag than what had collapsed around the *Bulotecus.*

What it really looked like, she thought, was that some foul god had cleared its throat. Its stink was powerful. More so today than yesterday. She watched its surface, crawling with sparkling nyaffle and wondered if the subtle metallic tinge meant that the hylden too had fallen victim to the disease.

The Iycestokians had processed the qloin. Miriam had allowed it. This was part of getting aboard, evaluating the situation, determining what to do next. Her eyes strayed up from the vast carcass to where Sena's ship hovered. The Pplarian craft was surrounded on all sides. There was little drama. The Iycestokian ships with their huge black hoods and undulating pieces, ringed her in all three dimensions but no guns had been fired.

"What is she doing?" asked Autumn.

"I don't know. Waiting for us I guess."

Earlier, the Iycestokians had gagged all three of them and shackled their hands behind their backs. Gags and shackles now lay in a neat pile in the corner of the cell. The cell consisted of a cramped but clean space with two berths, a window and a wall of bars. Miriam didn't suppose the ship took prisoners often.

On the other side of the bars was a narrow hallway that ran past the cell, the ends of which stretched beyond what perspective allowed Miriam to see.

The floor was textured duralumin and the wall that faced the cell was white. There was, however, a solitary guard.

It sprouted from a simple rectangular pot lined with what looked like shallow brown soil. The pot sat on a short corbelled shelf, eight feet away according to Miriam's diaglyphs.

In the pot was an organ, pale and rigid as a Pplarian phallus and covered with what looked like tiny black eyes. It rose vertically, at an organic angle. Fungoid. Whether it could see or hear or both, Miriam didn't know. She spoke in cant to Autumn. "Are you going to bite your tongue?" She was only half-joking.

"If I have to." Autumn smirked.

"You'd think they'd have come to check on us by now," said Anjie. She nudged the pile of restraints with her foot.

"I imagine they'll bring breakfast," said Miriam.

After a short interval, Autumn scowled and said, "Can you hear that?"

Miriam had no idea what she was talking about.

"It sounds like—"

"I hear it," said Anjie. "It sounds like someone screaming through the wall."

Miriam still couldn't hear it. "Maybe they're torturing the High King."

Autumn looked out the window at Sena's ship. "You know," she said. "There's enough blood on this boat to jump across."

Anjie nodded.

"There's only three of us left," said Miriam. "I think we should regroup. I think we should go back to Skellum."

"I agree," said Anjie. "We should regroup."

"But she's right there," said Autumn.

Miriam didn't know how to say it. Yes, Sena was right there. But Miriam knew Sena, far better, and Sena frightened Miriam. How did she communicate the wisdom of that fear without demoralizing her ancillas?

A door clanged open at the end of the hallway. The sound was accompanied by the loud echoing rattle of a wheeled cart moving over the textured floor.

It stopped almost immediately.

"I'm not eating!" The sharp voice of Dr. Baufent made Miriam smile. She could picture the physician sulking three or four cells down.

The sound of plastic scraping against metal was followed by a crash. Autumn looked at Miriam and covered her mouth. Only Anjie remained grim in the aftermath of what had probably been an entire tray of food, scattering across the floor.

A man spoke with a thick Ilek accent. "Suit yourself. Maybe at lunch you'll be hungry." While he spoke, Miriam heard keys being applied, probably to the physician's door.

"What's that?" asked Baufent.

"Nothing," said the man. "Just going to draw a little blood. We have to make sure you're healthy."

Miriam looked at Autumn.

"I'm healthy as a horse!" snapped Baufent. "Get your hands off me."

"They're checking for the plague," whispered Anjie.

Miriam nodded and put a finger to her lips.

"Please try to relax," the man was saying.

"What's going on out there?" demanded Baufent. "I heard screaming."

"Nothing," said the man. "Everything is fine."

"Ouch!" Baufent cried. "You cradle-custard . . . ouch! Sozzling . . . are you even trained to do this?"

"I'm sorry," said the man. "I'm doing my best." But his voice was tense and strained. He did not sound as if everything was fine.

The words were an invitation. Miriam signaled Anjie who started whispering fast frantic syllables, searching for holojoules. Just a drop. A small bead soaking into a cotton ball that might have been taped over Baufent's arm, for instance.

Anjie made the hand sign for yes and Miriam heard the result. Enough holojoules had been gathered to breach the specimen vial the Iycestokian had used to collect Baufent's blood. It shattered with a pop. The men—Miriam could hear both of them—gave out panicked cries.

It was Autumn's turn to start talking. She quickly gathered the ounces into a stronger equation. A far more dangerous sum. Miriam listened as Autumn turned the fresh holojoules toward the task of understanding what she could not see: the region out of sight, down the hall, the landscape of the breakfast cart.

There wasn't much energy to work with and Miriam felt a pang of anxiety that Autumn might squander the small gift they had been given. But then Autumn's equation changed gears and Miriam knew she had succeeded in finding a tool to manipulate.

With a final word, Autumn ended her sequence and Miriam heard a scream.

There was no point being quiet anymore. Miriam called out to the new supply, a coursing torrent pouring from the man's chest, spattering over the floor from where a butter knife had been driven between his ribs. She used it first and foremost to slice—with numbers—through the other man's throat.

This used all seven cuts from the first body and left her with seven from the second.

But seven was not a small number in holomorphic terms. It was the threshold of sacrifice. It represented enormous possibilities.

Dr. Baufent was shouting. The strange phallic fungus in its pot was screaming and men armed with living weapons were pouring through the hallway door. Miriam watched them slip in the blood as they scrambled down the hallway, searching for the perpetrators. They did not move gracefully. They seemed ill. She turned her math. Their weapons betrayed them.

Now there were gouts and torrents of blood, holojoules singing in the air.

Miriam and her sisters exited the cell through fringe space as the violence continued to spread through the ship. Miriam guided it carefully, avoiding Baufent, avoiding those they had flown with on the *Odalisque.* It was a courtesy. She took blood from the Iycestokians. A great deal of it. Fully two-thirds of the crew went into her equation. Finally it was enough for the three of them to cross lines.

Miriam looked back on the world as if it were a litho. As if they stood on a color image of a prison. A two-dimensional picture of a cell . . . and no more capable of holding them.

Miriam stepped off the image and moved past copper wires, tubing and thick-lensed dials caked with grime. On the edge of the vessel's cockpit she found a woman that might have been the captain of the ship. She did not look healthy.

Miriam felt the darkness boiling behind her. She skirted the lip of the abyss, pulling her ancillas with her. The window back to reality shifted beneath her feet at absurd angles: she saw the Iycestokian airship from top down, the foot of a passing bird—stark against the sky. She didn't have much time to deliberate.

She glanced into another room and saw a man with silver skin curled up on the floor.

"It's not worth it," she said to Autumn. "We need to regroup. I'm taking us home."

Miriam dragged them north. Her decision meant that she would not be Coven Mother. She would remain Sororal Head. But she had had enough. Her girls had had enough. She didn't care what happened to the High King of Stonehold. Her little group had suffered too much.

With the holojoules of a hundred eighty lives propelling them, Miriam found the places where the starlines intersected the planet and calculated her coordinates.

She pulled her sisters along the outside. They travelled vertically in a higher dimension, up reality's thickness, thumbing through the pages to find the right place to reinsert themselves.

At her back, Miriam felt the void. She had crossed lines before and while there was the worry of losing touch with her window back, this time it was different. This time she felt something *in* the space behind her. A presence she didn't dare look at.

Instead, she looked at riverbanks, a cloud, a weathervane on a barn. She looked at a pile of silver bodies in a village and the things that were eating them. She had to concentrate on these things, on tractors and naked footprints in the snow. She had to focus on her window in order to keep from turning around.

Something *was* there. Prickling her skin. Just over her shoulder. Behind the corner of her eye.

"There's something following us," said Autumn.

"Don't look back." Miriam gasped. She could see Skellum through the window.

"It's made of gold," said Anjie. "Gods it's so beautiful . . ."

Her back crawling, Miriam stepped through the image and shuddered violently. She stood in Parliament at the great black fireplace. Safe. With a bright blue day pouring in through the windows. A chill went from the crown of her head, all the way down her spine.

"Oh—" Autumn's voice sounded like she had misplaced something important.

"Don't worry," Miriam said. "We have the book. We'll find a way to open it. We'll go back for Sena—" She turned around. "I just couldn't risk it anymore. I couldn't risk you—" Miriam counted heads. All two of them. Autumn's face was pale.

"Where is Anjie?"

CHAPTER 39

Caliph heard the screaming but it sounded far away from where he was lying, encased in bandages, tucked in with warm fuzzy pain medication that the Iycestokians had administered. Sena's pink hair and little black nurse uniform gave him confidence that this was all a dream. Scene two. Act something or other. Invert it. Stir it with a wooden spoon.

He did not feel compelled to investigate the shrieks, which was a nice change, since they were fiction—and he was tired. Nor did he feel compelled to jump up off the bed and grab Sena by the . . . arm? There was little clothing to grab her by. He could grab her by those two short pony-tail bunches or the slender heels on her boots, but doing either would probably steer his reasons for grabbing her in the first place down the wrong road. And that would be terrible given the fact that so many people had died.

He was angry with her. Partly because of what she had done. Partly because the real Sena had ignored him—and only this Sena, the dream Sena, the one he made up, still paid him any mind.

The real Sena evaded him . . .

In her white flying machine.

The drugs made him think of her as one of the beautiful insects he had pursued with nets and burning fingers, with breathless leaps and desperate eyes—as a child.

He had broken many handles against the headstones, where the insects landed to fan themselves, only to watch them flutter away like silent laughter.

Could he blame them? The only thing to do, if he ever caught one, was stick a pin through its lovely body, drip poison on its head and tape its wings down inside a cigar box until it dried. Sena's fate would not be so different if he caught her.

He heard another shriek but still didn't feel compelled to investigate it. That was a relief because he was so tired. His head was thinking in circles.

Everything, the whole world, was a cool intravenous drip and nothing could be expected of him. That was why, instead of jumping off the bed and grabbing Sena by the arm and shaking her when she showed up miraculously in his room; instead of asking her what in Emolus' name she had been doing, he instead focused on the sparkling tube between her fingers. He didn't want to drink it. He remembered the pain from before. His bones tearing through his skin. But her expression was quintessentially sincere.

"I just want you to understand," she said. "Think of me as your Veyden spirit guide."

This made him laugh. He couldn't understand what she meant but he smelled the sweet familiar fume around her, which was lovely until the ship pitched and he nearly threw up. "Are you really here?" he asked.

For a moment he determined there was no one in the room. Then she said, "It doesn't matter."

"Why are you doing this? Why don't you just help us? Help me find Sig . . ." He was deeply interested in what the fictional Sena might say and which of *his* thoughts his subconscious would choose to impose on her lips: concocted by himself to soothe himself. When she said nothing he took the sparkling tube and swallowed the tincture.

"It's going to be different this time," said Sena.

And it was. This time there was little pain.

One eyelid blink and he stood in the house on Isca Hill, feeling the cold at one of the windowpanes and watching the snow come down in the front yard. A cap of white obscured the head of a statue with a broken sword and seraphic wings lost among the trees. "Soon-soon," he heard himself whisper. But he was not himself. He was not Caliph Howl. He saw his hand come up to the frosted glass, old and roped with purple veins.

His uncle's hand.

"Soon-[illegible]." Three, seven, six. His finger drew a shape in the crystals on the glass. Almost like a flower opening.

But it was not a flower. The Unknown Tongue registered with him even in this crude medium. The symbol was a nonphysical two.

The two represented the only hope Nathaniel had in the world. Caliph realized this. He experienced his uncle's thoughts directly, without filter, as if they had been his own. He could taste the wetness in the old man's mouth—so foreign. Feel the frailty of his slender bones and translucent skin.

The numbers rolled through Nathaniel's skull over and over. They were his mantra, his instructions. Three—seven—six. Prepare the page. Create the ink. Escape the world.

Six. Slippery six. The six's surfaces curved protectively around that lower curl. As if hiding something. Such a subtle shape. Almost a mistake really. Adjust part of its arc just a little and it would turn into a zero.

Prepare, create, escape. Twice. Once for each of them.

He drew the number two again on the frosted glass.

Caliph laughed a little at the notion of the Yịllo'tharnah but even as he laughed he felt something squirm between the lobes, down in the germinal recesses. A sensation he could ignore only if he kept thinking fast, sliding forward quickly and rationally—else the thin crust on which his empirical sledge traveled give way. And whatever squirmed underneath the ice, if he fell through—

Then his uncle's ice-black eyes cracked. And he *did* fall through. And all the glass in the long hallway of the house on Isca Hill shattered and Caliph looked out with no barrier between himself and those strange wintery trees that moved their branches like cnidae: a forest of pale hydrae in a murky pond, immortal and silent—

What were they? Were They the Yịllo'tharnah?

A floorboard in the hallway creaked and Nathaniel looked down. "What are you doing out of bed?"

Caliph saw himself, his own mirror-haunted eyes. His own small body, tense-fisted, dragging his pillow across the floor. He heard his own asthmatic breathing. He had tears in his eyes.

"I saw something in my room," said Caliph the child.

"Go to bed." Nathaniel looked back out the window. *Three-seven-six. Three-seven-six.*

Caliph could sense his other self. The perfect replica of that small person he had once been, rooted in the carpet as if in deep mud. Stuck. Too afraid to go back to bed, too afraid to speak and risk the consequences.

Nathaniel looked at the child, standing in the hallway with the trembling lip, straight brown hair and—

"Go to bed!" Nathaniel shrieked.

Then he turned and stormed down the hall, leaving the boy in snow-sparked moonlight.

Caliph went with his uncle. He had no choice. He was inside of him, feeling the startling energy of that body as it moved through the house by memory, charging through lightless passageways with confidence. Nathaniel climbed the stairs to his tower room, threw open the trapdoor and clambered into a space set with a canopy bed that resembled a black crown surrounded by walls of bare stone into which had been chiseled deep-plaited designs: symbols of dimensions interacting.

He pulled his thick red book out from under a plate of quail bones and opened it to a marked page. *The jellyfish glyph!*

It was not black like the other glyphs because it had been inked in pure, undiluted blood. Caliph knew this.

"You are my creation," Nathaniel said to the glyph. "My little island in the dark."

He stared at the glyph under moonlight until it glowed with a white halo, then lifted his eyes and studied the afterimage that wavered in the air of his room. In that image, more than the image on the page, lived *the squirming.* The white pieces of the glyph twisted and broke off like ice in black water, drifting into darkness—consumed.

"They're behind it. Always behind it," Nathaniel whispered. "Waiting." He chuckled with absurd glee, took a pencil and clicked the chemiostatic light on his desk. Then he sat down and wrote a small block of text in the margin of the *Cịsrym Tạ*:

> No answer for the seasons! Prepare or perish! Ha! Plant, harvest, lay up fuel lest we freeze. Or we can travel . . . Go south! But we must react! We must do *something.* Because one morning the snow will fall. It is inevitable.
>
> This is obvious, but notice how easily we accept it, like dull beasts. We know it in our bones. Our controls cannot reach the seasons, nor do we believe that they are sentient. So we do not scream at winter as we would scream at an animal for digging up our garden. Or too, when the child (despite scarf and mittens) fails to make it through the snow; the police find her later, stiff and pale in a ditch—they do not organize a search. They do not relentlessly hunt her killer or seek for justice.
>
> It would be absurd.

CALIPH stepped out of Nathaniel's body, straight through the wall, into the wintry hydrae flailing in the underwater woods, following the sweet smell of the tincture.

Light swelled around him.

The trees darkened. The black sky turned white and the white trees turned black. They looked young and ancient at the same time, well-pruned and snapping, with a summer-sounding profusion of silver leaves. There were shadows in those dreamy trees, of warm comforting umber and purple-dappled reflections moving in their shade.

Silver leaves spiraled from black isentropic branches. Sena waited, one knee knocked against the other as if embarrassed or nervous. She was hiding someone behind her, holding someone's hand. A little girl stepped out. Sena bent at the waist and whispered encouragingly in her ear.

Caliph began to distrust the vision.

But the girl smiled. She released Sena's hand and ran in shy uneven steps toward him. Caliph had no idea what to do, but he crouched down instinctively and felt her arms wrap around his neck. She smelled of cold fresh air, sweets and paper glue.

Odd.

Over her shoulder, Caliph looked at Sena. There was a canal of black water beside them that reflected the leaves. Beneath its surface slipped endless schools of ivory fish. The child's embrace was tight and trembling, as if she was afraid to let go.

While Caliph endured the awkward grasp—her entire body clinging to him—he noticed through the trees that he could see part of a city with nuanced domes perfect as soap bubbles. Like pieces of summer blown by children. But they were not whole and glossy. They were bubbles at the end of their existence, dry and ephemeral as spiderweb. Split seconds from vanishing forever into gold and lilac-colored light.

"Where *are* we?"

Myths and stilted verses translated out of musty books mumbled from his college days, out of Desdae; about a sweet forever after that stirred the poisoned tissues of his mind. The place to which the Gringlings had tried and failed to return.

Sena answered his thoughts. "This is the jellyfish glyph."

Did that mean he was in a glyph? Or did that mean this had been a glyph at one time? He thought about the shape. The rusty darkness of that design he had seen in the *Cịsrym Tạ.*

"Begun by Nathaniel," said Sena. "I wrote the rest of it. Now you're here."

"But I'm dreaming," said Caliph with light, musical condescension. "I'm drugged up on some ship in the desert . . ."

He did not feel compelled to be polite with his own imagination. He stared at Sena as he picked the girl up from the trail and held her easily in one arm. The child's breath startled him, less restrained than an adult's. It was loud and raspy in his ear.

"Don't do this to me," he said. He was talking to himself of course. But Sena glowed in the raking light through the trees: an icon, an advertisement almost, torn from the foggy streets, from the jumble of Isca's billboards.

"It's still hard for you to control," said Sena. "I'll help you. Stay with me."

But a furious blackness erupted from the house on Isca Hill as if an ebon bedsheet had been thrown out one of the tower's red windows. It flew down over the snowy front yard, casting Caliph in shadow.

Caliph felt the world roll. The yard became a white tablecloth snapped open.

Sena looked into Caliph's face. "Hold on, Caliph." The silver-leaved trees became a gleaming array of hoses and saline bags. Window light filled up the place where he was lying on a gurney. "This is a dream!" Caliph shouted. He pointed. "It's a dream! You're manipulating me."

"No." Sena's gold hair caught light, white as the sun. It burned like snow. The glow became a halo, too strong to look at. Its aura obscured her whole body. It burned out his entire view of the world. Everything went white.

Caliph could hear an alarm. He assumed it was an alarm because he could also hear voices shouting beyond the wall of his room. The tincture didn't want him to get up yet. Sena's voice was calling him back, down into sleep. He didn't even know if the tincture was real, or if it might just be some additional element of the dream.

He heard echoes in his head of Sena's voice, telling him that she had something else to show him. She was begging him to come back. She was pleading for him not to go, but he had seen enough. He was through with self-delusion. He was done with lying here on a bed when Sig's body was still missing.

"He's not dead," Caliph said with a drugged slur.

The alarm sounded strangely animalistic. Certainly not mechanical. A kind of singing.

Caliph got up, head throbbing. The room swung. The room nearly won; almost pulled him down. He steadied himself against the wall and noticed that the Iycestokians had taken remarkable care of him. Near the bed was a window that looked down on the wreck of the *Bulotecus*. His ribs were wrapped tightly with some kind of elastic. His eyes were swimming. He didn't remember coming to the window. The smell of the little girl, the light shearing through the bright trees, Sena's familiar posture on the path—

He shook his head—gently—and regretted it. Sharp pain shot through his neck, all the muscles stiff as taproots.

The room contained medical equipment.

A knock at the door preceded, by only a few seconds, the entry of a man Caliph thought he had seen before, just after his capture. Tall and thin, there was a certain franticness to the man despite his being smoothed down with southern pomade. He looked disheveled and frayed at the edges, like he was barely holding himself together, like his composure was a hard-to-pull-off act. Caliph noticed blood on the man's sleeve.

"Siavush," he said.

"Where's Sigmund?" said Caliph. "The big man. He was wearing a red shirt."

"We haven't found anyone that fits that description."

Caliph decided the tension in the man's face was linked to the alarm.

"You told Isham you had the book," said Siavush. He spoke from the periphery of Caliph's world in a hurried, terse way.

"I did," said Caliph.

"I'm confused then, because Isham is recovering, enough to talk, and he said you showed him a *yellow* book. But I had heard that the book in question was red."

"Well your information's bad," said Caliph as if barely concerned. "It's always been yellow."

"I see. We found half a yellow book, ripped through the spine, but it didn't seem to be anything. Just a journal. It did, however . . . by Mr. Wade's account, look like the book you showed him."

"If you want me to cooperate, you'll find my friend, Sigmund. Big man. Red shirt. He's down in the wreckage somewhere." *Lost under the sand . . .*

"We'll do our best, Mr. Howl. But we can't stay here . . . long." The "long" was peculiar to Caliph.

"Why not? This is a solvitriol ship. It's not like you're going to run out of fuel."

A scream filled the hall outside the room and the sound of running feet pounded away.

"Listen, I need that book!" said Siavush.

"Really? What's the urgency?"

"Where is it?" Siavush shouted. He drew out his pocket watch and flipped it open. Pastel light ebbed over his panicked face.

Caliph wondered what the rush was. He hated the sight of the solvitriol timepiece. "How do you do that?" He pointed at Siavush's watch. "Cope, I mean. With the fact that you've enslaved souls to run your machines in the south? How do you get to the point where you believe that's okay?"

"We don't have time for this, King Howl. I don't believe in souls."

"That seems a bit arbitrary in light of the blueprints—"

"Gods. You northerners really are—" Siavush stopped himself. "Solvitriol power runs on the residue . . . of some power . . . left over from the body. That's all. It's a trace. Some kind of energy that used to—do something in the body. We don't know what it is. But it's not a soul." Siavush snorted. "No tests we've ever run indicate that it thinks. Or that it can communicate. It's not a ghost, Mr. Howl. It's just what's left over. And we're practical enough to recycle." His finger, emerging from the bloody cuff, did a small circle in the air.

Caliph's injuries ached. "I suppose you're right," he said. "The north has always been a bit more . . . superstitious. Anyway, that's a beautiful watch. Could I see it?"

"I need the book. Now!"

Caliph reached out and grabbed the pocket watch. He pulled it up, high overhead. It was not until the chain had been looped around Siavush's neck that the Iycestokian understood what was really happening.

In small countries, like Stonehold, thought Caliph, men were still taught things forgotten in Iycestoke. Things that Siavush, in his slippers in the morning, would not understand . . . no matter how many pieces of northern journalism he might read over breakfast. In Stonehold, where the mountains could kill you. Where the wind and sea and sarchal hounds . . .

In Stonehold, where survival was a real struggle, men were taught how to survive. They did silly things. They wore swords.

But as Siavush's hands groped ineptly, without the slightest notion of how to save himself, even against a man so badly wounded, Caliph felt some sick-making pride in coming from a long tradition of what the north called *Stonehavian resolve* and what the south had always labeled simply as *brutality.*

Caliph did not stop even after Siavush's face was purple and his full weight pulled forward from the knees. His body *was* kneeling but it wanted to lie down.

After counting out a full minute, Caliph let the chain go. He dragged the body to the room's tiny closet.

Not possible.

Caliph was sweating. He felt inexpert at this. He felt like he might throw up. He went to the window and looked out. In his current condition he doubted he could heft Siavush's body through the window. Dropping it into the desert wasn't very subtle anyway.

"Fuck." This was ill-thought. But what else was he going to do? The alarm was still quacking its strange high-pitched song. It seemed strange that no one had come to check on him. It felt bizarre that there were not more sounds of running feet.

Where were the guards?

Caliph gave up on hiding the body and opened the door. The cramped hallway beyond was, perhaps because of the alarm, empty of people, but painted in blood. It looked like there had been a slaughter. The walls were coated. The floor was covered with a red half-congealed sauce.

Caliph felt his gorge rise. He started pulling off his bandages as he went, not wanting to stand out in case someone passed him in the hall.

Where is everyone? he thought.

Not knowing where to go or what to do, he followed the hallway to its end and met no one, headed away from the sound of the alarm in what he imagined was a good first step at getting his bearings.

He passed a room with an open door that looked in on the unmistakable resting form of Isham Wade. He was on a gurney of sorts in a cabin identical to Caliph's. The main difference was that Isham Wade had been hooked up to a system of insectile-looking machines. He looked gray. Silver really. His skin was horribly changed and speckled with black spots.

Plague? But how would Isham Wade have caught the plague?

Caliph hesitated a moment at the doorway. He thought about pulling the plugs. No. There was nothing to do here. Nothing that would make Caliph feel better. He looked hard at Isham Wade, angry and repulsed.

The man had already contracted his punishment. Caliph would not interfere.

He moved on into the hall's terminus, which was a wide space that surrounded an open locker full of weapons. Caliph stared at it while the alarm wailed. That sound might have explained why it had been left open, unattended. But it was not serendipity that made him stare. Rather it was uncertainty and fear, both over whether this was truly a weapons locker and whether finding it ajar had just saved him or put him into deeper peril.

He stared at the rack of sedate, dark, leathery things and questioned whether they were watching him. All he knew for certain was that they moved.

CHAPTER 40

The tantrum of shadows that whipped and splattered over walls, rooms and mechanisms had finally retreated. Nathaniel's ghost had left the Pplarian ship and gone south in a rage, bent and billowing and thorny. It cursed Sena. It howled and ranted on the mountains: on K'rgạs, on Bujạit and Jạg'Nạrod. It raged back and forth between Veydith and the Kallywạrthing.

Sena could hear it in the thin, tropospheric miles that girdled the world. It drew over the jungles like a black squall, gathering in on itself, a clock spring tightening.

He had not foreseen this. That she might sentence Arrian to Taelin's body had never entered his mind.

Sena felt a little swell of pride but the danger offset her euphoria. Would he unleash St. Remora?

Nathaniel had disappeared south, beyond the equator.

She hoped not. In the meantime she dug in the moist peat of a Tebeshian pot, beneath the alien stain of the flower's shadows, and snapped off part of the pimplota's root. Growing the pimplota from a twenty-thousand-year-old seed in the span of a few moments required only marginal holomorphic tampering.

The root came out of the peat, clean and waxy, like a mummified toe: purple, ghosted with hair-like tendrils and morsels of dirt. Juice coursed over her fingers. Nearly black.

She extracted the liquid with a small wooden herb press. It dribbled through a short spout into a shallow clay mixing vessel. Sena wiped her hands, willing her cells to repel the pigment. They came clean instantly. She sat down and drew out a silver vial. The same silver vial that she had taken to the Howl Mausoleum twenty-three months ago.

She would have used her own if she had any: Hjolk-trull blood. So incredibly rare, like those moths from the steppes, on the verge of extinction . . . the bacteria in their fur capable of miracles.

In one sense Caliph could be reduced to this vial, stoppered and preserved. Just an ingredient. Just a substance to be manipulated. Sena put the smooth metallic cylinder to her lips. She could smell iron and steel. It made her feel close to him.

She opened it and poured all but the last of his cells into the clay vessel. A few drops she spared. Then she added salts. Together, with the acids and tannins of the pimplota juice, the suspension formed an ink that would not deposit, thicken or mold. It would never fade, crack or flake.

This was the recipe for ũlian ink, the ink that had written the *Cịsrym Tạ.*

Sena corked the clay vessel and shook it vigorously, using math to quicken the reaction. It required no heat. She strained the liquid through a hair sieve and poured the resulting colloid off into a glass bottle.

It was time to test the ink.

She took out her gunmetal pen and depressed the beryllium filler. It slurped. Ink glugged from bottle to sac.

She adjusted it. A few test scribbles.

Then she took a sheet of parchment—not one of the three sheets of her skin—and began to draw. As she drew, she felt the sky tremble. The desert below her charged with static. She whispered and the ink called for information, organizing itself quickly, capturing the dimensions, the contents, the structure of her mind. Omniscience was not a passive thing in this process. She could not approximate here. Isomorphism was not enough. The analogous shapes of letters, the property of being legible was meaningless in the creation of Inti'Drou Glyphs. Precision became essential.

The enormous energy required to form the glyph came from her ambit and from what remained of the dwindling, evaporating holojoules she had coiled around the Pplarian ship. There was not much left. Most of the holojoules from the massacre at Sandren had slipped away. But there was still enough—just barely.

She pulled them straight into her pen.

Sena focused on the page until it felt like her eyes might cause it to burst into flame. Far away, the *Cịsrym Tạ* began to dissolve.

Its form and information, its substance, was reduced, reconstituted. The essence of the thing that it was appeared in the glyph on Sena's page.

It was simpler than other glyphs, being a compression of a single object—no matter how dense. She looked at it, its shape devoid of the Dark Tongue instructions so familiar in the shadow of every glyph catalogued in the *Cịsrym Tạ*—she did not need them. In addition to this, its shape unsettled her. Different somehow than she had expected. It threatened vaguely and she associated it instantly—not as her own creation but as a curiologic phenomena—with watery allusions to blossoms, universes and myxozoa.

The image stayed only long enough for her to appreciate it.

Could she do this? Had she gotten it right? But when the sound came out of her mouth, passing over her vocal cords, it was nothing that she could have produced before the Yịllo'tharnah had modified her. It was her first enunciation of a complete Inti'Drou Glyph.

As she spoke, the shape on the page disintegrated. The glyph vanished and in its place, defined by coordinates she had written into the page, lay the *Cịsrym Tạ*.

The book was back.

But its movement from Parliament to her airship was not the miracle of the moment. Teleportation had not been the purpose of her proof. Nor was bypassing the wards in Parliament's deepest vaults—the most secure vaults in all the north. Yes it pleased her, but this was not about thievery. What this was, she thought, was proof that she could do it.

Metaphorically, she had entered into the lowest scholastic grade of immortal entities that now surrounded her and had proven that she could learn to read and write and yes, *speak* in Their tongue.

She reached out and picked up the book. With the tiny vial—and the last drops of Caliph's blood—she released the lock, taking shortcuts she had been unable to take a year ago. She was above graveside incantations now. Beyond circles and candles and locks of hair. Because the Yịllo'tharnah had granted her immortality. They could not kill her now and so, only the blood was essential.

The latch on the book popped open and the hideous beautiful thing opened beneath her, symbols intact. Even Nathaniel's handwriting in the margins had been preserved. A perfect copy. *Not* a copy, despite being one. That was a confusion derived from language. This was the book. It *was* the *Cịsrym Tạ*. Its only difference lay in its coordinates.

She opened it to page eight hundred forty-seven directly, near the end of the book—as if she needed to check—and stared down at the page that still contained the jellyfish glyph.

Its shape was the shape of branes touching. The beautiful violence that embodied the instant of discharge. In this glyph's heart lived the mad excitement and headlong rush so typical of the processes of production: frozen at the moment in which new creation was released into the universe, ready for love and ridicule, nurturing and abuse. But there

were sweepings scribed there too, in the shadows of that burst of energy, bruises and casualties. Sacrifices made to the machinery of creation, remnants discarded on the workshop floor that told of the incredible effort of making something new.

Having succeeded with the *Cịsrym Tạ,* Sena spoke again. this time her vocal cords strained. The pronouncement was far more difficult but the glyph that Nathaniel had slaved over, the glyph that she had finished, vanished from the page.

She stared at the blank sheet in the book and nearly laughed with joy. It had gone out. It had gone out, gone out, gone out! It was real. It had changed from a possibility, from a dream she had only ever seen in a tincture journey, to a real place, a real island in the stars!

The empty page was a victory and for a moment she allowed herself to smile, to look from the fathomless cosmos, from the creation that the glyph had formed, down into another possibility. A tiny one. The secret dream sleeping in her womb.

WHAT if she had never opened the book?

But Sena knew. To look away would avert nothing.

In Their eagerness to break through, lay the makings of the pact. And she had made up her mind, forged her purpose from surprising cruelty, from the feral, animal ferocity of a mother protecting its child. It made her unpredictable. It made her capable of startling things. She would not turn away. This was her decision. She would not change it now. She would see this through.

Sena put the *Cịsrym Tạ* into her pack along with the three crisp sheets of vellum that she had cut from her back. Then she pressed the rest of the pimplota root into a jar that she sealed and wrapped.

She could see through the walls of the Pplarian ship to the great armada of Iycestoke that had surrounded her. They had not shot her down yet in the event that she had the book with her.

She could hear the armored troops on the craft that had silently positioned itself directly above hers. She watched them release drop ropes, saw the men descend and land on the white skin of the Pplarian balloon.

Atop the great modulating gasbag, they began their search for the hatch, the rungs that would lead them down to the decks, and to her.

Yũl had left. She was alone.

The great capacitance of holojoules from the murder below Sandren had now been fully spent and there was little purpose in staying here.

Sena gathered up her designer backpack, with the pimplota juice, the book and her other essentials.

Where are you going? Nathaniel made her jump. He had returned quietly.

"Come and see," she said. Then with a bloodless word, she vanished from the ship.

AFTER Sena spoke she stood for a moment in front of the Howl Mansion, looking up at the unbroken windows that had always filled her with dread. She waited for Nathaniel to trace her movement and arrive. There was no reason to hide from him. Doing so would only fuel his anger.

Snow buried the yard but brown weeds poked through and hissed at her. The mansion looked black, but the windows were red and seething, a scarlet sunset boiled inside each one.

You can't be serious, said Nathaniel.

Sena dropped her pack in the snow. She left the book, the supplies for the ink, all of it—sitting in the weeds. "Why? They betrayed our trust." She walked up into the wind above the yard and passed through one of the windows.

Nathaniel followed.

As I said, you can't be serious.

"I'm straightening this out."

You can't threaten Them. And what about the book—

"You'll go back and protect it, won't you?" Nathaniel resonated on a frequency Sena took for hoarse disparagement. "We're a team now," said Sena. "You and me."

Your half is bent on our destruction. Nathaniel had been here before, many times, on the other side of the glass, gathering secrets, collecting numbers. But he had never come *this* way. The road to the north was closed to him.

Sena looked up at an atmospheric phenomenon that passed for violent thunder. It looked to her like the sunlight was sweating through layers of cherry gelatin and tar: cloud layers bowed around the front of a black and crimson storm.

Gravel crunched under her boots.

The dead world of the Yịllo'tharnah was accessible only through Nathaniel's estate. The house was a cork in the hole that the great holomorph had cut out. He had built imperfect windows, scraped them clean with math. They provided a smudged view of what lay inside.

There were no furnishings here. No ecology. Sena felt like a child setting foot in a haunted place.

"What did you study here?"

Them. Of course. I found where They wait, separated from Their Queen, drowsing until She opens the doors. And there was the matter of wiring St. Remora's clocks to this place. A tricky business, threading it from the church, then pulling it through from here. I wonder if you are here to sabotage—

"Am not." She scowled, insulted.

This isn't the dimension where Næn struggles at the world's core, you know, with Her luciform brood? But you may have seen that in the Chamber? You've never been here before, have you?

Sena didn't answer, which only gave him cause to continue.

This dead plateau, with its netting of augered crypts, is where They hauled Themselves after the fuel ran out. They designed this place. Now They wait, suspended, gathered at one point, so that Their collec-

tive gravity might help to tear the fabric, loosen Their bonds and disgorge Them like slippery fish, following Their Queen from one world to the next, thrashing alien, renewed, reborn and ravenous.

Sena walked north, passing a singular column that stood mightily against the wind. Her diaglyphs measure it precisely: one thousand six hundred eighteen feet tall. "Isn't that your cue?" she asked. "Shouldn't you turn back soon?"

But the black gibbet of Nathaniel's shade continued to follow her, suspended several feet above the plateau, refusing to blow away.

I'm not leaving yet. It's ridiculous to scold Them for what They did to you at Sǫth. Your vanity is repugnant. They will not listen to you.

It felt strange to Sena that he was talking about these things rather than still assaulting her over his daughter. He seemed almost to pick up on this thought and abruptly change tack. *What made you betray me?*

But to Sena, there was something wrong even in this question. His angle did not originate from his daughter. It focused only on him. Why had she betrayed *him*? Sena stopped and looked at Nathaniel directly, puzzled, letting her thoughts seep out. The shade had no clear features. Only a hint of sharpness both at the place its nose might have been and also at the ends of its hands. Nathaniel's eyes were terrible black holes. "You care so little about her, do you?"

What's done is done. Your cruelty exceeds mine. Now that you've bottled her up, what will you do? Tell me again that we are a team?

She didn't believe it. He had not gotten over it so quickly. There was something he wasn't telling her. Something she couldn't figure out.

A fleet of shadows passed over the ground, causing Sena to look up firmly into the wind. Grains of sand bounced off her corneas but she did not blink as a legion of dead flyers careened overhead. They fled the great red storm on the horizon with bodies that undulated like tissues caught in wind.

I think I know what you are up to, said Nathaniel.

Sena felt her throat clamp tight. She hoped desperately that he did not. Below her, the hollowness of the plateau flourished with gauzy indigo things. They were many and one at the same time, silent yet moving and enormously cognizant of both her and Nathaniel's presence.

She did not warn Nathaniel of his danger. If he was undone here, she would be glad. If he was foolish enough to stay a moment longer, she would rejoice.

And he was. He stayed stubbornly, glaring at her while an army of pebbles inched in the wind, making sound as it crossed the vast key bed of solid rock, beneath which stirred the presence he had to fear.

The Yịllo'tharnah began to uncoil. They seeped out like carbonic gas and yet he pressed her, hatred ferocious enough to anchor him. *I think I* know *what you are up to . . .*

The huge black pillar behind him moved with shadows. Its lee side held a deeply carved depiction of some hideous creature or agglomeration of creatures and though embossments many feet deep had withstood the sand, they showed nothing more than the badly cratered semblance of a host of eyes and moving fur.

I will protect the book and wait for your return.

Finally, Nathaniel fled.

He was gone in an instant, slipping out between Their claws.

Sena heard the pebbles move. She looked down to where it seemed an entire ocean had once raged like a river for eons and worn the bedrock to a satin finish. Occasional pits, where softer minerals had been hollowed out, harbored little handfuls of gravel. There were whispery designs in the stone. A repetitious pattern of timorous shapes, cast random as dice. Sena's eyes traced the faint outlines of teeth, sockets and jumbled ribs—not of prehistoric fish—but of men and women.

Fossils of the old world.

With Their only prey gone, the Yịllo'tharnah unrolled slowly, lethargic and tired. Sena waited for Them as the clouds thinned above her head and opened on an enormous red star sinking into the valley beyond the plateau. A smaller brighter point of light, dwarfed by the scarlet titan, glimmered and followed its epic descent.

Here at the edge of the plateau, on the brink of a huge vertical miter in the world's crust, Sena noticed the angles of intersection with the surrounding geography, how they proscribed light and reflected darkness. It was a phenomenon she had never seen before. Darkness cast itself through lit canyons of sky in beams and pillars and gradients. Lovely and terrifying.

And then she realized how the vast valley before her, a megalodoppelganger of the Great Cloud Rift, resembled a sunken font and how the distant crumbling mountains, High Horn in particular, felt like the worn stumps of non-human caryatids in a row. As if this had once been a continent-sized temple, a building that could tip the world . . .

At that instant, Something groped skyward through the rock, touching her abstractly, mouthing her with its thoughts. A vague threat rose through the fossilized stone.

Sena was afraid.

A moaning sound coursed through her ears. Her dark trench coat snapped as if clothespinned to a line. How strange! They had inverted the colors.

Her coat had been red. But now it was black and the bandeau underneath had changed to crimson. She tried to change it back, to re-imagine her clothing, but realized that her ambit extended precisely to the limits of her skin, not a fraction more.

You look better in black. Red is your accent.

They were not Nathaniel's thoughts. These thoughts came from below, smooth, dark and vast as a polar ocean. They were not words. They were not even sentences. It was by approximation that she interpreted them. There was no humor, even sardonic, to their composition. Just as there was no sincerity. The thoughts were devoid of recognizable logic or opinion.

What made them so breathtakingly alien was that they did not mean what they appeared to mean. The Yịllo'tharnah had no opinion on color, or style. They were not commenting on her sense of fashion. Their thoughts communicated a simple yet multilayered threat. What They had really said was, "We are here. We see you. Notice that you have little power in this place."

Where is the book? the Yịllo'tharnah thought at her. Again it was a thought too large to encapsulate with words. Not a question at all but rather a caress—a kind of worship. They knew she had left it out of reach—like Taelin's necklace. They knew this and did not attempt to tear through vague parallel coordinates in order to make a snatch.

Sena felt the writing in her skin grow even colder as They retraced what They had written, making certain she had not modified the design. Her pages had been cut from the prescribed location. She had done nothing wrong.

Sena tried not to move or recoil. Their touch was as icy as the world she stood on, racing around its dying star. The Yịllo'tharnah touched her with the curiosity of a machinist examining a part for wear but she was still functional, well-oiled and shiny as the day They had made her. Her ambit was strong. They accepted her as perfect. The creation and the Creators were on level ground in this: both would last forever. She was beyond Their power to melt down, to recast. The gift could not be taken back. Which was why, Sena supposed, the integer had to be small.

Having traced the lines methodically, the Yịllo'tharnah withdrew. They were satisfied.

It was her turn to assess. "You tried to take the necklace at Sọth."

This was why she had come, despite Nathaniel's admonition, to scold Them. To try to threaten Them for Their betrayal.

The reply from beneath the plateau was grim and smarmy, a hint not of apology, but of acquiescence—like a lawyer, Sena thought, reluctantly amending the contractual loophole It had authored.

She stood atop Their tomb, feeling insignificant, a tiny mite perched on the corner of a great piece of furniture. Their promise was clear: not to interfere again. But when They were free, she knew, there would be no promise that They would keep. Pleading would not change that, even though her instinct was to plead.

Sena gazed at the stars just beginning to gleam in the quadrant where the storm had burnt the sky. There was no oxygen here. Bright, young, feral suns, billions of them watched this version of Adummim spin like a marble on oblivion's lip.

Her meeting was over. What could be settled was settled.

The number stood at two.

The Yịllo'tharnah had recognized her and the lines in her skin lost their temperature as the capreolate Entities above the plateau pulled down, chilly and bloated. Acres of invisible sweet tendrils sank beneath the stone and boiled softly in the dark.

Sena felt the sand ping against her cheeks and knew it was time to go. Something like a gasp filled the hideous cold desolation of the plain.

She spoke a bloodless word and turned to step from the murrey vista, through a tall and impressive window frame, out again into the snowy yard.

The ruined estate of Nathaniel Howl loomed behind her. The trees creaked from the edge of the mountain woods.

Nathaniel was there, waiting for her, hovering over her shiny backpack in the snow.

CHAPTER 41

Taelin realized that the Iycestokians had locked her in her room. She knocked on the door. She called for help but no one came.

She shrieked and wept and tore objects off the walls. She scooped up the little crockery of flowers from the aluminum desk and hurled it out the window. After the flowers went other things: her clothes, her pen and a tin of tissue. Her letter to Archbishop Abimael went too.

The Iycestokian nation must be punished for locking me up, she thought. *But how?* She looked around the room for a weapon, a letter opener, anything—

Then she remembered her razor. She snapped it up. The handle was still buttery with soap and blood. She took a moment to scream and pound on the thin door before whirling around.

It began to sink in just how austere the room really was, and how cell-like. She went for the curtains first; sliced them into strips. Yes. Iycestokian taxes would have to pay for that!

With the curtains in shreds she began cutting up the sheets and pillowcases, slicing up the mattress.

Sit down, said the inside-girl.

"I don't want to sit down. We need to get out. I'm on a mission from—"

You're making a mess.

"Shut up!" Taelin's shriek filled the room with sound. "Shut up! Shut up! Shut up!"

I will not. Father will come for me. I don't need to do anything. Just sit down and wait. Wait like I did in the dark.

"You're crazy. I have to get ready. I have to break my necklace. I have to get us to the jungle."

But Taelin did sit down on the edge of the cut-up mattress and for a moment held the razor to her silver-spangled wrist. "If you don't shut up, I'll end this!"

It wasn't true. She had tried before and lacked the courage. But as she bluffed, she noticed that her razor was an almost perfect match, colorwise, to the silver blotches covering her arm. The two very different things, knife and flesh seemed to blend together without any pressure at all.

It's my birthday today. You can't kill me on my birthday, said the inside-girl.

"Get out of my head!" Taelin threw her razor on the floor, then she picked up the aluminum desk chair. It was incredibly light and delicate, just like the door to her room. She swung the chair like a pickax. It rang in her hands. Its legs bowed but the door dented and shuddered under the blows.

Give up. We don't need to try to get to Ahvêllẹ. Father will open the way.

Taelin remembered her descent into the dripping gulf of nightmares, where the hoarse voice in her head had been real, where the inside-girl had been the outside-girl, the girl with the petrified eyes, the girl whose head Sena had sawed off and dropped into a shopping bag.

"Sena will save me from you!" Taelin screamed. "When the necklace breaks, I'll be free of you!"

The door bonged and twanged like a bell forged from the wrong sort of metal. Its upper portion started to bend when the latch gave way and Taelin followed her chair out into the hall.

"Nenuln's light!" She saw herself in a mirror hung above a table, flanked by two crockery pots of flowers. There was blood on the mirror. Blood on the floor, on the pots of flowers. She seemed to blend into the scenery, naked and coated with red grime. *What happened to my clothes?* She let go of the chair. Her palms were lined with deep aching trenches.

In the distance, something shrieked constantly, echoing around corners and nearby, just a few feet down the hallway from the table and the lovely mirror, a man on his hands and knees was vomiting. The man had one hand on his weapon, but he was busy. Taelin took it from him with a sense of déjà vu. It was a velvet gun. She hefted its soft bulk against her chest and stepped past its owner, bare feet unable to avoid the warm slippery spatters.

The hot light of an open airlock made her blink and the dry biting fragrance of the desert beckoned her past the vomit. Outside, in the blast-furnace heat, she could see shapes dancing crazily, haloed by the blinding sun.

CALIPH reached into the locker fully expecting to regret it. When his fingers brushed the first cool leathery shape, the hair on his arm sprung up. His eyes struggled over the object's long-hung thinness: like a plucked goose. It flinched slightly, then touched him back. It stretched out with an appalling willingness, coming off the rack like an infant reaching from its mother toward a stranger. Headless, simian and dark, Caliph could not tell whether it was actually intelligent.

The thing's cool skeletal embrace drew its small mass up close against Caliph's chest where it adjusted to his panicked movements. It flinched beneath his elbows, swinging its "body" around to his lower back. The creature, or thing, was lightweight and sinewy, hairless and flecked with ferruginous eyes: both on its central thorax and nestled in the deep soft flesh of all four of its "shoulders."

It was boned like an old woman.

Caliph had no idea what it did or how to use it. Still, the long hairless appendage that sprouted from the top of the weapon's rib cage, and which ended bizarrely in a single plumose frond, seemed to be the business end. Like the antenna of a moth, it quivered slightly and stayed erect, hovering behind his head. He had to crane his neck to see where it floated, preoccupied, seeming to taste the air.

I guess I'm armed, he thought. He still felt naked with nothing in his hands but if he didn't have to manipulate a weapon he supposed that was for the best. His whole body hurt, his neck in particular. He could feel where the Iycestokians had stitched him up.

The hallway he had followed ended here at the weapon locker but there was a wide archway that opened onto the airship's deck. He could feel the desert heat tonguing through the exit, mixing with the cool air of the hall.

He looked out tentatively. Nothing moved except the shadow of the feathered appendage, which lengthened before him. He watched it slide forward over the smooth metal decking, silently checking the kiln-dry air.

The deck itself was devoid of both weapons and men. Caliph tested its desertion by venturing to the railing and looking down at the wreckage of his former ship. The sound of the alarm faded behind him. He turned and moved toward what he believed was the front of the craft.

Most of the ship's crew had probably been assigned to the wreck site.

Even so, he stepped quietly into the shadow of an airlock cased in black flaking metal, veined with conduits. On his right, a glass housing flecked with orange water stains glistered from the pastel fluctuations of solvitriol energy inside it. The doors opened automatically, double-startling him, first with their sudden hissing movement and then with the thing behind them, like a person in a sun-sheltered cave. Skin shimmering and silver.

It was a woman with greasy red-brown hair, and the hint of a double chin. She stood there a moment, shorter than he was, staring at him while a single strand of milky saliva stretched between her lips.

Caliph recognized the disease despite its not having eaten her down to the bone yet. She carried a subtle roll around her midsection. What he couldn't understand was how she had gotten here, aboard the Iycestokian ship. Then he noticed the patch on her tight-fitting uniform sleeve. She was a crew member.

She bleated like an injured animal and walked toward him. Caliph's instinct was to try and help but when she touched him, when her hands clenched in his shirt, the feathered tail behind his head came down. A slender talon of bone emerged like a dewclaw from a hidden fold near the tentacle's end and punctured her through the chest. The attack brought the woman to her knees.

She looked into his face without any emotion. He reached out and grabbed her by her soft meaty arms, her shoulders, steadied her and eased her toward the deck.

She came down on her right side with the bone spine still inside her, limbs nerveless, eyes staring as if bewitched by the soul-lights in the glass housing beside the door.

Caliph didn't know what to feel for her. Partly he was numb as he stood up and watched the spine withdraw, retracting silently into a cartilaginous groove beneath the frond.

The breeze from the desert was hushed enough that Caliph turned his head at the sound of footsteps just inside the airlock. He could feel the frosty coolness of the ship's interior leaking out into the heat around him. The ghastly shapes of two more crew members with glazed eyes and silver skin were coming out onto the deck.

Caliph backed off, wary.

He looked over his shoulder for a means of escape and at that moment heard a dry brittle sound in the sky.

It came from the direction of Sena's ship. A crescent formation of hooded Iycestokian vessels flanked her as she sat motionless several miles out. The black hooded warships made a gloomy crackling sound that spread by means of lilting murmurs interspersed with terrifying sizzles and pops and other surprising crescendos. The sound birred out in every direction, then echoed back from the edge of space.

The crackle resonated in Caliph's body an eternal moment before the Iycestokian guns fired in unison and turned the Pplarian airship into a symbol. Caliph couldn't even scream.

His voice broke under the force, trailing off into a hoarse croak.

Hands grabbed at him from behind and he heard the tentacle of his weapon whine through the air. The weapon thrashed and stabbed and killed but Caliph's eyes were not on the silver people trying to maul him. He looked at the Pplarian ship that had opened like a white lotus, ejecting beautiful golden globules of light and giant starfish arms of cream-colored steam. He was listening to the reverberations of the guns. The entire sky warbled.

Caliph felt the hands now. They were hurting, clawing, digging but he still couldn't look away. Strong thin fingers pulled him, turned him. The white explosion vanished behind a tangle of dark torsos and arms. Why wasn't his weapon protecting him? He looked down and noticed several bodies. Apparently it had killed five or six crew members while he had been distracted. But now the weapon was sweating great burgundy droplets, as if it was fevered. As if it was sick.

The bone spine clawed feebly at one of his abusers before two grisly shapes pulled it from his torso and hurled it at the deck. Arms were everywhere, faces blocked out the sun.

Caliph still felt drugged. He swung his stitched-up hand at his assailants and felt the wound tear open. He hollered. It didn't matter. They surged again. A knot of carrion birds squabbling.

Caliph looked through them at the sky. There was a square of light framed by their moving limbs and heads, ever-changing, a triangle, a squashed octagon of stratospheric blue. But at least he could see out, see past them to something beautiful, something pure.

Ladies, gentlemen, members of the North-South Peace Protocol, we are here today, gathered at the great city-state of Sandren, a symbol not only of prosperity but of peaceful independence. I'd like to start by—

His talk unrolled in his mind, aimed at the blue sublime.

After a few moments he realized that he had lost track of the words and that the small aperture through which he had been looking had expanded. It was not framed by a frenzy of moving bodies anymore. The borders of his vision had stilled. He slid his elbows back along the deck, far enough to prop his head up and look around.

Half a dozen men and women in uniform lay around him, brushed by wind, dripping in milky goo. The sun was a blazing white flare. Too hot. But there was a cool softness on his neck, supporting him. And a tiny bit of shade in the shape of someone's head. He looked up at Sena's face, upside down, hovering over him.

For a moment he felt afraid. Terrified of her. Terrified because when she smiled it was not a familiar smile. Her hair was long and coffee-brown and her body was covered with red war paint. It was not Sena. It was Taelin, gooey and crimson and joyous.

* * *

The dappled silvern bodies fell away from Caliph Howl. Taelin fired one more time at a livid torso still struggling to rise.

Thick creamy strands spewed over the blazing deck and spread a bitter-sour smell. The grisly shape floundered and collapsed as the subtle venom paralyzed it and began its dissolution. Taelin stared unblinkingly at her handiwork. The changed crew reminded her of insects in tree sap; their silver-gold eyes bulged beneath the sun.

She set the velvet gun down and moved around behind Caliph Howl. He was barely conscious. For a moment he seemed to recognize her and smiled faintly. His stitches had opened up and he was bleeding badly.

"You are not going to die out here in the sun." With great effort, she dragged him up a ramp and into the cockpit where the coolers were blowing through the vents. He had already passed out by the time she got him situated on the floor.

It had taken all of her energy to move him and for a while she rested and listened to the desert howl. The cockpit was tubed with black pipes and glowing solvitriol bulbs. Most everything was written in Ilek with the exception of a chrome-and-brass fire extinguisher.

The inside-girl was being quiet. Taelin eased back against the wall. Sweat and blood gelled on contact with the cool metal; she felt her skin stick to it. She was on the verge of relaxing, when the room darkened dramatically. Maybe the ship had pivoted in the wind. A sound thrashed against the fine hairs inside her ear.

The only intelligible words she could pick out of the static-rich vibration were: *I found my daughter's head . . .*

Taelin shivered and stood up. She went back out onto the strange chitinous deck where the heat was baking the dissolving bodies. She picked up the velvet gun but nothing stirred.

Taelin looked toward the empty place where the Pplarian ship had been, but she knew that the Iycestokians could not kill her goddess.

Faith was the opposite of fear.

She was wondering where her clothes had gone.

Caliph Howl needs help, she thought. *I should go find Dr. Baufent.*

CHAPTER 42

A woman stood in the sky, surrounded by yellow-white chaos. Shrapnel, fumes and scalding steam cartwheeled through the air. Hülilyddic acid atomized from chemical cells in the Pplarian ship's mythic compartments. The explosion had dispensed a sour perfume that floated in helices around her.

The woman seemed preoccupied. Her fingernails sorted through her curls, scraping the scalp just above her forehead. This was visible in minute detail through the Iycestokian gunsights.

"Sir, she just disappeared."

"What?" The commanding officer leaned forward and peered into the sight. "What's wrong with you?" he asked. "She's right there."

The gunner looked back.

It felt like a glitch but there she was, miraculous and dazzling, standing in the sky. The gunner was afraid.

The deep rigid fear that springs from the impossible had filled him and it had already spread man to woman to flight lieutenant to brigadier general up the chain of command, as each person in the armada took their turn at the scopes and stared.

The scopes told the truth about the thing that couldn't be, but *was*: in casual defiance of their might.

SENA fears that Nathaniel might still undo her plans. She fears the future and the moment when she will have to look Caliph in the eye. What she does not fear, are the Iycestokians.

They have no way to cross her ambit.

She does not hate them. They have no idea what is coming or what has already passed. They are just following orders, just demonstrating their violent national pride.

What they believe is that the Duchy of Stonehold has a book, which they have been told to take by force. They do not understand the legend of the Sslîạ. Their guns have failed them and now they are confused, trapped within themselves, trusting to a shilly-shally episteme of vaccines and imperialism and all sorts of strategies divorced from what is real.

It is because they know so little that she decides to save them.

Returning from the Howl Estate she finds her airship flinderized, but this is a simple misunderstanding. The Iycestokians do not know what they want. They have made an error. She will give them what they need.

And she will do it out of kindness, out of sacrifice. She will take a piece of her ambit to work this miracle on their behalf. But they will not thank her.

She speaks and vanishes from the sky.

Nothing can stop her as she arrives in the capital of Iycestoke City, in Môlbũl Square where the three turfs of the ochlocracy meet. She uses raw math to quiet the quarters before her main argument goes off.

No terror-stricken cries lift from the silver crowds where disease has already taken its toll.

She is barely there an instant before she is back above the desert. But in that instant, her voice is in two places at once, sound waves still projecting.

In Iycestoke, an unnatural hush goes out over a six-mile radius of urban sprawl.

It begins with a watchman positioned at the entrance to Ninel's tomb: Iycestoke's sacred monument. But it does not end there. Next to him lies another man with a worn and haggard face. His collar flaps senselessly against his cheek. Beside him rests a pale silvery girl dressed carelessly in black wool. To her left is another body and to that body's right three more.

The crowd crumples in the moment when Sena is there. It continues crumpling now that she has left. Across the enormous vapor-wrapped city, every breathing creature plummets. The starlings and pigeons have fallen from the sky like cruel hail. They plunge to the streets, thumping against cobble and brick.

People sleep in unseemly positions, faces pressed to stone. Some kiss animal excrement, gutter grates and garbage. A few fall into puddles face down where they are doomed to drown.

Iycestoke sleeps.

"Shh—" and twenty million people more or less join the dreamless oblivion from which their bodies begin to burst.

It begins with the watchman.

His terrible stain spreads out behind Sena in the same instant that she disappears. It forks bizarrely like a pair of bloody wings, as if a plastic bag full of red paint has been hurled at the pavement.

Iycestoke is red. Its citizens are spell-slaves in the purest sense. She gathers holojoules from ten million bodies and leaves the rest sleeping like wild cattle shot for sport to dream and die. Already she is back in the sky above the desert, with the holojoules in her mouth. The gunners on the Iycestokian ships have just seen her flicker in the sky.

Nathaniel is frantic. He does not know what she is about to do. He reaches out tentatively to St. Remora and his soul machine, ready to bring his power source to life.

But when he hears the numbers coming out of her mouth, he sneers.

She is a merciful god. The Iycestokians are blessed. They will not find themselves in a labyrinth when the Masters come.

Sena knows that this is a betrayal of the trust between her and the Yịllo'tharnah she serves. But she smiles. It is payback for Their brazenness at Sọth. They are angry with her now. She has stretched the limits of Their patience and now she pushes it to the absolute edge. The Yịllo'tharnah are enraged. These souls will have a different fate. Unlike the rest of Adummim, the people of Iycestoke will not fall beneath a Yịllo'tharnahic yoke.

Sena takes the holojoules of ten million people and turns the blood of Iycestoke's civilians against their great armada.

It will not be true salvation, but it will be salvation's shadow.

THE Iycestokian fleet fell out of the sky. All safety devices on all one hundred seventy-nine of the huge hooded monstrosities failed. Crews and admirals were caught by surprise.

The sound of their plummet was not loud. The sound of their impact was. A chorus of metallic groans and deep geologic shrieks sounded a thousand feet below. The crashes did not echo above the blue and whisky-colored sand.

Sena took no joy in it. The black crescent of wreckage completed a nearly perfect ring far below her feet, gaps filled in by craft that had—erenow—orbited her in a sphere.

She looked down at the new geography and chewed her lip. God of a dying world. Light streamed from her shoulders, spitting rays through steam and dust and acid that had yet to fully clear. Emotionally, she was threadbare. Irritated at Nathaniel for his lunge toward St. Remora.

You reckless fool, Nathaniel hissed.

Sena walked across the sky, briskly at thirty knots, heading for the only ship she hadn't touched.

I found my daughter's head, Nathaniel said. *Floating in the ocean.*

"Call me callous but I don't think you really cared about her. I think there's something you're not telling me." Sena looked across the desert, north and west, across the Great Cloud Rift and out to sea. Nathaniel wasn't lying. Arrian's head was there, bobbing like driftwood. Why had he gone searching for it? There had to be a reason beyond familial affection.

This wasn't a game.

Nathaniel didn't respond to her assessment. He had left the desert and gone out over the sea.

Sena stepped from the sky onto the deck of the Iycestokian ship. Taelin was there, naked and blackish-red from head to toe. By comparison, her eyes and teeth looked incandescent. Dr. Baufent stood in the doorway, watching over Taelin's shoulder with a terror-riven expression. Her whole body stiffened at the sight of Sena.

Taelin rushed forward. She got down on her knees.

"Shh," Sena whispered. "Don't do that. Don't do that." She pulled Taelin off the floor. "Get up, Taelin. Get up. We need to get you washed. We need to get everything and everyone washed. And we need to move Caliph into a proper bed. And then we need to get this ship moving again. Are you with me, Taelin? Do you understand?"

Taelin smiled a grisly smile and nodded her hand up and down.

CHAPTER 43

Earlier in the day, the Sisterhood had swung Parliament's countless metal grilles closed across each towering windowpane. The pins were secured. Doors were bolted. Blood was spilt and the entire ground floor warded and sealed.

Despite this, the windows had shattered within moments of the onslaught and winter had billowed in. A forest of arms still flailed between the bars at every casement. Snow drifted through the central hall. The statue of the Eighth House in the atrium had become part of a frozen wasteland. Nevertheless, the silver mob did not break through.

Miriam mused momentarily over the not-quite irony that Mirạyhr's citizens had always been careful to muffle their criticism of the Witchocracy. Only now—after they could no longer enjoy whatever freedom a victory might earn—had they found the courage for rebellion, for revolution.

But as she stood in an icy balcony off the west wing, overlooking the wild fingerlings of the Wịllin Droul, Miriam knew this had nothing to do with domestic unrest. All that had happened was that somehow, after hundreds of years of clandestine warfare, the Wịllin Droul had gotten the upper hand. They had moved their dominion out of slumbering lightless reservoirs and unleashed their disease on an unsuspecting world.

Days ago, when word of the plague had first reached Sandren, many of the lower Houses had struck out through the cold. They had gone while Miriam was away, before the citizenry had turned. Before it was clear what was happening, sisters of the Fourth House and below had gone to be with their relatives.

If Miriam had been here she might have stopped them. Megan certainly would have stopped them. Those sisters that had stayed behind now maintained their vigil from Parliament's second floor.

Two hundred twenty-two women. Hardly a crowd. More like the number of tourists on a slow day, a scant sprinkling, nearly lost amid the frescoed empyreal chambers. They were all that was left to guard the seat of Shrạdnæ power.

Naobi burned five nights from full, pure white above the milling yard, which gave Miriam a clearer view of the numbers they faced. A thousand at least. Hundreds had frozen to death, but others had arrived. Their cries filled Miriam like the white moon filled the ice on the balcony railing.

Miriam looked up and imagined a vast ghostly squirming in the abyss beyond Naboi's vivid corona.

Polar lights? she thought.

After crossing lines from the desert how could she think that? They had lost Anjie between the worlds. They had lost so many girls. They had lost their position of power here in Skellum and now, they had also lost the book—a secret she was trying to keep from the Sisterhood.

To Miriam, the faint ebbing tendrils in the sky were sinister. As if the Devourer had come back and turned its ravening on them. Was this it? Was she the last head of the mighty Shrạdnæ witchocracy, destined to cope with the crumbling infrastructure Megan had left behind?

The sky swirled horribly above Parliament, black and hissing.

"Everyone's assembled."

Miriam felt ambushed. She had not heard Autumn approach. Now she could make out the ice crackling underfoot. It bothered her that Autumn had snuck up on her without even trying.

I'm a detriment, Miriam thought. *A liability.* Her injury could, in the course of any engagement, prove disastrous. Autumn knew it but said nothing.

Miriam smiled at Autumn whose calm, sweet-timbred voice, rather than reassuring her, reminded Miriam of all they had been through—and where they were going.

"All right," Miriam said. She kissed Autumn on the mouth, softly. Then she put her arms around her and held her close.

"It's going to be all right," she whispered. She could feel Autumn's shoulders tremble inside the embrace. Thankfully there was no sound.

"We're going to catch her," said Miriam. "We'll end this. I promise you. We're going to be all right."

MIRIAM left the balcony and the soft whickering cries of the ghouls and went into the yawning end of Parliament's largest meeting hall. All that remained of the Sisterhood was here, gathered by firelight and colorful metholinate lamps. Perhaps there were still qloins in Yorba or Greymoor but birds had been sent and none had returned. So this was it. All of them.

The room stilled as she took her position.

Miriam took a sheet of paper out of her pocket and unfolded it. She held it loosely, in one hand.

"Here we are," she began. Her voice cracked. She had never been comfortable in front of crowds.

"The questions you have are simple. 'How did this happen?'

" 'Where did this terror come from?' And most importantly, 'What do we do now?'

"All of us have lost friends and loved ones. I share your grief. As you know, until this morning, I was in the south, tracking Sena. Over the past three days I have lost some of my best friends. I was forced to leave them: in Sandren. And in the desert.

"We know from what papers were able to publish before sickness stopped the presses that the Wịllin Droul's disease is everywhere. It is in the north and the south, the east and the west.

"The people of other nations cannot understand the significance of this event. Sadly, it may be too late for many of them to ever learn. But *we* know. We know this sickness marks the end that our enemies have long threatened.

"We knew this would happen if the Wịllin Droul ever returned. The Sisterhood was founded on preparing for this war.

"I know some of you believe Sena has assumed the mantle of the Eighth House. That Giganalee passed it on to her before she died.

"Even if that is true . . . Sena must be stopped.

"How do we stop a myth? How do we stop a legend?

"We stop it with truth. We stop it with determination. We stop it because we must. And most importantly, we stop it *together.*

"We cannot fear the future. For the enemy's sickness we have wards. For the enemy's lies we have truth. Against their desires for destruction and chaos, we will bring the hammer of order and hope. We will meet them with blade and tongue.

"We will turn them, we will win. And when we prevail, when their false hopes have been heaped in the street, we will have fulfilled the thing this Sisterhood was destined to fulfill.

"Prepare yourselves. Tonight, we fly. Together we go south. Our enemy will know fear."

Miriam raised her slender fist.

A subdued cheer went up in the hall.

EVEN from under Parliament's roof Miriam could sense the cold empty wave-like motion of the sky. It leaned on Parliament's ancient steel trusses.

Dizzy and upset, she left the front of the room, barely acknowledging the applause.

Autumn would get the girls sorted.

Returning to Skellum had turned out to be critical. Another day without leadership and she might have found the whole of Parliament empty, the entire Sisterhood disbanded.

And that was the most demoralizing part of the Sisterhood's situation. The flawless had not come to Skellum. In Skellum there were no primeval horrors. Here, there were only fingerlings. It was just the disease and the onset of the transformation.

The Wịllin Droul had not found it necessary to send a single cabalist to the Shrạdnæ seat of power. No battles with ancient abominations here as there had been in Sandren. Miriam felt the hot embarrassment of that truth: that the Wịllin Droul no longer considered her organization a threat.

The Sisterhood could not stay in Skellum. Here they were trapped and useless.

In the Shifting Sands near Umong a pile of markers delimited the starline that the Sisterhood would follow. There in the wreckage, outside of Bablemum, the entire Sisterhood would arrive—perhaps irrevocably—in the deep south.

Miriam had used Megan's scrying dish to find Caliph Howl, filling it with her own blood. The sacrifice had bought her fifteen minutes of insight; the numbers in the bowl had told her he had arrived over Bablemum.

This was frightening because it meant, most likely, that he was still chasing Sena and that Sena had indeed arrived in the oldest city on the Tebesh Plateau.

Bablemum was where the Bedrigan Aquifer bubbled up. So ancient that the locals took pride in their *fossil water,* as if some antediluvian vitality imbued what came up through pipes and wells. A local company bottled it and shipped it all over the Tebesh Plateau at exorbitant prices.

Used to anyway.

The oldest city in the south had looked ominously silent through the blood in Miriam's dish.

Why would Sena lead him to Ŭlung? That dark watery stronghold within the aquifer? Was Sena just a puppet of the Wịllin Droul? If so, could the Sisterhood face the flawless at Ŭlung with any hope of success?

Miriam thought about the aquifer, which connected through underground seas and rivers, to the east, west and north. Prehistoric cracks that led beneath the Ghalla Peaks had allowed the flawless to poison Sandren. They could reach Stonehold. They could reach anywhere.

There was no telling how many of them were down there, sliding through the dark, tainting the drinking water of a million cities with disease.

CHAPTER 44

Despite having woken from a terrible dream, Caliph breathed easily. His body tingled with pleasant, torpid warmth. The dusty rawness of the desert, which had made his throat sore and shunted blood through his sinuses, had been replaced with gauzy humidity. Air soft as cobwebs dragged over his skin; he could hear the outside world, ebbing on the draft. Based on sounds, someone had put him to bed with the window open.

His ears opened like sinkholes, funneling sound directly into his brain. He was curious where he was, but still too sleepy to open his eyes.

Big occasional droplets dinged on tin, thumped on wood. Intermittent. There were tree sounds as well, or maybe grass, behind which murmured a faintly unnatural urban stillness. Soft electrical purring mixed with the unmistakable sob of tree frogs.

Caliph lingered, enjoying the after-rain smell and the softness of his pillow.

Faint flickers and far-off thunder encouraged him to stir. His last memory was of Taelin bending over him. He swallowed hard. His throat itched and his eyes were puffy and hot. The air tingled with sweet black molds and mildew.

He squinted; sat up; dug the crust out of his tear ducts and realized that he didn't feel nearly as well as he had thought. Though warm drugs still gloated in his capillaries, vague pains lingered.

He set his feet on the cool flooring and peered toward the window.

"Mizraim . . . Emolus—"

He got up and stumbled toward the astonishing view.

Beyond the window, the sky boiled with ultramarine storm clouds, immolated by Naobi.

He was still on the Iycestokian ship. He recognized the smell. But while he slept, it had moored at the edge of a city where great stupas, not of stone but of ornamental iron, enmeshed the clouds. Black cage-like shrouds surrounded and capped the city's more compact structures.

Purple lights in cupolas and minarets bled wetly through the grilles.

Copper wires and golden transformers traced the blackness with countercoiled designs. Signs glowed and bubbled in the empty streets. Tropical trees hissed as wind pushed through husk-like silken fronds.

He drank it in for several moments. Then he noticed a folded stack of papers, propped up, labeled with his name in Sena's handwriting. He picked the papers up nervously. They were paper-clipped together. Their contents had been typed.

He read them by moonlight and scowled.

Session #2: Phismas, Sae 9
Stenographer: X. Fadish
Subject: [redacted]

How are you feeling?

[redacted]

Good. What would you like to talk about today?

[redacted]

I see.

That's a lot.

Well let me try to respond to all of that. I'll start by saying yes. The Veydens do say that visions without actions are only dreams.

[redacted]

No. No one really knows where the Veydens got their pseudosciences from. Some claim they deciphered old stones in the jungle.

[redacted]

Yeah, well the Pplarian-Gringling link is really just speculation. You'd be hard-pressed to get a group of scholars to believe—

[redacted]

Sure, but nowadays, Greeny *culture* is practically invisible. We're like birds in the market. We've been skinned and chopped into anonymous pieces. Our origins have been sterilized.

[redacted]

I'm entitled to use it. It doesn't offend me at all. I like to remember that we're green. I like the stigma: of wealth and cunning, smelling like turpentine and expensive smoke.

[redacted]

No, it's *not* what we used to be about. We didn't used to sell our secrets to the companies. But now look at us: in posh apartments on the avenues, living above Ilek and Pandragon and Despche alike.

I'm proud of that, by the way. I'm proud that we're doctors, psychiatrists, holomorphs for rent.

[redacted]

Sorry, I don't give readings or sell talismans. I can point you toward some colleagues that will work out elaborate star charts. I don't do that either. My approach is more direct, which I assume is why you came to me.

[redacted]

Yeah. Those questions aren't really up my street.

[redacted]

I'll try.

[redacted]

That's right. You're pretty well versed for a girl such as yourself.

[redacted]

Yes. You're going to eat my heart with that silver spoon. Where were we?

[redacted]

Right. They call her the Sslîạ. It's like uh . . . deliverer. *The* Deliverer.

[redacted]

Well that's because it *is* a murky legend. You know this entity is not gender specific. Sslîạ is like—

[redacted]

Right. Exactly. There would be a lot of interest in making sure you get the right person for the job. (laughs) Assuming it was real.

Anyway, I simply don't know much about the subject. The only reason I know anything at all is because—you guessed it—shuwt tinctures.

[redacted]

No. I don't believe that. Keep in mind none of this is science.

[redacted]

I don't know if Pplarians have ever used shuwt tinctures. That's way off track.

[redacted]

Okay. Fine. The short of it, right? Is that some entity, the Sslîạ, uses these tinctures to travel around in time—sort of. It's part of some big apocalyptic bullshit scenario. So, in the end, supposedly, this Sslîạ uses the tincture to escape this epic black cosmic meltdown of the world or universe or whatever. He or she disappears and leaves everyone else in the lurch. That's it. That's all I know.

[redacted]

(laughs) You're funny. No, I mean, no one knows, right? This legend is old as dirt. I have no idea whether there's some grand purpose.

I've certainly never heard of one. The Sslîạ just . . . does crazy stuff, and then disappears.

[redacted]

Well I think there are some drawings. Old engravings or whatever. But you know they always show the Sslîạ hooded and gender-neutral. The actual entity of the Sslîạ is described as having wings. Wings of light. And the power to destroy the world, of course, which is symbolized as a sword. That's what this whole myth is about. The Sslîạ shows up, prepares the planet for the end of time—maybe that's your grand purpose—then it opens up the floodgates of destruction and disappears instantly on a drug-induced journey into forever after.

[redacted]

Yeah, it is nice. Why can't all recreational drugs have legends like this to bolster sales?

[redacted]

Right. These notes you've brought. You said they're from your grandfather's war chest? My opinion is that you should stop reading them.

[redacted]

Sure I can translate Veyden. I'm green, aren't I?

[redacted]

This one here? Gnôr-ak Gnâk Zith'yn Åuth-ịch Aubelle Aubiel Gnâk Næn'Ữln Thũ-ru Ryth-ịch El.

[redacted]

Yeah. I know that.

[redacted]

No.

[redacted]

Maybe you're thinking I'm an olive with its core cut out? Half-Veyden born and raised in Pandragor . . . long way from the jungles? So how can I be so sure of the deeper cultural significance?

[redacted]

Sure, but, I'm sorry, your translation is just wrong.

Look, I'll do it word for word, exactly. Darkness-in Light Exist (with a plural subject marker there) Many-of One Terrible Light White Moon'Gold Culminate-will Age-of Sadness. It's a bit esoteric but the translation isn't hard. Just that Næn bit.

[redacted]

Right, "white moon gold" is a bit ambiguous. That's because Næn'Ŭ̃ln is a religious word. It could be purely descriptive—a thing that's whitish-gold like the big moon—or it could be a proper noun. If I were to translate it for you into Trade I'd probably write it something like: In the darkness there are many lights, of which one Terrible Light, white-gold like the moon, will culminate an age of sadness.

[redacted]

Hey, if you want to think it means something different, use your translation instead. You won't upset me.

I just don't think you should focus on this. It's bad energy. It's easy to read fear into that little Jingsade-sounding whatzit that some Veyden probably copied from a carved block.

[redacted]

(laughs)

[redacted]

Well, I'm laughing because here you are, sitting in my den of iniquity, asking me about shuwt tinctures but treating me like your priest.

[redacted]

No. What I do is offer counsel on the use of an extremely expensive, extremely dangerous and extremely illegal recreational drug. Why? Because I *do* feel some moral obligation to help really rich people not kill themselves while they're getting high. It's that simple. What other brand of drug dealer hires a stenographer? I do it so that my clients feel at ease, to provide them with a level of comfort. This isn't a dirty brothel with syringes scattered all over the floor. This is an office, with comfortable chairs, a window and water in glass bottles.

You get to take these notes home and use them as a reference and a guide for your own shuwt experiences. That's all this is. I am *not* your priest.

[redacted]

Oh, good. For a minute there I thought everything was unraveling.

[redacted]

No. Yes, it is an incredible sum.

[redacted]

Yes, let's do both, thank your father.

[redacted]

No, I understand, you're right. For what you're paying you're entitled to talk about whatever you want. But like I said, I don't want you to get all crazy-religious on this stuff. It's just a drug. I don't want you to wind up dead. That's why I'm being practical . . . trying to turn you off from all this Sslîạ-legend-shit.

[redacted]

Uh, sure. Nenuln *is* a nice-sounding phrase.

[redacted]

You could use Sslîạ, you could use Nenuln. Whatever you like better. No one in the north is going to know what they mean anyway.

[redacted]

No names please. Will you strike that? Thanks.

Anyway, back to the tinctures. This is your second time with them so it's going to be less painful. It gets easier every time.

[redacted]

Is it a dangerous underworld drug? Yes. With repeated use, will it eventually cook your brain from the inside out? Yes. You signed the waiver.

But is it also a sublime concoction capable of drawing on humanity's collective past and personalizing it for you in a way that provides inspiration, insight and possibly even epiphany?

Maybe, yes. I think I'm offering that service.

Others are going to tell you that shuwt tinctures reveal hidden dimensions and enlighten you as to the actual nature of the universe. I don't say that. I suggest a conservative approach to the aftermath of a shuwt journey. Remember the ratio: ninety-nine percent meditation, one percent action.

[redacted]

Right. Let's finish up with a legal recap, shall we? First offense will get you . . .

[redacted]

Iycestoke is far worse. I don't know what they do in Bablemum but once the treaty takes effect I'm sure they'll follow the same laws as Pandragor.

[redacted]

I agree. It's just arbitrary legislation as far as I'm concerned. But they can't legislate my culture out of existence. Veydens have been doing this spirit guide thing for centuries.

[redacted]

Yes, but see, that's precisely why I don't offer those services. You shouldn't take tincture without a guide. But this whole movement of getting a dream shaman? I mean, that crap about the answers being inside of you is just a convenient way to sell things to people that don't have any friends.

[redacted]

Because we're talking about transcendence. And I'm of the opinion that you cannot transcend without permission. Without help.

That's the one part of the Sslîạ legend that I can buy into. I don't believe the notion that shuwt tinctures offer some kind of passage to divinity, but I do like the idea that, in the end, the Sslîạ doesn't really seem to succeed. The Sslîạ just disappears. Why? In my opinion it's symbolic of taking something to the extreme. It's symbolic of obsession, of elitist rhetoric, of going down the wrong road on your own. That's what happens. You fucking disappear.

[redacted]

Good. Right.

[redacted]

Yes. Use them but not more than once every other day and no more than twice in a week. Three doses in a ten-day period will probably set your brain on fire. So go two in a week and then stop. And I mean stop.

Cold.

I've never seen anyone take a third-day dose and not end up tied to a bed for the rest of their lives, assuming they survive.

[redacted]

Yep. I'll get you a copy of the session. No problem. Two-week rest intervals.

[redacted]

Yep.

[redacted]

Yep.

[redacted]

All right. Take care. I'll see you in three.

CHAPTER 45

The papers were smudged. Their margins were also badly crumpled as if they had been carried around for a long time, pressed inside a small book with their edges hanging out. They were at least a year old based on the political reference.

The questions pertaining to how Sena had gotten access to these personal papers and why she had placed them here made Caliph uneasy. A soft knock on the door brought a further lump to his throat. "Come in?"

The door slid open and much to his relief the familiar face of Dr. Baufent leaned in. What he didn't like was that she looked nervous, and not a little afraid.

"What's wrong? Where are we?"

"Bablemum." She didn't elaborate but inflected it as if to lay blame on him.

"How did we get here?"

Baufent looked at the papers in his hand. "Found those, I see?"

"Yeah."

The physician withdrew her head as if toward a sound from outside the room. Her hand came up, finger raised while she listened. All Caliph could hear were the dripping branches, the frogs and leaves and buzzing static of the city. A weird night bird also called from just outside the window.

"Yes. He's awake," Baufent called out to whoever had spoken. Her voice launched the unseen bird from its perch. Its wings sounded large and leathery and Caliph caught a glimpse of its head—an anvil-shaped aberration—as it flew away. "He'll be out in a moment."

She stuck her head back inside. "You'll be out in a moment?"

Caliph considered exercising his authority. Part of him wanted to bark at her, demand a full account of what was going on, whether Sig had been found—even though he knew that answer, didn't he? Instead he nodded and let her go.

He tossed the papers back on the small table and slumped into a chair by the window. He closed his eyes and Sig's face was there, teeth chewing at that ridiculous patch of hair. Caliph let out a silent, volcanic wheeze, hot and angry and cathartic. He allowed himself a few seconds of grief.

It wasn't enough.

Sig deserved more than stifled sobs. He deserved life.

Another knock at the door.

Caliph lashed out. "What!"

Baufent's voice was firm on the other side. "I forgot to tell you not to turn on any lights," she said. "It'll draw attention." Then her footsteps scraped away.

Caliph stood up, furious.

He inhaled the lukewarm humidity deeply, then wiped his eyes. There was a set of clothes laid out for him. He dressed violently, thrusting arms and legs through holes. He took his anger out on the seams.

Fly buttoned, boots buckled, he marched toward the door, eager to confront the unknown.

A lit octagonal hatch ten feet down the hall guided him toward the only possible destination. Tremulous people-shaped shadows spilled out into the hall. He barged in, then drew up, forced to reassess.

Taelin lay practically atop a tattooed man Caliph had never seen. It was an exaggeration, but she was perched on the same divan, leaning parallel with him into the cushions, one of her legs draped over his mighty thigh. His arm was around her waist.

Dr. Baufent stood by a lamp whose maroon globes bloodied the room. She did not look happy.

There were other big men, like the one groping the priestess. Heavily tattooed greenish skins and coarse red braids erupted from them, unable to be contained by rich clothing. Cuff links, and black sleeves and silk ties strained but failed to tame the crew of wicked gentlemen. They glared at Caliph.

Their leader was obscured, barely discernable among the powerful angles of the room. He was huge and broad, a trapezoid flowing, hacked from bolts of luxurious cloth. Easily twice Caliph's size, he looked down with fiery black eyes and said, "High King Howl. A pleasure to meet you."

"I'd like an introduction," said Caliph. It was a flat command leveled at Baufent.

She spluttered. She was not trained as an aide or a servant and must have found his order discomfiting. "Th-this is—"

"I am Kü'h," said the huge man. He had a thick southern accent but his Trade was just fine. "We are glad you are feeling better. I am . . ." he seemed to lose his way for a moment "in charge . . . of the Great City of Bablemum."

"In charge?" Caliph couldn't hide his skepticism.

"The lord mayor is dead," said Kü'h. "Only some of us are left."

"Dead how?"

"The disease."

"We know the Sslîạ brought you here," said Kü'h.

The word surprised Caliph. He recognized it from more than Taelin's drug counseling transcripts. It had also been in the journals Sena had given him.

"Sena came aboard while you were comatose," Baufent said quietly, as if passing Caliph the facts which Kü'h had molested. "But she didn't speak to us."

"Sena spoke to me," Taelin interjected happily.

Caliph didn't look at Taelin. He kept his attention fixed on Baufent. The doctor rolled her eyes at Taelin's comment. Then she continued. "Sena set the ship's course before she left. We stopped here, last night."

"The Sslîạ," said Kü'h calmly.

Caliph turned to Bablemum's makeshift magistrate. "Kü'h, can we talk? Privately?"

"Of course." Kü'h smiled. There was something wrong with that smile. If his entire city had been wiped out by the same disease that had steamrolled Sandren, why did he seem so calm, in control, even amused? Why wasn't he filthy and tired from fighting off silver-skinned plague victims and giant eel-men? Even more obvious, why wasn't he sick?

Caliph gestured to the doorway through which he had entered the room. He didn't know a thing about the ship's layout and decided to take Kü'h aside in the only direction that wouldn't make him feel lost.

Kü'h stepped into the darker hallway. When they were sufficiently alone, Caliph said, "There was an international conference scheduled in Sandren five days ago. We—"

"I know what happened," said Kü'h. "I know how you came to be here."

"So you know we're following—"

"The Sslîạ," said Kü'h.

Caliph didn't want to give in. He didn't want to accept that his world of metholinate trade, of meetings and treaties and signatures on paper was collapsing into a deep hole of esoteric words and occult legend. As much as he had wanted to escape the role of High King only days ago, he now very much wanted it back. He wanted all of it back, all the problems and threats and mincing tongues.

Those things were understandable.

"I'm following the woman who committed the crime. Who murdered all those people in Sandren." It was all he had left to hold on to. The last rational piece of action he could take. Caliph realized this even as he said it. But now that it was out of his mouth, he also realized that it sounded crazy. If the plague was everywhere, if even the mighty city of Bablemum was a silent ruin, where would Sena's case be tried? Were there any lawyers still alive? Judges? Did laws still exist? The world had changed under Caliph's feet. He was falling and yet he was trying to ignore that fact.

The realization disturbed him. As if some mechanism in his head had finally snapped to, he wondered, maybe, whether it was time to start thinking in a new direction.

"She is in the city," said Kü'h.

"Where?"

"With the Lua'grọc."

"The Lua'grọc?"

The lewdness in Kü'h's smile arose, no doubt, at Caliph's expense. Kü'h pulled his white shirt out of his pants and lifted it to reveal his muscular sage-colored abdomen. There was an ugly black mark above his navel.

"We are the Cabal of Wights," said Kü'h. "Or, as the witches of Mirạyhr call us, the Wịllin Droul."

Caliph sorted through everything he had read in Sena's books. "The Lua'grọc are one of the ancient races. But you don't look like some kind of mon—"

"The Cabal is not an ethnic organization, King Howl. We come from every region of the continent. Most of us do not have Lua'grọc blood in our veins."

"So you have medicine? You look healthy."

"We wear the Hịlid Mark," said Kü'h. He gestured to his waist, which was not far below Caliph's eye-level. "It is a ward. We are protected."

"So you're with them? The creatures spreading the disease?"

"Yes."

Here was the enemy. One face of it at least. And Caliph felt unarmed. There was no way he could fight this man. And what good would it do? Rather, this was an opportunity to understand, finally, what had happened.

"Why are you with them? Why do you want all of this to happen?"

Kü'h laughed, a sound that came from miles deep. "You expect poor, ignorant people to join a cult. People without hope. But that's not the case, King Howl.

"The affluent and powerful can also become disillusioned. The endless pursuit of money, fame, comfort, power? The desire for a sense of accomplishment before you die? Don't you feel it too?"

Caliph rocked back on his heels. "You don't think providing government for peoples' well being is worthwhile? You don't think doctors—"

"In the end," said Kü'h, "no matter who you are, or what you did, self-sacrifice included, all you've done is rubbed yourself in an effort to feel special—to feel good.

"Which is why I joined the Cabal of Wights, *Mister* Howl: to get underneath the protective shell that keeps us all feeling safe and normal. To get down to the ugly, tender truth."

"And what's the truth?" Caliph asked.

"Change is truth."

"You joined an organization that backs change? That's not so unusual. But why the disease? Why—"

"Why paint with yellow over blue?" Kü'h interrupted. "The answer is that you prefer it. That's all there is. Change. Not change with a purpose. Just change. That's why the Lua'grọc laugh in the face of their own death. It's a beautiful, empowering thing: to not care. To stand in awe and watch the universe devolve."

Was this true? Was this what Sena believed? Was she really with these psychopaths? Some kind of prophet flying at their head? Leading them? Caliph couldn't believe it.

And yet . . . she had killed all those people at Sandren.

He felt the planet crack in half and all the warm logic pour out of its center, leaving the world cold and empty. Maybe there were no courtrooms left. Maybe there were no crimes that could be rationally punished. But there was still one thing Caliph could do. He could find Sena and he could ask her, to her face, *why.*

"You worship Sen . . . er, the Sslîạ?" asked Caliph.

"The Sslîạ is the avatar of change. We embrace that change. But the Sslîạ is also a servant, an attendant. The Sslîạ prepares the path. The Sslîạ, by virtue of its own desire to escape the role it has been given, does the only thing that it can do."

"And what is that?" asked Caliph.

"The Sslîạ destroys the world."

"That's a lot to take in, Kü'h . . . especially on an empty stomach."

Kü'h's smile was dark and cunning. Caliph could tell that the huge Veyden was not underestimating him. "The Sslîạ told us that you had arrived. She said you would need food and safety, that you were already protected against the disease. Bablemum is no threat to you. We have come up to invite you to dinner."

"Thank you. We're all hungry. But I've just woken up and I need a shower. Can I ask for forty minutes?"

Kü'h's eyes were predatory. "Of course."

"Again, thank you."

Caliph reached out to shake the man's hand but Kü'h only simpered. "You are in the south now. We do not touch here . . . unless we are mating."

Caliph followed the giant man back into the other room. Without a word, Kü'h made a gesture and all his men stood up.

Caliph cringed at the demure moment of separation between Taelin and the Veyden who had been reclining next to her on the divan. The sight of it made him hugely uncomfortable.

When all the Veydens had left, Caliph turned to Baufent. "Tell me when you think it's safe to talk."

"I think it's safe," she said.

"Are we in danger?"

"I don't know." Her face was as gray as her hair. She looked exhausted. "He's not the lord mayor, that's for certain."

"What's going on? What happened?"

"You know as much as I do," Baufent snapped.

"I mean with Sena. What happened?"

"I can tell you what happened," said Taelin.

Shielded from the priestess, Baufent offered Caliph an elevated eyebrow.

"Taelin? Can you excuse the doctor and me for just a couple of minutes? I want to talk to her about my injuries."

"Sena healed you." Taelin beamed. She giggled softly and sauntered toward the door. "But that's fine. I know you want to talk about me." She blew him a kiss and then the curious octagonal portal slid shut.

As soon as she was out, Baufent exhaled. "She's lost her blessed mind. Completely. She practically worships your . . ." An awkward moment. Baufent's face was deeply lined. "Anyway, I have to admit, I'm starting to wonder whether I should join her church."

The humor was so dry that neither one of them smiled. Caliph was looking at his hand. The stitches were gone. There were no scars or traces of injury.

"Look, I'm sorry you're here. I know you didn't want to come—"

"Of course I didn't want to come!" Baufent yelled at him. "Do you realize where I am? I'm fourteen hundred miles south of where I should be. Fourteen hundred!"

"I know. We'll get you on a ship headed for Stonehold—"

"There aren't any ships." Baufent's voice was a chisel. She chipped her words directly from his optimism. "Did you *not* look at the streets? When Kü'h said only some of them were left, he meant it. There *isn't* anyone in Bablemum. There are no flights out of here!" Her cheeks sagged but her eyes looked bright and young and pleading.

Caliph couldn't reassure her so he changed tack. "What did Sena do while she was here?"

"You think that's going to help us figure—"

"I want to know!" he barked. "What happened while I was asleep?"

"I already told you."

"Tell me again."

Baufent glowered. "They had me in a cell. The Iycestokians I mean. Lady Rae let me out and told me you needed a doctor. We were on our way to the cockpit to tend to you when Sena walked onto the deck. She's the one who fiddled with the controls."

"How did she get on board?"

"The same way we all saw her leave the ship in Sandren. She just walked clean out of the sky!"

"And she left the same way?" It sounded stupid but he wondered if Baufent might have seen her go into the city.

"I didn't see her leave. All I know is that she took the Iycestokians with."

Caliph noticed for the first time how quiet the ship was. He remembered the silver arms flailing, the hands pawing at him. "So there's just the three of us now?"

"As far as I can tell."

"And you never spoke to Sena?"

"No."

Caliph found it hard to believe, but the fear on Baufent's face as she remembered the event was clear.

"Sena talked to Taelin. I stayed away. They moved you into the room over there." She waved her hand toward the place he had woken up. "Then the ship started moving. I came back to find out what was going on and Taelin said we were headed for Bablemum.

"I assumed she was delusional but she wouldn't let me give her anything to calm her down.

"Anyway, that's pretty much it. Shortly after that I realized Sena was gone and so were the Iycestokians."

"Did you check the cockpit?"

"I looked in. I'm not a pilot. I didn't dare to touch anything."

"And you said we arrived here last night?"

"That's right. We drifted in low, through the trees. Kü'h showed up right away. Said he'd seen us coming from a lookout in one of the towers. He basically showed up and said hi, then left and didn't come back until this evening. That's when I came and got you."

"Did he say he wanted anything?"

"He's offering us dinner," said Baufent. "Which I'd like to take him up on. We're down to a few canned goods in the kitchen."

Caliph was hungry too but he remained thoughtful.

"So," said Baufent. "Are we going? To dinner?"

"Indeed," Caliph mumbled.

After half a minute of silence Baufent asked, "What are you going to do?"

Caliph looked at her. She was powerful and fierce, defiant of her own lack of options.

"I'm going after Sena." When Baufent didn't reply he offered a few qualifiers. "It's all I have left. It's the only thing that makes sense. Sigmund's dead. Alani. So many people."

"Well can you at least get me fed before discarding me for your silly quest?"

"I'm not discarding you. What else do you want me to do? What makes sense? I couldn't have planned for this. How the fuck could I have planned for this?" He saw the truth of it register in her face. He saw her regret her words. "You can come with me," said Caliph. "Or you can do whatever you think is best. I'm not your king anymore. I'm not a pilot either. I can't fly us back home.

"I just need to understand what happened. How everything turned upside down. Even if it kills me."

"Again?" Baufent asked.

"What?"

"Even if it kills you again?"

He studied her face for cynicism but she was unreadable. "You really believe that?" he asked. "That my organs are in jars back in Stonehold?"

Baufent pawed the side of her face, a combination perhaps of pensiveness and nervous tic. "The organs you were born with? Yes," she said. "Yes I do."

CHAPTER 46

Sena stood at one of Ŭlung's many inroads, waiting for the Veydens. The flawless did not guard the borders to their empire. Those who stumbled in were presumed swallowed by the sewers.

You ate here last summer, said Nathaniel.

This particular gateway to Ŭlung was located in a cistern beneath one of Bablemum's restaurants, not far from where the airship had moored.

"Yes," she said. Despite her eternal lack of hunger it was true.

You made your pact with the flawless here?

"Yes."

I don't doubt they greedily accepted your terms. But you don't need to be here. You don't need to fulfill your promise to them. I've been infinitely patient, he said.

"Patient, is it? Not desperate?"

I'm far from desperate.

"So it seems. You just returned from the ocean . . . I've been wondering—"

Why isn't the High King dead? Why are you delaying the ink?

"When I need ink I'll have it, Nathan." He hated when she called him that. "But I've been wanting to ask you something—"

Don't try to turn this around.

"Why did you send me to Sọth—?"

For my daughter. And the pimplot—

"That's a lie. You never loved your daughter. You saved yourself in that garden twenty thousand years ago—"

You know nothing.

"I think we could have found a substitute for the pimplota seed, don't you?"

I don't know. You're the one going to the jungles. You're the one who wants to do everything with exactness—

"The platinum wires. The rubies? You actually tried to use stones. You've made mistakes. But I don't think you could have really believed—"

So you think my journals are a fabrication . . .

"Yes. An impressive fabrication."

You know the number is two, don't you? I knew it when you came back from the Chamber. Who are you planning to take instead of me? After the ink is made, who will you take? Who?

"I'm taking you."

Lie! Who?

"It's *you* Nathan. Who else can I take? If I don't want you to sabotage the glyphs? I have to choose you, don't I? Isn't that what you'd do?"

Metallic shrieking filled the lightless recesses of Sena's head. She was genuinely worried that he might snap. This was the moment that would decide how the rest of the night played out. Nathaniel's howls slowly dwindled into whimpers that faded across the world.

"You can't get out without me," she said, hoping he was still listening. "St. Remora can't speak for you. St. Remora can't manipulate a pen. It's you and me . . ."

But he was gone. What was he doing? She looked across the intervening miles to St. Remora for a sign. Had she had a heart, it would have been pounding. She looked south toward his stone house in the jungles. Nothing. She looked everywhere but he was powerful in insubstantial ways. In the numbers of nonphysicality, he was expert from long meditation at the edge of the abyss. He hid from her with puissant ease.

St. Remora ticked.

The jungles blew in a damp wind off the sea.

Sena waited, more afraid than perhaps she had ever been.

Fine.

It was a dry hiss, desiccated and startling inside her ear.

But I know about you. I know what's inside you . . .

Sena's stomach turned on itself. Her entire body went cold. "Oh? What's that?"

Guilt. You feel guilty about what you're doing.

"You'd have no remorse—"

No. I wouldn't. That's the difference between us. That's why They chose you I think. They're great connoisseurs of pain.

Sena didn't dare upset him with another question. She would let him say whatever he wanted. She would do whatever he asked her to do. Because she could taste the end from here. It was within her grasp. Yet if he found out, if he suspected—

I think you've waited to make the ink because you have feelings for my nephew. Tell me I'm wrong.

"You're not wrong."

You feel guilty, so you want him to know. You need to apologize.

Sena touched the corner of her eye with one fingertip. The strain was written in her neck, in her jaw.

So go apologize to him. You have the tincture. I will give you three hours to say your good-byes. But I warn you. If you set one foot inside my house at Ḳhloht—

"I won't."

The shade seemed to incline its head just slightly. Then it was gone.

From the basement of the restaurant came a bang, the sound of a metal door swinging full back. The tramp of feet descended. A light slowly infused the cistern.

Two Veyden men arrived at the bottom of a set of crust-caked cement steps and swung their lanterns over Sena's form. Despite their great size and the weapons they carried, they looked at her with pale green faces and glossy eyes.

"You don't want a light down here?" one of them asked.

"No." Her small form had materialized silently in the middle of the room when their lights had struck it. They were Wịllin Droul. They wore the Hịlid Mark. But they were not Lua'grọc, which meant they could still feel fear. It was fear they enjoyed. The awe of the cult kept them invigorated and honest in their efforts to serve it, and it was also their reward. Sena knew this.

"Have the flawless come up?" asked one of the Veydens.

"No. I'm going down to them," said Sena.

Both men shifted uncomfortably. They were terrified and giddy to the point of euphoria. "The Shrạdnæ Sisterhood has arrived in the eastern ruins—as you predicted," one of them said.

"Make sure they find the Grand Êlesh'Ox."

"Is that where the sacrifice will take place?" the first Veyden asked.

"Just do it," she said.

Both Veydens bowed.

"Tell Kü'h," Sena said, "that I want him to bring Caliph Howl to the tanks."

The Veydens wondered why. Why bring the king of Stonehold down to her council with the flawless? Would he be an offering? Would the flawless eat him? But neither man would ask this question. They were both too afraid.

After talking to Baufent, Caliph took a shower. The stall was plated in mirrors and pierced by recessed lights. Creamy pearls of gold-brown soap ejected automatically into his hand from a liquid dispenser hidden in the wall. The tacky spore-filled stink of the jungle slid off him. Only after that, he imagined, did the desert grit embedded in his pores come up too.

Under the lights, in the mirrors, Caliph looked at himself. Clean at last. He gleamed with uniform color save for a one-inch scar on his arm. He stared at it for a few moments.

Then he got out and toweled off.

He got dressed and went back to the room where Taelin and Baufent were waiting for him. He wanted to grill Taelin before Kü'h's men returned, but she wasn't talking. All she would say was that yes, Sena had talked to her, yes Sena had given her instructions, but that no she couldn't talk about them.

This came as no surprise to Caliph. He expected this sort of nonsense.

"I don't know whether you took advantage of her or not," Baufent said as an aside. "But I think she's suffering severe polymodal hallucinations. Multisensory. I'm not sure she can even tell what's real anymore. She keeps claiming that you and she—"

"What?" Caliph came momentarily unglued. "Gods no!"

"I see. Well, she's got a low-grade fever. I checked her, and her one arm is absolutely silver. She's fighting it off thanks to the vaccine, I think she'll make it, but . . . anyone she comes in contact with. Those Veydens for instance."

"I'm not worried about the Veydens," Caliph groused.

"Well, obviously they survived the plague here in Bablemum but . . . they might have stayed clear of physical contact. Taelin was all over that man—"

"I said I'm not worried about them."

"*I'm* a doctor. It's my job to worry about everyone."

"If you knew what I knew, you'd feel the same. Trust me on that."

"My stomach hurts," said Taelin.

"Give her one of your tablets," said Baufent.

Caliph rooted in a pocket for his bottle. What his fingers touched jarred him. He drew out a small cold steel flask, like a memento carried back from a dream. It did not belong here, in his hand.

Staring at it, Caliph forgot Dr. Baufent; he forgot what he had been digging for in his pocket. All he remembered was a little girl with cold fingers who smelled of sugar and glue and Sena smiling as if happy for the first time in her life.

He shook the flask but couldn't tell if it was empty.

"What's that?" asked Baufent.

He barely acknowledged her with a mumbled "Dunno. Some kind of tincture I guess." He unscrewed the cap and peered inside. There was liquid, like dark tea, and a smell that made his mouth water.

He clenched his jaw and screwed the cap back on. *What is going on?* He slipped the flask back into his pocket.

"Everything all right?" asked Baufent.

"Fine." But now, with all the things he'd read, he began to postulate, against his logical nature, what the dreams Sena had showed him might have meant.

He remembered the antacids and handed them to Baufent who took them with a growly look and gave one to Taelin. The priestess didn't ask what it was. She munched it like candy.

A knock sounded from the door that led to the airship's deck.

"Kü'h's back," said Baufent. Her voice held mild apprehension.

"You should be happy," said Caliph. "We can go to dinner."

CHAPTER 47

Umong was the name of a ruin that jutted like a rotten tooth fifty miles due north of Eh'Luhnah Ûsoh: Lake of the Sky. There were markers near the ruins—for the starline.

The starline had carried the Sisterhood, which was safer and less costly than the way Miriam had traveled from the desert. Still, whatever had taken Anjie remained between the worlds, and it pressed the starline. Miriam felt it as the Sisterhood went south. She arrived in the ruins with one hundred seventy girls.

It was a devastating blow. The witches had used the starlines with impunity for decades. They were the only ones that knew about them. How could they be attacked en route, while walking lines?

Despite the shock, the dismay and the confusion that every girl felt, Miriam forced them to regroup and get organized. And while they muttered that it didn't make sense, Miriam thought, *What did?* What did make sense? Certainly not that the Sisterhood had fallen to pieces, that the Country of Mirạyhr had been overrun with silver ghouls. That the Wịllin Droul had taken the entire world by surprise and that, last of all—and most ridiculous—that the Sisterhood's only hope of survival was to put every resource they had on chasing down one orphan from the islands . . .

Going after Sena, thematically, didn't make sense—mechanically it was the only thing Miriam had. The Sisterhood would serve out its purpose. She would see to that.

Miriam's skin prickled despite the warmth.

Though initially she had seen people near the ruins—huge green-skinned Veydens, looking like businessmen that had been stranded on a tropical island with only fine clothes to wear—they melted into the jungle at the Sisterhood's arrival.

The ruins consisted of a few scorched and green-carpeted walls that rose from an ancient pile of paint cans. Corrosion had made the cans thin. They resembled hollow cylinders of rust-colored paper, part of the metallic scrap dumped decades ago by the look of it, all shrinking slowly into a vine-solidified mound.

Miriam got the Sisterhood moving right away.

South of the scrubby savannah that spread north and west, tendrils of hungry green supplanted grassland. The city of Bablemum lay just inside the jungle. A seed of commerce and government bounded by ceontes and thousands upon thousands of miles of dense jade-colored rot.

The Sisterhood did not follow the road. Even though their arrival had been noticed, Miriam took them along the jungle's edge, through waist-deep grass. The sounds of birds, insects and leaves refuted the idea that this was a civilized place. There was no commerce along the road to the north. No people anywhere to be seen.

In addition to scrying on Caliph Howl, the blood-filled dish back in Parliament had shown Miriam other cities. Ekron, Iternum, Nilora and Os. Dadelon, Norwytch, Loonal and Gath. She had glimpsed Horth Gar and Afran. Everywhere it was the same. Disease and madness.

With a mix of compassion and regret, Miriam noticed the contrite and haunted circles around Autumn's eyes.

It took them the whole day to walk from Umong to the outskirts of the city, following the jungle's edge. As they neared, pushing through fields of round-bladed grass, Miriam noticed a few Veydens standing on rooftops in the outskirts at a distance of a hundred yards. They must have used their own brand of holomorphy to evade her diaglyphs. Perhaps witch doctors protected them from disease.

Keen as she was to establish contact and gather information, the Veydens withdrew before the Sisterhood could advance. But Miriam didn't have to follow them. They retreated in the direction of the Iycestokian ship, the place she had pinpointed as Caliph Howl's location.

Despite her unfamiliarity with the region, Miriam had no need of a map. The bowl of blood had given her the High King's position and her diaglyphs led the way.

She pushed out of the grassland, into the actual city, and found the metropolis quiet. As evening fell, she could tell her girls were exhausted.

They needed a place to make camp. A building. Power seemed to be cut almost everywhere. Small things worked. Signs burnt with bright colors, sucking their energy from golden wires that coiled into the air and ended miraculously like antennae. But there was one building with noticeably more juice, one that clearly had its own grid, like the localization of chemiostatic power in the north. It glowed, independent of the surrounding darkened streets.

Miriam sent scouts to determine if it was occupied.

Word came back that it was empty, powered on bariothermic coils near the back of the building, and that it seemed tactically sound.

"I don't like it," said Autumn.

"I don't either. But we have more than fifty qloins here." Miriam looked around. "I don't want to search for another place with power, do you?"

Autumn waved a hand back and forth.

"No. So we'll make camp here," said Miriam. "Then we'll get some food into the girls. And then we'll head for the Iycestokian ship."

It had been two days and one night without sleep. It had been a full day without food. Necessities were necessities.

Miriam led the Sisterhood into the building, which advertised an opulent set of suites. It was an old hotel where dignitaries had stayed, regal and impressive from the outside; posh on the inside. The foyer bore the taint of calamity: a vase of withered flowers, a discarded washrag twisted and hardened with dried blood. A cash register had been overturned and left empty on the carpeted floor. There were a few personal effects abandoned off the waiting area, in the west hall.

Ensuring wealthy guests didn't have to suffer an outage explained the localized grid. Miriam wondered how long the bariothermic coils would last. Ten, fifteen years without repair?

She assessed the building's lines of sight. Its position was good. It commanded a clear view of the avenue out front and looked down on all approaching streets. It was also only a few blocks from where the High King's ship was moored. When she climbed the stairs to the hotel's roof, she could actually see the airship, levitating amid the trees.

The kitchen had canned goods but no running water.

That made sense if the mayor had discovered where the disease was coming from. He would have depressurized all the mains just prior to Bablemum's gruesome end.

Bottled juice and alcohol would not go far. Miriam would have to find water soon. What they had carried from Parliament would not last the night.

By the time the Sisterhood had eaten, the sun was gone.

Miriam sent Autumn and two other sisters to the Iycestokian ship well after dark. They came back with word that the ship was only recently empty. Autumn claimed she could smell Taelin's perfume.

The High King was close by.

Miriam was ready to send qloins into the surrounding streets when message came that sisters posted at the front door had received a visitor.

Miriam went straight down to the foyer and found an enormous Veyden. He waited quietly, surrounded by drawn kyrus.

"He has the mark," said one of the girls.

So this Veyden was from the Wịllin Droul? This would explain their ability to evade the Sisterhood's diaglyphs and why they had shrunk from Miriam's approach.

Four girls surrounded the huge man, trepidation painted on their faces. Miriam planted herself in front of him.

"Sit down," she ordered.

He did so.

"What is your name?"

"Kosti."

"Why are you here, Kosti?"

He spoke reasonable Trade. "I need a token that I delivered my message. Something I can take back—"

Miriam called for a small case. Autumn handed it to her. Inside was a flashing array of gems, padparadshas: the Witchocracy's untraceable reserve currency of choice.

She took one, large as her thumbnail, glittering with orange and pink-colored light, and put it into the Veyden's hand.

"Now why are you here?"

Kosti turned the gem in his big green fingers. "I have a message from the Sslîạ." Miriam's heart stilled but she maintained her composure.

"Get on with it," she said after his unbearable pause.

"She will come. Tonight. Here."

Miriam watched him closely. Kosti's cagey eyes flicked first to Autumn's face, then once again to hers. He watched them with animal interest for signs of deception, but Miriam couldn't tell what he might be thinking. His facial tattoos blackened the serenity of unmoving cliff-like structures of bone. His skull was almost prehistoric, and undeniably frightening.

"Why is she coming here?"

"To make peace."

"What do you mean *make peace*?"

"To make peace is all the Sslîạ said." Kosti stood up from the red leather settee and slipped the jewel into a pocket on his satin vest. Apparently he felt his duty here was over. His yellow-green hands flickered with muscles. His braided hair swung like fronds from a tropical tree.

"Will you let me go and tell the Sslîạ that I delivered my message?" he asked.

"I don't think you'll go back to her, Kosti. You wouldn't want to risk leading us there. So no. I'm afraid I won't let you go."

She looked at Autumn and spoke in Withil. "Take him out behind the hotel."

TAELIN followed Baufent. They left the ship by way of a lightweight boarding bridge, which was anchored to a mooring tower.

Rather than coming himself, Kü'h had sent a detail of men to escort the High King. They were not proficient in Trade.

Taelin listened to them.

She kept her fingertips on the cable railing. As she moved down the center of the bridge, she felt the causeway bounce under her feet. At the far end, she stepped off, through an outer mesh of caging that decorated the top of the mooring tower. A proper stone dome formed the inner shell of this caging and provided an apse-like space, lit with wild torchlight and painted with a profoundly ancient-looking cyclorama. Taelin had to duck her head.

One of the Veydens spoke to the High King and gestured toward a set of stairs that led down. Although it was plain that Caliph didn't understand their speech, body language sufficed and the Veyden quickly switched to rudimentary Trade, still beckoning with his hand. "Come," he said. "Come, come."

The stairs under the painted dome funneled Taelin down a guttering orange nightmare. Flames flapped in the warm dense air, sounding like water.

Sometimes the inside-girl talked to her. Sometimes there was a dryer, older, darker whisper in her ear, telling her what to do. Or more specifically, what *not* to do. It was her mission from Sena to ignore both of these voices, which was difficult—especially when the inside-girl chimed in.

Father says you shouldn't listen to her. The witch is lying . . .

To help ward the voices off, Taelin rubbed the demonifuge between her thumb and fingers. It was cold and comforting against the warm humidity of this place. She worked it vigorously. Like picking at a sore, it drove her on, wanting to be open, slick and glaring.

As she followed Caliph Howl and the others down into the tower's belly, she pushed at the necklace's edges, felt the setting bend and stretch.

Shapes moved under the splashy torchlight. Taelin fumbled for her goggles. She tightened them to her head and rummaged in her pocket. She stopped while the others walked on and pulled out the secret tin. There were only three sticks left. She had rolled them earlier. She took one. The crinkling sound and the texture between her fingers offered prompt reassurance. She could feel the seeds sliding inside.

She patted herself, found her box of matches and snapped one. The wonderful smell effused, of the beggary seeds' first contact with fire.

"What is she doing?" Caliph's voice was far away. "Ubelievable . . ." There were hands on her arms now. She batted them away.

"Gods . . ."

"Does it really matter? Let her smoke."

"Just put her on a godsdamned leash!"

The goggles made the world lovely-tinted. The stonework inside the tower was transformed into puccoon patterns while the torches snapped—pretty sheets of coquelicot.

Supposed to be mine. Mine. One of the voices was like a feather quill scratching over paper.

Taelin didn't know what that meant, but she held the demonifuge close. She tried to block the voice out with another drag as she tumbled out of the tower and into the humming, dripping streets of Bablemum. She was following the crowd.

Glowing signs made strange oases of light. A few of them anyway. Neon colors bubbled. Liquid buzzing sounds soothed her indescribably.

There were thick curved walls, unlike the squared angles of northern cities. And there were tropical trees whose leaves dangled like belts of leather. Vines lit with pale florets threaded the masonry like star maps.

"I'm hungry."

No one heard her.

"I'm hungry!"

"We'll get you something in a moment, dear. We're going to dinner."

"That'll be nice," said Taelin. She looked at the physician's short solid body padding through the street, dark and compact, hair unmoving. Her profile in the strange light was vaguely rodent-like. "Are you married, Dr. Baufent?"

The physician snorted.

"No children?" Taelin pressed.

"I live alone."

"That's good," said Taelin. "Less sadness . . . back in Isca . . . you know? When the jungle eats us." She burst into laughter. Boisterous. Filled with genuine glee. "Oh, shit! We're going to dinner!" She bent forward at the waist, eyes closed, bellowing so hard she nearly dropped her smoke.

No one was laughing with her. In fact, she could hear them talking about her.

"Shut her up?"

". . . already smoking . . . it's dangerous to double up on sedatives."

"We can drag her."

She opened her eyes and stared down at a face cast in dark silver. Hairless and dead, it was attached to the body of a teenager that lay crumpled in the street. One of its eyes was filmy but still glistened with moisture. The other had been gored out, probably by a bird. It stank of rotting fish and its abdomen had been opened by scavengers.

Taelin stopped laughing. Her mouth opened wide as she lost her balance and stumbled forward, bashing her knees on the bricks, skinning her palms. She recovered clumsily, felt Caliph's strong grip under her arm.

She gasped for air. Heavy and fungal, tainted with a billon spores.

"Ahh . . ." Her mouth was open, drooling. "Ahh . . . I'm going to be sick."

"Give her one of your tablets," said Baufent.

"I already did."

Behind the voice of the High King were the voices of the Veydens. They sounded gruff but frightened, talking in their language of inverted vowels. They were saying strange things that she doubted Caliph would approve of. Assuming she had understood. She wasn't exactly fluent. They were talking about Sena. But she felt distracted from the conversation by the silver body. Rather *bodies.*

"Nenuln!"

They were everywhere! A sediment. Debris borne in on a violent tide, deposited without decorum, strewn limb over torso across curb and fender. They were tangled around doorjambs and bariothermic transformers. Ravaged. Some stripped to the bone. Rib cages strung with pemmican.

"Oh shit! Ohshit-ohshit-ohsit!" Her legs gave way again.

You know it was Corwin that saved me? He pushed me out of the way at the last moment. Then this beautiful glowing stone came down on his head. And he just . . . disappeared. Is that what you're going to do? Sacrifice yourself to save Sena? Push her out of the way while the Yịllo'tharnah come down on you?

Don't do it.

The inside-girl wouldn't be quiet.

The smell of the dead city was in her mouth, her eyes, her hair.

The dry whisper of the old man was in her ears, urging her to stop working the soft metal of her necklace, to stop bending it back and forth, back and forth.

"Soon—soon," Taelin whispered.

Taelin had lost her cigarette. She spun around in Caliph's grip. Her whole body felt sticky with sweat. "Gods you have beautiful eyes," she said directly into his face. "Cobra-brown."

Then one of the Veydens hissed that they needed to be quiet. That someone was coming. She felt the familiar stab of a hypodermic. People were always giving her injections.

She was laughing again, because the color of death was pink.

CHAPTER 48

When Taelin went slack, Caliph nearly dropped her. Her eyes were hidden behind the dark red lenses of her goggles. He hoisted her limp body across his shoulders, holding a leg and an arm. He tried to gallop toward the Veyden escorts that were motioning to him, windmilling their long olive-colored arms, trying to encourage him through a kind of stone doorway that led into a small court.

The doorway was vaguely coffin-shaped and he bashed Taelin's head unintentionally against the awkward frame.

"Fuck! Is she all right?"

"Bit of a bump is all," whispered Baufent.

As soon as Caliph was through, the Veydens panned their hands. Clearly they wanted him to be quiet.

Caliph had no idea what might have spooked them but he decided the best course was to exercise a bit of trust.

On the walls of the court, Caliph could make out several posters of children in southern dress. Their faces were made adult with makeup and they struck strangely sexual poses as they marketed some diversion located at 2229 Lẹd'Nhool N'gôd.

Sinewy feline shapes hissed from atop a pile of cryptic refuse—things partly organic and partly incomprehensible because they were intricate and foreign. The Veydens led them across the pavement.

Caliph could hear a hive of bariothermic coils. It buzzed against the foundations of the next city block. Initially the sound masked low gluttonous slurping sounds in the darkness. But as they neared the hive's brain-like convolutions, Caliph drew up.

Icy white fog from the tubing mixed with holomorphic sparkles. The pale light revealed a ghoul hunched over the body of a dog. The sound of eating became clear and Caliph almost let go of Taelin.

Before he could set her down, one of the Veydens had driven his spear into the creature's shoulder. The blade entered along the neck, behind the clavicle, following the creature's spine into its chest cavity. The Veyden jerked the spear around, presumably slicing up internal organs before wrenching it free.

Just as the event seemed over and they began to move on, something grabbed Caliph and jerked him sideways against the wall. Again, he almost dropped Taelin. Bolts stuck mindlessly from the mortar where they might have once supported fire escapes. He had gotten snagged.

Baufent asked if he was all right. He nodded but felt his irritation dilate. He did not like his lack of direction or his lack of control.

Where are we going?

He couldn't ask because the only word his guide seemed to know was *come.*

At the end of the barren court, an eight-foot wall blocked any possibility of progress. A ridge of cement topping the wall had been embedded with broken bottles and random shards of glass.

The Veydens drew up and Caliph wondered if they were lost. He turned to Baufent whose face was lacquered in wild color. A streetlamp beyond the wall threw its rays through the broken glass. Baufent's face caught a reddish-purple triangle over one eye and a thin strip of green across her lips and chin.

She looked terrified.

Caliph listened to the bubbling sound of the streetlamp. He was just about to ask her opinion when one of the Veydens wrestled with a metal hatch set atop a short cement cylinder. The cylinder was twelve feet across but only four feet high and the Veyden knelt on it, fumbling with something.

With an objectionable grating sound he finally drew the hatch up. A mephitic burp rolled out of the city's guts. Caliph peered in. Pestilential darkness sighed.

Why are we going down? thought Caliph. *We're supposed to be going to dinner . . .*

"Come," said the man.

"I don't know about this." Caliph directed his doubt at Baufent.

"I don't know about it either." She looked around, first at the serrated wall then back toward the stone doorway they had come through. "Do we really have a choice?"

"You always have a choice."

The Veyden was getting impatient. He patted the top of the cement cylinder with the flat of his hand. "Come, come!" The other two had already gone inside.

Caliph thought of the Iycestokian ship, floating back at the edge of the city. It was the only place he knew that represented relative safety.

But could he find his way back to it? What if he ran headlong into whatever had spooked his guides? Even if he did manage to reach the ship, carrying Taelin the entire way, he still didn't know what to do from there.

And where would he—

"Come!" The man's whisper resembled a shout.

Caliph glared at him. But the Veyden did not shrink. He beckoned, pulling with those great fingers, gesturing for Caliph to hand Taelin over.

Caliph looked at Baufent once more. She hesitated then nodded her assent.

"Okay," said Caliph, after which he didn't sigh or deliberate. He rolled Taelin off his aching shoulders and into the big man's arms. Then he climbed atop the cement tube and looked down. The fumes smacked him in the face. He felt dizzy.

The man reached out and steadied him.

Of all possible realities, this had to be the most improbable. He found no humor in the bizarre fact that he was climbing into a foreign sewer. He gritted his teeth, clenched them until it felt like they might shatter. Then he helped Baufent up onto the access point and lowered her carefully onto the rungs.

"Thank you," she said as she began feeling her way down into the dark. "I think."

She was sturdy and powerful but he knew that she shouldn't be doing this. None of them should be doing this.

THE walls of Bablemum's sewer system sloughed like diseased flesh. Pale leprous hunks of masonry buckled and spluttered into residual pools. Everywhere, it seemed, vesical-pipes dropped into the vault. Hydriform.

But the inlets were quiet. Barely dribbling. They moaned with air currents, purposeless in the vacuum of the abandoned cityscape.

Squelchy walls led in every direction but Caliph stuck to one, following the Veydens sack of netting, which cradled three glass balls—analogous to the city's lamppost globes. As with the streetlamps, these too were filled with an oily liquid that emitted a cadaverous luminosity.

They had been stored in separate niches at the bottom of the access point. The man had taken them out and slid each, clanking against the other, into the sack of netting. As he eased the last one in, some kind of proximal reaction had taken place and all three orbs began to bubble and glow.

Without the language barrier Caliph would have asked what they were and how they worked. Instead, he said nothing.

The sewer did not smell as bad anymore. The initial blast of fumes must have been lurking, trapped against the hatch. Down here, there was a breeze, cool and almost refreshing and Caliph realized that with such regular rain and no fresh waste being introduced, much of the sewage had already been flushed from Bablemum's system.

"I don't believe they're taking us to dinner," said Baufent.

"Me neither."

The man had given Taelin to one of the other Veydens, leaving one hand for the sack of lights and the other for his spear. It was bizarre. This man in fine clothes, carrying a spear through the tunnel.

They passed beneath occasional grates that sluiced in streetlight and sound. Caliph heard trees shush-shushing. Then the narrow slits to the upper world disappeared and he felt himself sucked into another sagging archway.

Finally, after tramping some way, the man's oily light burst out over an uncertain precipice. The man held the netting high, revealing a dam of sorts that dropped off on the left into churlish reeking darkness. The air here was stirred by a never-ending gray waterfall, which poured from higher up on the right, over a series of smaller flumes that stepped through a vast angled tunnel. Caliph smelled minerals here and thought of Bablemum's infamous mines. Maybe this was part of them, carrying out the dregs and sediment from what had once been constant digging.

The man was crossing the dam, dragging the light with him. Caliph let Baufent go first, watching over her not only from the darkness that quickly converged behind them but from the possibility of a fall.

Their path was furnished by a questionable catwalk that straddled a narrow viaduct. The viaduct was in turn supported by a series of pillars through which jetted the great cataract from the mines. Unlike the textured metal of the *Bulotecus,* the floor panels of this catwalk were poorly designed. Though they were grilled and therefore porous, they were also smooth and extremely slippery. Caliph kept a ready hand in the event Baufent lost her footing.

Unintentionally, he tasted the mist before clamping his lips shut.

The man with the lights used his single word again in an effort to coax Baufent along.

"I'm coming, you oversized toad!" She said.

"Take your time," said Caliph. "They'll wait."

"Of course they'll wait! Do you think I'm a damned fool?" Her voice was angry but her arms shook a bit at the slender and overly rusted rail.

"Take my hand."

"So you can drag me down too?"

"Take it."

Baufent snapped her fingers around Caliph's wrist. She looked at him meaningfully and said, "All right, hero. Get me out of here."

Caliph pivoted around her and took the lead. He adjusted her grip, reciprocating her wrist-lock, then, slowly, he began guiding her toward the Veydens.

They reached the end with only one close call and stepped from the catwalk back onto solid stone.

"Thank you," said Baufent.

"Wouldn't have to thank me if I hadn't dragged you fourteen hundred miles," said Caliph. He turned his hands upside down and pushed at the cushion of air between him and the Veydens, ushering them impatiently to get on with this ridiculous and dangerous excursion.

They did, guiding him through a pointed archway into a nondescript and sloppy cellar that echoed with some dolorous mechanism laboring far above.

A series of low, flat steps offered access to a strangely domestic-looking but dingy hallway. The floor had been tiled in tasteless ocher and lavender squares—many of which were broken or missing. The glass spheres in the net illuminated a rusted iron door.

Caliph felt the fumes of the waterfall pull past him and thought he could now interpret the sound as a chugging ventilation fan, though its location remained a mystery.

The Veyden guide rattled at the door. He did not seem to have a key or any other means of opening it but there was a chain attached to a strip of rusted metal that he could have slid within a frame. A peep slot, Caliph realized. It was the chain that the man had rattled.

Instantly, beyond the portal a faint sound of frenzied movement reverberated softly. More the ghost of sound than real sound, the clamor splashed and roiled only a moment before settling into ominous silence. For several long moments Caliph listened to the distant splish of the falls and the ghostly sound of glugging pipes. He waited for the peep slot to slide back, for someone to demand a password.

The Veydens waited too, frightened looks on their faces. Why were they frightened? Caliph had a bad feeling about whatever was going to happen. He didn't have a weapon. Baufent would be useless in a fight. And the three Veydens would make short work of him.

The peep slot did not slide back. It never slid back.

Rather, a harsh squeak followed by a rusted clank bounced through the tiled hall. On the other side of the door Caliph heard a metal bolt retract and the portal creaked open. A tantalizing fissure peered into the darkness. An audible gasp rose out of the black, as though lungs full of liquefied sickness had breathed too deeply.

Then the door swung wide and Caliph nearly screamed.

CHAPTER 49

What Caliph had taken for negative space beyond the door, was in fact a hunched but enormous bulwark-like body, draped in inky cloth.

The Veydens seemed to melt before it, trembling.

When this daemon-shape spoke, a kind of "Hlnugh'dugh!" sound, the solid metal door vibrated. Caliph could assign no recognizable language to the voice and considered that it might have been a feral croak.

Whatever was underneath the shimmering blackness was only vaguely man-shaped. Caliph had the impression that the longer he looked, the less man-like it became, as if in that first glance his mind had tried to bend what his eyes took in.

It reached out, which elicited a yelp from Baufent, because this thing belonged in a wax museum of static nightmares, not here, not shifting and sentient, not groaning in the dark.

When its hand or paw extended to the edge of the door, Caliph felt his sanity slip. The paw rose from what was not precisely an arm, anchored to a hump of evil muscle. It was the only part of the actual entity exposed beyond the cloth and when it took hold of the scabrous door frame it made the metal groan.

The room beyond the door was sunken so that Caliph realized he was viewing the monster only from the waist up. As it leaned hunchback, gripping the door frame, Caliph got the impression of a giant crone peering through her window at him. Its enormous pink hand, pale as pork fat, held the casement with the wrong number of fingers, each only two knuckles long.

Caliph could feel hidden eyes examining him while the huge filthy brown talons flexed and gouged the metal as if it had been clay.

He had nothing to focus on besides the paw. Black silk in a black sewer swung in the black doorway so that only this *thing,* this paw, a gift of raw fish, glistened in the Veyden's light.

The hand's corpulence was so swollen that it looked as if touching it might cause it to tear open. Caliph decided he was not looking at skin but at raw exposed tissue—that was alive with wriggling, threshing forms. He realized that they were not parasitic worms but pulsing veins, squirming as if the creature's circulatory system had a mind of its own.

When he heard the dreadful inhuman voice again—slurred inarticulate, and soft, semi-consonants melting into one another, he felt the blood leave his head. What kept him conscious was the shrieking sound of the paw coming away from the door frame, swinging back down into the pure black folds, disappearing and taking great hunks of metal with it.

The claw's absence made room for the Veyden to use the doorway but Caliph's guide was rooted in place. If the Veydens had betrayed him, they seemed just as terrified as he was. Caliph assumed that this strange reality was based on facts he had no access to. He wasn't trying to piece it together. He was looking for escape.

Back in the direction of the dam there was no light, just the distant roar of water. Baufent was still staring through the doorway, lips parted, cheeks trembling.

Caliph glared at the man who had led him here but then, the situation that had been impossible for him to understand became more so as, for no apparent reason, the monster behind the door reached out and grabbed Caliph's Veyden guide. The pink paw came through the doorway and enfolded the Veyden, large enough to engulf the seven-foot man.

In response, the man dropped his net full of glowing spheres.

Caliph scrambled for them but they were already beyond his reach. They tumbled over the threshold, down a set of steep stone steps and into the sunken room. Caliph watched them go. One cracked and intense liquid sprayed through the fissure, losing its luminosity as it wet the wall.

The Veyden screamed as he disappeared under the black canopy of silk. A mortifying crunch put an abrupt end to his wailing.

What were the other Veydens doing? Caliph couldn't see. Darkness had swallowed everything. He heard a second man scream. It too was cut short and followed by gruesome crunching. Caliph remembered his guide's spear. It must have fallen somewhere. He dropped to his hands and knees, desperately searching.

That was the moment he heard her voice.

It spoke in a language he didn't understand.

A prickle at the base of his hairline crawled up the back of his skull as Caliph's eyes adjusted to the new level of gloom. Past the hideous black-draped shape that still swayed guardian, he detected a strange halo of light whose origin seemed remote.

It bled from behind a familiar, slender, diminutive silhouette.

Sena stood at least thirty feet away, perhaps at the center of the space beyond the door.

THE other Veyden wasn't making noise. He might have crawled back toward the roaring cataract, feeling his way through the dark. Caliph didn't know.

Baufent stood over Taelin's senseless form, staring into the only light left: a pallid radiance that streamed—or so it seemed—from between Sena's shoulder blades.

"The flawless won't touch you," said Sena.

Caliph didn't know about that. The sounds of chewing, of breaking and grinding had only recently stopped. They had been terrible, and like the aftermath of a devastating quake, the silence that followed was both profound and uncertain.

He looked over his shoulder one more time at Baufent. Her eyes darted to him. She seemed to know what he was going to do. Without a word, she communicated her demands. *Get back here! Don't you dare leave me!*

He motioned her to stay put, then looked down the stairs, past the hulking thing toward Sena's halo.

Crossing the threshold was like entering a crypt. The room smelled of things long settled.

"What are you doing down here?" His voice was unsteady. "What happened at Sandren? What is all of this?"

He put the huge silk-covered thing behind him as he crossed the room but it was still there. It creaked against reality's floorboards, almost insupportable.

He refused to look at it, keeping his eyes on Sena.

The steps had been uneven and slick with the fluid burst from the glass spheres, but the floor of the room was equally treacherous. It was relatively dry but each step sank in, an inch or more, into a peat-like sediment. It was like walking on cake.

"Why are you here?" He tried to keep his voice level but detected the sound of pleading in it. He was unprepared for the truth.

"I'm not *with* Them, Caliph." His heart swelled momentarily. "But I wanted you to open that door." The metaphor she had used on the airship came back to him. "I wanted you to see these things behind it because you never believed me. You never listened to me about your uncle's book. I just needed you to understand."

From behind, Baufent called out to him, desperate, pleading. Her voice prompted a vague sense of responsibility that he ignored.

The room was some kind of empty septic tank and as he crossed it, it sank its cold moldy teeth into his chest. He detected a slope. Some cement structure meant to control the flow of sediment. Sena stood on top of it. She was only a few steps away now. She said something in the language Caliph couldn't understand and the thing at the doorway moved away. Caliph heard other movements in the tank. Other vast shapes, which he had not even noticed, began to disperse, hauling their giant forms into equally sized culverts.

"You have to understand something," she said as he approached. "It's you and me. Just you and . . ." Her voice trailed off for several seconds, hinting at deeper meanings. ". . . me."

"Is it?" A tatting of mold on one of the room's pillars seemed to absorb the phosphorescent light coming from her back. "I don't think it's been you and me for a long time now."

Little was clear to Caliph except that Sena was standing in this horrid tank, surrounded by miscreations.

The long chase had worn him down. He had made up his mind, finally. But the realization made him miserable and desolate. He felt sick. Sick and weak and exhausted. He reached out and grabbed her by her fashionable jacket, hands knotting into fists.

He shook her violently. He took her by the throat. She was light and her body jerked limply under the force, as if she was helpless. She winced. He threw her on the ground.

"What did you do!" he screamed at her. "What did you do!"

All the dead people poured out through his scream. He could feel them as if they were there. His responsibility. As if they were staring at him right now. Alani and Sig and all the rest.

Sena did not look up from where he had thrown her. Light trickled between her leather collar and the back of her neck. It lit her hair. He could see flecks of sewer mud. Glops of black gunk from a puddle near her arm had splashed up and spattered her shoulder.

Chest heaving with shame and anger and uncertainty he stood over her with one bizarre thought in his head: *what now?*

He certainly wasn't going to sink down on his knees and touch her, help her up, clean her off. What he *was* thinking of doing was unspeakable.

"Drink it, Caliph."

He couldn't see her face. He swung his chin to one side and cocked his head. Incredulous. He wasn't listening to her. He would never listen to her again.

But already he had reached inside his pocket and found the tiny metal flask. It was leaden in his hand.

"No," he said. "I won't. This is over. This madness. It stops here. You're going to fix it." He was embarrassed at how childish his words sounded. "Get up," he told her.

A few huge shapes shifted in the black wings of the chamber. Apparently not all of her immense underlings had left. He sensed some of them might be drawing closer but he didn't dare to look. Were they her bodyguards? Would one of them now reach out and break him in its mouth?

Baufent's voice called again, thousands of miles away.

Sena's whisper drowned the doctor out. She whispered to the flawless first, passing them some instruction. Then she whispered to him. "You know everything you need, do you? To make your decision? Is that it, Caliph? You know so much?"

"You've been dosing me with these tinctures. Who knows what—"

"Your third dose isn't going to kill you. Drink it." She rolled onto her side and looked up at him. There was an ugly smear of mud on her face.

"Fix it," he said. "Fix what you did!"

"I will. You drink it and I'll fix it. I'll fix everything."

"Fix it now!" He wanted to call her a murderer, but felt the hypocrisy of the thing. He wanted to blame all his frustrations on her, starting with her inattentiveness over the past year to everything from the plague and his dead friends right down to this moment standing in this deplorable room. But he couldn't. No matter what holomorphy she had used, he had chosen this. He had arrived here under his own power.

"If you don't drink it, I won't stop you. You can strangle me if you want. It's what you're thinking. And I'll let you do it. But what will happen next, Caliph? Think about that. What will happen next?"

Caliph did think about that. She was crazy. She had always been crazy. And that was why he was here. Because he had always gone along with it. But not anymore. This was it. This was the last time.

"I drink it and you fix everything? Can you can really do that?"

"I can really do that, Caliph."

He hated her. He hated her more in that moment than he had ever hated anyone, because even now with her lying in the shit of civilization, at his feet, she was still somehow more powerful than he could understand.

"Gods-fucking-dammit!" He could smell the drug before he unscrewed the cap. The memory of it. Its taste and aroma were already burned into his brain. What was he going to do instead? Go back to Baufent and help her drag Taelin up to street level? And then what? Find food? Barricade against the creatures?

So maybe this *was* the easy way out. And he was a gutless shit-heel. He had always suspected himself a coward. And maybe this was the worst moment of his life. He hated the sense of inevitability. With the flask open, the sweet tea-and-mint smell sickening the air, he tipped it into his mouth.

CHAPTER 50

The Veyden messenger that had told the lie—that Sena was on her way to make peace—was dead. Autumn had taken him out behind the hotel as ordered. Shortly after her return, Miriam had noticed how things had changed: how everything had a wrongness to it.

As the Sisterhood's attention had been pulled inward, diverted from the exterior of the hotel and focused on the mysterious Veyden messenger, the lights in the Grand Êlesh'Ox had shifted color. They were not dimmer. But they had turned from yellow-orange to olive-green. Then slowly, ever so slowly, the ornate textured wallpaper began to peel.

When some of the furniture started floating, spare inches above the floor, Miriam knew what was happening.

The humidity doubled. Then it doubled again. It was like breathing water. The whole building felt like it had been scuttled. Miriam's feet barely kept contact with the ground.

Outside, in the wide avenues, shapes were massing—orderless and green, shadowed by distance and atmospheric moisture, flickering with a hint of silvery, reflective skin.

The Wịllin Droul were coming.

From all quarters, from every building, street and drain, a huge circle of hungry variegated forms drew in around the grand hotel. It was clear to Miriam that the Sisterhood had been led into a trap.

Miriam blamed herself for this mistake.

From the Grand Êlesh'Ox, the collective smell of the Sisterhood's skin, warm and fragrant, bled out into the avenues. Her girls were leeches, dangling in the watery air, baiting in a great gathering of silvery schools.

The snuffling groans, the chirrups of titillation and ecstasy were audible as the hoard surrounded the building. Miriam watched hungry eyes gather in the streets, eager for the slaughter. Some eyes were visible. Many more were not. Mounds of rags stood and swayed. The Wịllin Droul clogged every alleyway; they filled every adjacent window.

Talons and fat lumpen heads scraped the brickwork around the hotel's foundations. Tentacles wrangling from fishy jowls; they tasted over sashes and drip caps. The creatures had ringed the Êlesh'Ox with wards. All exits were sealed from the outside, with fish-blood holomorphy; with puissant ancient skill.

"They're everywhere," said Autumn. "We have to get out."

"They've sealed the corners," said Miriam. Even with the Sisterhood's own blood, which Miriam was not prepared to spill, moving in the absence of the starlines—as her qloin had done in the desert—was not possible. In order to attempt it, they would need to get out of the hotel, out of the streets, out of the damping holomorphy that the Wịllin Droul had draped over everything.

Miriam didn't feel like she should have to explain all this—especially to Autumn—so all she said was, "Put a qloin above the delivery door."

"Already done."

"Good," said Miriam. Even that single word had to be forced with great effort past her teeth. She wasn't going to try and run. In some ways, she was grateful that the Wịllin Droul had sealed them in. The Sisterhood had already seen too much failure and death; too much running. Tonight would be different.

As the Wịllin Droul surrounded the building, Miriam took comfort in the idea that Sena might have orchestrated this ambush. That, at least, would be better than being outwitted by fish. She wondered if it had always been Sena's aim to destroy the organization that had burned her mother.

If so, there was something to admire there in the ruthlessness of the planning. In light of what the Sslîạ was *supposed* to do, it struck Miriam as peculiarly meticulous that Sena would, on her way to whatever oblivion awaited her, arrange to destroy the organization that had given her so much. Given and admittedly taken away. Was this why she had flown an airship into the south instead of simply walking lines? To lure the Sisterhood to the Wịllin Droul's ancient seat of power?

Huge bodies threw themselves against the hotel's outer walls. Miriam heard windows breaking in the back.

As the clamor rose, there was no doubt that Sena would not show up for this finale. The Sslîạ had more important things to do. Giganalee had been right. Who else but Sienæ Iilool could claim the mantle of the Eighth House? And the Eighth House did not use its hands. It used its minions to get things done.

"What if we jump?" asked Autumn. "We can go roof to roof. We can use their blood to fuel an escape."

"You don't think they're on every rooftop for a quarter mile in every direction? Waiting for us? Have you counted them?"

Autumn licked her lips.

It was fitting, thought Miriam, that the girl from the isles, who had arrived out of Greenwick so long ago would have hands like these. The fingers of the Eighth House were silver, slippery and ichthyic.

"We have to try," said Autumn. "We can't give up."

"All right." Miriam made the southern hand sign for yes. "But I'm not going to run like I did in the desert. Tonight I'm going to stay here. Take half the cohort and tell them to try and escape across the roofs. The other half will lead a distraction—with me. We'll try to hold them in the street. The rest of you are free to go."

"I'm staying with you." Autumn's eyes told of disappointment. She wanted for Miriam and herself to be in the half that fled: that escaped. *Who will lead the Sisterhood?* was a question neither of them asked.

"All right," said Miriam. "Go and get them sorted." *But Autumn, baby . . . they're not going to make it.*

"Yes, Mother."

Autumn did as she was told.

This was how the world would end, thought Miriam. Amid the gluttony and screams of those insensitive to the miracle that they were still alive. Amid the chaos of disease and universal pandemonium, those that represented the last vestige of intelligent life would squander their advantage in this avenue, on this city block.

She chuckled bitterly as she hustled down the hotel's main staircase, conspicuously unafraid, incapable of changing what was going to happen.

The hotel was dark. Miriam had ordered all the lights put out. Witches covered its rooftop, crouched on dormer peaks, ledges and cornices like gargoyles. Their sweat unfurled from waxed cotton and drifted, tantalizing the crooning horde below. The horde began to hop and lurch excitedly, cracking paving stones with their collective mass.

Miriam waited for Autumn in the foyer. She peered out through a jalousie while the building's foundations shook. The panes of glass rattled in their frames. She sensed the Sisterhood shift within the hotel, anxious. Sisters appeared in the stairwells.

Autumn squeezed her way through them, down the wood and tile steps. When she reached Miriam, she spoke in Withil. "We're ready."

"All right."

Miriam ordered the doors thrown open.

At the front of the building, a wide porch cupped the curvature of the facade. From it, a flight of stairs ran directly to the street. Miriam walked out, kyru in hand. She stood at the head of the steps and gazed down hatefully into the multitude. Sickly fingerlings, thin and newly changed, mewled below her as if waiting for some sign.

Although their insatiable hunger had pulled them close to the Grand Êlesh'Ox, Miriam decided there was no real order to the ranks. The flawless of Ŭlung stood shrouded in black canopies, surrounded by their spawn, paws like pink cake batter dripped from their sleeves.

Other flawless had also arrived. She recognized their diverse forms from Sandren, Iycestoke and the White Marshes of Pandragor. They did not represent a uniform horror. They took many different shapes. Similarity was sparse but a turgid opaline sheen marked them as one.

In the avenue, Bablemumish sculptures of black marble, pewter and beryllium found new uses. They allowed the Wịllin Droul to coil their limbs around sculpted legs and arms and thereby support their grotesque fatness. They had modified the air so that gills could breathe. They had changed gravity so that huge bodies could have some relief—but it was not complete and they were still heavy and this was not the same as swimming.

For a while, the Lua'grọc held back, perhaps savoring the moment. Miriam noticed Autumn come out of the hotel and stand beside her. Her sweet ancilla. She did not regret the moments when they had been just that: cephal'matris and ancilla—when she had been forced to give orders, and Autumn had been obligated to carry them out. The hierarchy had never been an impediment for them. For them, the protocols had only ever allowed them additional ways to show each other respect. To love each other. She had never ordered Autumn around like a subordinate. Ever. There had always been that understanding between them, that they were partners. That they were a team.

Other sisters came out onto the porch, kyrus glittering.

Miriam was almost ready to give the command when Autumn smiled as if for an ambrotypist, modeling the perfect young athletic face of the north. The lean sweat-dappled cheeks and arms. Then she drew back and pitched her kyru into the horde.

The blade landed in a white forehead and blood like lake water rolled out. The windows and peaks of the Grand Êlesh'Ox began to mumble with voices. Witches pulled at currents of holojoules in the Unknown Tongue and threaded the power of the Wịllin Droul's blood into divergent equations. A bubble of humid dreams surrounded the hotel and sealed the witches in, but they could still use hemofurtum to fight.

An orgy of self-mutilation began among the fingerlings who, under the numbers of the witches, started clawing off their own skins. Their blood fueled other deceptions as some of the flawless turned their long striped talons on one another. Bodies flew. Limbs and organs cartwheeled through sultry blood-flecked air.

Then chirrups and barks and groans welled from the numberless congregation and endless ranks surged at the Êlesh'Ox.

Miriam watched the heavy bodies stampede toward her as she talked. With every few words another of the Lua'grọc died. But they were without number and without fear.

Lacking a final moment of glory, Autumn disappeared less than ten feet in front of her, swallowed up at the base of the steps. When that happened, Miriam did not scream and throw herself into desperate battle. Instead she dropped her kyru and stopped talking. She looked up at the cloudy sky, hinting at more rain, away from the abortive ancient things that floundered up the staircase and trampled her under claw and limb. The rough brush of their hides, the slapping wetness of their bindings, the stink of their gasses was gagging.

She gasped from the impact, breath forced out when their weight ground her against the right angles of the stairs. They broke her bones. They crushed her rib cage like a sack full of kindling.

And there was blood. An elemental figure in a holomorph's death. Hot red wax running down the stairs. She searched for any sign of Autumn between the shuffling legs but her head was pointed in the wrong way and the world was getting cloudy.

The greatest equations were products of suicide. She opened her mouth in a bid for final retribution. To gather all of what had spilled out of her into one conclusive strike: a detonation that would kill hundreds. But Miriam's lungs were empty and she could not fill them.

CHAPTER 51

Sena watched as the tincture unfurled its pseudo-reality, its time-bent brand of postulations-cum-potential-for-meddling.

It was Caliph's third journey. Though the pain of entry into dream was not so bad—the damage this dose did was extreme. She had lied: he would not recover.

But that didn't matter. Nathaniel was right. This was her chance to say good-bye, and to apologize.

The tincture brought them both, Caliph as traveler and Sena as guide, down hard in the House on Isca Hill.

In this dream, Caliph was coloring at the kitchen table while his uncle stood in the sunlight holding the *Cịsrym Tạ,* reading. She hoped Nathaniel would not follow her. She hoped he believed what he had said and was allotting her this time for closure.

Sena looked around the room. A man in formal uniform was cooking eggs and strudel at the stove. Over Caliph's shoulder Sena could see that he was drawing red and purple monsters. Their shapes were like simple clouds with serrations instead of soft curves. Their almond-shaped eyes had slits for pupils. Their mouths were jagged.

She wondered why his mind had gone here, of all possible memories. Perhaps the monsters in the sewer had chased him to this quiet morning where similar fears were explained with crayons.

The smell of breakfast was delicious. A bell rang in the house and Nathaniel did not look up from the book. The servant picked up a towel and wiped his hands.

"Let Caliph get it," said Nathaniel.

Caliph sat at the table, engrossed in his images, pressing hard against the paper so that each stroke made a soft smack when he pulled the crayon away.

"Caliph! Get the door!"

Sena watched the command register. Caliph didn't look at his uncle but his young eyes grew wide. He glanced peripherally as he slid off his chair.

In an act of betrayal, the crayon rolled off the table. It clattered loudly. The sound of it pulled him up short though he had already marched halfway across the room.

He turned around, looking frightened, then walked back. He picked the crayon up and set it on the table, making sure it didn't move again. A quick glance at his uncle confirmed that Nathaniel was staring at him. Then Caliph walked fast out of the room, legs leading, butt tucked in, wary of a swat.

Sena followed him down the dim passageway between the mansion's kitchen and its foyer. Little Caliph glanced over his shoulder but Sena was invisible to him. All he cared about was that his uncle was not behind him.

When Caliph reached the foyer he struggled with the huge door, trying the dead bolt several times before understanding which way he had to flip it. Then he tugged with his whole body, barely managing to drag the portal back.

The day outside was young and brutally cold. Fine snow sifted from the sky and icy golden light flared into the foyer around three women. Sena was stunned. She had not expected this.

"Hello," one of the women said. Her eyes glittered with miniature carvings. "Is your uncle home?"

"Yes." Caliph stood there, staring at the women.

"Can he come to the door?"

Caliph put his lips tightly together and nodded. Then he walked stiffly to the passageway and called out, "Uncle Nathaniel!"

Instantly the black billow of Nathaniel's robes gusted down the hallway. His lips were bloodless, his expression one of infinite irritation.

"Who is it?"

"Some ladies," said Caliph.

Nathaniel entered the foyer and stared at the women on the front steps. His scowl deepened. He pulled his robes around him and snapped his book shut.

"Nathaniel Howl," said one of the women but her eyes, all the witches' eyes were on the book.

He sneered at them. "Unable to get in through the windows, I assume?"

"We're willing to make a transaction," said the witch.

Nathaniel didn't laugh. Instead his lips pulled back from his teeth in the manner of a cornered animal. "Really? Belting the three of you nightly until my heart wears out?" He shook the book at them and did not invite them in. "You'll stay out there until I'm ready. And when I'm ready . . ." He giggled softly. "Well, I'm sure the three of you can piece it together to be gone by then."

"You think you'll survive long enough? To get ready?" The cephal'matris took half a step closer, keenly aware of her inability to enter the house, but threatening nevertheless.

Sena saw Nathaniel's eyes dilate with inhuman blackness. He took several steps toward the threshold, book in hand, smiling rapaciously. The entire qloin drew back. It was impressive, even to Sena, to see them cower.

"Yes. Yes I do believe I'll be around," said Nathaniel. "Long after the three of you are not. Yes. I'll be here. Rest assured. Arrangements have been made."

"The Sisterhood can make you the richest man north of Eh'Muhrûk Muht." Sena looked at the cephal'matris' quavering eyes. She was lovely and young and scared, sent out by Megan to do what could not be done.

"Why not the richest man north or south?" asked Nathaniel. "Why not the richest anywhere? I'll tell you why, you pathetic pully-haully whores. Because you can't give what you don't have. You are not remotely powerful enough to offer me what I want. What I want, I will get. Myself! And you," he pointed at her directly, "will go back and inform that whitewashed cunt you call the Eighth House of my decision. Have a wonderful day. Ladies."

He shut the door and turned to Caliph who had been sitting on a tall back chair in the foyer, listening quietly to the exchange. "Women are receptacles, Caliph. You have to give them something to hold. Pound it into them really. That's why, in the end, I'm going to survive. Because I can see the future, boy. Did you know that? I can see it. Just like my daughter, with her immortal eyes. Her perfect immortal eyes. They'll carry whatever burdens I give them. And it's going to be wonderful. A brilliant success."

Caliph swallowed hard as his uncle stormed out of the foyer. "Don't answer the door again," Nathaniel shrieked.

Sena marveled at this serendipitous insight.

His daughter? Here was undeniable proof that all his notes had been careful deceptions. Not a surprise. But what *was* surprising, and the thing that sent a shiver through Sena's immortal flesh was that Nathaniel had *not* sent her to Sọth to rescue his daughter . . .

But to rescue her *eyes.*

How could she not have seen that? The double fake! Pretending he loved his daughter and then when the lie was uncovered, he was able to make it seem that Sena had guessed right, that Arrian had meant little to him—when in fact the opposite was true.

He needed his daughter desperately as any holomorph needs a drop of blood.

Now it made sense, his smug announcement that he had found Arrian's head, floating in the ocean.

He must have known full-well that the rubies would never work. Yet he had left no part of his deception to chance. His ambit was every bit as strong as hers and just as she had hidden her thoughts from him, he had done the same.

He had foreseen her. He had known it would come to this.

Sena swallowed hard. Now she was thinking, remembering how Nathaniel had raged when she had come back from Sọth without the body, but how calmly he had mentioned finding Arrian's head.

Arrian's eyes would last an eternity.

And all of this, every detail down through the centuries, all the research Sena had waded through at Desdae, in the south, in the long dark hours at Isca Castle: all of it had been compiled by Nathaniel Howl with the sole purpose of fooling her.

Sena was dumbstruck. How could she not have seen this coming?

It was as if Caliph had seized this one moment of clarity, this admission from Nathaniel, and remembered it subconsciously. He had guided her to it as if he had known that it was important.

Pshaw, Nathaniel hissed. And Sena stood up straight in Caliph's dream. Because this was not the Nathaniel from the past. This was the real shade, the lich-thing come crawling over her brain. *You think Caliph guided you to this memory? You fool.*

"Why?"

Because I want you to know—that you had to be shown. Doesn't that hurt? You simply weren't smart enough to win.

"You could have convinced Arrian to give up her eyes," Sena said with belated understanding. "She trusted you."

Which was something you would never do.

"But I left her there," said Sena. "You didn't think I'd leave her body at Sọth."

A coincidental victory. And momentary.

But Sena grasped mentally at this slender ray of hope.

Sena could not believe that she had avoided his trap—almost—and that she had done it by accident.

Not good enough.

"Would you have tried to cut your pages from Arrian's back?"

No. I'll use yours. You won't be going anywhere. Neither will your little grub.

Sena's mind went to her womb. Her thoughts locked up. He knew. He knew and he was doing something about it—out there in the real world while she was stuck here, inside Caliph's tinctured head. *Yella byũn!*

He had told her to use the tincture to get her out of his way, while he executed his plan. Sena looked out of the dream, just in time to see Stonehold drop dead.

The eruption that radiated from St. Remora didn't melt the falling snow. It didn't disturb the white-caked wires strung above the streets. It made no sound at all as it uncoiled in the heart of the city, while the city's populace still slept.

Vaccinated as it was, Isca wasn't to be spared, it was to be harvested according to Nathaniel's plan.

The god-pudding calved in St. Remora's depths—birthed dead but dreaming from that crimson world. It landed in Isca with a squelchy ripple of ethereal sound. The first of the Yịllo'tharnah to *physically* arrive. St. Remora's clockwork pulled it out: lightless, formless and asleep . . . a fetus still tethered to the dark . . . its plasmatic black subtrahend contracted, sending an unconscious blast outward, a feeding reflex—exactly like a solvitriol bomb—barreling through Isca.

Quick as a scavenger, Nathan Howl wrought his equation and sucked the dislodged lives out of Isca like egg whites, leaving the Yịllo'tharnah stillborn.

Sena turned and ran. She had to find Caliph. Her plan had just fallen apart.

Caliph rested on his back. The ceiling of his uncle's lab was coffered white. In one of the squares a spider had made an invisible web. Caliph could see a moth dangling in the threads, sucked dry. It seemed to struggle when the breeze from the windows disturbed it. He sensed that this was not real. That all of this had happened before. He knew he was in a tincture dream. But he could not control it. All he could do was go where the dream took him. He was a passenger. A voyeur looking back on his own life.

Caliph's eyes noticed things: fly flecks on ceiling paint, cracked plaster, discoloration where there had been a leak in the roof.

He turned his head toward the lab's bank of windows. Several were open. The old whitewashed metholinate pipes came up through the floorboards. He followed them with his eyes, around the window frames and up through imperfect holes in the ceiling. He could feel how nervous his tiny body was, heart racing like a hamster wheel.

Caliph watched and listened to the summer branches roll like waves beyond the windows. White winged insects shuddered and flashed, carefree amid the churning green. Humid summer smells mixed with medical antiseptic as his uncle turned and swabbed his arm.

Overhead, a tin ceiling fan whispered while the brittle chirr of insects rattled in the heat.

"Good boy," said his uncle. Then there was a sharp pinch in the tender place at the crook of his arm. "Stay still."

Caliph winced and arched his back slightly. His head pushed into the pillow.

"You're Hjolk-trull," said Nathaniel. "You know what that means?"

Caliph's eyes were streaming from the corners; the pillow soaked up his fear. He shook his head slightly because he could not speak.

"Well the Hjolk-trull are descended from Gringlings, who are descended from Limuịn . . . who are descended from gods. That makes your great-grandfather quite powerful, doesn't it? If you believe in him. But I'm afraid he doesn't care about you."

Nathaniel rummaged with some metal tools on a nearby tray. He tore a length of fabric tape and plastered it over the spot where the tubing came out of Caliph's arm. Then he flipped a switch on a small machine and Caliph watched his blood run up through the coils. He felt dizzy.

"I don't believe in your great-grandfather," said Nathaniel. "He exists, I'm sure. But I don't *believe* in him. The scientific fact is that your blood is special. Aren't you happy to be helping me?"

Caliph nodded. The old man's eyes glittered with lightless mirth.

"Now hold still. We're doing a test. I don't have all the ingredients I need, but let's see what we can accomplish without them." The small machine made a sound that Caliph imitated by popping his lips. It was an airy pumping noise.

Pop, pop. Pop, pop, pop.

"Be quiet," said Nathaniel.

Pop.

Caliph stopped but watched his blood run through the tubing, into a kind of pen that Nathaniel had picked up and was now adjusting.

"What are you writing?" asked Caliph.

Nathaniel chuckled. "I'm not writing. I'm drawing. You like to draw and so do I."

"What are you drawing?"

"A jellyfish," said Nathaniel. "To float in the abyss, in the dark, alone but beautiful."

Caliph couldn't see the drawing from his position on the gurney but he could see his uncle concentrating, whispering. Outside, the trees kept rolling, rolling, churning. His head felt like it was on the end of a stick that was being swung around the room. "Uncle?"

Nathaniel continued to whisper and draw.

"Uncle, I don't feel good."

The white laboratory ceiling had a black ring around it. Fuzzy. The ring was getting fatter and the hole in the ring was getting smaller. Most of the ceiling was hidden.

"Uncle?"

"Be quiet."

The whole room had nearly disappeared and Caliph reached up with his other hand to scratch at his eyes. Something was wrong. He couldn't see. Everything was black. His head felt funny. And then he was falling. There were rocks all around, hitting him in the face. He was falling in blackness. The rocks were falling up and he was falling down. The rocks hurt. He was crying.

The rocks hit him in the face. Slap, slap.

"Wake up, boy."

Caliph could see the white ceiling again but it was fuzzy. His arm hurt and he was sweating, giant drops. His fingers tingled as if both arms had gone to sleep. The machine was turned off.

"Well I guess that has to be enough," said Nathaniel. "I don't want to kill my calf, do I?

"Do I, Caliph?"

The lab blacked out and Caliph snapped up straight. He heard Nathaniel's voice again, but this was not a memory. This was something new.

You can't touch her the way you want to, Caliph. She's gone infinite. Infinite.

And you can't trust her anymore.

CHAPTER 52

Taelin looked up into the face of Dr. Baufent. "Hi," Taelin said. Baufent looked serious. Baufent always looked serious. "What's wrong?"

"Nothing," said Baufent.

Taelin didn't believe her. The doctor sat across from her on a bench in what looked to be a restaurant. There were copper fixtures and dark wood on the wall. When Taelin sat up she saw eyebrow windows above the booth, looking out at street level on an indistinct mass of shambling feet.

People, she thought happily. Her head hurt and she was hungry. She reached up and touched a swollen goose egg exactly on the scar at the middle of her forehead.

"You took a bump while we were carrying you," said Baufent. The doctor seemed wholly uninterested in what was going on outside the window.

"How did we get here?" asked Taelin.

"Up some stairs, through several doors," said Baufent. "The High King's witch helped spirit you up."

"We're in a restaurant! Have we ordered? Where is everyone?"

"I don't know," said Baufent. "Sena said to wait here for you to wake up and that you'd know what to do."

Oh, thought Taelin. *It must be time!*

"Where's the High King?"

"I don't know. He abandoned us. It's just you and me." Baufent looked indescribably glum as she said this. Gray and tired and hopeless. She looked like she needed sleep. More than that, she looked utterly beaten, as if the thing that had been her had been pulled out and trampled and thrown away. There was no fight left in her face.

Taelin pulled out her necklace. She looked back out the window where a dismal dawn made droplets flicker like tiny white flames. She began to work the soft metal of the demonifuge in her hands. Squinting past the rain, into the gray breadth of Bablemum's tropical avenues, she could see the Lua'groc massing. Ghouls with leaden skin crawled from sewers followed by taller, thinner men and women that moved like insects or crayfish. Squeezing from the ground came fatter forms, grotesque and slippery, bulging and toad-like, skinned in silver and gold and pink. "Don't worry," said Taelin. "Sena's a goddess. Do you want to play cards?"

The things in the street seemed to be rejoicing.

They seemed to be eating.

"I'm going for a walk," said Baufent suddenly. She stood up in a curt manner from the booth, put her hands in the deep pockets of her red coat and shuffled toward the door.

"I don't think that's a good idea," said Taelin.

Baufent gave a humorless smile. "Good luck, girlie." She opened the door, stepped outside and shut it behind her.

Taelin poked her nose over the window ledge again, looking out, trying to see what might happen, but there was too much commotion. Too much noise. Baufent's entry to the street changed nothing. The celebration continued and Taelin slipped back down into the booth to continue working on her necklace.

Sena could hear snow falling around the eleven asymmetrical dials. Flakes toasted in orange light, glowed like bits of burning paper. As if there had been an explosion.

Though St. Remora still snuffled and coughed, the city of Isca, the last city to contain *real* people, had settled. A hush clung like ice to every building. She saw where footprints in the new-fallen snow, of factory workers and children delivering the *Iscan Herald*, had ended in low piles of wind-rumpled felt. The snow came down over the dead in an act of reverence. In an act of symbolic mummification.

All two million of the dead were coming after her, churning through the ether, wielded in the immaterial grip of Nathaniel Howl. The dead were his scepter, his stick of thunder, his trumpet blasting. Arrian's head floated in the ocean and its eyes were missing.

Sena ran through the tincture dream, looking for Caliph. She still had her colligation, but if she exhausted it now, there would be nothing left for later.

She had meant to say good-bye, to show Caliph their daughter again. She had wanted them to be together, just one last time: all three of them. And the tincture could have provided that. It could have bent logic just enough to allow her to have, for a few seconds, that perfect family that she had never known.

But Nathaniel had found out. It could only be her fault: some stray unguarded thought. Or maybe the secret had leaked from Caliph's head.

All she knew was that there was no time left to say good-bye and that she was in serious trouble.

CALIPH smelled his uncle, which was a musty blend of citrus and furniture dust mixed with a fume of urine and cold air, as if an elk had sprayed the bark of a tree, after first snow, high up in the mountain woods.

He rode the tincture without choice, tumbling down a thread of memories. He was alone, directionless, and it felt like his brain was on fire.

His uncle was here, choking him—not as a person chokes another person but as a fable, a sort of inescapable story that posited Caliph as its central character, which Caliph had no control over and which he felt, with the unaccountable clarity bestowed by nightmare, would end as fables generally did: gruesomely. The walls of his uncle's house closed in on him like a black envelope, the same sort that contained the solvitriol accord. He was being crumpled, crushed . . .

And then Sena's hand took hold of his and pulled.

SENA dragged him hard, out of the tincture dream and into black champagne, into an endless bubble where the universe swarmed. Gibbering sputtering shapes eclipsed the stars. She felt a tug. Some force pulled her backward. She was a swimmer experiencing a bite. Then the Yịllo'tharnah let go. It was a warning. A reminder.

She held onto Caliph tightly, regained momentum and emerged.

"*Yella—!*" Sena shouted and stamped her feet. The tug had dragged her off course. She had not arrived *inside* the ruins of Arkhyn Hiel's stone house, but on a rocky fossil-rich escarpment twenty yards to the north. Somewhere, she imagined the Yịllo'tharnah were laughing.

Caliph was sweating profusely. Sena slapped his cheeks in an effort to bring him around. He would not survive this tincture journey. His brain was bleeding. She shaved some of her ambit to stanch his hemorrhaging—just enough to see him through to the end. She couldn't afford to waste power now. Not with what was coming.

"Where are we?" he mumbled. He looked positively green as his eyes drifted over the stone palace that pawed the sky.

"We crossed lines," she said. "We're two thousand miles south of Bablemum." Sena felt Caliph steady himself beside her on the escarpment. His legs wobbled but he got them working. He scowled at the barren, shadow-raked clefts before panning his eyes, once more across the remnants of the palace then down into the more unusual ruins of Ooil-Üauth.

This was the vista Arkhyn Hiel had once enjoyed from his terraced lawn. The topsy-turvy dirty white and pink annulated stacks of Ooil-Üauth thrust from the valley like the stilled ends of colossal earthworms. They were misaligned with both jungle and sky. What streets might have existed were shrouded by trees.

Caliph stared at the tall narrow domes, traced with day glow. He looked bewildered.

Beyond the blunt ugly crests, which seemed set in frozen upheaval, Naobi trembled above the ocean, flanked by two morning stars. Wind came straight up the face of the hill. It stirred every plant and filled the breeze with slapping sounds.

With it came Nathaniel. He roared out of the north.

Sena braced for impact.

"You see the ruins, Caliph? Not the ones down in the jungle." She pointed with her whole arm. "The stone house, right there. Go inside. Find his skull. Smash it. I'll hold him as long as—"

She couldn't believe the force that struck her. It shook her. It pushed her. Her feet slid back, grinding against the stone. She was surprised because she had thought herself to be immovable. Her ambit shone as she pushed back, gleaming like a star.

Nathaniel's power struck her so hard that she felt the planet shift. She lost several inches of ground. Then her feet caught. Her willpower anchored her to the spot but Nathaniel's pressure against her moved the world. Adummim tilted on its axis, into a new direction.

He was moving her, whether she liked it or not.

CALIPH did as he was told not because he felt overly confused or childish but because he believed, for the first time, that she was right.

Nothing had made sense since reality had failed him in the skies over Sandren. That was how he felt. Reality had failed him and it was a personal betrayal.

He was doing *this* now, which was not founded in reality. Reality had abandoned him and so he abandoned reality. He was doing what Sena said because he trusted her, despite everything.

He believed in her not because she had earned it but because he had always thought himself to be a better-than-average judge of character. That was why he had stuck it out all the months she had been gone. And now, since there were no facts anymore, or courtrooms or juries, he tossed aside the judgments that logic had forced him to levy against her. He went back to what he felt, which was trust in a raw half-buried sparkle of goodness that had managed to survive the brutality of her Shrạdnæ childhood.

Caliph trusted—perhaps too much. He climbed the escarpment, scrambling for the ruined stone house. Behind him, the spectral presence of his uncle filled the sky. He could feel the size and shape of Nathaniel's power, like something sensed in dream. The gravity of this moment was not delivered by things seen or heard. Caliph heard nothing but the shrill cry of jungle crickets. He saw nothing but the ruined house. But Nathaniel's existence was something he could sense.

Caliph entered the house through one of many ruined windows. He skidded on tumbled blocks, coated with living green scum. Amid the ubiquitous growth everything looked the same.

He could see what had once been a doorway was now choked with a swollen tumor of roots.

Amid the creepers and moss and dismal predawn light, shapes were hard to separate. The room he had entered was open to the sky.

Caliph felt the ground shudder under him and glanced back through the ruined walls to where Sena stood quietly, faced away from him. He could see nothing beyond her but black trees tossing in the wind. Yet he sensed Nathaniel. And he sensed the wall separating him from his uncle. That wall was Sena. And she was beginning to break. Nathaniel's might began leaking through the chinks in her defense.

What are you waiting for? Sena's voice sounded in his head. *This is why I brought you here. To be free of him.*

Caliph looked across the room, fifteen feet at most, and suddenly he saw it. Dark brown and spongy. Glittering with intricate wires. Where the umber bone was not exposed, a skullcap of green carpeted it. The thing leaned into a pile of corruption that must have been Arkhyn Hiel's forearms—as if his body had finally given out while resting his head on the desk. As Caliph approached it, he saw a sprinkle of bright pink spore caps quavering in a tiny cluster on the brow.

In that moment that Caliph viewed the skull of this stranger, all the books Sena had given him, all the passages she had marked, broke free from their association with her. They stopped representing her designs, her cryptic research, her plunge into something he could never understand. And instead, suddenly, whether by her design or not, they belonged to him. They were *for* him. Suddenly what had happened to him as a child had a context. He understood it in a broader theater. It was not his fault. It had never been his fault.

"I don't want revenge," said Caliph.

It isn't revenge, Sena thought at him. *It's your moment to be free. Take it.*

Caliph looked at the thing on the desk. Its face was a travesty.

Both sockets had been filled with heavy black jewels and on the upper row of teeth, a third gem replaced one of the incisors. The whole head was wrapped in a thin filigree of platinum wires, delicate as thread. Despite much of them being buried in moss, they reminded Caliph instantly of the lines on Sena's skin.

Caliph heard Sena cry out with a mixture of surprise and pain.

He didn't know whether crushing this head would somehow fix everything or whether this was about his own personal salvation but he picked up the skull.

The platinum wires crumpled. Some of the bone had been replaced by a soft, green film. His fingers crushed through this slimy membrane to a slippery jagged interior that swarmed with fat, segmented life. Tiny creatures poured out of every available orifice.

Caliph swore and dropped it.

It disintegrated on the floor into a shattered mess of black and green and wet-gleaming metal.

And then there was only cricket song again.

The sound in the wind lost cohesion and dissolved into something natural: a breeze blowing in from the sea.

He bent down and plucked one of the gems from where it sparkled on the floor. When he did, he felt an immediate chill, then Sena was standing beside him, looking frightened. She was holding out her hand.

TAELIN had trouble hearing. She could still make out amphibian chirps and barks wrapping around the restaurant's brick-framed windows but she had also noticed that one of her ears was bleeding.

A few moments ago, she had heard Baufent say, "They're going to find us." But now the doctor wasn't talking anymore. In fact she wasn't even sitting across from her at the table. Baufent had disappeared.

It didn't matter. Past and present didn't matter, praise the Omnispecer. All that mattered was the future, which Taelin could see. The future was bright and golden.

Taelin did not fantasize about changing things. The past was the past.

Except maybe for Corwin.

She had that one clear memory of him, before he became High King of the Duchy of Stonehold and got her pregnant. A clear picture of his smiling face as the two of them sat on the cement steps of her grandmother's house. He held a stick in one hand, that he had been using to play with those tiny red bugs. So simple back then. She couldn't remember how the house had caught on fire. She supposed that was the one thing she would change. Because it wasn't fair that she had sent him inside to rescue her box of colors—and the necklace.

She bent the demonifuge back and forth between her fingers, working the soft cool metal with a vengeance.

Poor, beautiful Corwin with his lovely brown skin and cobra eyes. She remembered him nearly making it out of the house as the door frame collapsed on top of him in a salvo of fire and heavy timber.

It had crushed him and simultaneously hurled him down the steps and into the backyard. Then her father had drunk the tincture and disappeared. She had picked the necklace up and noticed the tiny red bugs streaming down the foundation, hurrying from the flames for the safety of the grass.

If she could change anything, that would be it. She would bring her dead king back to life.

"Corwin . . . Corwin . . ."

Taelin stared into the demonifuge. Its color was like the inside of a fire barrel in the cold streets of Isca. Palmer stood beside her, looking in.

"Should I do it?" she asked.

Palmer passed her a beggary blunt and shrugged. "You gotta do the right thing," he said.

"I know. I don't really think she needs my help. But that's the brilliant part of being a god I suppose: you give over the handling of things to other people . . . almost like a gift."

Palmer looked at her like a devotee with those pure blue eyes.

Then Taelin heard the necklace snap.

The orange-yellow bliss in the fire barrel expanded dramatically.

Taelin stared into her hands at the broken setting. The cold golden light that was not a light swelled between her hands. Like the mouth of a bag opening, she thought. So lovely.

Albescent yellow sea foam glowing at dawn. Lovely cold mountains like radiant thunderheads ballooned through the stretching aperture. A bright batter. A birthing. It moved like lava underwater but did not dim, or crust over, or solidify. It swelled like a storm wall inside the restaurant. Mustard white. A juggernaut coming.

Taelin gave a little cry as her goddess enveloped her.

The magnificent body slobbered through the fully effaced hole. It dragged whimsical, ghastly improbabilities behind it. A necklace of alien placentas.

* * *

UNDER churning volcanic blackness, red meteorites plunk the ground. There are screaming people. Some crumple when they are struck. Others catch fire. Taelin can see a man with soft green eyes standing in front of her as the rain comes down. His face brims with regret. His hand reaches out to her . . .

SENA saw the necklace break.

She watched Nathaniel's skull, his phylactery, shatter—not at her hands, but at Caliph's. That had been important to her. That was why he was here. She wanted the victory over his uncle to belong to him. And it did. That part of the ordeal was over. The hurricane of souls devolved into the unfocused milling of the damned. All the dead of Isca floated aimlessly, confused ghosts in the jungles of the south.

There would come a time, as the twisted eons burnt down, that little by little, Taelin's soul might escape—one particle at a time—over the course of millennia. One day she might reorganize somewhere in the deep cosmic black—along with Nathaniel.

The stars were full of ghosts.

But that time would not come soon.

As the necklace opened Sena heard a crackle in the sky. This was the place Nathaniel had found, at Ooil-Üauth, which had taken lifetimes to solve, to pinpoint the spot where the second door would open. Sena looked up at the two stars that still flanked the moon. So bright. Unconnected with this world's constellations. This moment was Sena's chance, but Nathaniel's assault had interfered with her strict schedule. Næn was free. Næn was ravenous. And Næn was coming.

Huge ruffled pseudopodia uncurled, delicate and beguiling. Næn took no special notice of the souls she absorbed. Taelin had been drawn into the ever-swelling lung-like recesses of her extra-dimensional form. Buildings melted. Streets cratered. In Bablemum, paid with the Sisterhood's blood to leave the jungles empty, to not be present in the ruins of Ooil-Üauth when the second door opened, the Lua'grọc burned as the End of the World was finally born.

They had been unable to resist the blood of their ancient enemies and, as their god came at last, they died in joy to feed her.

Sena saw Næn fill Bablemum, balloon and then abruptly turn, lured by the huge number of souls Nathaniel had brought from the north. Millions of them. They were like a great bait ball in the sky.

But more than them, it was her: the Sslîạ, standing on the brink of escape. Næn moved toward her automatically, intent on her destruction.

Sena was afraid.

Her eyes, which saw everywhere, witnessed the Chamber under Sandren where the golden holes had stretched and broken. They were dark now. The wet stone made of dreams had fallen away, great pieces dropping into Yọloch's relentless surf.

Beneath her feet, Sena could feel the fringes of the continent collapsing, the world eaten at a harrowing rate, racing across the steppes, the desert, the jungle, coming toward her. And it made her sad. She felt Caliph's sorrow, vicariously.

Because the number was only two.

CHAPTER 53

Caliph sees Sena drink from a small steel flask. He knows it is tincture by the smell. Then he sees her toss the flask aside, touch her stomach with one hand as she reaches for him with her other. She looks worried.

Her face is lit by the gray dawn and gathered into tense angles.

Caliph notices how time feels differently now. As if everything has already happened. Maybe it is part of the dream, part of the tincture. He can still feel the poison coursing through him as Sena pulls him along, down the escarpment. Wind is blowing.

"Come on Caliph—"

He cannot feel his feet against the ground. The boulders, the treacherous clefts and snarls of vegetation might as well be paved causeways. Everything is running smoothly now, just the way he likes it.

They enter a desolate quadrangle. The trees cradle the poisonous colors of a new set of ruins.

"It's a necropolis," says Sena.

He hears the leaves moan.

These new ruins, the necropolis of Ooil-Üauth, are so striking he knows he must still be dreaming. No real place could look like this. Far above his head, strange jungle foliage rumbles with air currents. Trees like kelp slosh against a dead blue sky.

He makes his way among huge cucullate structures, like beehives, mathematical and sharp, some tumbled down and broken, all organic and contradictorily vague.

For a moment he loses track of Sena and finds himself alone.

Only in dreams can you be so alone, *he thinks.*

Only in dreams can the entire universe be emptied of your species and leave you to haunt the cosmos, a solitary morsel of meat.

He looks up into heavens the color of paint mixed with ash.

The sky hates him.

He stumbles into the middle of the square, feeling catarrhine, barely capable of balancing without all four feet on the ground. He swaggers, hardly standing. For a moment the heat is incredible, then that whimsical-strong ocean breeze tongues the trees. Stray currents swirl into the square and goose bumps rake his skin.

The jungle moves. It unrolls and blooms and sways. It mouths the ruins and the beach, slobbering, drizzling nectar from millions of blossoms. Caliph appreciates the sticky mist coating the back of his neck, spattering against his cheeks, like strange rain, like bat urine. Sweet, aphrodisiacal and repugnant.

Jungles are not really black. But this one is: in perfect counterpoint to the variegated colors of masonry, blossoms and acid-pink water that laps at the beach.

Hurry, Caliph.

Ah. He has found her again.

Movement stirs at the north end of the square. Darkness pours from the undergrowth in tendrils and clouds. Black butterflies, big as his hand. Even the shimmery lunulae of their hind wings glister like fresh tar.

"So beautiful."

He has found her. Through the wings and disembodied spirits. Eyes made of blue crystal. No. Black. Her eyes have turned black.

She stands at an altar or a lectern and beckons him. It, like the necropolis, is made of dreamt stone.

Its shape is long and threatening. It looks old. Like something that has existed from the beginning. Because of it, thinks Caliph, even if tourists crawled all over this place, ferried from some nearby village in solvitriol cabs, this would be a terrible—

"Are you all right, Caliph?"

He feels pressured into saying yes, because of the desperation in her voice. She sounds hurried.

And then, as if the idea is planted, he has a moment of clarity, which can be compared to only one or two other experiences in his life.

He starts talking without fully understanding what he is saying. But he can feel that he is onto something. "Did you read the papers last summer? When you were away?" he asks her while she is doing something frantically at the altar. "They were so full of the news about Bablemum?" He almost laughs. "The treaty? You know? How the city was going to go back to Pandragonian rule?

"I remember they published excerpts of letters sent from citizens of Bablemum to Emperor Jünnű, begging him not to do it. They wrote to senators, diplomats, even foreign powers, asking them to intervene. Even I got one.

"As if—right? But they went door-to-door for signatures. They held

rallies. 'Don't follow through with this treaty,' they begged! Because it was going to, you know, modify a whole lot of lives. Change laws. People's freedoms and families and everything were on the line."

Caliph gasps as a blast of ocean wind takes him straight in the face. "But you know what? Nothing changed. The day arrived and the treaty went into effect as planned. Because you can't fight inertia. Not even when you know it's going to be a disaster. Not with all the reasoning in the world. Because the receipts win out. The money and time spent have too much weight. And people want what they paid for, even if it's going to kill them. So the police moved into the streets. And no one could do a damned thing about it. People jumped off buildings that night rather than become Pandragonian."

He looks at Sena closely. "That's what happens when whole cultures are annexed. That's what happens when the world loses its ability to steer. And you know, I guess I thought . . . that people were more sensible."

"I'm just the sexton," says Sena. "I dug the hole." Her mouth is beautiful. Her teeth are an omegoid array of enamel shields standing in pink gums. Her tongue dances behind them.

He doesn't know why he notices this.

"Why are you doing this to me?" he asks. "Why fill me up with drugs?"

"No matter what I did, I couldn't get to three." Sena looks more sincere and more bereft than she ever has before. "This is about transcendence. And you need permission. You have to forgive me for that. I hope you'll forgive me for that."

Caliph believes that there are interminable seasons bracketed by proterozoic soup and stars—wheeling over him.

"I wanted to tell you," she says. "But I couldn't. It was too dangerous. Your uncle could have—"

But Caliph barely hears her. The sky is not yet light but there are shapes in it. He watches them press and queue like the shadows of frenzied shoppers pressing against frosted glass. There is a red glow behind them as they bang for the clerk, demanding that the bolts be snapped back for their turn to enter, trample and consume. For some reason he imagines all the windows of his uncle's house blowing out in prismatic splendor as the Yịllo'tharnah molt across the sky. They are black laughter, exultant and empty.

"Hold my hand," Sena whispers.

Caliph laces fingers with her. She has done terrible things. But perhaps she is about to follow through on her promise—and fix everything.

Her hands feel cool. Cooler than the gooey air. The reflection of his face, in her black eyes, is serene and resolved. She guides his forearm over a bed of hollow tines.

The lectern-altar is a ghastly cackle of stone and ancient residue. When his arm is in position, she helps him press it down. The hollow slivers go through him effortlessly, popping from the skin in glistening pincushion-array. He gasps, sets his jaw, says nothing. Blood pours from him into the stone channels, down the drain and into the tubing of a pen.

He looks up, dazed by the creamy pink fume rising over the trees. He doesn't know that his brain is bleeding.

SENA lifts the pen with the heavy tubing. A small bottle screwed into the hose mixes pimplota ink as it fills with his blood. When her quill touches the first page, the world shakes. When her pen lifts the tremor ceases.

She can tell that Caliph is disconcerted. He knows now that this is real. He remembers when his uncle did this to him as a boy. The quill's nib is sharp and supple and drips with the ink of worlds.[25]

But she must focus all her attention on this act. She cannot search for power and she cannot afford to draw it from herself.

She reaches for the colligation. She pulls holojoules, endless incredible amounts of holojoules from her black amphorae still frozen in Isca. The temple atop the great frustum is empty. It floats, cold and desolate in its realm above Incense Street. But the gelid pots of blood are still there, preserved.

Sena uses all of them.

It hurts her to do this. She feels each pen stroke in her skeleton. The scrape of the quill against the paper is deafening. As sensual as satin or milk poured in morning light. She feels the stone lectern beneath the vellum, formed of Adummim's geology through ancient dreams—set here as a traitor, for this purpose, to murder the continent.

But the lectern has changed its politics, aligned itself with the new power. The grain of its smooth rock surface kisses the underside of the sheet as she writes in cool defiance of the apocalypse around her.

NÆN fanned over the equator and pressed the ruins where Caliph was just beginning to feel the kind of unity with Sena that he had not felt for many months. He began to understand things, as if he was inside her, part of her. He began to love the sheet of vellum she was drawing on,

[25] Ŭlian ink.

profoundly, though he was unsure why. It was primal, like loving sunlight and fresh air. Ancient as his mortal need to be touched.

Sena set her teeth and concentrated. She finished the first glyph and pronounced it. She felt her stomach empty. Her sight dimmed. Her depth perception was gone. She began on the next.

Caliph tried to take a step forward but his forearm was still impaled in the bed of tines. He jerked up short. Sena held his hand. She paused to settle him like a curious child.

The sky was turning from pink to gold. The Goddess of Light was breaking on the horizon.

In a moment of mixed emotion Sena leaned forward and kissed Caliph. He felt it as a sticky soft plucking. His lips were thin and dry; hers were jungle slugs. Then Sena hurried to finish her work, composing the final dots and dashes of the glyph.

Caliph's arm ached deeply.

There were forests of waterspouts holding up the sky above the ocean. The Great Cloud Rift had fallen into the planet's core. Its god-tons of rock had sloughed away and released the radiant unsleeping horrors through cracks a hundred miles wide.

MEADOWS burn. Mountains and deserts dissolve like sugar in a buttered pan.

But Sena is not capturing the world in a glyph.

One of her eyes is already gone. She steadies the second sheet. Above the altar, Næn looms as the ink spreads. A yellow-white cloud in a sky gone black, shredding the atmosphere in her wake.

"I think I'm going to fall over," says Caliph.

It is his first complaint. He has leaned on his impaled arm, put all his weight onto it, but having given so much fluid, even that will no longer support him.

"You did good," she says. He cannot see the horror that is right on top of them, nearly blocking the invisible doorway in the sky.

CALIPH looked at the woman he loved. His insides were hollowed out and packed with fear—because he felt himself dying. He watched her incisors dig into her lower lip. The final words he heard her say were "Fight for it, Caliph. Fight for it!"

It seemed to him as if she had been writing on two different sheets of paper at the same time. As if he were looking at separate worlds. Sena existed in both of them, in all of them.

Then all separate realities collapsed into one and something horrible and amazing burnt through the fabric of every universe and melted their fibers together. An object. A great red orb. Its path and position was identical to the planet's size and movement around the sun. A crimson world flowered inside Adummim, cold and gleaming. The white and golden mass in the sky reached out for him.

Caliph's mind was far away as the end enveloped him. He was thinking that there would be no more new days. No luncheons or silk stockings. Bureaucracy, pastries, love, ice cream, vague connections on the street corner at the steaming vendor cart, the dirty hand delivering you your change . . .

The eyes reflected in store glass staring through themselves at what they wanted to be . . .

These had been burnt up in this ceremony in the jungle.

For a few spare seconds, Caliph saw humping mountainous forms judder in the red world's unbroken oceans of mud. Risen. Shining with a slurry of clay and starlight. For that single instant, Caliph stared. Then the thousandfold tendrils of negative space splashed toward him. Næn reached for him and he screamed.

He thrashed brokenly against the hot suffocation, molten slag, organic compost instantly stewed to mush. Fumes of burnt obsidian and sweet methane filled him like a balloon but enormous pressure held him down. He was being squeezed. Crushed. Devoured.

Caliph flailed, arm and leg, across the brink of oblivion. His body came apart. He felt Sena's hands adjust his bones. Her fingers slipped under the strips of his skin and followed them down with the practical brevity of a seamstress. Then he heard Sena speak a single word and he snapped together, hard and slippery. Strong as stone. He felt the tincture carry him out of his old body into this new one, into a new place, a place that was difficult for Them to hold onto. He had become a perfect orb, black and slippery, moving through Their grasp. He focused all his determination . . .

And then, fast, he was out. Like a melon seed pinched between thumb and finger, shooting from darkness into strange light.

He passed through the Nọcrịpa and held his breath as if underwater. He kept his eyes in front of him and did not look back. He was fighting for every inch, every moment, going for speed, blinded by stars that did not move.

He did not give up.

In a different time, the light tunneled, natal and traumatic, but it also thronged with warmth.

The light became orange and blue—leaves in autumn. Supple black branches spindled over a canal, lit with catoptric perfection. In the water, dappled movements swarmed: fish like white lilacs. And through the trees, Caliph saw pale mythic domes and spires quaver—somehow susceptible to wind.

In the dream, the tincture is gone. Burnt up. He has moved on. Someone in the dream asks him a simple question that he cannot understand.

CALIPH looked down at a girl on the path, divorced from logical timelines. Her hair was curly and dark brown. But her eyes were crocus-ice-blue. Her skin was pale and glittered with subtle platinum lines. The loveliest child he had ever seen. Standing in the cold.

"What did you say?"

"I said that's a nice one, isn't it?" She pointed at the ground.

"Oh. That *is* a nice one." He crouched down. There were actually two shiny husks on the path at their feet, like stones, each resting by a strange whorl-like pattern in the clay. Both were like summer beetles fallen in autumn. Both were broken and empty.

Aislinn bent at the waist, like her mother would have done, and picked one of them up.

It was still beautiful. Caliph hadn't thought of it as such until she said so. To him it was small and ugly. But Aislinn said it was beautiful and then she pressed its cold hard shape into his palm. It bit him strangely, like a talisman.

Aislinn touched his other hand. All her fingers wrapped around two of his. She tugged, swung his arm.

"You should keep it," she said. She assumed her propensity for stone collecting was something shared by everyone.

He slipped it into his pocket. "All right, I will. You want to go home?"

"Yes."

He picked her up. The girl rested her head on his shoulder, draped her arms over his back. He knew where he was going. Into the mist-drenched sweetness of unending autumn. He could smell it—whenever he breathed. He could feel it on his skin, a crisp pomaceous tartness: cold from hanging in trees against the stars.

His head was clear.

The girl traced the lines on the back of his neck as she always did. As she had done since she was half again as small.

He carried her toward Ahvêllẹ, toward the shining crest of the jellyfish glyph. There was no one to ridicule their ascent as some mawkish final illustration in a children's book. Even if there had been, Caliph would not have cared. He was glad to be mawkish.

He found no sorrow in having changed. No sorrow that he wasn't breathing.

APODOSIS

Though I fail, my success is enough.

Isn't it?

Because when there is no way out, you must go deeper in. Then you will find that the direction you have taken does not end. Your walls will crumble. Your path is endless.

I learned this from you.

You taught me to be relentless.

I cut three sheets of skin from my back. The third was meant to keep all three of us together. But it could not, and therefore, onto it will go this letter.

I knew even a year ago that it wasn't going to be me. I hoped. I wished. I went to Sandren to double-check. But I wasn't destined to be hurled into the sea: a message in a bottle, born by knowable tides toward an island paradise—newly made.

It was Nathaniel's paradise. I only finished it. I had other things to worry about. It has been complicated, trying to get you both out while Nathaniel watches my every move.

When I wrote your glyph did you feel yourself come apart at the seams? Did you feel how I stitched you back together, so carefully? So tight? And then, into your new home, your new phylactery, the tincture packed you. All of you. Your body, the very fabric captured in my eye. The seed of *you*.

I know that feeling. To be cut apart, turned into a symbol. Perfected. Your design shining like a gem.

And this is the part where you will think, *How strange!*

That she put me into her eye.

I used to laugh at the old holomorphic prescriptions. They read like fairy tale recipes for spells. (I never told you the outrageous equation for opening the *Cịsrym Tạ*. I am so sorry for the scar I gave you.) But these recipes contain more than numbers, which was hard for me to understand. Initially, I laughed at their strangeness but now I know, only the *preposterous* should be set aside. The *unknown* is what I embraced.

There is no more fitting phylactery for the things I wanted to save—than my eyes.

With my eyes, I looked to the future. They apprehended what was important, sorted through the clutter, focused on that which I desired. They were the seeds of all my actions and filled with what mattered most to my heart. It is true that I carried what I loved best in my eyes.

I find it unaccountable that such alien horrors as the Yịllo'tharnah should have so much insight as to my nature, to set the number at two and force me to wrestle with these emotions. Perhaps it amuses Them, that the Sslîạ should be faced with these introspections at the end, that I must go blindly into the future, on hope, my ambit divided and reduced. My eyes plucked out, my tongue silenced.

But at least now, it is done.

I spent all summer preparing the math that could change you, like the Yịllo'tharnah had changed me. In this I feel some success. Know that this was never about preserving a species or salvaging the *greatest mind.* It was never about saving a people. It was, in every instance, about transformation. About leaving the split, gooey chrysalis behind.

This is not betrayal. This is evolution.

I wanted you to understand that I did not consult with kings or clergy or ask for the opinions of philosophers or conservationists, holomorphs or seers. And this was on purpose.

Why?

Because, quite frankly—fuck them.

This was my decision. And I admit it was selfish, like everything I have ever done.

Our daughter went first because I owed her that. Because, among many things, I regret the tiny bones I left in the ground at Desdae. Tell her I love her. I had to fight for her because she was so young, because she couldn't have escaped under her own power. You went next, on your own. You had to fight for yourself because I was already overcome. And you won, as I knew you would.

It is what I wanted. You are finally free—from everything. This is a repetition of the sacrifice my father made for me. I am proud to be caught in the noose, hanging like a question mark at the end of the day, for both your sakes.

I have written this before my fate has reached me, in secret, away from Nathaniel's prying eyes. But I hope for what is to come.

Right now you are chasing me. Right now you don't understand what I have done. One day you will open this book and you will find this note tucked inside its cover, passed to you like we did in class.

I have made notes to help you remember.

In the bookcase of the house you now live in, you will find the *Cịs-rym Tạ*. And therein, in Inti'Drou Glyphs, is a trace of me and you. Seeds floating in sunlight over Thilwicket Fen, strung out on the breeze that buoys them. In the evening slant, by the shadow of a road, glows the packed clay of my youth with a boy named Caliph Howl. I love this memory. It comforts me beneath the groaning of the world, spinning in blackness, while the Abominations send tremors through my core.

You will read it. You will discover the possibilities. But that is not why I chose you. I picked you because I love you. And there is no other reason.

I see something clean as clouds flowing across the Healean Range, sky bright as glazed porcelain painted by sun and shallow sea. In the book rests your future—captured—in an instant held. Drifting on the trajectory of our throw.

I can already feel the pressure on my back and the miles of still-accreting sediment begin to weigh. I will be the first fossil of the new world. My ambit—so small.

But They cannot dislodge me or draw me out. I am not Nathaniel Howl, soul uncoupled from body and mind. I am only buried under mud and heavy numbers, beneath the new continents, as *They* once were buried.

As we ignored them, I am: a grain of sand, muffled by Their pallial secretions, stuck until the tides go out again.

—S.

PRONUNCIATIONS

Ạ *A* in *father*. Mirạyhr.

Å *O* in *home*. Dåelôc.

Â *I* in *high*. Barâdaith.

Æ *EY* in *whey*. Sienæ.

Ẹ *UE* in *hue*. Mrẹsh.

Ê *E* in *bend*. Nêlẹạ.

Ị *I* in *ill*. Nịs.

Î *E* in *eel*. Înẹ.

Ķ Approximated with a glottal sound between *k* and *h*. Ķhloht.

Ợ A slightly softened vowel articulated between the *o* sounds of *over* and *on*. Sọth.

Ô *O* in *oat*. Dåelôc.

Ü Approximated by a punch to the stomach. A guttural *u* similar to that in *fun*. Ooil-Üauth.

Ữ *OO* in *tool*. Brũak.

Ụ *OW* in *now*. Nụmạth.

Ǔ A diphthong combining the *e* of *hem* and the *oo* of *tool*: eh-oo. Ǔlung.

Y In words unique to Adummim, *y* is almost always pronounced as the *e* in *eel*. Mirạyhr.